
The kiss that followed was passionate for both Tyler and Charlene. Moments later, when they pulled apart, gasping, each sensed their actions this night would change their lives forever.

She knew she shouldn't let things get out of hand, but Lord help her, Charlene's resolve completely disappeared. Admitting that she wanted him would be foolish on her part. Making love to him would be a mistake of monumental proportions that could potentially hurt both of them. Still, it didn't lessen her desire for him. If anything, she wanted him more because she knew, ultimately, when he found out that she wasn't Corinne, he would hate her for playing such an underhanded and conniving trick on him, on all of them. Still, when she claimed his mouth and her hands circled his neck, for the first time in months Charlene's grief gave way to the comforting arms of a man…a solid, caring, and handsome man.

A man she knew she shouldn't be with. He was, after all, her sister's husband.

LIES IN
DISGUISE

BERNICE LAYTON

Genesis Press, Inc.

Indigo Love Stories

An imprint of Genesis Press, Inc.
Publishing Company

Genesis Press, Inc.
P.O. Box 101
Columbus, MS 39703

ISBN: 13 DIGIT: 978-1-58571-392-9
ISBN: 10 DIGIT: 1-58571-392-9
Manufactured in the United States of America

First Edition

Visit us at www.genesis-press.com or call at 1-888-Indigo-1

DEDICATION

To my husband, Derrick, and my daughter, NaTiki, thank you for your ever-present love and encouragement. Your constant support and guidance has once again been my strength as I brought another novel into existence. Your steadfast belief continues to inspire me, not just to write, but to believe, to hope, to imagine, and to dream. I'm so fortunate and blessed to have you both in my life.

To my Sisters—I'm glad for all that we've shared and for the special love between us.

Bernice Layton

ACKNOWLEDGEMENTS

As always, I give thanks to my family and friends. My heart is filled with gratitude for your love, support, and encouragement.

Special thanks to my mom, Susie. I couldn't be more blessed in life than to have a mom like you. Thank you, Mom and happy reading!

To Danise (Lu)…and her cat, August, who walked all over my manuscript pages, thank you both so much. We made another great team to bring *Lies in Disguise* to life. You have to know I still laugh every time I think about our talks about the character, Charlene. Thank you for bringing Flo to life, and I'm keeping your review pages—gotta love orange. I'm looking forward to your review of the next draft, "Auntie." Our telepathic thing is awesome. Thank you, my friend, you took the time to review my work and gave your honest, on-target and often-hilarious feedback. I'm honored, and filled with gratitude.

To Angie and the "Nurses" once again, your support has been so encouraging. Thank you Gladys, Chesapeake, VA is awesome. I am truly honored to call you my fans.

To Deborah Schumaker, Executive Editor, Diane Blair, and the rest of the staff at Genesis Press, Inc., thank you so much for your guidance and expertise.

To Mavis Allen, thank you for your review and edits. Hope you like this finished novel also.

If I've forgotten anyone, please know that I thank you for any assistance you may have given me. It is with heart-felt gratitude I say, thank you!

PROLOGUE

Three decisions made spontaneously in a single night change the lives of all three decision-makers…and the effects are long lasting.

The night is March 25.

A sister can be seen as someone who is both ourselves and very much not ourselves—a special kind of double.
~ Toni Morrison

CHAPTER 1

Corinne McDonald Mills searched the contents of her purse.

"Where is it?" She'd been looking for a slip of paper containing a telephone number. Two days ago, after discovering the danger she could be in, Corinne felt she had only one option.

Finally finding and unfolding the piece of paper that contained her twin sister, Charlene's, telephone number, Corinne's heart wrenched. Running her finger over the tightly squared piece of paper, her breath caught in her throat. Her shame went so deep.

It was March 25. In a matter of hours they would turn thirty-five years old. Charlene was her only sister, her identical twin, and yet Corinne felt the familiar ache that always hit her when their birthday came around. Truthfully it was more often than that. The ache also hit her on holidays. She had so many regrets since she'd banished Charlene from her life.

The fact that she'd been born with an identical twin had been the one thing that Corrine couldn't change.

Since coming to California almost ten years ago, Corinne McDonald had changed many things about herself. She'd first overcome her Southern accent. Then she'd completely eradicated everything and anything that connected her to her hometown back in Virginia, including changing her name to McDonaldson.

She'd fabricated a lie, and it grew.

She'd told everyone she was an only child and that she had no parents. As a bright, pretty, and intelligent young woman with excellent business savvy, Corinne quickly moved up the ladder in every job she held. When she saw a posting for an administrative assistant at the prestigious Mills Shipping Company, she'd studied hard to learn everything she could about the shipping business. When she interviewed for the position, she'd been hired immediately. Within months, she'd set her sights higher…on the man who would one day take over the family business, Tyler Mills. Following a planned and calculated courtship, Corinne had one goal in mind: marriage to the affluent and handsome man. She knew if she married a man like Tyler Mills she'd never have to worry about money again.

Over the years, Corinne wondered how Charlene was doing but never once did she contact her…not even eight years ago when she'd discovered she was carrying twins.

Her husband, Tyler Mills, was shocked about having twins. But before Corinne could concoct an explanation for carrying twins, Tyler's mother, Mona Mills, explained that the twin gene went back several generations in the Mills family. Still, Tyler had insisted on having the babies tested before they left the hospital. When the test confirmed that he was the father, Tyler had been apologetic and contrite. So much so, he'd excused Corinne's past indiscretions, which he'd suspected but couldn't prove.

It was Corinne's love for her twins that prompted her to unfold the piece of paper and whisper aloud Charlene's name. She didn't have to wonder what her sister looked like now. Lifting sad and reddened eyes to the mirror for a split second Corinne saw her twin sister's face in hers.

"What have I done? Oh, Charlene, please forgive me," she whispered, then looked down at the small picture frames containing pictures of her twins, Shane and Shelly. "I love you, my babies," she said, picking up the telephone and dialing the phone number on the now worn piece of paper.

Charlene McDonald snapped her cell phone shut again.

No, she'd decided she wouldn't make the call. She'd had enough. That is enough excuses and put offs from her estranged twin sister, Corinne.

It was their thirty-fifth birthday.

Charlene McDonald thought her only sister, her own flesh and blood, would have at least a desire to call and wish her happy birthday. But she hadn't. She hadn't in many years.

It had been eight years since the twins had spoken to each other.

Nursing a second cup of tea, Charlene felt the tears sting her eyes. *So I made a stupid error in judgment. Okay, two errors in judgment...but that second one was major to Corinne.*

The first one occurred when they were seventeen years old and Charlene had done a stupid thing. She'd dressed up, put on make-up and her shortest shorts, and gone out on a date with Andre, the hot saxophone player from the high school band. Charlene had purposely pretended to be Corinne. Her stunt was to prove to Corinne that Andre had only one thing on his mind concerning Corinne. He'd wanted another conquest and not a steady girlfriend. Everyone in their high school knew what Andre was after, but because Corinne wasn't close to or trusted anyone easily, she refused to believe them...not even her own sister.

Then things went from bad to worse on that date. Apparently Andre didn't want to take no for an answer. When his advances became too insistent, Charlene decided she'd had enough of pretending to be coy, prim, and proper, because she wasn't any of those. She'd succeeded in giving Andre two punches...one to his groin and the second to his nose, which she ended up breaking. The next morning when Andre's furious parents came to her father's house, they were not alone. They'd brought along a horribly swollen and bandaged Andre and a deputy to arrest Corinne for assault and battery. The entire neighborhood was in an uproar, made worse by Corinne's furious denials.

The gig was up then. Charlene had to come clean because if she didn't Corinne was surely going to jail.

"It-it was me," she said guiltily. After explaining what she'd done and why, Charlene glanced around to see her father standing on the front steps shaking his head in disgust. Corinne on the other hand stomped down the steps, walked over to Charlene and right there on the sidewalk in front of the neighbors, the deputy, the mailman, and Andre and his parents, Corinne and Charlene got into a down-in-the-dirt, knock-down, drag-out, hair-pulling cat-fight.

Their father, Daniel, waited a full three minutes before stepping in to separate the girls. He told the onlookers that something had been brewing between his girls for quite a while and maybe a tussle would shake them of their ills. Then he'd dragged both into the house as they continued to kick and claw at each other.

Their punishment lasted a whole month, during which time Corinne didn't speak to her sister at all. Several months later, Corinne moved out of the house, and within a couple of years she'd moved out of Virginia and settled in California. She'd left no forwarding address.

Over the years, Corinne maintained brief contact with their father, but rarely did the sisters speak. Several years after that, nine to be exact, a second humiliating incident occurred between them. That incident was unforgivable and Corinne severed all ties with Charlene.

Sitting alone in her cozy kitchen, Charlene sighed. Her pride wouldn't allow her to make that impossible first step of making a simple phone call, not yet.

Taking a deep breath, she flipped the cell phone open again…for the third time. "Okay," she said out loud. "I'll call her house and say…what?" What indeed? What does one say to a sister she hasn't seen or spoken to in nine years? "Hi. How ya doing, sis?" Thinking that sounded silly even to her own ears. Charlene snapped the phone shut.

"Damn." She couldn't do it. What a coward. Squinting through her wire-rimmed reading glasses at the date on the wall calendar, Charlene realized sadly how much she'd missed the sound of her sister's voice. Leaning back in the chair, she also realized that she had no one but herself to blame for what happened. It was all her fault, no doubt about it.

Charlene had been the one who'd instigated the second incident nine years ago that led to the big blowout that ended the relationship with her beloved sister. It wasn't like any other fight they'd had before. The fight occurred just moments before Corinne exchanged wedding vows with Tyler Mills, a wedding that neither Charlene nor their father had been invited to.

When Corinne called to tell their father of her upcoming marriage, Charlene had been listening on the other extension. When her father asked if she loved the fellow, Corinne's response had been, "Dad, for real, nobody gets married for love anymore. It's about security and never having to scrape for food or live on welfare."

Hearing the hard edge in Corinne's voice, Charlene couldn't remain quiet any longer. "Corinne, please don't marry that man if you're not in love with him." She'd asked her father to hang up so that she could talk to Corinne privately.

Corinne reacted with venom. "There you go again, still trying to butt into my business. What I do is none of your concern, you got that, Charlene?"

Hurt, Charlene pressed on. "So that's why you haven't even invited Daddy to your wedding? That's just dumb Corinne and from what I've read in the paper about the man you're gonna marry, Tyler Mills, he's some kind of a player, anyway," Charlene had retorted. "It seems to me that neither of you should be gettin' married, especially if you don't love each other."

"He loves me and he can give me everything I've always wanted and dreamed of," Corinne had said. "I won't be like you, Charlene, stuck in that town and working in some convenience store, then marrying some idiot with nothing to offer and having a bunch of kids."

"Well," Charlene retorted. "I certainly wouldn't marry a man I didn't love."

"And that's where we differ. I'm done talking to you."

"No wait," Charlene wasn't ready to end the conversation, but Corinne had hung up.

In an effort to save her sister from making what she thought was basically a dumb mistake, Charlene set out to find as much information as she could on Tyler Mills. It took two weeks, but what Charlene discovered wasn't pretty. While attending a teacher's conference in Miami she'd spotted Tyler Mills up close and personal with a beautiful woman who was not his fiancée. Charlene even found herself a little bit jealous. Why wouldn't she be, she thought. Why wouldn't any woman? Tyler Mills was considered the most sought-after bachelor in Baldwin Hills, California, and Corinne had latched onto him…for his money.

Charlene snapped two pictures with her camera and rushed to call Corrine. Of course, Corinne accused Charlene of lying again. She'd said that Tyler had business in Miami and wouldn't be such a fool to do anything like that. In the heat of that phone conversation, Corinne's tirade was unrelenting.

As identical twins, they were never close as one would expect twins to be. Even now, after so many shared birthdays had come and gone, Charlene could still feel the pain of Corinne's hurtful words all over again.

Charlene felt she'd done the right thing by going to California to try and talk Corinne out of marrying a man she didn't love, a virtual stranger, for his money. Charlene had snuck into the back chapel to speak with her sister. Until that day, she had not seen Corinne in many years.

"Corinne, wh-what are you doing? That man is a liar. Why are you going through with this weddin'?" Charlene had argued in a voice barely above a whisper.

As the assembled choir members sang several selections, none would have known what was about to take place in the back of the chapel when Corinne turned and came face-to-face with her twin sister, Charlene.

Upon hearing the once familiar voice, Corinne turned and fixed a glare on the only other person who shared her face…her features, her hair color, her body type, and her blood type.

The same dark amber-hued eyes stared back at her, wide and timid. "I told you that you were not invited to this wedding. Why are you here?" Corinne slowly narrowed the distance between them, advancing on Charlene. Her intent was to move Charlene back to the wall and out of sight should someone enter the chapel at that moment. "This is my business, sister," she hissed. "You don't even know Tyler." Angrily grabbing at Charlene's arm, Corinne pushed her sister further against the wall. "How dare you do this to me again, Charlene? How dare you come out here with your false accusations and jealousy and try to ruin things for me? Once wasn't enough for you?"

Incapable of speaking, Charlene shook her head in denial of her sister's allegations. She was shocked and saddened to hear Corinne's hateful words.

Corinne's onslaught continued. "You want me to be as miserable and alone and unhappy as you are, don't you? Well, you know what? I had enough of that growing up with you. Your constant aches and pains and hospital stays and your overall pathetic weaknesses drained the life out of our mother." Corinne took a step closer. "I'll be damned if I ever let you do that to me."

Corinne's beautiful face contorted in anger. "I've had enough of going without, living off the scraps of others, and depending on welfare, and you remind me of a past that no longer exists for me," she'd hissed at her twin. "Get out of here right now, or I'll have you thrown out."

Charlene stood her ground, refusing to give up. "Corinne, how can you say such horrible things to me? How could you blame me for being a sick child? That wasn't my fault. But please listen to me, I didn't lie. I saw him with my own two eyes, kissin' that woman." Charlene let her hands drop to her sides in defeat, but her eyes shone brightly with unshed tears. "And why would I lie about that, huh? Why would I use my hard-earned money to come all the way out here and try to stop you from makin' a big mistake? But you're right. I don't know him or his family, and why is that? Because you refuse to even acknowledge that you have a father or sister, and that's just stupid.

I'm your twin, Corinne! Your identical twin, and that's a fact whether you choose to acknowledge it or not!"

Corinne shook her head so hard that her bridal veil slipped and sat awkwardly atop her beautifully coiffed hair. "Maybe you need to change your reading glasses, Charlene. And for your information, it wasn't important for you to know Tyler or his family." Inching ever closer Corinne said, "and you never will."

Charlene was conflicted. She didn't recognize this person, or the evilness spewing from her mouth. Her throat tightened with emotion. "Corinne, either you're insane or you've grown more desperate than I could have ever imagined. But you go right ahead and trade your life away like some pathetic, desperate woman!" Charlene hadn't mistaken the look that crossed her sister's face, just seconds before she'd watched Corinne step over to the open door in the back of the chapel and crook her finger.

Three security guards had rushed to the private room on Corinne's silent command.

A stunned Charlene was placed in handcuffs and whisked away, but not before Corinne, adjusting her silk veil, told Charlene cruelly, "You'd best remember this…I don't have a sister, and I definitely don't have a twin."

Over the years, the few times Corinne had bothered to call home to check on their father were strained and short and even those calls had dwindled over the last few years. After their father died, Charlene had called Corinne and she'd cried. But she didn't show up for his funeral. What she did do was send Charlene a check to cover some of the funeral and burial expenses. Charlene believed that Corinne was taking to heart her parting words that day in the back of the chapel. She had erased the fact that she'd ever had a twin sister.

Charlene suspected that Corinne's anger stemmed from her having to fight for everything she wanted because they'd grown up poor. Tyler Mills and his family represented what they'd never had: prestige, wealth, respectability, and privilege, all the things money could afford.

For all these long years, Charlene had done as her sister demanded of her that day. She'd stayed away and living almost three thousand miles away made that easy. What wasn't easy for Charlene was that she'd missed her sister because despite what happened, she still loved Corinne and she continued to pray for her and wish her the best.

But it was time to change things. They were older. They were turning thirty-five years old.

And Corinne and Tyler had two children, fraternal twins, and Charlene was desperate to meet them. The one picture Corinne had sent to their father had been taken on their second birthday. Their sweet little faces were burned forever in Charlene's heart and sat in a frame on her nightstand. On a larger scale, Charlene resented Corinne for keeping her children away from their aunt and grandfather. But from the moment she'd heard of their births, Charlene had longed to see them and thought of them constantly.

When Charlene's father died eighteen months ago, it also ended the snippets of information Charlene got of Corinne. Even the newspaper she'd occasionally got from their town in California rarely showed a picture of the couple or of their children. She'd read before that Tyler was quoted as saying his children were off limits and they would be protected from the harshness of the media. But he was open game. Tyler Mills's business intellect had landed him many acquisitions since he'd been named CEO of his father's shipping company. It made news across the country and the company, Mills Shipping, was a Fortune 500 company.

Determined to meet her niece and nephew and see Corinne as well, Charlene was more than willing to accept whatever Corinne would direct at her. Charlene no longer cared. She was tired of being alone. She had kin. She had family. It was her sister's family. Swiping at the tear sliding down her cheek, Charlene sat up in one quick move.

Just like that, she made a decision and flipped her cell phone open again.

She didn't call her sister. Instead, Charlene quickly called the airport and purchased a ticket on a flight to California. It was leaving in two days.

Charlene toyed with the phone in her hand. She contemplated changing her mind and canceling the flight, but just then her phone rang.

———∿∿∿———

Tyler Mills sat in his office at Mills Shipping.

It was a business his father had started over thirty years ago. His father had recently stepped down as CEO. Much to the disappointment of his younger brother, Ryan, Tyler now held that position. Although Tyler played it off, there was some friction between him and his brother about that. But Tyler knew that Ryan didn't have what it took to run a large conglomerate such as Mills Shipping. In the short months since being pinned CEO, Tyler was responsible for securing several highly profitable contracts. He knew Ryan wouldn't have stood a chance, because Tyler had been a shark circling the waters for those contracts…and he'd gotten them in one big gulp.

But no sooner had he celebrated the last shipping contract, Tyler had another pressing contract to deal with, one that weighed heavily on his mind. It was personal.

He again read a document on his desk. To him, it would put an end to his misery and his pain and his nine-year marriage to Corinne Mills. But Tyler also realized ending his marriage to Corinne would be the most unselfish thing he'd ever done. He had to do it, for himself, yes, but also for his children…mainly for his children.

Tyler had known long ago that his marriage to Corinne was in trouble. In fact, it had been in trouble for a very long time. Corinne had become sullen, snippy, demanding, and downright difficult to be with. Nothing pleased her. Not him or the lavish life he'd provided her. She wanted for nothing…but there was something, only he didn't know what it was. He'd never known. But Tyler suspected it was Corinne's loneliness that ate away at her. She had no family, so Tyler sought to correct that, and after a year of pressuring her to forgo using birth control, Corinne had become pregnant and blessed him with a set of twins.

Tyler was well aware of Corinne's dalliances and flirtations. He knew she thought she was discreet. She wasn't. He needed proof of her latest affair, however. Humiliated, Tyler had contacted a private investigator to follow Corinne…just once. Tyler didn't think he could stand days or weeks of investigation and waiting. No. He wanted only one picture. Then he would confront Corinne.

Slowly opening the file folder under his hand, Tyler held his breath and his heart broke. There were two pictures. The first, a color photo showed Corinne sitting on the lap of man. His hand was beneath her short skirt. They were laughing, kissing, and sitting on a park bench. The second, a long-range shot, showed Corinne and the man in bed. They were nude. The man's face wasn't captured fully because it was buried in Corinne's neck.

Immediately, pure and profound jealousy hit Tyler. This was his wife. Then his outrage caused his breath to unexpectedly come out in waves of anger. Heat rose up from his shirt collar and forced him to loosen his tie. This is what he'd wanted, right? But he was not prepared to see it. He wasn't prepared to have his suspicions confirmed and staring up at him.

He wasn't prepared to see his wife and the mother of his children in the arms of another man, and certainly not in bed with him.

With mounting fury, Tyler thrust the pictures behind the divorce documents. He was going to make things very simple. He was going home to confront Corinne, and when she protested he'd show her the pictures. *Then what?* Then the hard part…he was going to put her out. Eventually, he'd be able to put her out of his heart.

And that, Tyler knew, was going to have a long-term effect on him and his children because they loved her dearly, as much as he did. It had to happen tonight. The children had spent last night and tonight with his parents. Tyler knew his family figured he'd planned a quiet, romantic weekend alone to celebrate Corinne's birthday. That was so not the case. Not now.

Slamming his briefcase shut, Tyler left his office. His face was grim.

As he headed home, he thought Corinne wasn't going to like her birthday present…not one bit.

CHAPTER 2

The years fell away like tumbling blocks.

That's what Charlene thought watching Corinne crossing the hotel lobby. Standing, she ran her hands nervously down the sides of her best black slacks.

Then there was only two feet separating them. "Hi," Charlene said hesitantly.

Corinne's eyes took in every detail of her twin sister. She thought she was beautiful. "Hi yourself, and happy birthday, sis," she whispered. Swallowing back the painful lump of regret and guilt, Corinne stood back and smiled. "Well, look at you. Charlene, you're beautiful."

Never one to accept compliments, Charlene shook her head. "No, you're the beautiful one. Even more than you were the last time I saw you, on your weddin' day." *Oh, why did I go there?* She rushed on. "Anyway, happy birthday to you, too…well, a day late." Charlene couldn't hide her nervousness. She never could. But the fact that they were talking civilly after so many years just seemed weird. Suddenly alarmed, she pulled her lips in, fearing she'd say something that would set Corinne off. That lasted five seconds. "Corinne, um…" she began.

Within seconds Corinne closed the distance between them and embraced her twin tightly. Each held back a rush of tears. They stepped back but continued to hold hands. Corinne eased Charlene over to a secluded sitting area just as the waitress appeared. "Charlene, would you want something to drink or eat? I know you had a long flight," she said.

"I'm fine. I had lots of refreshments and a meal, too. About that, Corinne. I surely didn't expect first class accommodations, and I want to pay you back for that ticket," Charlene said.

"You don't owe me anything, Charlene. Hey, wasn't it weird that we called each other like that?" Corinne asked, remembering what happened when she'd called Charlene at home the day before and found out that Charlene had scheduled a flight that would arrive later in the evening. Upon hearing that, Corinne had called the airport and rescheduled Charlene's flight, bringing her to California a day earlier and in first class.

"Yes, it was. You know, as twins, you and I never had that telepathic thing, did we?"

"No, not really," Corinne said, "and we never dressed alike, either, did we?"

"No, not really, but look how we're dressed today," Charlene said, noticing their almost identical outfits.

Each sister looked down before running their eyes over the other. Each had on black slacks and a long-sleeved silk white blouse. Charlene ran her hand down the sleeve of Corinne's white blouse. "This is a beautiful blouse, Corinne, really fine."

Corinne laughed lightly. "I'll get you one just like it. Hey, we have the same brown hair and you wear yours out to your shoulders and parted on the side like I do."

"That's because we're still twins, Corinne. It's not unrealistic to think that we wouldn't share similarities. I think it's kinda cool," Charlene said, timidly reaching for Corinne's hand.

After squeezing hands again, Corinne pulled back. "Yes, it's pretty cool, and I've missed you. Hey, I have to show you something pretty awesome and wonderful and cool."

Charlene watched Corinne unfasten the gold chain from around her neck. Swallowing hard, she watched Corinne open the oval locket before passing it to her. Charlene's hands shook as she held the locket in the middle of her hand. "It's them." There was no holding back the rush of tears, which she wiped away with the back of one hand. "Oh, Corinne, they're beautiful," Charlene said as she gazed at the small pictures. "Just adorable. Tell me all about them. What are they like?" Charlene asked, anxious to hear every detail.

"They are adorable and sometimes they're a handful, but they're the most precious things I've ever created. Every year I get a new locket and put a new set of pictures in it." Corinne hesitated briefly. "I want you to meet them, Charlene."

Taken aback, Charlene's eyes widened. "You do, really?" A smile suddenly split her face. "Tonight?" she asked, hopeful and unable to hide her excitement, but at the same time a feeling of apprehension waved over her, forcing her to look deeply into Corinne's amber eyes.

"I think tomorrow morning is probably better. They're spending the weekend with Tyler's parents. But, um," Corinne hesitated briefly, "but it's important for them to be around family, and I have to tell you, Shane, my son, well, he reminds me so much of you. He's a little quiet and he likes to draw, too," she said. "You're their auntie, and I feel awful for not letting you meet them sooner."

Unable to contain herself Charlene closed the space between them. Embracing again for several seconds, each choked back emotion and then laughed.

Corinne spoke first. "I'm sorry I didn't make it back home for Daddy's funeral."

"It's okay. It was a very simple service. It was just what he wanted, nothin' big. Besides, he told me I'd better not spend a lot of money on his funeral," Charlene said. "By the way, I really did appreciate you sendin' more money to pay for the hospital bills. I did try to get Daddy some health insurance, but it was too late. None of the insurance companies would approve a policy with a precondition like that. I really wish Daddy had stopped smokin' long ago. But, Corinne, I do want to repay you, somehow."

"You don't owe me anything, Charlene. You were wonderful to take care of him like you did. Daddy told me how bad he felt that you'd put your life on hold to take care of him."

Charlene rolled her eyes upward. "What life? My life was work and Dad. I have no regrets about takin' care of him until the end. He was so sick and all. But really, I can repay you some money. A thousand dollars right now," Charlene dug into her pocket for a band of bills.

Corinne grasped Charlene's hand, stopping her movements. "No, keep your money. But I do want to talk to you about something. You see, I'm kind of in a bit of trouble," she said in a quiet voice. "But I can't talk down here, so let's go up to my room."

"What...your room?" Stuffing the bills back into her pocket, Charlene glanced around the hotel lobby. "I thought you'd just picked this place for us to meet because it was convenient or somethin'. Corinne, you're stayin' in this hotel? Are the twins and Tyler stayin' here, too?"

"No, they're not. It's just me."

"Since when?" Charlene asked incredulously.

"Since night before last," Corinne said.

There was no mistaking Corinne's sadness. Charlene had picked up on it, but it was mingled with something else, an edginess that chilled her. "What's happened, Corinne?"

Raising a hand to her mouth, Corinne inhaled deeply. "Oh, Charlene...can I trust you?"

"Yes, you can trust me with anythin'. We're no longer kids, Corinne," Charlene said.

Corinne breathed a sigh of relief because she did trust Charlene. "Can I trust you to take care of my children…my precious babies?"

―⁓⁓―

When the sisters left the sitting area of the hotel lobby, they headed up to Corinne's room to talk and reconnect. Several hours later, at two-fifteen in the morning, the sisters sat in Corinne's grand hotel suite still talking and catching up on the previous nine years.

As they talked, the long years of separation continued to tumble and fall away.

Charlene couldn't believe what Corinne had told her, of her affairs and the current problems in her marriage. Her husband had confronted Corinne. But then Charlene couldn't believe that Corinne could get involved with a man who had ties to criminal activity. But then she wondered how much did she really know about this adult Corinne.

Standing, Charlene began to pace the floor. "Corinne, maybe you're wrong about this J," Charlene said, repeating the name Corinne mentioned. "Maybe you misunderstood what you said you overheard that day?"

"No, there was no mistake. I know what's going on in his company…they're using him, but things have spiraled out of control and I know what's going to happen. When the last shipment is sent, in about three months, two innocent men are going to be killed. But if that shipment makes it to Mexico, many more will die." Crying harder, Corinne reached up and grasped Charlene's hand tightly. "Listen, if-if something should happen to me I need you to take care of my children and to help Tyler. Please, will you do that for me, please?" Corinne begged.

"Corinne, nothin' is gonna happen to you, but this man, he's gotta be stopped. You have to go to the police," Charlene said.

"No, no police. You don't know these people, Charlene. I can't risk anything happening to my children, or to Tyler." Corinne held onto her sister's hand.

"Does this man know what you did? Hidin' that memory card you got?" Charlene asked.

"Oh, God no. It's a micro-memory card with tons of data and documents, everything I've saved and managed to get. If he knew, Charlene, I'd be dead. I wouldn't be sitting here with you. He does know that I have original invoices of his shipments, and he wants them back."

Charlene gulped down another glass of water. "Okay, so when are you seein' him again?" The thought of her twin being involved with such evil men frightened Charlene.

"I thought I would see him tonight. When we talked earlier he said he had a birthday gift for me," Corinne said, checking her watch.

"Good Lord! How can you take anythin' from the likes of him? He's the reason you're in this trouble!" Kneeling before Corinne's chair, Charlene watched her do something familiar that she hadn't seen in years. Corinne shrugged her shoulders and that meant what she'd just said wasn't important but what she was about to say would be a real bombshell. Shaking herself out of her reverie, Charlene suggested a plan of action. "Go to Tyler and tell him everythin' if you won't go to the police. He'll protect you, won't he?"

Fighting off a sudden wave of anger, Corinne scoffed and shook her head no. "Maybe at one time I would have said Tyler would protect me, but not now. When I went home the other night I-I was going to confess everything to him. I was going to tell him about the shipments and the man, everything...and I was going to beg for his forgiveness."

"Well, what happened?" Charlene asked.

"Ha! What happened was a shock to me." Corinne let out a sardonic half-laugh, half-sob. "Tyler presented me with a birthday cake and his birthday present."

"So what happened that brought you here, Corinne?"

"When I got home, Tyler told me he was filing for a divorce. He knows about the man I've been involved with. He doesn't know who he is, just that he exists...and he put me out of the house," Corinne said, forcing her eyes closed as she recalled how Tyler had asked her to join him in the living room.

Following unsuspectingly, she thought it was going to be a romantic evening after the many months since he'd moved out of their bedroom. But it wasn't that at all. Not giving her any indication of what was about to happen, he'd watched her blow out the single candle on a small birthday cake. Then he presented her with a beautifully wrapped gift box.

Smiling, she'd guessed that the lightweight box contained a nightgown. Maybe something flimsy that she'd envisioned herself putting on for him. Maybe they'd make love, something they hadn't done long before he'd moved out of their bedroom. As Corinne had carefully unfolded the white tissue paper, her smile faltered when she realized that instead of sexy lingerie, the box contained papers…divorce papers. In shock, she could only gape down uncomprehendingly at the document, a sinking feeling clawing at her chest.

"Tyler…" she'd said. "Wh-what is this?" Looking up, she found his face tight.

"It's exactly what you think it is, Corinne," he said coldly.

Only then did Corinne realize how angry he'd been. He'd been seething inside from the moment she'd walked into the house. "Tell me what I think it is, Tyler." Her heart was pounding as she focused on his face.

Sarcasm laced his response. "It's your birthday present, sweetheart. Don't you like the wrapping? I did it myself."

Corinne clutched her throat. *No, no. This can't be happening.* "Tyler…" But he'd made it obvious he had nothing else to say to her. "Tyler, you face me like a man and talk to me." Corinne slammed the box on the table. "Explain this!" she screamed.

Turning back, Tyler walked right up to her. He picked up the divorce papers and flipped them to her. "Okay, but first you explain this!" He'd pulled out the two pictures and slapped them into her hands. "Better yet, don't bother, because I don't want to hear it. I don't want to hear any more of your lies!"

Corinne stared at the picture where she lay naked in bed with her lover. What could she have said? She could have said plenty. But then the fighter in her came out as she realized she stood to lose everything if Tyler divorced her. She stood to lose the life she'd created and the lifestyle she'd become accustomed to having. Yes, she'd turned her back on him, but divorce, no. Not like this. Not now. "I don't think an explanation is needed, do you? But what about your lies, Tyler!"

"Don't you dare throw your crap back on me. I have no lies with you and I'm not the one you're fucking in that picture. Spare me your lies and get out of this house!"

The force of his anger caused Corinne to stumble back against the couch. She almost fell down. "What? You're crazy if you think I'm leaving this house." Panic loomed in Corinne's chest. "This is my home and…" Corinne had stopped mid-sentence when she'd realized what he'd said. "Wait a minute…I'm not for one second leaving my children! You're out of your mind if you think I'll ever leave them." Dread and fear turned her face beet red.

"You don't have a choice. If you don't get out of this house tonight, then tomorrow I'll take these pictures and they'll be filed with those divorce papers. By the way, I'm demanding full custody of the children." Tyler forced himself to look away from her face.

Oh, please no…not my babies. "Tyler, listen to me, I'm…" Corinne had made a feeble attempt to talk to him, despite the anger and resolve she saw in his features.

"I don't want to hear it! I'm done. I've had enough and I want you out of this house, tonight!" Tyler refused to give into her fake frightened look. He knew she wasn't. She never was scared or frightened. Lifting her hand, Tyler placed a single sheet of paper in her palm. "That's your hotel confirmation. Stay as long as you like. It's a five-star suite, just as you like it."

Corinne glared up at him in panic. In a state of shock, she'd picked up her purse from the coffee table and stormed through the living room, out into the foyer, and out the front door. She'd died a little with each step she took. Never in a million years would she have thought Tyler would threaten to take her children from her.

The hard cry didn't come that night for Corinne. It came in that moment of recollection with Charlene cradling her tightly in her arms.

Charlene was stunned after hearing what Corinne had endured and what Tyler had done. "Oh, Corinne, maybe this is why my heart was achin' so a few nights ago. The pain was so strong it woke me from a deep sleep. I'm so sorry for what you've been going through."

Pulling herself from Charlene's embrace, Corinne reined in her sobs and managed a tiny smile. "So maybe we do have that telepathy thing because the other night when I checked into this room you're the first person who came to my mind and the only person I thought to call."

"And that's when you called me." Charlene nodded. It was a birthday greeting after all.

"Yes. I ordered a pot of tea from room service, and then called you."

"And there I was sittin' in the kitchen sippin' a cup of tea myself. I'd just hung up the phone after schedulin' the flight when you called," Charlene said.

"Charlene, I'm so sorry for forcing you out of my life. It was a dumb, unforgivable, childish thing to do and I've suffered for it. This is my punishment."

"It's in the past. It's over and I'm here now and nothin' will change that, okay." Charlene squeezed her sister's hand just as her cell phone rang.

Corinne trembled when she recognized the number on her caller ID, but she sat up and answered on the fourth ring. "Hi...oh, really? At this hour?" Her eyes lifted to Charlene's. "Well, okay, J. I'll see you shortly," she said and snapped the cell phone closed.

"You're not gonna meet your lover now, are you? Corinne it-it's almost three in the mornin'. Please don't go. Wait until tomorrow. Then we'll go to the police. With the evidence you have, we can stop those two men from being killed. Then we can talk about how to salvage your marriage," Charlene said, watching Corinne unfold herself from the chair.

"No, I'll be fine. I'm just going down to the parking lot," Corinne said, smoothing out the wrinkles in her expensive jersey slacks. "You see, like me, Charlene, he's married, too, but he's really a sweet guy and all. He just got caught up with the wrong people who've lined his pockets with a lot of money by using his business as their cover. He can't turn on them, not now."

"Corinne, I'm not lettin' you go. It's dangerous," Charlene said, grabbing her purse.

Corinne reached for her sister's hand. "No, Charlene. You rest for a bit. I'll be back in an hour. We'll order a pot of tea and some food and catch up some more. Then we'll talk about Tyler because I do want a life with him and our children okay?" She winked.

Charlene didn't feel good about her sister leaving. She mumbled, "Okay." Unconvinced that Corinne would be fine, she watched her go to the door. "Hey, Corinne, I-I love you, sister."

Corinne turned back and hugged Charlene tightly. "And I love you, sister…I never stopped," she whispered and kissed Charlene's cheek. "Never, ever, did I forget you, always remember that."

―∞―

Charlene knew she'd done a stupid thing by following Corinne. But she couldn't just sit there in that beautiful suite waiting for her sister to return.

Barely waiting for Corinne to step into the elevator, Charlene ran down the six flights of stairs, taking them two at a time. She came out on the far end of the lobby, where she practically collided with two housekeeping employees. She hastily asked them if there was a side exit to the parking lot. When they eyed her suspiciously, she said, 'boyfriend issues,' and pulled out two twenty-dollar bills for each of them. They both pointed to a door to her right.

Ten minutes later Charlene was hiding in the bed of a pickup truck in the parking lot, her head barely poking over the side. But it was enough for her to clearly see Corinne about to step from the passenger side of the snazzy black car she'd been sitting in. Mostly in shadow, she couldn't make out the driver's features. *This guy must be loaded to have a car like that,* she thought a little resentfully.

She was beginning to feel foolish and started to rethink her decision to follow Corinne when, out of the corner of her eye, Charlene saw another car slowly approach from the other end of the parking lot. She thought it was odd that the driver turned his lights off and stopped. Frowning, she glanced back to see Corinne lean in to give the 'J' guy another lingering kiss. Feeling uncomfortable about spying on them, Charlene shifted her position and pushed her hair from her sweaty forehead. She wasn't used to the warm California weather and found her silk shirt sticking to her body. Just as she was about to loosen a couple of buttons, she spotted the car with the lights off begin another slow approach. It was headed straight for Corinne.

Maybe it was the telepathy thing they'd spoken of earlier or just a sixth sense, but Corinne had stepped from the car and looked up over the roof of the car to the pickup truck parked across the road. Her eyes immediately locked with Charlene's. She didn't seem at all surprised that her sister had followed her. With a slight shake of her head, she leaned over to say a final word to her lover. Then, straightening, she watched as he drove off.

Charlene felt as if she was watching the scene play out like a movie, but in slow motion. Charlene's eyes shifted from Corinne back to the car with the lights out. Vaguely, she thought that if she squinted a little, she might be able to see the face of the man stepping out of the car. Good, she thought, because she had every intention of reporting him to the hotel manager. It was dangerous driving in a parking lot without headlights.

Then her eyes dropped to his hand. He was reaching into his jacket.

Looking back at Corinne, who was about to cross the lot than quickly back to the shadow man, Charlene realized in horror that the man had obviously been reaching for the gun that was now in his hand! Shocked into stunned silence, she couldn't even scream. Her instinct was to jump down from the truck bed and run to Corinne. Her one thought was to protect her sister. She had to stop her from crossing to the open parking lot.

Too late.

Corinne glanced back, following Charlene's gaze, noticing the car and the man for the first time. She stopped and watched as the man started walking purposely towards her. Something in the way he was approaching her must have alerted Corinne that she was in danger. She had to get to Charlene. She had to protect her.

Shaking herself from her stupor, Charlene was already on the move. Scrambling out of the back of the truck, she sprinted across the road, grabbing Corinne, who seemed frozen in place, by the hand and practically dragging her out of the lot and down the road. "Oh, my God, Corinne, run!"

Hearing the panic in her sister's voice mobilized Corinne and she tightened her grip on Charlene's hand and together they ran away from the hotel towards the cliffs.

Earlier that day, Charlene had marveled at the cliff's spectacular view of the ocean, but now all she could see was shadows and darkness as they plunged perilously closer to the edge in an attempt to evade their pursuer. Daring a quick look behind them, Charlene wished she hadn't. The black car was picking up speed and bearing down on them!

Seeing the fear on Charlene's face, Corinne also dared a look back. In doing so, she lost her grip on her sister's hand. Reaching out to catch her balance, she stumbled on the loose gravel. With the car almost upon them, Corinne instinctively shoved Charlene out of the way, but the vehicle veered to the right and slammed into her.

Charlene took the full force of the impact. She felt herself falling, hurtling headlong over the cliff into darkness. She clawed desperately, frantically for anything to break her fall and somehow managed to snag a protruding branch, but it wasn't strong enough to hold her for long. With a snap, the branch gave way and Charlene continued her descent, free-falling over sharp-edged, jagged rocks, striking them on her way to the bottom of the cliff. By the time her battered and broken body reached the bottom of the abyss, she was already unconscious.

At the same time, Corinne lay crumpled, painfully struggling to move, rising just enough to hurl something over the edge. She never felt the silent bullets that pierced her body, killing her instantly. And she would never know that her dead and lifeless body would be placed inside the black car, driven away, and set afire.

CHAPTER 3

Tyler's eyes were red and scratchy from lack of sleep. But he was too restless to sleep.

God help me. He'd wanted to call and check on Corinne. He'd been up for two nights worrying about her. He'd almost called her at the hotel, but refrained from doing so. The pictures of Corinne and her lover continued to flash behind his eyes, flaming his anger anew. So why did he keep dwelling on them? But Tyler was also grappling with how he was going to tell the kids that their mother would no longer be living with them. Hell, he didn't even know how he was going to tell his parents. He could just hear his mother now…accusing and blaming him.

Cringing at the thought, he went downstairs to the kitchen and realized he'd given his housekeeper the week off. He set about making a pot of coffee.

It was eight o'clock in the morning and he would be picking up the twins at nine. It was Saturday, their fun day with their parents. To be practical, he wouldn't delay telling them about their mother. Sadly, he realized their fun day wasn't going to be fun at all.

Filling the coffee pot with water, his eyes went to the refrigerator door and saw the birthday cards the twins had made for Corinne. Smiling sadly, Tyler guessed Shane would grow up to be an artist. He thought his son's choice of colors on the small poster board were exceptional, and he could see that Shane had drawn Corinne sitting out on the back patio looking far away, something she always did, regardless of the weather.

His daughter, Shelly's, drawing was confusing and caused Tyler to frown. Her poster was a wonderful sloppy mess and he knew she didn't care. Circles of every crayon in her box had been used to haphazardly and hastily make the card. Shelly was such a tomboy, he thought. No silly girly ways about her. To her, drawing was a boring waste of time, but she could build a sand castle and could put Shane's Transformers together in minutes.

His children were going to be hurt by his decision to divorce their mother, but there was nothing Tyler could do except to love them even more. He would tell them they could see their mother any time they wanted. He would never be so cruel as to keep them apart. Chiding himself, Tyler knew he shouldn't have told Corinne that he was filing for custody of Shane and Shelly. But he wouldn't let them be hurt by her actions, either.

He alone knew the claws she could unsheathe and the pain she could inflict. He couldn't remember the last time they'd even had sex. Yes, he could. Ten months ago. He didn't even know why she'd decided to sleep with him that night. He suspected she'd just gotten tired of him asking and did it to shut him up. He was miserable afterwards, and so was she.

The ringing telephone pulled Tyler from his troubling thoughts. Glancing at his watch he guessed Shelly was dressed and ready to begin her fun day. "She's so bossy, just like her…" Tyler caught himself. He picked up the cordless phone. "I'm on my way to pick you up, honey," Tyler said.

"Pardon," the male caller said. "Hello, I'm trying to reach Tyler Mills."

"I'm sorry, this is Tyler Mills. Who is this?"

"Yes, Mr. Mills, my name is Dr. Dom Holland. I'm calling from Cedars Sinai Hospital." The doctor was silent for a moment. He cleared his throat before he spoke again.

"Sorry, I thought it was my daughter calling. How can I help you, Dr. Holland?"

"Mr. Mills, there's been an accident…"

Tyler backed into the kitchen counter. His mouth silently repeated the word *accident.*

"My children, my parents…" The thought was too farfetched to imagine that anything could happen to any of them. No. It was probably somebody at work, he thought. Then he heard the doctor clearing his throat again.

"I'm sorry, Mr. Mills. It's not your children or parents. But there's been an accident. It's your wife. Corinne Mills is your wife, is that right?"

Tyler was experiencing several emotions all at once. "Yes, that's right. Is she all right?"

"She's in pretty bad shape, but for now she's alive, Mr. Mills."

Feeling his legs about to give way, Tyler gripped the counter with his free hand. "Pretty bad shape...wh-what are you talking about? She's at the hotel down on..." Tyler's thoughts were becoming jumbled and speaking was becoming an effort. For the life of him, he couldn't remember where the hotel was located now. It was the same hotel he and Corinne used to go for a quick getaway, very early on in their marriage, that is.

"Yes, the accident occurred near the hotel," Dr. Holland said quietly.

"Near the hotel, but there's nothing up there except..." Tyler struggled. It was a scenic area and the hotel was set back off of a cliff.

"Mr. Mills, your wife's accident occurred off the main road that leads to and from the hotel. I have to tell you...your wife...fell over the cliff."

Every nerve in Tyler's body quaked and he thought he would be ill. Surely, he hadn't heard the doctor correctly. "You said she's alive, for now. What does that mean?"

"Mr. Mills, get somebody to drive you and come to the hospital as quickly as you can."

Tyler was trying to read between the lines of the words the doctor spoke. *What did he mean, 'as quickly as you can?'* "Dr. Holland, you're not trying to tell me that my...that Corinne is...that she might..." He couldn't even muster the word *die*. It was ridiculous. "Doctor?"

The doctor cut him off, giving one more directive before ending the call. "Mr. Mills, get here as soon as you can. Come to the E.R. I'll meet you there."

Tyler stared down at the phone and clicked the off button. His muscles had gone slack and he couldn't move. Then the phone in his slack hand rang again. He lifted it to his ear. "Yes?" He heard his daughter's jubilant greeting.

"Daddy," Shelly sang.

"Hi, honey, put your grandmother or grandfather on the phone right away, okay?"

"Okay, they're both right here, Daddy."

~~~

From the time his parents, brother, sister-in-law, and sister raced to the house to get him everything had become a blur for Tyler. Arriving at the hospital a short while later, the family was escorted into a private waiting room. Tyler was thankful for that because the media was already camped out in the hospital corridor, eager to get a story. As they waited for Dr. Holland to come in and give them a report on Corinne, the police came in to question Tyler, specifically asking why his wife would be out on that hillside at that time of morning.

"All I can say, officer, is that Corinne always loved looking out at the water." When the officer gave him a skeptical look, Tyler explained further. "Whenever we've gone there she'd always walk over and um, gaze out at the water, admiring the view."

The officer scribbled onto his pocket-size notepad then looked up. "Would she walk that close to the edge and at that hour, Mr. Mills?"

Tyler blew out a breath. "Look, I don't know. All I can say is that she was often reflective when I'd find her there…just staring out." Feeling uncomfortable, Tyler watched the officer nod and walk out of the room.

Everyone was jumpy, scared, and edgy. Each recalling what Tyler had told them…that Corinne had left the house extremely upset after they'd had an argument the night of her birthday. Now, Tyler could only wonder if Corinne was so distraught that she'd do something as unthinkable as try to take her life. No. He wouldn't believe that. She'd simply walked too close to the edge and lost her footing in the dark, that's all.

Tyler's mother, Mona Mills, tried to put everyone at ease. It was something she usually did with a graceful smile, or a soft word or two. Mona was the matriarch of the Mills family. A family she kept together. A family that was open, loving and loyal to one another.

"Listen," she said, "we've all prayed and now the angels are holding her, healing her. Corinne has us and we're all prepared to help her come through this terrible ordeal." But then Mona's comforting words began to falter because she just didn't know how badly her daughter-in-law was injured.

Tyler's brother Ryan and his wife Trish sat holding hands beside a clearly worried Tyler.

Tyler's twenty-three-year-old sister, Terri, was one who was quick to speak her mind. "Tyler, Mom's right. Besides, Corinne's way too stubborn to let anything serious keep her down for long. Well, besides missing out on buying another designer outfit or berating somebody. Hey, you remember the time when she chewed out those painters for not properly mixing that paint?" Terri laughed. "I mean, come on, who paints a wall that god awful shade of orange, anyway? It still sucks, if you ask me. It makes my eyes bleed just looking at it."

Dismayed by his daughter's uncensored opinions, Melvin Mills told Terri that nobody was listening to her and to 'put a sock in it.'

Everyone chuckled, a temporary reprieve to ease the stress.

Standing at the door, Dr. Holland was glad to see the family had a sense of humor. He knew they were going to need it in the months to come. That is, if Mrs. Mills survived.

Clearing his throat to get the family's attention, Dr. Holland stepped further into the room, which immediately became silent. With a wave of his hand he encouraged everyone to remain seated. He was escorted by an attending nurse in the event one was needed. Having recognized Tyler from various magazines and news reports, Dr. Holland walked directly over to him. He decided to give him the full details of what his wife had suffered.

Tyler stood and met the doctor's eyes directly.

"Mr. Mills, your wife suffered some serious injuries. I just got out of surgery resetting a bone in her leg. It should heal properly. She has several broken bones, multiple abrasions and cuts, some of which required sutures, and a severe concussion. She has a deep laceration above her brow that a plastic surgeon can probably repair to reduce the scarring. Right now, our primary concern is a skull fracture. Because of the severity of her head injury, we've listed Mrs. Mills in critical condition."

Having already braced himself for bad news, Tyler took a deep breath. "Can I see her?"

"In a few minutes." Looking around, Dr. Holland addressed the room. "She won't know you're there because she's in a coma. Her body suffered a terrible beating in that fall. Obviously, there was lots of blood loss, too, and we're monitoring all of her vitals."

Melvin held tightly onto his wife's hand. "Doctor, she's going to walk out of this hospital. You'd best believe that, young man." Even as he said it, Melvin noticed the finger he was pointing at the doctor was shaking, betraying his confident words. "She's a wife and mother and she can be a tough girl when she wants to be," Melvin said, crossing over to Tyler and squeezing his shoulder in a comforting gesture.

"I believe you, sir, and I also believe she's a fighter," Dr. Holland said.

Tyler barely heard what the doctor was saying. He kept hearing that Corinne had fallen over that cliff. Why was she so close to the edge like that, he wondered? *Surely, she wasn't so distraught that she'd…No! She wouldn't do that.* Tyler was too shocked to even consider that Corinne could die. *No, I won't think that.* He was saved from saying what he was thinking when his brother Ryan's arm replaced his father's and Trish squeezed his hand reassuringly.

"Come on, let's go see her," Ryan said with more conviction in his voice then he felt.

As much as Dr. Holland tried to prepare the Mills family, he knew they were in for a shock when they saw their loved one.

Nobody was prepared to see Corinne lying in that hospital bed, Tyler least of all.

She was almost unrecognizable. The part of Corinne's face not covered in bandages was horribly swollen, discolored, and covered with some type of glossy salve. Several tubes snaked out from under the white cotton blankets and dangled all around the narrow bed. The steady beeping of various monitors keeping track of Corinne's vitals seemed particularly loud in the otherwise quiet room. Slowly, quietly, the shocked group moved closer.

To Tyler she looked so fragile and small and damaged. A section of her hair just above her ear had been shaved clean and a small plastic tube had been inserted. Lifting his hand to her forehead, Tyler moved a stray curl off her face. There he saw that a deep gash had been sutured. At the top of her head a thick bandage covered her head. Gently running his hand over her body, he assessed Corinne's injuries for himself. Her right arm rested across her abdomen and he took notice of the various tubes coming out of the veins in her arms, as well as from the back of her hand. The left arm and leg sported a cast.

Her ring finger was bare and that brought back their last conversation at home…when he'd thrown her out of the house. Corinne had hesitated only a second before walking out of the room. She'd taken off her rings and dropped them into the gift box. They'd landed on top of the divorce papers. To see her so hurt, so incredibly mangled and holding onto life, Tyler was hard pressed to contain the sob that escaped his constricted throat. "Corinne…I'm so sorry."

Mona Mills was at her son's side in an instant. "Tyler, she's going to be okay. I feel that. I know she's in pretty bad shape right now, but you wait, Corinne will heal and she'll be as strong and healthy as ever. Besides, she's got you and those beautiful children to come back to, and we'll all be there to help her," Mona said, watching the grim set of her son's mouth. "She'll be chasing those kids around in no time at all."

Tyler felt the last of his strength leave him. The thought of his children seeing their mother like that would be devastating. He recalled how he and Corinne recently had to explain death to the children.

After a stray kitten had wandered onto their property, the kids had instantly fallen in love with it. Tyler had taken the kitten to the vet and the prognosis wasn't good. The sick kitten had to be put down. When Tyler had returned home without the kitten, he had to explain that the kitten had died. Their rush of tears tore at his heart. But Corinne explained that the kitten was in heaven with other sick kittens. As a tribute to the kitten they'd only known for a brief period, they'd placed colorful rocks in the flower bed in the backyard where the kitten had been found.

Remembering that day just a few weeks ago, Tyler would have never thought how quickly their lives would change. Yes, he realized his children were going to be scared and sad…but so was he. Because he realized for all his words the night he banished Corinne from the house, he still cared for her.

This time he didn't bother to hold back his sobs.

CHAPTER 4

Intense pain, horrible pain, unlike anything she'd ever experienced before, came in waves, receded momentarily, only to come back again stronger and even more intense.

Through the haze of agonizing pain and consciousness, Charlene's brain couldn't grasp anything. Occasional blinding lights would flash before her eyes and there was nothing she could do to stop them, but thankfully they were always brief.

For the life of her, Charlene couldn't even think of what that light could be or where she could be for that matter, and then...*A touch*.

Soft whispers, unfamiliar sounds, and voices were constantly and oddly comforting to her. Then she tried to open her eyes and couldn't so she gave up the effort and drifted back to that quiet place...a place where the horrible pain would retreat and stop its punishing assault on every inch of her body.

Tyler stood in the hospital room, his back to the window. He didn't want to watch yet another sunset from this room. Instead, he glanced at the abundance of get well cards that had been sent to Corinne. All of the flowers and baskets had been collected at the nurse's station and taken to other hospital patients since neither was permitted in the ICU.

After five days so far, the flowers and baskets continued to arrive daily. Tyler's eyes were drawn to the cards created by Shane and Shelly.

Tyler recalled having to tell them about Corinne's accident. Thankfully, his family had been at his side. He thought the twins would need consoling, but wise beyond their years, they ended up consoling him. Once again, he realized that he and Corinne had created wonderful, amazing children. They were identical in their emotions and their dislikes, but they loved equally, and for that, he had to thank Corinne. She was a good mother.

As a wife…she wasn't so great.

Tyler had to wonder if he blamed Corinne for their problems. Yes, he did. He blamed her for falling out of love with him and turning to another man, not once, but several times. But why had he finally decided to confront her that night, he wondered. He'd set the stage to have the upper hand in what he thought was going to be a battle. Oddly, it hadn't been.

For the hundredth time in the past five days, Tyler wished he hadn't put her out of the house, and certainly not that night. If he hadn't, she wouldn't have been at the hotel and he wouldn't be standing here looking down at her lying so silent and so still.

Now Tyler recalled what happened that first evening when he and his family had returned to his home with heavy hearts and unsure of what Corinne's future would hold.

Arriving back at his home, Tyler had more reason to feel remorse.

Everyone had spilled into the living room, but it was his mother who'd picked up the gift box from the coffee table. There she spotted the rings, the untouched two-day-old dried-out birthday cake and the pictures. Mona Mills missed nothing. With everything else on his mind, Tyler had completely forgotten about these things. Before he could stop her, Mona had already begun flipping through the documents, the divorce papers, before raising scornful eyes to him.

"Mom…" he started in a warning voice.

Passing the box to her husband standing beside her, Mona held onto the pictures but angled them for only Melvin to see. Without taking her eyes off her son, Mona ripped the two eight-by-ten-inch photos into pieces then stuffed them into the pocket of her slacks. Before looking away, she shook her head negatively at Tyler.

Melvin glanced over the title of the document and he too gaped at the rings, suddenly realizing what it all meant. "Are you kidding me, Tyler?"

"Look…Dad, Mom, some things have happened between me and Corinne…" Tyler left off when their tight faces registered their disbelief. They were angry and disappointed in him.

Mona thrust a finger at the untouched cake. "On her birthday, you did that." She inclined her head to the gift box in Melvin's hand. "How could you do such a cruel thing? That's unforgivable and out of character for you, Tyler. And in the face of Corinne's current state, it was not only a cruel thing to do, but could be a deadly one as well!"

With their interest piqued, Terri, Ryan, and Trish crossed over to Melvin and looked down at the documents in his hand. They too saw the rings lying in the gift box.

Trish spoke her shock. "Oh, my God. Tyler, you filed for divorce from Corinne?"

Terri shook her head and slowly exhaled. "Guess you got tired of her spending all your money, huh, big brother? I'm surprised you'd go the divorce route. It's a bit drastic, isn't it? I mean, it's not like she was creeping around, or was she?" Terri asked with wide eyes.

Grabbing Terri by the arm, Mona propelled her daughter from the living room with a direct order to go into the kitchen and put on a pot of coffee. Then, after slamming shut the double doors leading into the living room, Mona turned and advanced on her son. "Start explaining," she'd demanded. "Where did those pictures come from?" There was no denying that Mona was the head of their family. When she demanded answers, she not only expected them, she got them.

"I had them taken," Tyler confessed, not quite meeting his mother's sharp eyes.

"By a private investigator, no doubt," Mona scoffed. "Why would you do that?"

"What do you mean why? Mom, you saw the pictures before you ripped them up. I don't think they need further explanation, do you? Or would you prefer to tape them back together for everyone to see?" Tyler responded, giving his mother a direct look.

Running a hand across his face, Mel sensed Tyler's controlled anger. "You have copies?"

Tyler felt his father would be more understandable. "Yes, of course I do."

"Well, son, you've wasted your money, now destroy them. You hear me? Destroy them today," Mel had said heatedly, rare for the quiet man to raise his voice.

Nodding, Mona agreed. "Yes, you most definitely will destroy them, as well as that document," Mona said, pointing to the divorce papers he'd had drawn up but not yet filed.

Tyler was shocked that his parents somehow thought they could dictate how he lived his life. "What? Excuse me, but have you two forgotten that I'm a grown man and that neither of you can tell me what I can and cannot do?" For an instant he thought his mother might actually smack him. She was close enough and the look on her face showed she just might.

Mona tapped a finger to Tyler's chest as she simply nodded her head. What she really wanted to do was push him back until he fell on his arrogant ass. "Don't you think you've already done enough, Tyler?" Mona asked. "You sent your wife fleeing from her home and she ended up at that hotel! You set the stage that sent her there, and I'll be damned if you think you're going to just walk away from her. Not now you won't, buster! Corinne is your wife and mother of your children." Pausing to pull a tissue from her purse, Mona stepped back, creating distance between them. "You're hurt, and I get that, but this situation is bigger than your hurt pride. You suck it up," she snapped and dabbed at her eyes.

Only then did Tyler realize that he hadn't figured his family into the equation and the ramifications of putting Corinne out of the house and his plan to file for divorce. He'd forgotten his family, primarily his mother, who maintained that the strength of the family was a whole unit. He should have known that she wouldn't take lightly his decision to divorce Corinne, regardless of what Corinne had done. "Hurt is an understatement. It's not me in that bed with her!"

Feeling the pressure of everyone's eyes on him, Tyler had little time to prepare himself for the difficult task at hand when the housekeeper had just arrived with Shane and Shelly.

That was five nights ago when their amber eyes spilled their tears. Tyler's heart was ripped to shreds when each promised to take care of their mother as soon as she got home from the hospital.

Turning from the get-well cards tacked to the corkboard to a comatose Corinne, Tyler prayed for strength to forgive Corinne's indiscretions for his children's sake.

CHAPTER 5

For the longest time she had no idea if it was minutes or days that had lapsed, but Charlene had been trying to pry her eyes open. And just when she thought she could, she couldn't. At times, it seemed a safer option to keep them closed anyway.

The flashes of bright, blinding light continued to disturb the quiet place she'd settled herself into, and the whispered voices and gentle, tender touches continued to soothe her. She looked forward to them. A whispered voice hovered above her just then and Charlene tried to latch onto it. Then something soft and lightly scented touched her face. So gentle, she wished she could reach up and touch it, if only to see if it was real.

Then she heard a sound that she recognized. It was a sniffle. She thought she could relate to sniffles and wondered if she'd been around fresh water lilies because they made her sneeze. If that's the case, then it had to be...April, she thought or... *March...our birthday is...*

The image was so fleeting that Charlene wondered if she'd actually seen it. Two little girls playing. *No, skipping with popsicles...one strawberry, one lemon.*

Then it was gone. The image felt good. It would have made her smile…that is, if she could.

Come back, please.

The voice above her whispered again, and this time Charlene grasped it with her mind. She somehow sensed the voice could help bring her from wherever she was.

———

When she was finished dabbing gently around Corinne's facial abrasions and contusions, Mona Mills asked the nurse to remove the small basket of flowers from the room. "Honey," she said, "I don't know why those flowers are in here, but could you please remove them? They're doing a number on my allergies." Returning her attention to bathing Corinne's face she said, "Now, where was I?" Mona sighed. "Oh, yes, I was telling you about my old friend, Helen. Like I was saying before the fragrance of the flowers hit me, as teenagers, Helen and I were thick as thieves. We were real party gals. But we were good girls, we weren't loose. That's what they called fast girls back then. Loose hussies, as my mother used to say." Mona chuckled again.

Charlene was still grasping. She understood the words and began trying to string them together. She understood some of the words and the light giggle that followed.

Mona wrung out another face cloth and bathed Corinne's neck and ears. "Anyway, Melvin practically forced me from the house to go out for lunch. We went to that new restaurant overlooking the water. But wouldn't you know it, no sooner did our dessert arrive in walks Helen and her husband, Grant. They both looked like the wind blew through their sails something terrible, age-wise, I mean," Mona whispered. "Helen and I had a falling out and haven't talked in years, but you know what…"

What? Charlene sense the voice moving away, leaving again. Then there it was again, the blinding light, but with it came the smell of antiseptic. *Antiseptic?* Then she was chilled. Cool air moved up her body and hands, many hands seemed to touch her. At first frightened, then she was floating. She was going back into the comfortable place again. But she missed the warm, gentle hands that touched her face so tenderly and the voice that spoke so pleasantly.

He shouldn't go, he thought, hanging up the telephone.

Tyler had received two calls from the hotel where Corinne had stayed for two nights. He'd put off going to pick up her personal things that were boxed up and in the manager's office. He had no energy to do anything except go to the hospital, pop in at the office, and go home to look after his kids. At the insistence of his parents, he'd temporarily moved in with them. He knew it was a good move for Shane and Shelly as well as for himself.

"Hey, who was on the phone?" Terri asked as she came into the kitchen.

"That was the hotel manager. I need to go pick up the things Corinne left there."

"Oh. I'll go with you," she said.

Thirty minutes later the small unopened box of items rested in the back seat of his car. With his sister Terri sitting in the passenger seat, Tyler drove a few feet down the road from the hotel and then pulled the car to the side.

Terri noticed his closed eyes from the side of his dark, tinted sunglasses. "Tyler, it's going to be okay. Corinne will recover. I was there yesterday and she's looking better already, you know, because some of the swelling is gone."

"But she's still in a coma. You heard Dr. Holland's update when he met with us last week. He'd said the longer she stays in a coma the more likely Corinne will have brain damage, and the children have been asking for her."

"Then let them see her," Terri implored. "They're worried about their mommy, Tyler."

"I know. I've told them she's healing in the hospital after her accident, but it's too soon for them to see her," he said looking at the area of the cliff and seeing faint skid marks. Getting out of the car, Tyler walked across the two lane road and looked over the edge. It had to be twenty feet to the bottom where the water slapped against the rocks. Without a word Tyler returned to his car and drove off.

Driving until he reached the bottom of the hill, Tyler made a sharp left and the road ended. Getting out of the car, ignoring Terri's questioning look, he walked over the area where the hotel concierge had told him Corinne had been found by a honeymooning couple walking along the water's edge very early in the morning.

"Oh, no," Terri murmured and immediately pulled out her cell phone and punched her parent's number. She reached her father. "Dad, please come up here, Tyler is acting weird and he's walking in the water and rocks and stuff." Disconnecting the call, Terri got out of the car and gingerly followed behind Tyler. "Hey, big brother, I really don't like this. My cute boots are getting all wet and dirty."

It was unmistakable. Looking up the rocky hillside, Tyler saw brown blotches covering some of the rocks about ten feet up. It had to be blood. Corinne's blood, he realized. Tyler stepped over stones that crunched under his feet to climb up several feet until he reached a branch sticking out of the hillside of the hillside. His fingers stretched until he was able to pluck and snatch a piece of material he'd spotted caught up on the branch.

It was a piece of white material. It was a piece of the blouse Corinne had worn the night of the accident. He'd recalled a nurse at the hospital telling him that her clothes had to be thrown away. Tyler spotted something else caught up on another branch jutting out of the side of a boulder and reached for it before making his way back down. With tears blinding him, his eyes trailed up to the top of the cliff. It wasn't twenty feet. It was at least thirty. Corinne fell some thirty feet. He couldn't stop the tears that ran from beneath his sunglasses.

Just then, his father arrived on that desolate stretch of beach. "Son, she's alive. Broken and tore up a bit, but she's alive. You just remember that, okay?"

"Okay, Dad," Tyler said, turning around at the sound of his father's voice. Releasing a breath he opened his hand. The object he'd grasped from the branch was Corinne's pendant containing the tiny pictures of Shane and Shelly.

~~~

Several days later...

She had a headache, but the searing pain was only on one side.

Charlene wished she could just pull the irritating comb from her hair. She guessed she must've fallen asleep again with the claw-type comb in her hair. *No wonder my head hurts.* Someone was talking again. It wasn't the soft whispered voice that she'd gotten used to. Rather it was the other one, the deep, more masculine voice. *Yes…it's a man. Who is he?* Holding onto the man's voice and looping his words together, Charlene was able to follow what he was saying.

Tyler was having another one-sided monologue at Corinne's bedside.

Dr. Holland had encouraged the family to talk to Corinne even if she couldn't respond. "So anyway, Shane's not too happy with me right now, but if he throws another stone at Mom's gazing balls in the backyard, well, let me just say, Shane's getting an old-fashioned whooping." Tyler chuckled. "I blame Mom and Dad for spoiling them. I mean it, Corinne. I'm tired of running out to buy more of those damn glass gazing balls. And you know if Mom finds out then I'll be the one getting a whooping and—"

"If Mom finds out what?" Mona asked, coming into the room and kissing Tyler's cheek.

"Nothing." Tyler stood up and hugged his mother. "Something between us," he added.

"I like that. Everything is between the two of you, Tyler…the good and the bad," she said, moving to the side of the bed and pressing a kiss onto Corinne's not-so-puffy cheek. "Tyler, I've already spoken to the home nursing department here at the hospital and Trish and I have interviewed two registered nurses already. The one named Florence Green specializes in trauma patients and physical therapy. I think you should meet with her. Of course, it's your say which one to hire."

Mona smoothed down Corinne's hair. "The doctor said the hairline fracture is healing nicely, but we should still get her haircut and trimmed." Looking down into her daughter-in-law's comatose face, Mona held back a sob. "Corinne, honey, please come back to us soon. Your babies miss you desperately." Mona adjusted the blankets and then ran a hand along Corinne's arm before crossing the room to where Tyler stood staring at the get well cards.

Corinne? What? Wait...I'm not Corinne. Corinne...is my...twin. My sister! Corinne run! My babies? I-I don't have any babies.

In a panic, Charlene's eyes flew open.

Everything was fuzzy and hazy as though looking though murky water. The overhead light was painfully bright. *My babies...* The voices were now distant but still there. Charlene tried to open her mouth. She had to let them know she wasn't Corinne.

Why would they confuse me with Corinne? I haven't seen her in years. Too long.

With the sudden clamor of noise, the light hurting her left eye and the comb pricking her scalp, Charlene closed her eyes again. *Better, now. I'll rest a bit longer, then I'm gettin' up and tellin' those people they're confusin' me with my twin sister...people used to always do that.*

———⟆⟆———

A week later, she remained in a coma and Tyler was back at Corinne's bedside sitting in the chair that had become his spot. He'd often fall asleep in it while working on his laptop.

Tonight he didn't have his laptop and his body was slumped in that chair. He was tired and remorseful as he began another one-sided conversation. "I did it, Corinne, and I feel like crap." He absently smoothed the blanket covering his wife's unmoving form. "Yeah, we were all having dinner and out of the blue Shane threw a handful of cooked carrots at Shelly. Well, the fight was on. Mom was scolding and Dad was trying to get between them and Terri was laughing up a storm. Then Shelly managed to get away from Dad and socked Shane right in the jaw." Tyler couldn't hold back his chuckles, picturing that scene all over again.

"Truthfully it was funny because none of us knew what was going to happen next. I mean, I'm sitting there choking on those damn chicken nuggets they insisted on having for dinner, too stunned to even reprimand Shane at first. Then our little princess Shelly walked right up to Shane and…BAM! She popped him in the jaw." Tyler couldn't contain his laughter. "All I could do was to tell him he was never to throw cooked carrots at a woman again. So guess what Miss Shelly said to that?"

What? Charlene was holding onto the story because she understood it.

"Well, she turns to me and says, 'Daddy, I'm not a woman…I'm a girl! Is Hannah Montana a woman? Duh, no!' " Tyler's chuckles reverberated in his chest. "After Shelly filled me in on who Hannah Montana was, I scooped Shane up and punished him. No video games for a week. Not even the new one I just got him, and I was looking forward to playing it, too." His laughter stopped suddenly and Tyler exhaled deeply. His voice had become labored as if it took way too much energy to talk now.

"I didn't want to punish him, Corinne. In my heart I understand that Shane's angry and lashing out. He misses you. He said he wants to talk to you. I know he doesn't mean to be bad, but he thinks you're gone like the kitten. I promised him you weren't. Our little boy is scared," Tyler said quietly, his emotions forcing him to squeeze his eyes shut for several seconds.

"When I went back down to the dining room ready to reprimand Shelly for hitting Shane, Terri was still snickering. She cheerfully told me that my butt was now in deep trouble. I'd noticed Mom had that funny curl to her lip. You know, like somebody's about to get it big time. So Shelly said she'd told Grandma that Shane had thrown rocks at three of her pretty gazing balls, breaking them into pieces, and that I had covered for Shane by going down to the Home Depot and buying new ones." Tyler suddenly started laughing. He found he wasn't able to stop as he struggled to say what'd happened next.

"Corinne…Mom chased me around…the dining-room table…with her shoe. She kept saying she was going to break…my balls…into pieces…too," he'd managed to say while grabbing his stomach and covering his mouth, least he awaken other patients in rooms down the hall.

Suddenly Tyler's laughter subsided and stopped altogether. "I didn't want to punish Shane," he said sadly and rested his elbows on the bed before dropping his head to his folded hands.

He's sad now, Charlene thought, and without any other notion whatsoever, lifted her hand and touched his arm. She noticed his arm felt warm, and very real. *I'm not dreamin' this.*

Rubbing at his eyes, Tyler didn't immediately feel the light touch on his forearm. Then collecting himself, he stilled instantly. That's when he felt it again. Without lifting his head, his eyes slide to his left arm and there he watched her hand gently pat his arm.

His eyes flew to her face at the same time his hand captured and covered hers. "Corinne?" He stood up and stared down into her opened eyes. "Corinne, can you hear me?"

Charlene couldn't speak. Something was preventing her from speaking. It was preventing her from telling him yes, she could hear him, but no, she wasn't Corinne. She was forced to blink rapidly against the bright overhead light. She couldn't even raise her left hand to shield the light because both arms were painfully sore. What she could do was squeeze his strong, yet comforting, hand lightly.

Relief washed over Tyler.

"Oh, God, Corinne, you're okay. You had an accident but you're going to be all right. Can you understand me?" He smiled when her hand tightened around his again. "I knew talking about the kids and their antics would do it." He sensed her getting agitated. "It's all right, baby. You're in the hospital because you took a terrible fall." In that second of staring down into her face, Tyler didn't believe that Corinne would ever be the same. "You're going to be fine. I-I need to get the nurse. I'll be right back, Corinne," Tyler said, and flew from the room.

No, don't go…please come back. I'm not Corinne…I'm Charlene. I'm Charlene McDonald!

Soon the flurry of activity overwhelmed her but she could only lay there, unmoving. Again a chill moved over her body, and then endless needles pricked her skin. But he was still there, she felt him…the man with the gentle touch, strong hand, and deep voice. He was watching her. Charlene thought he looked frightened, but relieved. *Who is he?*

Tyler couldn't believe it. Corinne was awake. It didn't mean she was okay, just that she was awake. He watched the team of doctors and nurses attend to her, checking the monitors, taking blood samples, checking her vitals. Her left eye was still swollen and bruised, but her right eye was as clear and as bright as ever. He knew that she had to be scared. She looked it, although he'd never seen her scared. A nurse approached and asked him to leave so that they could finish attending to his wife.

At the end of the hallway, Tyler pulled out his cell phone and called the family. Then he called his best friends, Darrell and James. Both had been sources of strength and support since Corinne's accident.

Dropping into a chair, he realized he'd had Corinne's locket in his pocket and decided when the doctor was finished with his examination he'd put it around her neck…where she'd always worn it.

———∿∿∿———

Some days Charlene could open her eyes and feel mentally connected to time and space, like the fact that she was in a hospital. Although her thoughts were scattered, she was aware of a few things. First, the people who talked to her quietly all confused her with Corinne…folks always did, she thought. Second she'd had a terrible fall. Everybody had said so, but she had no memory of falling. Third, she wondered why her father hadn't come to visit her yet.

She'd been listening to the bits and pieces of conversations as people came and talked; all seemed to be caring and attentive people. Except for one, she thought.

It was a man's voice that whispered in her ear. For the life of her, Charléne couldn't make out what he'd said. But she felt his lips against her ear.

———

Mona was glad she had a strong stomach. When the attendants came in and out of Corinne's room to check or clean her tubing or to bathe her, Mona always stayed nearby, often holding Corinne's hand. This was the mother of her grandchildren, and for that she was to be cared for and protected. She didn't care what Tyler had accused her of.

"There you are, dear, all cleaned up," she said. Mona's mood was pensive. She was equally worried about her daughter-in-law as she was about Tyler and her grandchildren. "I should have never stuck my nose into yours business, Corinne, and I'm sorry I did," Mona said after planting a kiss on Corinne's cheek. She then quietly left the room.

CHAPTER 6

Several days later, Tyler was at the office. He had to make sure a major contract he'd drafted was sent to their legal department. Having entrusted the day-to-day operations of the shipping business to his plant managers, he'd been able to take the time to care for his children and spend time at Corinne's bedside.

Since Corinne's accident he'd only stopped in the office periodically to sign a document or two and to attend the weekly staff meeting. Even though he couldn't focus on business, he knew his staff understood and were capable of running the business in his absence.

The previous evening, Dr. Holland met with the family. He'd suggested Corinne be moved to hospice for long-term care because she remained in a coma. Their hopes had been dashed when the doctor previously told them that Corinne opening her eyes and moving her hand were likely involuntary movements.

Standing at her bedside with his parents, Tyler told Corinne just that. "Corinne, I don't want to do it, but I think a hospice is better for you instead of bringing you home right now."

Melvin's face was grim also as he caressed Corinne's arm. "Don't you worry, missy. You're going to a top-notch facility. It'll be the best that money can buy," he said.

Mona adjusted Corinne's cover. It had become a nervous gesture. "I still think she should come home, Tyler, but I understand it's your decision," she said.

"It's for the best, Mom, and in a few weeks I'll take Shane and Shelly to see her."

Charlene understood it all and she felt their regret at having to send her away. *Oh, I want to wake up. I want to tell them I'm not Corinne. I can do it. I'm not a sickly child any longer. I'm stronger. I can open my eyes and move my hand again...*

"Helen..." Charlene said in a croaked, hoarse whisper as her right hand grasped the hand adjusting the cover around her. "Helen..." she said, stronger this time. Then she opened her eyes.

Mona's hand shook and her knees quaked. "Oh, my goodness..." Her eyes flew to Tyler's and Melvin's as they gawked down at Corinne.

"Corinne..." Tyler said as his hand curled around her fingers. "Corinne. Do you know me?" When her fingers tightened, Tyler prayed it was a sign that there was no brain damage.

Charlene looked from him to the woman who was leaning close to her. Her vision was hazy and the side of her mouth felt as if it was bandaged, but she'd managed, "Helen?"

A smile lit up Mona's face and she did a little hop. "I'm not Helen. I'm your mother-in-law, Mona. Welcome back, dear, welcome back."

Charlene cleared her throat and repeated the only word she seemed to know. "Helen."

Glancing up at Tyler and Melvin, Mona smiled. "So you were listening," she whispered.

Tyler reached up and pressed the nurse station call button. He noticed her eyes watching him intently, oddly. "Hey, it's me, Tyler."

Dr. Holland, with a resident and two nurses, rushed into the room. Each stopped in their tracks when they heard Corinne Mills address her husband.

"Tyler?" Charlene sensed she knew him. She sensed he was important. *To me, how?* "Tyler?" Repeating the name again. "Do I-I know you?" she asked, lifting her eyes to his handsome face. She'd seen that face before, perhaps on television. She didn't think she'd ever met him, though.

Tyler chucked and sighed heavily with relief. "Yes, you know me. I'm…"

Then it hit her. In absolute shock, Charlene's eyes widened in horrible recollection.

They all think I'm Corinne, my twin sister. Tyler? Tyler Mills is…Corinne's husband! Somewhere in the distant, Charlene heard her own voice yelling loudly, *Corinne, run!* Then she heard *my babies…*

A painful spasm rippled through her head and Charlene's body was rocked into a violent seizure.

The two nurses rushed to lower the bed as the doctors began attending to her. Each barked out orders for the family to leave immediately. But the beeping monitors with flashing numbers held them immobile. The seizure caused Charlene's body to thrash about on the narrow bed. Perspiration covered her face.

Tyler and his family all stood close together at the foot of the bed. They could only look on in horror. The pain etched into Corinne's face was hard for them to take.

Ryan held Tyler back from going to Corinne. He knew he'd only be in the way as the doctors and nurses tended to her. Mona cried out for her to stay strong and to stay with them.

When the earthquake that seemingly ran through Charlene's aching body finally abated, she was left with aftershocks and twitches she couldn't control. There was a metallic taste of blood in her mouth. Settling down, Charlene knew the strange faces staring back at her from across the room were frightened also. Raising her hand, she moaned, "Helen."

Separating from the group, Mona rushed to Corinne's side and grasped the trembling hand. "It's okay," Mona said, struggling to keep her quivering voice calm and soothing. She took the damp cloths from the nurse and wiped Corinne's face. "What's my name, dear?"

"Mama?" Charlene whispered.

"Close enough, it's Mona." Mona turned to Tyler and held out her hand for him. "And here's Tyler, your husband. You just gave him a fright, but he's okay too, aren't you Tyler?" Mona asked when Tyler walked over on shaky legs and lifted Corinne's hand.

"Sorry," Charlene mumbled. But she was scared herself, because she couldn't understand what was going on. "Scared."

Tyler kissed her forehead lightly. "I'm the one who's sorry," he said quietly.

Despite the agonizing pain, Charlene recalled the last thing she remembered doing was running, then everything went blank. "Who...was I...runnin' from?" she asked Tyler, her words slurring as the pain medication began to take effect.

Tyler looked perplexed at her question. "Running? I thought you were staring out at the water again. Were you were running from someone?"

The fragmented pieces were like watching quick previews of a movie clip. Fast, fleeting, and making Charlene want to see more. Problem was she couldn't hold onto them for any length of time. Hearing the man's question, she returned his stare. "I-I...don't know," Charlene mumbled, becoming frustrated. *'Corinne, run!'* "Corinne is..." she began.

"That's right, your name is Corinne and we're your family," Mona was saying. "And very soon the doctors will let us take you home. You'll recover in no time at all and you'll be taking care of your babies once again."

"My…babies," Charlene whispered. *These people are wrong. I just don't understand why they think I'm Corinne.*

Dr. Holland asked them to leave the room so that they could better access the patient.

A man in a white lab coat filled Charlene's vision. "Welcome back, Mrs. Mills. It's taken several weeks, but it appears you've awakened from your coma. We need to do some tests, physical and mental assessments to evaluate you. What do you say? Do you feel strong enough to answer a few questions? We'll stop if you get too tired."

Charlene watched the strangers leave the room. Incredibly after several seconds she realized what they were all thinking—that she was Corinne. Surely, this was some kind of joke. She and Corinne hadn't played that silly 'guess which twin it is' game since they were teenagers, at least not since she'd taken Corinne's place to get a driver's license for her. So what had happened since then she wondered. Just then she realized something the doctor had said.

Wait a minute…several weeks?

Dr. Holland explained the accident and her injuries. When he told her she'd taken a fall over a cliff and had been in a coma, the incessant beeping of monitors caused him to motion the nurse standing nearby to administer a sedative right away.

CHAPTER 7

Over the course of the next two weeks, Charlene had gone through a battery of tests, evaluations, and intense physical therapy. The psychological evaluation showed a severe memory lapse. She had no idea of time, her age, or address, and she couldn't match names with faces. She knew she had a father, but didn't know his name, and when asked her mother's name, Charlene responded, "I don't know. Is it Mona?" But she sensed that was wrong.

She continued to have mini-seizures that left her drained of energy. The man she now recognized as Tyler was always there…she knew he was her sister's husband. The doctor prescribed anti-seizure medication to decrease the severity and frequency of her episodes.

The doctor reported that her injuries were healing faster than expected. Her broken arm and leg were healing to the point where the doctor ordered soft casts for them. Charlene continued to complain about fuzzy vision in her left eye and it remained red, but the swelling was almost gone. The deep gashes above her eye and on her forehead were healing, but were painfully tight. She was completely deaf in her left ear.

Through it all, Charlene remained in a state of disbelief and shock because she had no idea how she'd fallen or how she'd come to be in California where Corinne lived.

But just a few nights ago she'd awakened from a dream about Corinne. When she'd struggled past the pain of remembering, she was positive what she'd dreamed might have actually happened.

It felt very real to her.

In the dream she and Corinne had been standing face-to-face, smiling. Then they were sitting together talking for so long that she'd had to get up and stretch her legs. She thought they might have been munching on sandwiches and chips as they talked.

What concerned Charlene about the dream was that in it, she appeared to be as she was now, an adult by the looks of her clothes. But that had to be impossible because she hadn't seen Corinne since…when? Straining to jar her memory, another fragmented memory sliced through. It was clear and very understandable. It was Corinne's wedding day.

Lifting her hand to her throat Charlene was surprised to discover a chain. Struggling to sit up further, she clutched the oval shaped pendant in her hand. Oddly, she recalled holding it before and knew that it could open. She couldn't open it so she let it be.

Later that day, Charlene was awakened by the orderlies cleaning her room. Assuming she was asleep, they chatted freely.

She heard one say, "I tell you this Mrs. Mills is one lucky woman. Her hospital bills have already reached high six figures and are still climbing. And, I heard her husband went down to the finance office and wrote out a check for what the insurance wasn't covering." The woman snapped her finger at the other. "Just like that…not even a problem to dish out that kind of money. Hope she recovers to thank him properly, you know what I mean?" She cackled.

Their gossiping grated in Charlene's good ear. How dare they be so cruel, she thought?

"I heard that marriage was in trouble. Can't be him. I've seen him down in the cafeteria, all worried. Seen her around town a few times, too, always dressed to the nines and he ain't never with her."

The other female orderly piped in again. "I bet you're right. A few years back my brother's painting company was hired to paint a wall in that big house of theirs. Well, he later told me it was some ugly sunset color. But Mrs. Mills had fussed him out because the color wasn't right. But, it was for *her* bedroom, ain't that something?"

Charlene heard the 'tsk-tsk-tsk' along with the squeaking wheels of the cleaning cart.

"I guess that handsome Mr. Mills won't get a proper thank-you anytime soon. She's a bit of a mess with those injuries and all." Snickering slyly, they left the room.

Charlene's eyes fluttered opened. Corinne and Tyler's marriage was in trouble, but Tyler had paid her hospital bills. "Six figures and climbing..." Charlene counted on her fingers what six figures meant. But because Tyler Mills thought she was his wife, he'd paid her hospital bills.

In her mind she could hear Corinne's voice but could only discern a word or two. She wondered when Corinne had told her that her marriage was in trouble. Had they talked recently? Charlene glanced at the opening door, putting an end to her troubling thoughts when another visitor peeked in the door before coming in to stand beside her bed.

Terri stepped closer to the bed and sang out a greeting. "Hey," she said, then, clearing her throat, Terri enunciated her words slowly, but loudly. "Hi, Co-rinne, how are you today?"

Charlene wanted to laugh. The young girl's pretty, cinnamon-brown face was split into a bright smile. Her hair was braided in a hundred tiny braids that swished against Charlene's arm as she leaned over her. Charlene fingered the silky ends through her fingers as they dangled above the sheets. "Pretty," she said. "Not deaf, this ear," Charlene said, pointing to her right ear.

Grinning sheepishly, Terri said, "Sorry, my bad." Frowning, she smoothed down Corinne's hair. "Your hair is a mess. Don't worry, it'll be trimmed now that the bald spot is healing."

Not missing the young woman's expression, Charlene tried to lift her hand to her hair but couldn't do it. "Bad?"

Terri managed to smooth back Corinne's tumble of matted hair. "Hmm? Oh, you want to know how bad the bald spot is, is that right?" She watched her sister-in-law nod slowly and awkwardly. Terri was brutally honest and the comical twisting of her lips said plenty.

"Well, let's just say a comb shouldn't go anywhere near it or even to the side where they shaved and that tube thing is sticking out from behind your ear. That cute doc of yours said it was to allow fluid to leak out. Yikes." Terri made another face but quickly covered her mouth. "Sorry, Corinne, but it's pretty bad. I mean, right now you can't even think about trying out for *America's Next Top Model*. Before the accident, yeah, but not now. Girl, they wouldn't even let you in the door." Seeing Corinne's agitation, Terri became flustered. "Hey, it's healing up nicely. I'm sorry, Corinne, I-I didn't mean to upset you."

Charlene touched the girl's hand. "Mirror."

"Huh? Mirror? Oh, you want to look into a mirror?" Terri sat on the side of the bed, dangling her feet. "I-I don't know, Corinne, you might freak out. Honestly, I know I would."

"Won't."

"You promise?"

"Um-hmm." Preparing herself, Charlene watched the young woman hop down off her bed and head out the door. Returning a few minutes later, she watched her hop back on the bed with a mirror in her hand.

"Now, remember you said you won't freak out," Terri said, then angled a large mirror she'd found at the nurse's station up to Corinne's face.

Shocked beyond anything she could have guessed, Charlene was unprepared for what she saw. The conversation of the gossipy orderlies replayed in her head. 'She's a bit of a mess with those injuries.' Charlene realized it was an understatement.

Her face was bruised in many areas, except for her nose, and she wondered how that had escaped injury. But everywhere else was bruised, discolored, or stitched up. She could only open her eyes a fraction. She had several sutures inching up above her eyebrow and the gash was still horrid looking. Angling her head to the right, she saw what the young woman meant about her head being shaved. It was, but a thick bandage was there. Lifting the mirror higher by nudging the girl's elbow up, Charlene saw the spot at the top of her head.

Bald spot, my ass, Charlene thought, struggling to control her facial expressions.

It was a two-inch long gap that was stapled closed. To her it looked as if someone had busted open a melon then used a staple gun to snap it back together again. *Don't freak out. Don't scream in horror, and don't cry.* "Wh-who're you?" she asked the young girl on her bed.

Terri tried to lower the mirror but Charlene wouldn't let her. "I'm Terri, your sister-in-law, Corinne. I'm Tyler's sister," she said quickly.

"What happened?" Charlene asked, sensing this visitor would tell her the absolute truth. But when the young girl simply said she fell, Charlene closed her eyes and forced herself not to cry. Besides, she sensed the tears would run down her face and sting her cuts and scrapes.

Terri seemed unsure of what to say, at first. "Okay, now I'm only telling you this because I kind of feel responsible for how things went down between you and Tyler, you know a while back. He's still pissed at me about that."

"Huh?" Charlene responded, only half following the girl's rapid speech.

"Well, you remember how I told Tyler I overhead you on the phone?"

"Huh?"

"Oh, right, I heard your memory fades in and out. But you see, I'd told Tyler about hearing you on your cell phone. You were all quiet and then crying," Terri said. "Anyway, it was midnight and I kind of implied that you were probably talking to a guy because you kept saying how you 'couldn't believe that you wouldn't see him again.' " Terri wouldn't meet her gaze. "I just know you were talking to a guy. Anyway, Tyler blew the roof and well, you know the rest because he moved out of your bedroom. Truthfully, he was all set to come back to our house. But if it wasn't for you getting sick that same week, I know Tyler was going to move out of the house, Corinne, and it would've been my fault. I really need to learn to keep my mouth shut sometimes," Terri said, picking at her burgundy-painted fingernails.

Charlene understood. "How...did I fall?"

Terri told her everything she'd heard about how Corinne fell over the cliff. Terri drummed her fingers along the bed rail. "Listen, Corinne, um, you and Tyler, well...you guys just needed some space after everything went down, you know, to chill for a bit, that's all," she lied.

In the mirror, Charlene's eyes dropped down to the pendant around her neck. "Mine?"

Glad that Corinne didn't press her for more details about why she was really at that hotel, since she'd also overheard that Tyler had kicked Corinne out, Terri unhooked and lifted the pendant from Corinne's neck. "Yes, it's your locket." Opening the tiny toggle, Terri held the small oval frames for Corinne to see the pictures.

Charlene stared at the two pictures, a boy and a girl, twins. *My babies...please take care of my babies, and Tyler.* "My babies..." Charlene repeated distant words in a strangled voice. *They're not babies anymore, they're...eight.*

"That's right. Well, they're just little bad-asses if you ask me, especially that Shelly. But, I got her number and that smart lip of hers, too, but, yeah, that's them and they miss you," Terri said, then lifted her eyes from the locket to Corinne's stricken and pale face.

Charlene's mind was tumbling, over and over as if she were falling and…

She remembered clutching that oval pendant before. But it was so much more than just a locket. *My babies*…Staring unseeingly into the mirror, Charlene saw several things, many things flashing and playing out in the images flickering and swirling in the mirror, almost like it was a magical mirror.

She held onto everything she saw and the memory attached to each. The first class airline flight and the ritzy hotel, black jersey slacks and her favorite white blouse…a black car, no lights on…gun…she and Corinne running for their lives. "Oh, my God…" Charlene croaked.

"Oh, my God," Terri repeated and gaped at Corinne shaking body and bleeding nose, as she was almost uprooted and knocked to the floor by Corinne's suddenly thrashing legs.

Another seizure hit Charlene.

Terri was too shocked and panicked to remember to press the emergency nurse call button or to pay any attention to the man who'd come into the room or the way he'd stared so deeply into Corinne's frightened face.

When Terri finally hit the button, she glanced anxiously at the door for the sounds of hurrying feet…the man had disappeared.

CHAPTER 8

At midnight, as she lay in her hospital bed, Charlene found she could remember and write more with fewer interruptions by hospital staff and visits from Corinne's family. She had asked a nurse for a pad and ink pen and, over the course of the past week, she wrote everything down as her memory returned, whether it made sense or not.

For their part, Tyler and his family didn't seem to care about her appearance or how much money they were spending on therapists and specialists who worked with her on her recovery. Their tireless efforts encouraged her to push her body to the point that she was healing faster than expected. Doctor Holland was encouraged by her progress.

The prior afternoon, Trish had brought her clothes to wear home. She'd commented on how much weight 'Corinne' had lost. And although her speech was somewhat slurred and she was, to some degree, disabled, Charlene felt everyone appeared eager for 'Corinne' to go home.

Their unselfishness tore at Charlene's heart. As much as she wanted to tell them that she wasn't Corinne, she knew they wouldn't believe her. They'd all been told that it would take time for her to return to her usual self, and that she had suffered severe head trauma that may cause confusion, depression, and anger.

At first Charlene didn't believe it, but, despite all the intense physical therapy, injections, and soft casts, she felt weak and frail. Charlene vowed silently that with their support and money paying for those specialists she was going to get herself in optimal health and then she would tell them. They had to know. They had a right to know what she already knew and felt in her heart…that Corinne, her only living relative, was dead.

Despite her memory lapses, Charlene had been a quick study of Corinne's family. Each had a personality that she'd quickly picked up and jotted down in her notepad. She hoped as she recovered and lived with them that she remembered everything she'd picked up of Corinne's personality also…just long enough so that she could play at being her twin to find out what happened to her.

—⁓—

Days later on a sunny California morning, 'Corinne' was going home.

Charlene glanced out the window at the passing terrain. It was all so beautiful, almost as beautiful as the interior of the limousine she sat in so comfortably. It was her first time in a limousine, but the severe headache she was experiencing didn't distract from the luxury of it. After she'd been helped into a wheelchair, the attendants informed her that the ambulance to take her home was waiting on a private ramp, meaning no media would be there.

Charlene immediately scoffed at being wheeled into the ambulance. One of her final memories of her father was seeing him carried from their house and put into an ambulance. He never returned home again.

She pleaded with Tyler and Mona to find another way to take her home, and, seeing her agitation, they opted for the limousine.

As she sat in the limousine Charlene wondered if she could pull off what she was about to do...pretend to be her twin sister. To her way of thinking, she didn't have a choice if she was to get to the bottom of what happened to Corinne that night they met.

A remorseful sob escaped her lips and Tyler immediately clutched her hand tightly in his. Charlene glanced up at him through her darkly tinted sunglasses. She remembered gasping when he'd brought the sunglasses to the hospital earlier. Not because they were so dark. They were exactly what the doctor ordered. It was the three-hundred-and-fifteen-dollar price tag dangling down her nose when she'd put them on that caused her to gasp.

"There," he'd said. "I like them, beautiful." Looking beyond the fading bruises, Tyler still thought his wife was beautiful, Charlene thought to herself.

Charlene thought he was just being kind. She knew she was anything but beautiful. Inside she felt ugly and hideous. *I'm the bride of Frankenstein, stitched and pinned together.*

Charlene had rarely talked since coming out of the coma. But when she did her sentences were brief and clipped, like today, so that no one would detect her Southern drawl. One of the things she remembered when she'd greeted Corinne in the lobby was Corinne teasing her about how 'country' she'd sounded, whereas Corinne had totally lost her Southern accent. Corinne had told Charlene how she'd practiced by speaking slowly and using brief sentences. "Scared," Charlene said in a quiet voice.

Tyler eased his arm around her shoulders. "What are you scared of?"

Before being able to answer him, the limousine came to a stop in a wide circular driveway and Charlene's eyes widened behind the dark tinted sunglasses. The large house with a wide front porch would be classified as an estate or mansion. "Really scared, now," she mumbled, letting her eyes run up to the second level where enormous, wide windows stood.

Tyler grinned. "Oh, come on, my family isn't that bad. Well, okay, they are, but I've only moved us back in with them until you recover fully," he said. "I figured you'd have round-the-clock care, and it's much easier on the twins." Tyler wanted to say that the house was so large that she wouldn't have to worry about seeing so much of him, but he didn't.

"The twins..." Charlene spoke of what she was really scared of. *The twins. Corinne's children and her blood relatives...* Only now did she realize what she would be doing to them. Since she'd awakened from her coma and was able to speak, Charlene had spoken to the children a few times on the telephone. She didn't know one voice from the other. But each chatted with excitement about 'mommy' coming home and how they would take care of her. Holding back another sob, Charlene smiled when she spotted Mona come out onto the porch and walk down the steps to meet the limo. Instantly, Charlene's fears disappeared. She was comforted by the older woman's lovely, smiling face. Odd, she thought.

I can do this. I have to do this because I have to find out what happened to us that night. I'll do it for you, Corinne, and for your children. I swear I will because I promised you I would.

———

Tyler carried her up the four steps to the porch and at Mona's insistence carried her into the house. But then Mona shooed him away when he pretended his back was aching from the effort. "Aaww," Tyler huffed, feigning a backache. "It's like carrying a piece of furniture." He succeeded in coaxing a small smile from his wife.

"Fun-ny," Charlene said when he'd set her down on her feet, then let her eyes circle the open foyer. The interior marbled flooring stretched on endlessly, disappearing out of sight into the back of the house. She could see several rooms tasteful and elegantly designed rooms from the wide foyer. From what she could see, it was a grand house inside and out. A large formal living room was to her left and another room, possibly a great room and den, were across the foyer to her right. Straight ahead was a formal dining room, and beyond that the large kitchen, completely modern, yet with a welcoming, homey feel. The house was expensive, yet understated and beautifully decorated. Charlene would bet it rivaled any Southern-style mansion back home in Virginia.

After Mona gave her a tour to reacquaint her with the layout of the house, the patio, and pool area, they returned to the living room where the rest of the family had gathered to greet her. "Now as I told you, and I know Tyler has also, honey, this is just temporary until you're well enough to go back to your own home." Mona sent Tyler a direct look. "But I'm delighted you're here, all of you."

Charlene had stopped listing to Mona because straight ahead were the twins. Each was cautiously approaching her with Melvin nudging them along.

It was incredible, she thought. The twins looked so much like Corinne. Right down to their beautiful and soulful dark amber eyes. Charlene knew they were just as frightened and apprehensive as she was. She felt it.

She was vaguely aware that Melvin was welcoming her home and absently mumbled a greeting, but didn't take her eyes off the children who'd just stopped in front of her, holding hands. A flash of memory hit her...she and Corinne running down the road near their house, holding hands until Corinne tripped. Swallowing the painful knot away she said, "I know. I look at mess, don't I? I'll bet you think I got hit by a bus, right?"

Shelly frowned. "No, we don't. We know you fell off a cliff like the lady on television."

Charlene smiled. "What lady?"

"That lady on the show Daisy watches. She was all broken up, too, but she has plastic on her face now," Shelly said.

Tyler angled his head to Daisy, the housekeeper, whose eyes danced up comically before covering a grin with her apron. Daisy eyed Shelly but addressed Tyler. "I got it, Tyler. No soaps around this one and, Shelly, that lady had plastic *surgery* on her face."

Shelly shrugged her shoulders. "What's wrong, Mommy?" Shelly asked, watching her mother's pale face collapse.

Hearing Shelly's innocent words, Charlene couldn't help but think of the similarities of the soap opera and what she was doing. Had it not been for Tyler tightening his arm about her waist, Charlene would have crumbled to the floor. "I'm fine now, but I-I missed both of you." Charlene lifted her eyes to

Shane, who so far had remained silent. "How're you, Shane?"

The little boy pouted. "Why do you have those big sunglasses on in the house?"

"Because my eye hurts," Charlene said, guessing Shane was the quiet one. "The sunglasses keep the bright light out as it gets better."

"I hurt my eye before, too," Shane said, rubbing his right eye.

"It bet it hurt a lot, didn't it?" Charlene inched slightly closer to the kids.

"Um-hum."

Everyone sensed the importance of the children warming up to their mother again. No one interrupted the reunion.

"Well, I sort of want you to see it, but I don't want either of you to be grossed out by it. I'll show you, but then I'll put an eye patch on. You won't be scared if I show you, will you?" Charlene sent Terri a smile, remembering the girl's words to her in the hospital.

Excited at the prospect of seeing it, the twins spoke simultaneously. "We won't."

Everyone chuckled watching Shane and Shelly inch cautiously, but curiously, to examine their mother's face. Satisfied and even a little disappointed that it wasn't 'too' gross, they stepped back but stayed close to Charlene. Mona suggested everyone go into the family room where a scrumptious buffet had been laid out by Daisy.

Ten minutes later everybody was sitting around comfortably listening as Charlene quietly told the twins about her injuries. In turn, the twins pointed out their own bumps and scrapes.

With several stitches almost going up beyond the natural arch of her eyebrow, and now partially hidden by her hair, Terri picked up Charlene's sunglasses and tried them on. "Girl, I sure hope that doesn't leave a deep scar, you know what I mean?"

Charlene shrugged. What did she care about a scar and constant pain? She was alive.

"Can I put my head on your lap if I'm careful?" Shelly asked, touching a fading bruise on her mother's cheek.

Charlene lost it then. The tears came out of nowhere and all she could do was nod her head. Then she cradled Shelly, followed by a reluctant Shane, who snuggled up closer. Her heart literally broke. These were Corinne's babies and she felt the love these two lovely children had for their mother. It was unconditional and overflowing despite her injuries, and it was amazing.

"Don't cry. Daddy said we could help take care of you. Didn't you, Daddy?" Shane said.

Tyler nodded, sitting beside Corinne on the couch. "Yes, I did, and we all will," Tyler said, looking down at Corinne as she tenderly touched the children's faces and then hugged them close. There was no doubt she'd missed them as much as they missed her.

"Okay," Mona said, getting up as a woman in her late fifties appeared in the doorway. "I think it's time for Corinne to get some rest and here's Florence now."

Florence Green crossed over to her charge. "Hello, Mrs. Mills, my name is Florence, but please call me Flo. I'm your nurse and also your physical therapist. Now, don't you worry about a thing and I'll have you doing jump ropes in no time."

The twins held their heads together, whispering. "Mommy doesn't jump rope," they giggled.

With Tyler's assistance, Flo helped Charlene to her feet. "Oh, just you wait, my dears. I will have her jumping ropes, won't I, Mrs. Mills?" Flo chuckled, arching an eyebrow.

Charlene immediately liked the woman. "And hoola-hoops, too." Charlene relaxed when the twins squealed in laughter.

CHAPTER 9

Registered nurse and physical therapist Flo Green didn't lie.

As soon as she got Charlene upstairs she went to work. First she helped her patient change into workout gear. Then physical therapy was underway. It was grueling, painful, and necessary. Charlene's complaints were silent, but her groans and grunts weren't.

Charlene had had little time to dwell on her new surroundings during her first two-hour workout. Earlier Mona had informed her that she and Tyler would share the suite Corinne and Tyler had shared as newlyweds. Now, two hours later, with a few minutes to herself while Flo drew her bath, Charlene glanced around the room. It was bright and cheerful and as tastefully decorated as the rest of the house.

The first thing she noticed was the king-sized bed. Another area of the room contained a sitting area so large there was enough room for a loveseat sofa and two wingback chairs. The rooms were fragrant with the pleasant scent of freshly cut flowers that had been arranged in vases throughout the room.

Charlene had never seen a bedroom or house so fine in all her life.

With the use of her crutches, she hobbled over to the large walk-in closet. There, she saw a few pieces of Corinne's designer clothing hanging inside and she couldn't keep from touching the delicate fabrics. The finest thing she'd ever owned was…*my white silk blouse*. She clearly remembered wearing it when she'd arrived in California. With a sinking feeling in her chest, Charlene also remembered what'd happened to it. "Oh God, Corinne," she whispered, holding a long, elegant robe hanging in the closet up to her nose and inhaling a light floral scent.

Tyler leaned against the bedroom doorframe waiting while Corinne walked around inside the closet. When she came out he stood up straight, walked in, and closed the bedroom door. "I, um…didn't know how long we were going to stay here so I grabbed some things from your closet back at our house." He watched her. "You okay with this…being here, I mean?"

Charlene nodded, again realizing how tall he was. "Do I-I have a computer?" She spoke slowly, deliberately and briefly…just as Corinne had done when she too pretended to be someone she really wasn't. Tyler responded yes she'd had a computer and offered to get it for her. Charlene was silently thankful; she had much to research, and she was eager to get started.

"I'll go to the house tomorrow and get it for you. Corinne, I haven't asked you much about your accident, but do you remember the last time we were in our house talking, or the night you left and went to the hotel?"

Tyler had come to a decision on the drive there. He would make it perfectly clear to Corinne that they were not back together. Yes, he would take care of her, and yes, he would help care for her; yes, because he still cared for her. But no, they were not a couple, not anymore. She would never make a fool of him again.

"No. Not really. Why?" Charlene seemed to be watching him very closely.

Although Tyler sensed she was telling him the truth, he couldn't be sure. He knew Corinne had years to perfect her lies and her well-controlled facial expressions. So well, in fact, that he didn't have a clue about her affairs. But he'd suspected Corinne had a lover. And what of him, he wondered. He'd never confronted her about it and couldn't come up with a reason why he hadn't. Pulling himself from his thoughts, Tyler murmured, "Just asking."

Charlene picked up the edge in his voice. She sensed he was holding back what he'd really wanted to say. She hadn't noticed, but just then the conversation of the gossipy orderlies came to her mind. They had implied that Tyler and Corinne's marriage had been in trouble and that they slept in separate bedrooms. Charlene was immediately stumped when another thought hit her as her eyes glanced over to the large bed. *Surely he won't sleep in that bed with me?* She didn't have a chance to ponder further because Flo came to collect her for her bath.

—∿∿—

Several hours later, Charlene refused the dinner tray Mona had sent up to her. Instead she wanted to have dinner with the children. She couldn't wait to look at them and touch them again. Every minute counted, and she was eager to spend time with them. Steeling herself for another appearance as Corinne, Charlene made her way downstairs to the dining room with Flo's help.

Melvin met her at the entrance to the dining room and beamed. "Well, missy, I must say I love the eye patch. Makes you look dangerous. How're you feeling?" He looped her arm over his and escorted her into the dining room.

Charlene nervously adjusted the eye patch. "I'm okay, um, Melvin," she said, remembering his name. She liked the tall man. He was quiet and looked so much like both his sons, Tyler and Ryan. At the dinner that followed, Charlene discovered that Ryan, Trish, his wife of almost a year, and Tyler's sister, Terri, all lived there at the family home.

As dinner was served, Mona explained she'd had Daisy prepare some of Corinne's favorites: pecan-encrusted salmon, rosemary potatoes, and several vegetable dishes.

Charlene thought the food was way too fancy for a regular weeknight meal, but ate what she could with small bites, mainly the soft vegetables. But suddenly aware of everyone discreetly watching, she sat her fork down and looked up at them.

"Mona this supper, um…dinner is excellent, thank you. I'm fine, so please, y'all, um, everybody eat your meal," she said. Turning to the twins, who sat between her and Tyler, she said, "And I'm watching you, Shane. I heard about the carrot throwing incident." She winked.

Tyler looked up quickly. He recalled telling a comatose Corinne about having to punish Shane a few weeks ago. It was too unreal to think that she'd actually heard him as he sat by her bedside talking non-stop. "What did you say?" Tyler studied her.

"I think somebody told me that Shane threw carrots at Shelly and she socked him in the jaw," Charlene said, dropping her gaze to a mischievously grinning Shelly. She could recall Corinne having that exact expression when she'd done something spiteful, most often to her.

On Charlene's right, at the head of the table, Mona chuckled. "Ah, yes, that was the night I found out about my gazing balls," Mona said, first sending Terri a warning glance to stop her sudden burst of giggles. "Just let something happen to the new ones out there," she said, tilting her head in the direction of the patio. "I have lots and lots of shoes, Tyler, dear," Mona quipped.

That did it. Everyone roared with laughter and Charlene joined in timidly. She thought Corinne was fortunate to have had such a wonderful and caring family.

———∽∽∿∽———

Stark fear followed by blinding pain filled Charlene as she slept.

She'd been holding onto a branch. Below her was nothing but darkness. Above her was the star-studded sky and Corinne's voice. It was loud and strong. *You'll get caught. Trust me, I've made sure you won't get away with anything and you won't kill those innocent men…* It was in that moment as she hung onto the branch that Charlene had seen a shiny object sail over her head. Her eyes followed it and the tree branch finally snapped under her weight. Charlene clearly remembered falling down the same dark path as the shiny object.

Before hitting the sandy coastal ground, her body bumped into the boulders and rocks along the way. She had been reaching out blindly for that shiny object when her hand grasped another branch poking out of the rocks. Charlene realized she had fallen. Did she lose her footing, perhaps? *No, there was a car…the black car…it hit me!* The car intentionally ran into her and sent her over the edge of the cliff. The fading, large bruise on her upper right thigh was proof of that.

Charlene awakened with a jolt. She remembered the black car slamming into her. In sleep, her hand rubbed the still painful area on her right upper thigh and she fought to hold onto the picture of what had happened just before the car hit her.

Then it happened again. A seizure gripped her.

After a few minutes, exhausted and with perspiration covering her face, Charlene slowly became aware of her surroundings. Worried faces hovered over her. She knew she'd had a seizure and when her eyes lit upon Shelly whimpering as Trish and Terri tried to calm her. Charlene saw the child's fright. She had to say something, but with Tyler and Mona flittering around her it was difficult to collect her thoughts enough to say something soothing to the frightened little girl. "Shelly, I-I'm all right, honey," she said, finally.

"You almost kicked me, Mommy," Shelly retorted fearfully. She sniffed loudly.

Managing to sit up, Charlene held out her hands for Shelly. "I'm sorry. I would never do that." She saw the little girl hesitate, confused and still unsure if it was safe. Then making up her mind she scrambled down out of Trish's arms and onto the bed. Charlene was relieved when Shelly eased herself into her arms. "I'm so sorry. I never meant to frighten you, okay?" When Shelly nodded, Charlene smiled and glanced up at the worried faces. "I'm sorry. I seem to have awakened the entire house. I'm okay, but I'd like to get up now and go wash my face."

"I'll help you," Tyler said, lifting Shelly and handing her off to Terri. "I'll come and tuck you in after I help Mommy get settled in."

With Tyler helping her get up from the bed, Charlene looked around. "Where's Shane?" Tyler reminded her that Shane was a sound sleeper and that he could sleep through a tornado.

Try as he might, Tyler couldn't ignore how soft her skin was to the touch. Instead of embracing her in a loving, tender husbandly way, he treated her like a fragile invalid.

Somewhat relieved that at least one of the children had not witnessed her exhibition, Charlene allowed Tyler to lead her to the bathroom but asked Mona if she could assist her.

But Charlene couldn't deny the fact that without his arm around her waist, she couldn't have stood. She hated being so weak and dependent. Getting past the fact that he'd been sleeping in the same bedroom was another issue she'd had to deal with silently. But he'd insisted on staying nearby and slept on the foldout loveseat across the room. Despite everything that had happened between him and his 'wife,' Tyler was still being the attentive husband.

Charlene pushed away the disturbing thought that a strange man slept just feet from her.

~~~

After the frightening seizure episode, Tyler and Mona asked Flo to move into the house full time. Both women were delighted as they were becoming fast friends. Flo pushed Charlene hard, and, despite the agonizing pain afterward, Charlene had taken on her physical therapy with a purpose. She knew in order to find out what happened to Corinne she needed her strength. But that didn't help her faulty memory of the night she met her twin or with her daily dealings with the Mills family.

Charlene knew the family had been informed of her memory loss and other behavioral issues that could occur as a result of her head injury. So what was making her so restless the past week, she wondered? It certainly wasn't the new short haircut she was sporting. Charlene was simply bored. Healing her body was one thing, but her mind was turning to mush with nothing to do. Conversations with the adults of the household were forced and awkward because she didn't know them.

On the other hand, she and Flo talked about everything and anything. Mostly, Charlene listened patiently as Flo indulged in useless and oftentimes funny gossip. Charlene felt comfortable and relaxed around her. Perhaps it was because Flo had no expectations of her being someone she wasn't. She didn't have to pretend and was free to be herself. But she did hide as best she could her Southern accent.

She liked the Mills family. But she also got the feeling that Corinne, although a member of the family, was mostly indulged and tolerated. At times, she picked up that they appeared overly polite and tactful when speaking around her. This gave Charlene her first clues to begin her work on finding out what happened that fateful night.

When Tyler brought Corinne's laptop computer to her, Charlene struggled for days to figure out the password to get into the files; even the passwords had passwords or secret questions. When she asked Tyler about the password, he'd told her he didn't know but offered to look at it and even suggested clearing the hard drive and starting from scratch.

Charlene definitely didn't want the hard drive cleared. She needed to check everything on Corinne's computer. When she had free time to herself, Charlene typed all of the notes she'd been jotting down in the journal she began in the hospital. The task was difficult because she rarely was left alone. Someone was always with her or nearby fearing she'd have another seizure. But every chance she got, she tried to put the pieces of the puzzle together. Then one day, feeling stronger, she'd attempted to navigate the wide staircase alone. She was doing just fine, that is until Tyler walked in the front door, looked up, and saw her. He raced up the steps two at a time. He wasn't pleased.

"What are you doing?" he demanded disapprovingly. Without giving her a chance to respond, he lifted her up in his arms and promptly returned her to the bedroom and put her in a chair. Then he gave Flo a tongue lashing for allowing her patient to walk down a flight of stairs unattended. After asking Flo to leave them alone for a few minutes, he turned to his wife.

That had been their first argument.

Charlene objected to the way he was talking to her. The second Flo closed the door, Charlene told him just that. "Hey, I'm an adult, so you'd better stop talkin' to me like I'm a child." But hearing her own voice resonate forcefully, Charlene backed down a notch.

Tyler fired back. "Then stop acting like one! You're recovering, Corinne, and that means you don't push yourself beyond your capabilities."

"As if you had a clue as to what my capabilities are," Charlene huffed, but then caught herself when Tyler's eyes shot daggers at her. *Back off, Charlene*, she said to herself.

"Well, you're absolutely correct there," Tyler said, leaning over so that he couldn't be overheard by anyone passing by in the hall. "I *didn't* have a clue. But you know that I do now, don't you, or has that bit of your memory faded as well?"

Although stunned at the harshness of his words, Charlene hadn't recoiled. Instead she stood up, forcing him to straighten up and back away from her. She had been holding back a retort of her own, but had a feeling it wouldn't have been something the proper and refined Corinne would have said. "I don't remember a lot of things…but then again I do. I remember what a liar *you* were." Fuming, Charlene realized that if Corinne had believed her when she'd told her about seeing Tyler with that woman all those years ago she wouldn't have been standing there breathing fire up in the man's face.

Thrusting his hands in his pocket, Tyler stepped back. "You have no room to talk. But you get better real quick, you feel me, Corinne?"

Oh, boy, did she. As much as she tried to force it away, Charlene hadn't forgotten that he'd put her sister out of her own home, forcing her to go to that hotel. "Yeah, I feel you, and don't you get in my face again, Tyler Mills, or you're gonna be needin' some rehabilitation yourself." Charlene watched his lips tighten, with what? Regret, guilt, and shock? Whatever it was she couldn't say, but she'd seen that expression cross his face before.

Gnawing on her lip, Charlene realized she *had* seen that look many times since she'd come to the house, too. She'd seen it while watching him reading or chatting or playing with the twins. Another troubling thought formed in the back of her mind the past couple of weeks, and only just then came rushing back again; could Tyler have *wanted* Corinne dead?

Charlene chided herself for thinking such things. No way would Tyler want Corinne dead. And for what it was worth, Tyler was her family now. But still…

Charlene decided that at this point Tyler Mills was number one on her list of suspects.

━━⟪∾⟫━━

A week later, on a beautiful afternoon in mid-May, Charlene was depressed. The house was so quiet. Tyler, Ryan, and Trish all worked until five or six in the evening, Terri had classes until four, and Mona, who served on several charitable organizations, wouldn't arrive home until that evening. Although semi-retired, Melvin went to the office with Tyler almost every day. The twins were at school and the school bus wouldn't be dropping them off until three-fifteen. She missed them terribly when they went to school. She looked forward to Shane and Shelly making a beeline up to her room to see her. They usually chatted endlessly about their activities at school, as well as some tattling.

As Charlene was now able to manage the stairs without any assistance, she headed down to the kitchen. There she shocked Daisy by offering to help with dinner. Before she knew it, Charlene began preparing a meal she'd made a hundred times before.

—◦◦◦—

While Charlene and Daisy prepared dinner, a meeting was taking place across town.

The two men reviewed their notes. Then one, older, the leader of sorts, looked up and addressed the other, younger man…his trusted associate. "How can this be? Corinne Mills is supposed to be dead. Who is this woman?" he asked, sliding the picture across the room table.

Capturing the picture under his hand, the younger man adjusted his tie. "It's obvious, isn't it? She must have had a twin, and that's who went over that cliff," he said. The younger man told the older man that he'd seen Corinne Mills being wheeled out of the hospital to a waiting limousine.

"We didn't know she had a twin. Actually, I don't think anybody knew. That woman could be someone who simply bears a remarkable resemblance to Corinne Mills."

"In any case, that brings me to why we're here today," the older man said, rising from his seat at the head of the table. "Find out everything you can about her, but more importantly, you find out who went over that cliff and who survived. And find out who has my property. Does the new *Mrs. Mills* have my documents? If she does, I want them back."

CHAPTER 10

If she hadn't seen it with her own eyes she wouldn't have believed it.

That's what Daisy thought as she dropped a handful of finely chopped green peppers into the huge bowl of ground beef. Daisy struggled to recall the last time she'd seen Mrs. Mills prepare anything besides a sandwich or breakfast cereal for the twins. But watching her measure spices and herbs simply had her flabbergasted. She just had to say something. "Ah, Mrs. Mills…well, I'd say you've done this before," she said, arching an eyebrow as she watched breadcrumbs folded into the mix.

For a brief time, Charlene had forgotten who she was pretending to be until Daisy addressed her as Mrs. Mills. Each time someone addressed her as such, Charlene would cringe inside; that is, after the pain that seized her heart subsided. *Corinne.* Reflecting on what Daisy had said, Charlene guessed that Corinne probably didn't do much cooking. She searched for appropriate words to allay the suspicious eyes of the housekeeper. "Daisy, why do you call everybody in this house by their given name but me?"

Sipping her tea, Daisy recalled what Tyler told her about his wife's head trauma. She liked the new Mrs. Mills. "Well, that's because you told me to call you Mrs. Mills."

"I see. Well, as of today, it stops. I insist you call me Ch-Corinne."

Daisy's face brightened. "I'd like that a lot, Corinne, and, who knows, maybe we can cook together again," Daisy said quietly.

"I'd like that, too. Now let's mix this up and put this baby into the oven." Charlene grinned at Daisy's laugh. Flo, who sat nearby completing her notes, joined in the laughter.

As the dinner cooked, Charlene donned a t-shirt and a pair of jeans she'd gotten from Terri and waited for the twins to get home. Then she helped them with their homework.

———∿———

Having come downstairs to the kitchen from the back of the house, Charlene followed Daisy into the dining room as she placed the large serving tray in the center of the table. Charlene said nothing as she lifted the lid in grand fashion, but knew all eyes were on her.

When Daisy was finished, Mona sent an inquisitive glance over to her daughter-in-law. "What's going on?" Mona noticed Tyler watching his wife with great interest.

"I was so bored today that I helped Daisy fix dinner," Charlene said, shrugging.

After a few minutes of stunned silence at the table, Mona cleared her throat. "Lovely."

Terri guffawed. "Oh, Lord! We're all gonna die, and I have a history test tomorrow!"

Ever polite, Trish giggled lightly but was quick to cover it. "How nice of you to do this, Corinne, it-it really looks delicious." Ryan, she noticed, was already munching on a roll.

Melvin came around to Charlene and kissed her cheek. "Good for you, Missy. I'm a bit scared myself, but I can't wait. It all smells wonderful."

Charlene squeezed his arm gratefully. "Thanks. It's meatloaf. I used to make it a lot," she said, glancing at Tyler, who sat on the other side of the children, watching her. They'd spoken very little since their argument, and that suited Charlene just fine. She was glad he'd moved to a bedroom down the hall.

Ryan and Melvin uncovered all of the remaining dishes, which included mashed potatoes, green beans, buttered corn, macaroni salad, and hot, buttery rolls.

Skeptically, Tyler finally spoke up. "You cooked all of this?" When she answered that she supervised, Tyler said, "What about your arm?"

"It's fine." She turned to look at Tyler. "Don't worry. I did nothing that would impede my recovery." With the direct look she gave him, Charlene threw his harsh words right back into his face. She knew everyone watched her and Tyler with great interest. From Terri, Charlene learned the only reason she was there with Tyler was because she'd been injured.

Tyler didn't respond but his eyes slid over her as she passed the children their plates. He couldn't help but notice that she did indeed seem to be recovering. According to Flo's assessment she was doing very well. Her facial abrasions were healing and the bruising was becoming less noticeable. Although the cast had been removed from her left leg, she limped if she didn't use a crutch. She still occasionally sported a flexible brace on her left arm, but she'd failed the hearing test in her left ear. Tyler thought she was still beautiful and even liked her new haircut. *Lord, help me*, Tyler thought silently as he filled his plate.

With Shane and Shelly's eyes bouncing between their parents, they shared a knowing look. No one paid any attention as they whispered and giggled to each other.

But no one was happier than Mona as she blessed the table. She, too, couldn't hide a smile as she watched her son and daughter-in-law.

Charlene still couldn't use her left hand easily. In the kitchen, she'd had Daisy and Flo to help her, but now she simply couldn't lift her left arm enough to fix her own plate. Tyler was right, she reluctantly admitted, she'd over-exerted herself.

Noticing a tightening of her lips, Tyler sensed her discomfort. He'd seen the pain she was trying to hide. "Why don't you let me fix your plate? Everything looks great, Corinne." Tyler took her plate and filled it while a relieved and grateful Charlene sat back.

Watching everyone obviously enjoying the meal, Charlene was pleased. It was such a simple meal, a poor man's meal, really, but her father loved it. "I needed something to do," she said. "My brain is turning to mush."

"That's because you need to go shopping. Your favorite designers' spring lines are calling out to you," Terri said out around a mouthful of mashed potatoes.

Charlene didn't respond because she'd been trying unsuccessfully to cut her piece of meatloaf with her fork. The children ate without complaints and Charlene was suddenly filled with emotion watching their little fingers as they ate. She could even imagine Corinne feeding them as babies and as toddlers. It was a lovely visual as she tuned out everyone's chatter. *Oh, I wished I'd seen them growing up from babies.*

Tyler watched her and caught the sad expression that crossed her face. "The meatloaf is excellent. Why aren't you having any?"

Terri smacked the table, groaned, and grabbed her stomach. "Uh-huh. I told you. We're all gonna die…Mom!" She groaned loudly, teasingly.

Ryan, Trish and the twins all laughed at Terri's clowning around, and even Melvin chuckled, but a tight-lipped Mona patted the table with the palm of her hand, sending Terri a warning.

Embarrassed, Charlene confessed, "I-I can't…I mean, I'm unable to cut it," she said, fighting off a painful spasm in her left arm. She desperately wanted another pain pill.

"I'll do it for her," Shane announced and reached over to Charlene's plate. He proceeded to stab large chunks off her meatloaf, most of which went flying across the table and landed on his grandmother's plate.

With everyone laughing, Charlene smothered the boy's face with kisses then breathed a sigh of relief.

⁓

Several hours later, Charlene sat alone in the backyard watching the sky. She reflected on the two slip-ups she'd made during dinner.

First, when Mona asked what she'd meant when she'd said she used to fix the same dinner. Stammering over a reply, Charlene said she'd remembered it was her father's favorite meal and she'd not had it since he died. Second, she'd declined Trish's offer to go shopping with her after she'd commented on the t-shirt and jeans Charlene had on. Truthfully, it was what Charlene was used to wearing. As an art teacher she couldn't afford the fancy, expensive clothes like she'd spotted in Corinne's closet. Some had never been worn, as evidenced by the labels and hefty price tags still hanging on them. She reasoned that Corinne would never miss an opportunity to shop for more clothes.

Charlene couldn't remember the last time she'd gone shopping for clothes, but she knew exactly what days to go to the market for the two-for-one specials or double coupon day, and she knew the exact due dates and amounts of her household bills back home. Charlene didn't think for one second that Corinne had ever worried about such things, or even cared. She was positive Corinne had forgotten how it was for them years ago…how it still was for her.

Closing her eyes she let her mind drift back to the night they talked until that cell phone call came. Straining to recall every moment they had together, Charlene sensed her sister wasn't happy. From what she could tell, Corinne had turned herself into a different person. She had done what she'd always wanted to do: marry into money. But then she was having an affair and had been put out of her own home, with Tyler ready to file for divorce.

Regrettably, Charlene realized all those years since seeing her sister, she'd imagined Corinne and Tyler happily in love with their beautiful children, living the fairy tale; only that wasn't the case. Charlene realized the money Corinne so desperately wanted had not brought her happiness.

Charlene was left to wonder how Tyler fit into the mystery of Corinne's death. Financially, he had the means to do whatever he wanted. She wondered to what lengths he would go to rid himself of an unfaithful wife. The thought both chilled and frightened her. Suddenly aware that she was no longer alone on the patio, she opened her eyes to find Tyler sitting in a lounge chair across from her. His stare was intent and suspicious.

"You okay?" Tyler noticed that sadness again when she'd finally opened her eyes. He'd come out onto the patio and sat watching her. She'd been deep in thought. He wondered if she was missing her lover. She told him she was fine.

"You don't look fine. Do you need Flo to get you some meds?" She shook her head.

"So what's wrong?" Tyler wondered why he'd asked. Did he care enough to hear her tell him what was really wrong? Did he really want to know what or who she was thinking about?

"I-I just want to get better. I feel useless," Charlene said honestly.

"Yeah, got to get that new spring wardrobe, right?" Sarcasm laced his words.

Charlene scoffed. "Shopping is the last thing on my mind. I was thinking about Shane and Shelly. They, um, they fear Mommy will leave them again," she said quietly.

"And you will. When you've recovered," Tyler said, sitting forward.

Take care of my babies…With Corinne's words ringing in her ears, Charlene met Tyler's unwavering glare, not feeling the tears staining her cheeks. "I can't leave them, not now. So please, please don't ask me to leave them. I-I have to take care of them, don't you understand? I have to. I-I'm their..." Charlene whispered, unable to continue.

Tyler was struck by a thought that, undeniably, something about her was off. Somehow she was different. His eyes searched hers, waiting for her snappy retort. It never came.

Tyler shook off the feeling of unease. "So what did you think was going to happen? That I would forget everything…forget about him? The man you've had afternoon trysts with? No wonder you're bored. I'm sure making meatloaf doesn't compare to an afternoon of steamy sex in another man's arms, now does it?" He didn't mean to raise his voice, but he couldn't help it. He was angry and he'd lashed out with what he'd wanted to say all along. He was angry at her for allowing another man to take her away from him and their children. When she said nothing, Tyler stood up in frustration and walked over to the pool a few feet away. He stood with his back to her watching the water lap against the sides.

Oh, good Lord, please help me out of this. Charlene frowned and got up. Leaving her crutch she eased over beside him. "Listen, I-I don't care what you think about me. Nothing matters to me except…" She halted and began again. "Except the children and their well-being. They need…they need a mother."

Tyler rounded on her. "Like you've been?"

Recoiling, Charlene stared at him. Was he implying that Corinne wasn't a good mother? *Oh, please no. That can't be right. The children loved Corinne. She loved them.* Charlene clearly remembered Corinne telling her that the twins were the only good thing she'd ever done in her life. Charlene reached out and grasped Tyler's arm. It was more of a move to maintain her balance than it was to recover from his shocking words. "She…um, are you saying I wasn't a good mother before the accident and…everything?"

Surprised by her tone as well as her hand lying on his bare arm, Tyler was caught off guard. In that second, he was equally shocked and repelled for wanting to pull her into his arms and hold her. Too kiss away her hurt and pain, and maybe his, too. He longed to feel her body against his. Recovering his senses and angry at his moment of weakness, Tyler quickly moved away from her and away from the warmth of her hand on his arm. "I never said you weren't a good mother," he called out over his shoulder as he walked to the back of the house.

Charlene had little time to react when he suddenly jerked his arm away. Since she'd left her crutch by the chair, she could do nothing as a painful spasm rippled up her left leg, causing it to buckle from under her. With nothing to catch her, and her breath caught in her throat from the pain, Charlene slumped and fell silently into the pool.

Seconds later the rest of the family spilled out onto the patio. Mona spotted Tyler several feet away absently fingering a velvety rose petal from one of the many pink rose bushes flanking the patio. She asked him where Corinne was. She was curious, but mostly she asked the question in an effort to get him away from her prized roses.

Turning, expecting Corinne to still be standing by the pool, Tyler had no time to react. His eyes flew wildly to the pool and his gut reaction kicked in…as did everyone else when they all saw Corinne struggling under the water.

Charlene saw the sky and many faces as it dawned on her what had happened. She'd fallen into the pool. It was then she began to move her arms and struggle against the water, which was hard to do when the pain gripping her left leg intensified.

It took Tyler all of three seconds to dive into the water. But he wasn't alone. Ryan, Trish and Terri all dived with him. Mona's scream forced Daisy, Flo, and Melvin from the house and out to the patio. When Tyler and Ryan heaved Corinne up and onto the grass, she wasn't moving.

Flo ran over and immediately began CPR. She barked out instructions to Tyler, who was staring in shock. "Don't just sit there, turn her head so the water comes out!"

Within seconds, Charlene began coughing and gagging. Then she clutched at her leg where pain radiated so blindingly hot that she cried out, frantic for the pain to stop. But she was choking and coughing up water, making it difficult for her to speak.

Tyler could do nothing but hold Corinne's hands in an attempt to stop her from clawing at her leg. "What's happening?"

Flo knew exactly what was happening. It was damage to the nerve in Corinne's leg that caused her muscles to cramp and throb. Calling out instructions, she sent Ryan up to the bedroom for her medical bag.

When Ryan returned, Flo immediately administered an injection of pain medication. "Come on, you're a tough one. Tell that pain to go on 'bout its business, girl." She took her patient's vitals. "How did she fall into the pool in the first place?"

"I-I don't know. We were talking by the pool and then I..." Tyler said, lamely.

"You what? I hardly think she jumped into the pool," Mona said, leaning over a now-lethargic Charlene and noticing the crutch several feet away. "What happened?" She repeated.

Tyler's gaze followed his mother's. "I didn't realize she didn't have the crutch when I...when I walked away."

Exhausted, Charlene's concern was about the twins. "Where's Shane, Shelly...?"

Tyler smoothed her hair from her forehead. "They're okay. They're asleep already. Corinne, you fell into the pool. Why didn't you call out to me or swim to the edge?"

Having never learned to swim, Charlene could only say that she was scared before the medication took over and she gladly submitted herself to its tranquilizing effects.

⌐⌐⌐

Tyler stayed awake all night checking on and listening for Corinne. Regardless of their marital situation, he hated seeing her in such pain. He thought back, seeing her in the pool. Her frightened and wide eyes beneath the water bothered him. She appeared not to know how to swim. How could that be? She was an excellent swimmer, and she'd taught the twins to swim when they were barely toddlers.

He reasoned he was just tired and not thinking straight. She was in pain, that's why she couldn't swim to the edge of the pool or stand up in the five feet of water.

CHAPTER 11

Another bout of depression hit Charlene the following night.

Flo told her that depression was expected. If what she was feeling was clinical depression, then Charlene wanted it gone. It was so much more than just having the blues. The feeling was altogether different, and she didn't like it one bit.

"It's too much," she whispered, reflecting on yet another blunder on her part.

When Corinne left Virginia, like Charlene, she couldn't swim. It was now obvious to her that Corinne had learned to do what she hadn't. Charlene couldn't swim. It was that fear that had paralyzed her after she'd fallen into the pool.

For the rest of the week, Charlene didn't share dinner with the family. She took her meals and her physical therapy in her room with Flo. Shelly and Shane had been the only bright spot in her days, and she loved them more with each passing day.

One thing that Charlene had accomplished during her period of voluntary seclusion was that she'd finally gotten into Corinne's email. There were hundreds of them, and Charlene began the task of reading each one. Picking them apart for details, clues, anything that would get her closer to what happened that night.

A week following the pool incident Charlene stumbled on another police blotter report on the internet. She'd been searching them since Tyler had brought Corinne's computer to her.

A body of a woman had been found, partially burned, in a car that had been reported stolen the night of the accident. The police had no leads and there had been no report of a missing woman. As she read the bulletin, Charlene was overcome with a terrible ache. It filled her with incredible sadness and then it was gone; somehow she knew that it was her twin. "Corinne. I pray you didn't suffer. I won't stop until I get the people who did this terrible thing to you, and I'll carry you in my heart for all eternity."

"Hello, dear," Mona said, coming into the room.

"Hi," was all Charlene could muster up as she eased the lid of the laptop down. For several minutes, she listened as Mona pleaded with her to talk about whatever was troubling her.

"Flo says that depression is common in head trauma patients," Charlene said, but sensed that Mona didn't believe that was all it was. "Okay, Mona, um, you know I'll have to leave this house when I'm recovered because Tyler said he's moving back to his house. He's taking the children, and I-I won't see them," Charlene said sadly.

Mona waved a hand. "Honey, have you forgotten that it's your house, too, and those are your children, also. Tyler is not so stupid to keep them from you. But he's hurting, that's all. I have to tell you something. Are you up to hearing it?"

"I guess so," Charlene mumbled absently, then listened quietly and without interruption as Mona explained about seeing the picture of Corinne in bed with another man.

"So you see, Tyler's anger runs deep from that betrayal," Mona said, rubbing the younger woman's arm affectionately. "Listen, honey, I'm not casting stones or even blaming you. Tyler had been so glued to his father's side learning the ropes to take over as CEO that he literally left you and the twins alone for weeks on end. He blames himself for that. But I have to tell you that since you've been here I've watched him and I've watched you and..." Mona smiled. "Well, love can grow again, my dear, and be even better than it was before."

"You mean between Tyler and me?" Charlene asked incredulously. The thought of such a thing floored her. She wanted one thing from Tyler...the truth. And she was determined to found out if and how he figured into the death of her sister. "Mona, I appreciate what you're saying, at least what I think you're saying, but trust me, nothing can or will happen between us," Charlene said in a firm voice, not even touching on the issue of Corinne's unfaithfulness.

Mona stood. "All right, but I know what I see and I know my son," she said, kissing Charlene's forehead. "Start by getting him to move back into the bedroom." Mona walked to the door, but then paused, turned back and let her eyes circle the room. "You know, you two made babies in this room." She turned around and closed the door behind her.

Oh, yeah, and guess what, Miss Mona? That is so not gonna happen again.

Shrugging off Mona's parting words, Charlene began to feel the walls closing in on her as she experienced pangs of regret. She knew whatever relationship they had would come to an end when she disclosed who she was. She also knew she would have regrets because she didn't want to hurt the family, especially Mona. She didn't want them to grieve, but knew they would, and she would be cast out as a stranger who'd lived amongst them and tricked them all. "But that's not going to happen until I find out who took Corinne away," Charlene said, lifting the lid of the laptop and returning to her task of reading emails.

After reading many emails in Corinne's inbox, Charlene cross-referenced key words she had created from her notes. She already noticed a disturbing subject matter. Some of the contents of Corinne's emails proved that Corinne was apprehensive about something. Her email responses in her outgoing box had a threatening tone, all relating to shipments.

$\sim$

Charlene had been at the Mills' home for six weeks and her depression had not lifted. Despite Flo's reports that her body and mobility had progressed exceptionally well, Flo sat down to have a heart-to-heart with her patient.

"Honey, I have to tell you that as far as your body is concerned you're recovering very well. Your bones have healed. The bruising is fading fast and your scars, well, you already know some won't fade completely, but we've talked about that. But I have to file a psychological assessment with the home health nursing department at the hospital. Your Dr. Holland will also get a copy of my report and make adjustments where he sees fit. Honey, it's not good, and you know it. Your insomnia and depression concerns me a whole lot…" Flo raised her hand, stopping her patient from interrupting her. "You can't hide it from me, Corinne. Now, speaking openly and honestly with you, I think your depression stems more from your relationship with your husband. Even the kids can see that something's wrong. Don't you see them watching the two of you and then they get that whispering and giggling going on? Now, what message are you sending to them and your husband?"

Caught off-guard, Charlene could only think how she was failing in her promise to Corinne to take care of her children. She thought poor Flo believed her only problem was with her 'husband' and failing marriage. Yes, Tyler was a part of the problem, because in her heart, Charlene blamed him for her sister's death. It had become a daily struggle not to lash out what was in her heart. But more than that, she blamed Tyler for taking Corinne away from her all those years ago.

She blamed Tyler for promising Corinne a better life and not delivering. That's what was uppermost in her mind. She also thought about her students. She was the only art teacher in the small middle-high school and she missed all one hundred and fifty of her students. Her spur-of-the-moment one-week vacation to the west coast for R&R had turned into a tragedy.

Two weeks prior, Charlene had sent an email to the principal of the high school where she taught art and art history. She'd requested an indefinite leave of absence, citing personal problems. The principal, Mr. Marsh, had written back expressing genuine concern. He knew she made little money and suggested they could start a financial collection for her. It was then Charlene felt her deceit hit another level, realizing she sat in an estate house with a housekeeper, limo at the ready, and round-the-clock nursing care. She begged the principal not to do that and promised to contact him again soon.

So many lies. She was lying and deceiving so many people, all concerned for her health and welfare. With Flo's curious eyes upon her, Charlene collected herself and mumbled a response to Flo's question. "You're right, Flo. We're sending a terrible message to the twins."

Flo looked relieved. "Good, now get your family business back on track, honey. Start with your man and the rest will follow." Getting up and adjusting her bosom, Flo's lips twitched. "I think you're ready to handle any activity that might occur in that big bed there. That's professionally speaking, of course." Flo cackled at her patient's wide eyes. "Why don't you stretch out your legs by walking down to the bus stop and meeting your children?"

Charlene did as Flo suggested, and two hours later she sat in the middle of the driveway with Shane and Shelly. Each was focused on the task of drawing a large colorful flower with fat chalk sticks. Charlene was so glad to be out in the sun with them. After she'd fixed them a snack of peanut butter and jelly sandwiches, she suggested they celebrate spring by drawing flowers. When she further suggested they do it outside on the smooth concrete driveway, none was happier than Shane.

Watching the boy, Charlene remembered that Corinne had told her that Shane was much like she was, shy and slow to warm up. Yes, that's how Charlene would describe herself, especially as a child. She'd learned that Shane had also been sickly when he was younger, much as she had been. In Shelly, on the other hand, Charlene could see Corinne, right down to her bossiness, impatience, and annoyance with details, as well as her need to be right about everything. Yes, Charlene thought, Shelly was exactly as Corinne had been as a child…and unfortunately, sickly Charlene had many times been on the brunt end of Corinne's exasperation.

"Mommy, look at Shelly's flower. It looks stupid, doesn't it?" Shane giggled, taking another gummy bear from the bag sitting in the box with the chalk sticks.

Charlene realized when she'd first came to the Mills home that Shane had an eye for art, also like her. So naturally he thought Shelly's flower was a colorful mess. And it was. But Charlene also realized that Shelly could tune her brother out in an instant. "You know what?" Charlene began, leaning forward to pop another gummy bear into her mouth as she drew another flower petal on her own flower. "I think Shelly's flower is just beautiful. Don't you, Shelly?" When the child bobbed her head, Charlene continued. "Just because you're twins doesn't mean you have to like and do the same things. You're individual and beautiful little people."

"You're beautiful, Mommy," Shelly said. "Even with your hair all cut up. I like it now."

"Thank you. One day my hair will be long again so I can make a ponytail like yours."

"I don't think Daddy likes it," Shane said, getting up to hug her. "But I like it."

Shelly's next words shocked Charlene to the point her hand quivered, causing the yellow chalk stick she'd been drawing with to crumble against the concrete driveway.

"Are you an alien? Because we think you are," Shelly said.

"Wh-what do you mean, Shelly? I-I'm not an alien," Charlene croaked.

"Shane and I think you might be an alien, that's all."

Shane picked up the broken pieces of chalk. "Not an alien, dummy. I said a clone," he said, looking up at Charlene. "It's you, isn't it, Mommy? You're not an alien or a clone mother, are you?"

Shane's identical amber eyes searched Charlene's. They were nose-to-nose.

Charlene's hand clutched her chest. "Oh, my God! Wh-what are you saying?" It wasn't difficult for her to realize she hadn't fooled them. *Oh, no, it's too soon.* She couldn't believe that the twins had figured out that she wasn't their mother.

"It's okay. We think our real mother is still sleeping in the hospital and you were sent here to take care of us until she wakes up," Shelly said, digging into the bag for a gummy bear.

Rubbing at her suddenly aching temple, Charlene realized they weren't afraid. "Sweethearts, um, both of you promise me you won't talk about this with anybody, not yet. But know that I would never, ever hurt you, you understand?" She sat Shane back at arm's length and watched them nod in unison.

"We won't tell anybody," they chimed and threw their arms around her. Then Shelly returned to her flower.

"I knew you were a clone mother," Shane said, returning his attention to his flower.

Charlene relaxed and prepared herself to have an honest talk with them despite the fact that her stomach was suddenly in knots. "And how did you know that, Shane?"

"Because clones have big heads and funny eyes and that's what Uncle Ryan says about those clone people on that sci-fi show he watches on television every Friday night."

Try as she might, Charlene couldn't suppress the nervous giggle tickling her ribcage. "Listen, you two, I'm not an alien or a clone. I'm a human being just like the both of you. If I fall and skin my knee it's gonna bleed just like yours will."

Shelly reached up and ran her hand across Charlene's forehead. "What if your wires come out and your head blows up? That happened to the clone mothers on the show."

"Yeah, and your body shakes all up again." Shane scrunched up his face.

Charlene thought their graphic description wasn't all that far from the truth. "Okay, first I think you guys shouldn't be watching sci-fi. Second, my body might shake because of the seizures. That has nothing to do with wires in my head because there're no wires up here," she said, pointing to her head. "Just gummy bears right now."

For several seconds the twins giggled infectiously. "Terri told Daisy that you had tubes sticking out of your head and yellow goo came out," Shelly said and walked around to lift Charlene's hair, where there was a scar above her ear.

Charlene hugged the little girl. "When I was in the hospital, the doctor put a tube above my ear for medical reasons. It's gone now and I'm fine, Shelly, honestly."

"Is our real mother fine?"

With her throat tight, she said, "Yes, she is. She's beautiful and she's in a good place."

"Okay, then do you want to be my BFF?"

Dazed, Charlene could only murmur a reply. "Huh?"

"My BFF," Shelly said, "my best friend forever."

"Yes, I will, forever," Charlene whispered. She was surprised to watch the twins reach for more gummy bears and then return to their flowers. It was as if the matter was dropped. "Will you remember your promise? You won't tell anybody, at least not yet?"

"We won't, and we'll keep calling you Mommy, okay," Shane said, with Shelly nodding in agreement and feeding Charlene another gummy bear.

This was the scene Tyler saw when he drove up the street. He almost drove past the house obviously not expecting to see children playing in the driveway. But when he realized it was his parents' house and those were his kids, he stopped the car, stunned, as he sat squinting through the windshield. He was surprised to see Corinne down on the ground with them. He parked at the curb, exited the car, and walked up the driveway.

"Daddy!" Shelly squealed. "Look at my flower. Mommy says it's beautiful."

Crossing over to kiss Shelly, then Shane, Tyler teasingly gave the drawing a critical appraisal. "Um-hum, um-hum, it certainly is," he said. "I like it. It's a daffodil, right?"

Charlene watched Tyler cautiously as he talked to the twins. She was still reeling from her conversation with them. She watched their twin brain power at work. Right before her eyes they'd swiftly dropped the matter of the clone mother and happily greeted their father.

"No, it's not a daffodil, Daddy. It's a daisy for *our* Daisy. She'll like it, won't she?"

"Of course she will," Tyler and Charlene said simultaneously.

Shane frowned. He knew the drawing looked nothing like a daisy at all. "Daddy, what do you think about Mommy's flower? Can you guess what it is?" he asked.

Tyler wasn't looking at the wide yellow rose petal Corinne had expertly drawn in the driveway. He was looking at the exact same one printed on the front of her t-shirt. "I think it's lovely, just like Mommy looks today," he said.

Charlene pushed the troubled thought to the side and smiled up at Tyler. "Thanks. Have a gummy bear," she said and held the bag up to Tyler.

"Any cherry ones?" Tyler asked, peering into the bag before meeting her brown eyes.

"Why don't you join us? Pick up a piece of chalk and create something that celebrates springtime," Charlene said. "Tomorrow, maybe we'll plant flowers." She winked at the twins.

Tyler thought she was glowing with the sun beaming down on her. "Ah-ha! So that's what this is all about. You know Mom is going to strangle you for messing up this driveway, don't you?" Tyler whispered, then popped two gummy bears into his mouth.

"No, she won't. Mona loves our flowers. Besides, she's been peeping out the second floor window. We're actually drawing for her."

"Who are you and what have you done with my wife?" Tyler asked, absently picking up a piece of chalk. Ignoring the fact that he was in an expensive suit, he sat down Indian style and proceeded to draw a tree with four branches and four little stick figures.

Hearing his words, Charlene went completely still, but sent a glance to the twins who apparently hadn't heard what their father had asked her.

"I didn't know you could draw like this, Corinne," Tyler said.

"There's a lot about me you probably don't know, um, even after all this time. Have you ever asked me to draw anything?"

"Guess not," he said. "I just know that orange paint covering that wall in your bedroom back at the house is atrocious," Tyler said.

Charlene remembered the gossipy orderlies' conversation back at the hospital. "Maybe I'll repaint it if it's that bad," she said, squinting at him, the sun in her face.

Tyler glanced back to see Shane and Shelly with their heads together whispering. "No, you won't," he said in a flat voice. "The previous situation remains in effect."

Watching the foursome from the second floor window, Mona shook her head sadly. Her eyes were drawn to the gloomy look on her daughter-in-law's face.

—◊◊◊—

The following evening Charlene was relaxing in a bath. With her eyes closed she again played out the night she and Corinne talked. Every day she'd taken herself back to that awful night in an attempt to recall everything Corinne had told her, searching for hidden clues.

Struggling past her fear and the pain that came with it, Charlene's focus tonight was on the man she'd seen Corinne kissing that night.

Corinne had referred to him as 'J' or 'Jay'. Charlene couldn't see his face because he'd been turned away from her and his sleek car had been a distance away. Of what she could see, Charlene thought he was a handsome man with medium brown complexion and that he was tall, recalling how high he sat in the driver's seat. Corinne's words replayed. "He's a sweet guy...the business is used as a cover...he can't get out." Despite what Corinne had told her about the man, Charlene sensed he was somehow involved in her sister's death. He'd been one of the very last people to see her that night when he drove off, rather quickly, from the parking lot...

Charlene shivered at the sudden memory. Why did he drive off like that, she wondered. Most men would wait until the woman was safely inside. But J or Jay had left in a hurry, leaving Corinne standing in the parking lot alone. That's when they'd made eye contact.

Hoping more would come to her tomorrow, Charlene sank lower in the tub with the water touching her chin. She was about to replay another pressing issue-the twins' discovery, when Tyler walked into the bathroom and began frantically searching in the medicine cabinet a few feet away. He didn't see her because his back was to the bathtub.

"Ahh! Where're those damn eye drops?" Tyler's allergies were getting the best of him, causing his eyes to itch. Finally finding the bottle of antihistamine eye drops, he placed a drop in each eye, held his head back and sighed with relief. "Oh, yeah."

Charlene covertly watched Tyler and became unsettled at the thought that ran through her mind. Secretly ogling him, she let her eyes trail down his back. He was tall—at least six feet, one inch, and handsome. *Goodness*. He stirred something in her that she brushed off, and assuming her mind was still on Corinne's lover.

But that wasn't it, either. When an unusual rush hit her body, Charlene reflected on her last boyfriend, Mark. She thought he was a sweet guy, too, and their breakup had been amicable. She'd had no time for a boyfriend because most of her time had been spent between teaching her classes and returning home to care for her sick father. That was almost a year and a half ago, and was her last intimate relationship. She couldn't even say what made her think about intimacy because she certainly didn't look at Tyler as anything other than her brother-in-law. But both Mona and Flo's words rushed to the surface. Charlene frowned as she watched Tyler place a cold washcloth over his eyes. *Nothin' is gonna happen between me and him. But if I find out he had anythin' to do with Corinne's death, then a whole lot of somethin' is gonna happen to Tyler Mills. I'll sure see to that*, she thought.

Then she sneezed.

Surprised, Tyler jerked his head up and whirled around so fast he banged his head into the opened door of the medicine cabinet. "Ouch!" He stood for a moment with a hand to his head. "Why didn't you say anything?"

"Why didn't you knock?" Charlene asked.

"Because the door was open, and, besides, I thought you were out at the park with the children," Tyler retorted, dropping his eyes to a small break in the bubbles in her bath. He couldn't help but stare at her full breasts bobbing just below the surface of the water. Vaguely, he heard her say that Trish took the children to the park. "Sorry," he mumbled after ogling her breasts, which she hastily covered with her arms. He didn't turn away from her.

Charlene sneezed again. "Would you call Flo up? I need to get out. The water has cooled off," she said, not moving an inch lest she give him more to look at.

Lifting his eyes from the rapidly dissipating bubbles, Tyler told her that Flo was in the den on the computer. Then, grabbing a thick towel from the towel rack, Tyler held it open. "Come, I'll help you out."

"What?" Charlene gawked at him. "No. Would you just call for Flo, please?"

Holding the towel open, Tyler stared at her. "What's wrong? I've seen you naked a thousand times…okay maybe a hundred times," he said sarcastically. "And I've helped you give birth to two six-pound crying babies." She wasn't shy, so he was at a loss for her hesitation.

Oh, no, you haven't, Charlene said to herself with a sardonic grin. Unfortunately, she knew if she continued to sit there he would surely wonder what was wrong with his 'wife'. But as more bath bubbles popped, Charlene realized she had no choice but to get out of the tub. He'd made it loud and clear that he no longer loved or desired his wife anyway, so Charlene thought she could play out the charade.

Get it over with and get up.

Grasping the hand rails that had been installed for her use, Charlene eased herself up from the water. She was thankful for the frothy bubbles clinging to her. Immediately Tyler's strong arm went around her waist, encasing her in the large towel.

Holding onto her with his right arm, his eyes skimmed over her. They missed nothing as he convinced himself he was just making sure she didn't slip as he lifted her from the tub. When he looped the towel around her, he couldn't help bringing her body closer to his. He felt her shudder and realized she was chilled, prompting him to quickly pat the towel over her arms and shoulders. Her body was so slender he'd been able to wrap the large towel around her almost twice, sending the frothy bubbles to fly around them.

Charlene had no choice but to hold onto Tyler's forearms when he lifted her over the rim of the bathtub. She had to hold onto his shoulders for balance. She thought he was being tender as he mechanically patted the towel over her wet upper body. She remembered his hands caressing her hand or her face when she'd come out of the coma. Even then she'd recalled wondering how it would feel to be held in such strong, tender arms. But she also hadn't known who he was, either.

Gently drying her skin, Tyler cringed at the sight of her bruises. Although not as bad as they were before, they were still physical reminders of what she had endured. The long scars going down her left arm and leg were closed but pink. Because of his height and her damp hair, now parted, Tyler could see the scar on her scalp. It was a good two inches long and matched the one just above her left ear. He'd recalled her doctor's latest report indicating the hearing loss in her left ear could be permanent. Of what he could see, her upper back and torso were scarred, also.

It struck him anew just how much she'd suffered and how close he'd came to losing her, the mother of his children. His guilt went deep at having sent her from their home. It somehow didn't matter now when he could see the physical reminders of how she'd struggled and fought as she fell. It was his fault that she'd been at that hotel in the first place. Tyler knew he shouldn't have gotten so angry that he'd lost control of the situation. He'd expected her to fight back when he threatened to expose the pictures. He'd expected her to lie, and he'd expected her to stomp up the stairs and slam her bedroom door. She hadn't done any of that. *But what should I have done*, he wondered. *I should have let the situation die out like I did before.*

Picking up another towel from the rack, Tyler carefully dried her hair. Her fragrant conditioner wafted its way up his nose, instantly affecting him.

Charlene was beyond thinking that he was simply assisting her following her bath. The sudden contact and closeness seemed much more. At least that's what she thought when she experienced a full body shudder that made her knees knock together and her stomach quake painfully. *Oh, no.* She didn't utter a sound when his cheek grazed against her ear.

Tyler thought she was some kind of witch casting a spell on him. He couldn't think of anything except her. Although areas of her skin were scarred and bruised, he couldn't think of anything except kissing those areas. She was soft and fresh, and, without the will to stop himself, Tyler lowered his lips to her ear and leaned into her body. He whispered to her, "What are you doing?"

Charlene was incapable of answering. She didn't hear him. *How do I get out of this? I certainly don't need this complication.*

Immediately, Charlene realized that, like the children, Tyler would be devastated when he learned that his wife had died that awful night—just one night after he'd forced her from their home. Yes, he'd said there was nothing between him and Corinne except for the twins, but she knew he would be remorseful...and he should be.

Still, knowing what she did and feeling how she felt, by the time Charlene sensed his next action, it was too late. Standing like a statue, she fought against the heat of his body. Then Tyler kissed her.

Tyler was filled with longing as he folded his arms around her body. Being careful, he ran his hands down her back, bringing her closer as his mouth swooped down upon hers.

Tyler's body shivered. Although starved for a woman's touch, he was gentle as he kissed her. She didn't reciprocate, but kept her hands on his forearms for balance. Lifting his mouth from hers, Tyler gazed deeply into her amber eyes.

Charlene returned his unwavering gaze. *This can't be happenin'.* It was obvious to her what Tyler wanted from his wife. As she struggled to get out of a situation, Charlene had been forcing away an erotic vision when he'd skillfully angled his body snuggly against hers. When his lips were inches away from connecting with hers again, she turned her head.

Tyler dropped his head to her right ear, where he knew she would hear him. "Neither of us wants this, right?" But he tried pulling her against him anyway.

Charlene shook her head as if to clear away the fog. *Mercy! This fool thinks I'm…his wife!* She quickly stepped back out of his arms and gripped the towel tightly around her. "I-I'm sorry, but did you say something?" she asked in a voice as cool as ice.

"It wasn't important," Tyler said gruffly. But for some reason it was, because after several long months, he wanted her regardless of the fact that he knew she didn't want him. Her coldness was always proof of that. But if she'd given him any inkling otherwise, he would have picked her up and carried her from the master bath and to the bedroom.

Forcing the storm brewing in his body to retreat, Tyler ran a hand over his closely cropped hair and closed the distance between them. He wasn't at all surprised when she backed up again. He simply reached behind her and closed the back of the towel, which had loosened from her grip. "I'll send Flo up," he murmured and walked out of the bathroom.

——⁓——

After two days of avoiding Tyler as much as possible, Charlene joined the family for breakfast, something she rarely did before her therapy.

Following Shane and Shelly into the dining room with the use of just one crutch, Charlene stopped short. She hadn't expected Tyler to still be at home. She'd learned previously from Terri that Tyler, Ryan and Melvin had been going into the office early the past week. "Oh, good morning," she said nervously from the doorway.

Mona was more than delighted to see her. Rounding the table, she greeted Charlene excitedly. "My, my, you look wonderful and colorful, doesn't she?" She sent Tyler a meaningful look, which he ignored, quickly returning his attention to the morning paper.

Trish snickered at Charlene's outfit of neon green capri pants and a juvenile t-shirt. "Corinne, I can't tell you how much I like seeing you wear simple clothes. You look so relaxed and carefree. Oh, but I do hope you dress up for the party tonight. Maybe wear one of those originals you purchased a while back..." Trish stopped talking abruptly, realizing she'd just reminded everyone of Corinne's last shopping spree that had cost Tyler thousands of dollars and had effectively put them on the outs for several months.

Charlene took a seat beside Shane. "What party, Trish?" she asked, taking a bite of the piece of toast Shane passed to her.

"It's their anniversary party, Mommy. You probably forgot, but you bought a new dress," Shelly said, following Shane's action and giving Charlene a piece of melon.

Charlene realized that Shelly was reminding her about something their mother had obviously done. She thought it better to concentrate on chewing the large chunk of melon. When the twins insisted on taking turns feeding her, Charlene erupted into giggles. "You two are always feeding me." Her heart overflowed with love for the twins and she forgot about everyone else. Then, glancing up quickly, she caught Tyler watching her with hooded eyes.

Burying her nose into each of the twins' necks, Charlene hugged them tightly. "Yes, I forgot about the party. I have mush brains, remember," she said, kissing their giggling faces.

Mona mentioned that everyone was taking off today and suggested Tyler should take his wife back to their house to get the dress Corinne had previously ordered.

"No, I can't do it. I'm going downtown with Ryan to pick up his anniversary gift for Trish." Tyler winked at Trish. "Get Terri to do it. I'm sure she can cut a class or two."

Terri sent her sister-in-law a sympathetic grin before rolling her eyes at Tyler. "I only cut the classes with the instructors who remind me of you, Tyler," she retorted. "Anyway, I can't do it, either. I'm getting my hair done today."

"I certainly don't want to cause any problems." Charlene realized she had no idea where Tyler and Corinne lived, but she would love to see the house…maybe she'd find a clue to aid her search. "I'm sure there's…" she broke off suddenly. How could she tell them that she dreaded the thought of leaving the house? "Look, I'm still pretty scarred, and most times I need at least one crutch to walk.

I'll pass on the party if you all don't mind and hang out here with Shane and Shelly." The twins delighted squeals meant more to her than a party.

"We'll eat popcorn and gummy bears, because Mommy likes them, don't you, Mommy?" Shane said, resting his head against Charlene's chest.

"Yes, baby. I love popcorn and gummy bears," Charlene said, "sometimes together."

Since his mother and father had been giving him an expectant, yet disapproving eye, Tyler relented. "I'll take you to the house for the dress." Just then they all heard the sound of a school bus horn. Tyler told the twins it was time for them to go.

"Thank you, Tyler. I'll walk them to the bus today if you don't mind," Charlene said.

"Why should I mind, unless you plan on running off with them," Tyler quipped.

Oh, how I would love that, you ass! The look Charlene gave Tyler mirrored her thought.

Tyler tilted his head toward her after kissing the twins goodbye, his eyes sliding down her back as she got up to follow the twins out of the dining room.

Following the twins, Charlene *accidently* bumped into Tyler's chair at the exact moment he raised his coffee cup to his mouth. "Oops, sorry. I'm so clumsy," she said and smiled sweetly. "You'd think I'd have the hang of this crutch by now, wouldn't you?"

Glancing up from the large coffee stain spreading across the front of his cream-colored dress shirt, Tyler sneered at her retreating back.

~~~

He cast a doubtful glance at the younger man. "Please tell me there has been some progress since we last spoke," the older man said.

"Almost," the other said anxiously. "There's a party tonight. I'll approach her then."

"You realize that shipment cannot be delayed. I've paid you a lot of money to handle things on your end, and so far you've disappointed me. If that shipment doesn't go according to plan, there will be serious complications all around." His tone was direct and threatening to the younger man.

"I'll talk to her tonight and call you."

"You do that." The older man watched the young man walk out of the office. He hoped he hadn't misjudged him. He flipped open his cell phone. As he waited for the voice mail greeting of his associate/henchman/enforcer to end, he spoke quietly to himself. "This is what I get for not following my instincts. Had I done that, Corinne Mills, or this looka-like, would be dead…and I would have my property back by now."

CHAPTER 12

Charlene was overcome with emotion when she went to Tyler and Corinne's home.

It was a lovely home. Everything was new and stylish and bright. To Charlene it was exactly the house Corinne used to talk about having when they were kids.

While Tyler went into his study somewhere off the living room, Charlene walked about the first-floor rooms. She imagined Corinne walking beside her and giving her the grand tour. The sunroom that was just off the stately kitchen sported a large bay window. It was full of plants, most needing water. Filling up a pot with water, Charlene went about watering them. In the kitchen, she crossed over to the refrigerator and couldn't help but smile at the two birthday drawings taped to the door.

Taking the drawings and holding them to her chest, Charlene left the kitchen and passed through the living room. Stopping to stuff the drawings into her pocketbook, she recalled what Corinne had told her about the scene that unfolded there between her and Tyler. She could almost see Corinne standing there with flashing angry eyes after Tyler had confronted her with the divorce papers and the pictures.

Leaving her crutch in the living room, Charlene climbed the stairs.

She wandered about the wide hallway and then stopped at Shelly's room. The room was an organized mess. Charlene smiled to see a train set on one side of the room. Many little toy animals sat in carrier cars. Not many dolls with frilly clothes; instead Shelly had lots of stuffed animals and many pairs of sneakers that were all jumbled together in the bottom of her closet.

Next, Charlene made her way to Shane's room. He was the neat one. His bed was fashioned after a race car. Checking out his chest of drawers, Charlene touched his little boy shirts. Little action figures lined the tops of the dressers and the windowsill. Under one window, he'd built a fort and a rescue was taking place…two little glass kitten figurines were sitting on the edge of the windowsill, waiting to be rescued by the action figures below.

Charlene was stunned to see the figurines. She had seen them before. Scooping them up, she stuffed them into her pocket. Turning to leave, she spotted a picture of Shane and Corinne on his desk. In the picture, Shane sat on his mother's lap. "Oh, Corinne, he's beautiful and sweet, both of them. How proud you had to be of them," she said.

Composing herself, Charlene left the room and walked across the hall to what she thought was Corinne's room. Pushing the door open she realized it was Tyler's bedroom and quickly closed the door without going inside.

The largest room was the master bedroom suite. It was Corinne's room. The bed was neatly made up and the same jacquard prints covering the bedding adorned the windows. Charlene's eyes surveyed the room. It was a profusion of green and yellow. There was a sitting area that clearly Corinne had used. It looked like a quaint living room. The Native American artwork in that area caused Charlene's breath to catch in her throat.

A built-in book shelf was filled with an assortment of books, too many for Charlene to even guess what Corinne preferred reading most. But there had to be at least twenty picture frames holding pictures of the twins, along with her and Tyler.

Charlene picked up each one for closer inspection. She could see how the twins grew up. "Lovely," she said, then heard Tyler calling up and asking if she was ready. "Be right there," she responded. What struck Charlene most about the sitting area was the one painted accent wall. Easing down on a foot stool, Charlene let her eyes take in the color. The combination of yellow, orange, and red caused her eyes to sting until tears spilled down her cheeks. To anyone else it probably was an awful color choice, but Charlene knew that Corinne picked the color as a tribute to their teenage years.

Many years ago, she and Corinne had snuck into a house on their block that was being renovated.

Tiptoeing through the vacant house, they'd imagined living in such a house instead of the one that they'd lived in…a rented fixer-upper. After running their hands across the wide kitchen counters they stepped out onto the back porch. Corinne had been the first to spot the cans of paint stacked up on top a of pile of debris set out for trash collection.

Opening some of the paint cans, they found three that were partially full with the top layers mostly dried out. They'd taken the cans back to their house and mixed the three colors together. It was just enough for them to paint one wall in the bedroom they shared.

Smiling at the memory, Charlene realized Tyler was correct. The color was atrocious in the beautiful setting of Corinne's room. Their father had pretty much said the same thing. But when they'd finished painting the wall, she and Corinne thought it was beautiful.

Charlene's head began to spin. "It's too much. Corinne, please help me," Charlene whispered. She waved a hand toward the wall. "This hideous wall tells me you never forgot us."

"Corinne," Tyler called out quietly, coming in from the hallway.

Crying in earnest now, Charlene could only look up at Tyler. She couldn't tell him what was wrong when he walked in and knelt in front of her. The image of Corinne baring her heart and crying an abundance of tears flashed suddenly in her head.

Guessing she was probably thinking about her last night in the house, Tyler took her hand in his. "Corinne," he began.

"No, no…" Charlene began. *I can't live this lie any longer. I just can't.*

"Oh, no." Tyler noticed beads of perspiration on her forehead, followed by a trickle of blood running from her nose and rapid blinking. Quickly lifting her in his arms, he carried her over to the bed. He ran to the bathroom for tissues and a wet face cloth. When he returned seconds later, Corinne had gone into a seizure. Hovering beside her on the bed, Tyler ran soothing hands along her twitching arms after wiping blood from her nose. As previously instructed by her doctor, he let her come out of the seizure on her own.

Several minutes later, exhausted and weary, Charlene became aware that she was on the bed and that Tyler was sitting beside her. "It happened again, didn't it?"

"Yes, you had a seizure," Tyler said, wiping her face with the cloth. "How do you feel?"

"Shelly's word for how I feel is yucky," Charlene said, making a face.

"I don't know why she's been saying that lately," Tyler said with a chuckle.

"It's a girly thing. You wouldn't know about it."

"Try me," Tyler said, having finished wiping her face clean.

"You won't know everything she's thinking about, but in a few years when her hormones are flying off the chart and boys start chasing her, all I can say is watch out." Charlene knew she wouldn't be allowed to see the twins then. The thought saddened her.

"I'm not worried," Tyler said. "Besides, I have a feeling she'll be the one chasing the boys. She's such a tomboy, and bossy, too. Like her mother." Tyler saw her face crumble.

"Yes. She has her mother's bossiness," Charlene murmured. Corinne was the bossy one growing up. "Tyler, um, will you also remember that Shane is like his mother, too. His quiet, sensitive side that rides just beneath the surface hurts quickly and deeply and he won't tell you. He'll just turn into himself," Charlene said, avoiding Tyler's eyes.

"There you go again trying to turn our boy into a sensitive punk." But Tyler had read between the lines of what she'd said. "I'm not going to keep you from them." Tyler sat up to talk to her. "Listen, I know what I said to you the last time we were in this house together. I was angry and pissed off over the situation. I said a lot of things that night that I regret saying," he said as he gazed into her eyes. "I should have handled things differently."

Charlene had to ask him a question that Corinne had wondered about that awful night. "Why that night? It was…" She watched him drop his head briefly before meeting her eyes.

"I know. It was your birthday. I hadn't planned it like that. I'd had the divorce papers in my desk for over a week and then I got the pictures that evening.

Well, it just seemed the time to deal with it." Actually, he'd remembered wanting her to feel as miserable and as heartsick as he'd felt when he got the pictures.

Seeing his distress, Charlene chose her words carefully. "So much has happened and we're different people now, um, but had you asked *that* Corinne Mills, who ran from here that night…well, she would have stayed and never left this house again. *That* Corinne left in turmoil and heartache, but she knew you were hurting, too. And the thought of not waking up with the twins was just so incredibly painful, but walking out with at least some pride seemed more important that night…" Charlene's quiet voice wavered. "There's no more room for anger."

"How can you say that? I was mean, and, yes, I was hurt," Tyler said.

"A part of *that* Corinne…" Charlene's voice wavered again. "She died that night. I don't have time to waste now. Life's precious. It can end in a flash…or in a tumble over a cliff."

Tyler searched her eyes. He was glad they were having this conversation. "But it's my fault that you were there. If you'd died, how could I live with myself? How could I look into our children's eyes, identical to yours, and not be reminded of what I had done?"

"You weren't the reason for…Listen, you're not the reason *that* Corinne Mills was on the road that night, Tyler." Seconds later, Charlene was shocked when Tyler lowered his head on her shoulder. He didn't embrace her. She didn't embrace him. She simply lay

there, staring straight ahead, letting her eyes dance
down the awful orange wall.

"I love you, Corinne."

When each drifted off to sleep seconds later,
Charlene would later wonder if Tyler had whispered
those four words, or had she.

———∞———

The one year anniversary party of Ryan and Trish
Mills was in full swing at nine o'clock that Friday
night. With Mona having overseen everything, it was
a spectacular event and everyone was in a festive
mood. That is, everyone except for Tyler and Corinne.
Their tense faces weren't lost on the family members
who quietly watched them.

When they'd first arrived at the reception hall,
Charlene was taken aback by the number of people
coming up to greet her, all wishing her well. She felt
most of them genuinely liked Corinne. With a slight
smile plastered on her face, Charlene focused more on
not fidgeting in the form-fitting dress. The original
dress she was to wear had caused her a new fear when
Trish had opened the zippered bag. The beautiful
peach-colored cocktail dress was sleeveless, backless,
and had a long split up the left leg. It would show all
of her scars, bruises and more.

Waking from their afternoon nap, Tyler grabbed
the first dress hanging in a garment bag from the
closet. Neither he nor Charlene looked at the dress
until they returned to his parents' house. When

Charlene again made excuses why she shouldn't go, Terri and Trish searched their own closets to come up with a black ankle-length dress with long sleeves. The dress fit her perfectly. She let them style her hair in a way that covered the scar on her temple. She didn't believe it when they all told her she looked beautiful. With the twins dancing around her, Charlene was tempted to run back upstairs and change into a pair of jeans.

Now, looking longingly as many couples took to the dance floor, Charlene was reminded how much she loved to dance. Before her father became ill, he used to dance with her in their backyard. On many occasions Charlene often danced by herself.

She spotted Trish and Ryan dancing closely together. She thought they were very much in love. She noticed that Ryan seemed to watch her, as if waiting for her to fall flat on her face, which was still a possibility. But she guessed Ryan's feelings toward her were simply a reflection of the brotherly friction between him and Tyler.

Charlene realized she was an outsider to this type of life. Their clothes spoke of money, as did the fancy décor…right down to the chilled little bowls holding the shaped balls of butter. She knew that Corinne had blended into this life of money. She recalled Corinne's mannerisms and speech were those of a cultured, wealthy woman…unlike herself. It remained a constant effort to pretend to be someone else.

She desperately wanted to leave the party and go back to the house and hide.

Tyler had all but disappeared for most of the evening. He'd moved from table to table, where his friends gathered and surrounded him. With everyone dancing, Charlene made her way to the ladies' room. Alone. *Yes, that's exactly how I feel…totally alone in this place of pretty, dressed up people eatin' fancy foods.* Exiting the ladies' room a few minutes later, Charlene wandered over to a large window overlooking the side garden. Decorative lights bounced off the spray fountain in the middle of tropical foliage.

Pressing her head against the cool glass of the window, Charlene was suddenly approached by a man from behind. He stood so close that his body touched hers, pinning her against the window. His breath was hot and rushed against her neck as he whispered, "Baby, I miss you. Listen, you've got to watch yourself. He knows you have his property," the man whispered, running his hand across her flat, tensed stomach and kissing the side of her neck.

Charlene was not only disgusted, she was now trapped by the man's body pressing against hers. "Wh-what? Get off me," she hissed.

"Please, baby, for both our sakes, Mr. Hunt knows you have the real orders. It's all incriminating evidence, so please give it to him or…" The man paused, looking behind him before rushing on. "Or we're both dead," he said, rubbing his hand down the front of her thighs suggestively. "Oh, you feel so good," he said, kissing her ear.

"Get off me, now!" Panicked and disgusted, Charlene grunted and pushed back, becoming increasingly frightened as he moved against her.

"Okay, baby...I-I'm sorry. I just miss you so much. Why haven't you called me? You had to know that I'd be worried sick about you. I'd had to sneak in and out of that hospital waiting for a chance to see you. Oh, Corinne, baby. I feel horrible about what happened to you."

His next words shocked Charlene and instantly stilled her movements, as well as her instincts to scratch his eyes out and hit him below his belt.

"You're my Corinne, aren't you? Yes, yes, of course you are...what am I saying? Hey, did you have a twin or lookalike who got hurt...burned in that car?"

Then he was gone.

Once she was alone, Charlene collapsed against the window. Collecting herself, she spun around, her eyes wildly scanning the outer part of the lobby. Her mysterious visitor had disappeared as quickly as he'd come. He'd spoken in her right ear, so she heard every word, and felt his every disgusting touch.

Charlene had little time to dwell on the man when Mona spotted her and quickly walked over to her. "Corinne, there you are! Are you all right, dear?" She seemed to notice Corinne's frightened expression.

Charlene struggled to recover her composure. "I-I had to pee real bad," she blurted out. When Mona chuckled, Charlene held onto her arm tightly for both security and balance.

Charlene's eyes continued to wander around the room for a glimpse of the man who'd accosted her just moments before. He was nowhere in sight. That's when the realization hit her. Everyone had to present their invitations upon entering the reception, so more than likely the man was an invited guest. She looked for a man with a lecherous grin on his face, but didn't find anyone looking like that.

A short while later, as guests were preparing to leave, she spotted Tyler again. He was talking to a beautiful woman he'd danced with several times. That, too, was something that bothered her. Okay, so yes, she couldn't dance like the other couples could, but to everyone Tyler and Corinne were a married couple. In her mind, Tyler had made it known that something was amiss with him and his wife; that's how *she* felt sitting there. Pulling her eyes away from Tyler and the woman, she was dismayed to find many in the room watching her. Looking away she desperately wanted to go home…to her home in Virginia.

When the stretch limo returned to take the family back home, Tyler announced that he was going to hang out with a few friends and would get a ride home later. He'd made his intentions clear. He wasn't coming home tonight.

∽

The following morning at Saturday breakfast, when Tyler made his way to the dining room table it was obvious by his ruffled appearance that he'd spent the remainder of the night partying or otherwise engaged. Everyone thought he'd probably done both.

Charlene did, too, but she had little time to focus on Tyler's disheveled appearance. He was the least of her concerns. While Tyler was most likely in his dance partner's bed, she'd spent the night tossing and turning in hers. She cared little that he'd been sexing the night away. Instead, she'd focused on the details of the encounter with the strange man. A shudder ran through her when she recalled his breath against her neck when he whispered those frightening words. It wasn't so much that he'd said she had to watch her back…it was that he'd implied Corinne had a twin who'd burned in the car. That in itself confirmed to Charlene what she already knew to be true.

It was Corinne whose body the police had found partially burned. *Oh, dear God.*

Charlene reflected back to that awful night again. Corinne had said she hadn't told anyone that she'd had a twin sister. She didn't want anyone to know how she'd grown up…poor and forced to live on government assistance. But last night, Charlene spent the night typing on the laptop computer. She'd added to her ever-growing pile of pages of information, but key words the man had whispered stuck out…*Shipping manifests, invoices and incriminating evidence. Some man named Mr. Hunt who wanted his property back or she and he would be dead.* What did it all mean? Charlene wondered.

Mona interrupted Charlene's musings by commenting on the success of the party, thus putting an end to the strained silence around the table. Mona sent air kisses to Ryan and Trish.

When Shelly and Shane made teasing kissing noises, Charlene couldn't help but lean over and kiss Shane loudly on his cheek. The boy smiled and dropped his head, shamefaced.

"Kiss me, too, Mommy," Shelly chimed in and was delighted when she got her own sloppy, noisy kisses.

Charlene wasn't prepared when Shelly scrambled back to her seat and said, "Okay, now kiss Tyler, Mommy. It's what mommies and daddies are supposed to do." Charlene didn't miss the meaning behind Shelly's words. She could only gape at her.

Tyler, who'd been broodingly reading the morning paper and nursing a hangover, heard his daughter's comment. "You know, sweetheart, I do prefer if you call me Daddy. It makes me think I'm special to you," he said, taking a sip from his coffee cup.

"But you are special to me, Daddy, and so is Mommy because she almost died and went to heaven. I can call her *Corinne* if I want to, but I don't want to," Shelly said, sitting back in her seat, looking contrite. "She said she wants us to still call her Mommy," the girl added.

Charlene felt as if she'd just stepped on a tightrope. She realized that either Shane or Shelly could slip up and reveal she wasn't their mother, just as Shelly just slipped.

"I know, sweetheart," Tyler said, now meeting his wife's eyes dead-on above the heads of the children. The fire in her eyes didn't escape his notice, either. "But Mommy is getting all better...she's recovering very quickly, aren't you, Mommy?"

All Charlene could do was think about Shelly's innocent words. Her deception was once again thrown back into her face. *What kind of monster am I to play such a dirty trick?* Realizing that Tyler was waiting for her response, she nodded. Yes, she understood exactly what he'd meant. He wanted her gone, and quickly. *Son of a bitch!* He wanted to get on with the divorce. And that ticked Charlene off in a big way. How selfish he was to think about himself, she thought. He simply didn't want a reminder of his guilt staring him in the face every day.

Well, later for you, Tyler Mills, because it ain't even about the likes of you.

She'd made a promise to her sister and she was keeping it, she thought. Charlene pushed her chair back and stood up. She was unsure if she was going to pounce on Tyler for his sarcastic comment or not, but something was about to happen because the air was thick with tension.

Having listened to their exchange, Mona also understood the meaning behind Tyler's question. She lifted inquisitive eyes to him. "You know, Tyler dear, when Corinne has fully recovered, this home—*my* home—will still be her home if she so chooses. As the mother of my grandchildren she has a place to call home." Mona stood. "It's best you remember that, son."

Tyler was in no mood to fight with his mother. Turning to her he responded in a firm voice. "And, Mother dear, you must remember that for the children and me this *place* is temporary and our original situation remains unchanged," he said, looking at his wife.

Pushing aside total embarrassment, Charlene rounded the table and embraced Mona. It was meant to smooth away the confused brows of the twins, who were trying to process the conversation around them. Charlene winked at them before placing a noisy kiss on Mona's cheek, too.

"Thanks, Mona, but I agree with Tyler. That situation remains unchanged, as evidenced by his behavior last night and this morning." Charlene then turned to Tyler. "So yeah, let's put what he wants first. Let's put that before everything that's important. He's such a big-headed jerk he can't think beyond his inflated self-importance," Charlene said sweetly.

Hearing that, Shane and Shelly's eyes went wide as each whispered in the other's ear.

Tyler stood up and tossed his napkin to the table. "Just wait one damn minute…"

In that instant, having overheard the heated words out in the kitchen, Daisy rushed in and scooted the twins out, telling them their favorite cartoons were on in the kitchen. But the second the door swung closed behind her, Tyler exploded. "I'm a jerk?! Is that what you said?"

"I didn't stutter, but actually I said you're a big-headed jerk! That's exactly what I said. Trust me, mister, I cleaned it up because the children were in here. What I wanted to call you was an ass! And you wear both titles well." She sent him a sour look.

Everyone was shocked to witness the blowout. Terri, on the other hand, was actually enjoying the spectacle playing out across the table. She picked up another piece of toast, munching on it and waiting for the next round of fireworks. Ryan rested his hand against his mouth. He was pleasantly enjoying watching Tyler coming apart. He also noticed his parents watching the blowout with keen interest. He hoped they thought Tyler's behavior unbefitting the future CEO of the family business.

"I'm an ass? I don't think so, and certainly not after all the crap I've had to deal with from you. Lady, you'd better check your date book," Tyler snapped as his anger resurfaced.

"Screw you! I have no date book, and if I did would it be any of your business? No! But you, Mr. Stay-Out-All-Night, it was mean of you to behave like that last night. If it was your intention to humiliate your wife in public, amongst family and friends, then you succeeded, you jackass!" Charlene knew she wasn't arguing the point of his behavior for herself because she didn't really care. He wasn't worth her energy. She was fighting for Corinne. Because for all intents and purposes that's who she was supposed to be. Had it been Corinne and not her, Corinne would have been the one sitting there last night, humiliated, embarrassed, and with sympathetic eyes and hushed whispers aimed at her. Silently she said, *For you, Corinne, I'm puttin' your dickhead of a husband in his place…somethin' I sure hope you would've done.*

To say Tyler was shocked was an understatement. Arguments between him and Corinne were a usual occurrence, but rarely did she fight back with words. Instead, she'd sulked for days on end until he apologized even when he knew he hadn't done anything wrong. "It was not my intention to humiliate you, but what about you, wifey? What about all of your bull-shit that I've had to endure? What about your needs that you had fulfilled elsewhere? Did you not think that I was embarrassed or humiliated by your behavior? If you didn't, or in the event you don't remember, think real hard and try pulling *that* from your faulty memory!" He couldn't stop the words he'd said because, truth be told, he'd held them in far too long.

With her hand on her hips and now up in Tyler's face, Charlene couldn't ignore Terri's amusement and sidebar comments any longer. Obviously neither could Tyler, because both looked at her and shouted in unison. "Shut up, Terri!"

"Tyler, what do you think I've been doing for the past two months? I've been pushing the physical therapy so that I can get better. I *need* to recover. I *have* to recover. I feel like I am a burden to you and this entire family. I hate that. I can't even look at myself in the mirror. There's not a part of my body that's not bruised or scarred, and Shane wants us to compare scabs! Do you think I feel pretty or sexy enough to even think about a date? Well, I don't! But last night I dressed up at the insistence of all of you, even though I didn't want to. And I still felt horrible. I felt like a taped-up, cut-up, pinned-together rag doll. I hated it, but what I didn't need last night…" Try as she might, Charlene's voice grew hoarse with emotion. "What I didn't need last night was for you to show everyone just how messed up I am. You didn't even sit at the table and eat your meal, or stay long enough to butter you bread with those stupid butter balls. Because of me, right? But forget about me because I don't matter to you. But what about the rest of your family and what you showed them, especially Ryan and Trish. It was their night. So, yeah, all of that makes you a jerk in my book." Charlene stepped threateningly closer to him and pointed her finger in his face. "And you don't *ever* get to throw past issues in my face again…you got that?"

Tyler let her finish her tirade. As a matter of fact, he realized that had been the most Corinne had ever snapped back and he was slightly stunned. "Yeah, I got that. But just so we're clear on a few things, I'm glad you're getting better…for you. I want you to recover so that you can get on with your life. I want our children to have a healthy mother because they're still frightened. And I'm sorry you felt so bad last night. I didn't intentionally do anything to embarrass or humiliate you, regardless of those *past issues*. But if you think that, hey, go right ahead and call me names. I don't care. In any case, it doesn't change our situation, now does it?"

Melvin stood up quickly, noticing Corinne's suddenly twitching body. Then her nose bled. "Missy…" His words forced everyone to react, guessing she was about to have a seizure.

Vigorously shaking her head and trying unsuccessfully to keep her shoulders from twitching, Charlene snatched a napkin from the table and pressed it to her nose. She stepped back from the hands reaching out to her, Tyler's included. Luckily, she didn't have a full blown seizure, but she did feel like she'd just sat down on a jackhammer. "No, it doesn't change the situation," she said and hurried out of the dining room and up to her bedroom, where Flo waited.

When Tyler sat back down and reached for his coffee cup, he met his mother's scornful eyes. "Go ahead, Mom, jump on the bandwagon and get your slice out of me, too," he said.

Mona smiled. "All right, dear. You know I hold mealtime a highly important function for us as a family, that's why I've always insisted we all eat together. It bonds us and helps us to connect daily. But, Tyler, now *you* listen up, that will be the last time you talk to your wife like that at my table or in my presence. You understand what I'm saying to you? She didn't deserve the remnants of your night's activities…whatever they may have been!"

Tyler rubbed at the knot of tension in the back of his neck before responding. "Yes, I understand perfectly, Mom. But answer me this, will you? When did you become such a champion of the Corinne Mills Fan Club to the point that I'm at fault in your eyes and obviously it's the opinion of this family?" As he asked the question, Tyler looked around the table.

Mona studied Tyler for several seconds. Then with a tilt of her head and a smile upon her lips that never was intended to reach her narrowed eyes, she answered him. "Oh, let's see…hum…well, in the words of your own daughter, 'when Mommy almost died and went to heaven,' that's when."

With that Mona pushed through the dining room door and stormed into the kitchen.

———

Following physical therapy, Charlene spent the remainder of the day researching information about the shipping business, specifically Mills Shipping. Her previous suspicions about Tyler proved futile at first. But since their blowout, she wondered if Tyler had gotten so upset with Corinne over her betrayal that he could have had her killed.

After breakfast that morning, there was no doubting that he was upset with Corinne, Charlene realized, but he loved his children. Tyler was a doting and loving father. He would probably do anything to protect them. But could he have planned the unthinkable act to rid himself of Corinne, an adulterous wife?

No. Charlene couldn't believe that. She simply didn't want to believe that. She recalled the incident in the bathroom and when he'd comforted her during her seizures. He was attentive and oftentimes playful, but she simply wasn't sure. After all, she didn't really know him. Tyler was a stranger, but something was clouding her mind from seeing into his soul.

Charlene thought herself to be a good judge of character. If someone was mean-spirited or wicked, she always picked up on it. She didn't sense anything like that in Tyler, but it didn't mean he wasn't somehow involved in Corinne's death.

CHAPTER 13

Charlene struggled to keep her depression to the edges of her mind, lest Flo report that back to Dr. Holland. She'd spent much of her time researching Mills Shipping. She found nothing pertaining to a Mr. Hunt, but she was forging ahead.

She needed to search Corinne and Tyler's house again for manifests and invoices. Remembering what the lecherous man had said, Charlene wondered if Tyler was using the family business for something criminal. Since that was more of a possibility than him having had Corinne killed, she had to wonder if perhaps Corinne had stumbled onto what Tyler may have been doing under the radar of regular shipping business. She recalled conversations she'd overheard between Melvin and Mona about the increased business and revenue since Tyler had been at the helm. They praised his expertise. *But was it all legal and on the up-and-up?*

Charlene needed help, and that meant coming clean about who she was. Since the twins knew she wasn't their mother, time was of the essence. With each passing day, she worried that one or the other would inadvertently say something to alert the family she wasn't Corinne.

But who can I trust? Who would help me?

Just then Flo breezed into the bedroom singing "Oh, What a Beautiful Day."

Charlene smiled. Yes, the fifty-something, feisty, down-to-earth woman was just the person. Stuffing her papers into a large satchel she asked Flo if she could drive her to her home.

Seeing her patient smiling, Flo was more than delighted. "Well, honey, if you're gonna smile like that, absolutely! I was going to run to the mall to pick up a new set of scrubs, and your place is on the way." Flo clapped her hands. "Well, come on, girl let's get moving so we don't waste this day," Flo said, pulling her patient to the door.

At twelve-fifteen that afternoon, Charlene had propelled a now weary-looking Flo into the living room of Tyler and Corinne's house. She'd nodded when Flo exclaimed how beautiful the house was. "Yes, yes, Flo, have a seat," Charlene said and began to pace.

"Oh, okay." Flo's eyes ran over her patient, assessing her outwardly. Something was afoot because she was a nervous little thing. "Corinne, honey, you feeling all right?"

"Flo, can I trust you completely?" Charlene asked, stopping to sit beside Flo.

"Absolutely! Girl, I'm like your lawyer. What's said between us stays between us," Flo said, and then frowned. "Oh, wait a minute, that's about Vegas, isn't it?" Flo's lips twitched at her own joke. "Anyway, that is unless I think it could jeopardize your physical and mental health," Flo said, patting her hand reassuringly. "Now, what's got you in all in a twitter today?"

Holding onto Flo's forearm to keep the woman from moving, Charlene began. "Flo, this isn't my house. The first time I came here was when Tyler brought me here last week to get the dress for the party, remember?"

"Yes. Oh, but honey, don't push it. Your memory will come back…well, most of it, and if it doesn't, well…" Flo stopped talking at the negative shaking of her patient's head. "No?" Flo said, mimicking by shaking her head also.

"No," Charlene said. "Flo, listen. Right now my mind is solid and the part of my memory that is solid as a brick is in knowin' who I am. I'm not Corinne Mills. My name is Charlene McDonald." Charlene let that sink in, and then reached out to stop Flo from dialing her cell phone when the woman mumbled about calling the doctor right away about a personality issue.

But Flo sensed this young woman wasn't having a meltdown. Dropping her cell phone back into her purse, Flo crossed her arms under her bosom. "Okay, you start talking, 'cause my North Carolina ears have been picking up a definite Southern drawl from you when we're alone." Pursing her lips, she added, "That can't be faked, so, as your confidant and lawyer, aka nurse and friend, tell me what's going on?"

"You're right, Flo. Corinne was my identical twin sister…" Charlene began.

An hour later, after hearing the entire story and after a seemingly endless number of questions, Flo's jaw hung open. "Holy cow! You know, I believe you. I don't know why, and maybe I need my head examined, but darn it, Corinne, I mean, Charlene…I do believe you 'cause everything now fits into place. It's like a completed puzzle, almost."

Charlene sank against Flo's hefty arm and let out a relieved sob. "Please say my name again. It's been months since I've heard it."

Obliging, Flo eased her arms around her patient.

"You have no idea how badly I needed to hear my own name and hear my own voice," Charlene said.

"Okay, Charlene. I have to tell you this is something straight from a Lifetime movie, and Charlene, the husband is always involved and they catch him in the end," Flo said. "But honestly, I don't get that from Tyler. He cares for you and the kids. He really does. I can see it."

"He cares for the mother of his children. That's not me, Flo. I'm their auntie." When Flo asked if she'd developed feelings for Tyler, Charlene had to think for a moment. "Truthfully, Flo, I don't know what I feel. He's my brother-in-law who paid a lot of money for my medical care. Aside from him, the twins are the only family I have left."

"Mercy! What a mess. Well, okay, what do you need me to do, and why are we here in your sister's house?" Flo asked, letting her eyes scan the elegant and spacious living room.

"I need to find out who killed my sister, but first I need you to do something for me." Charlene squeezed Flo's arm.

Flo patted Charlene's hand reassuringly. "I'm on it. What is it you need me to do?"

"I need you to go to the L. A. County Coroner's Office and claim my sister's ashes. I want them. Please, will you claim them? List yourself as her aunt or something, but just get them and bring her back to me," Charlene said with difficulty and pulled out the police report she'd printed from the internet. "Her DNA will match mine and any missed markers or tracers or whatever those things are called will be listed as undeterminable because of the fire. You already have my blood samples at the hospital. Take whatever you need and have tests run if you need to prove my DNA."

Flo read the police blotter reports Charlene pulled from her bag and then stood up. "My God. Okay, I'll go now. I'll get my new scrubs later. What are you going to do while I'm gone?"

"I'm going to search this house for clues to what Corinne's troubling emails were about."

Flo shook her head, recalling Charlene's earlier suspicions about the Mills family business. "Honey, be prepared for what you might find. Because if you do find the evidence that ties Tyler to some criminal goings-on with his daddy's business, then are you prepared for those children, your only relatives, to also lose their father to a prison cell?"

"Oh, God," Charlene groaned. "No, Flo, I'm not, and honestly I'm praying he's not involved. My instincts tell me he isn't, but there's a possibility," Charlene said.

"I hope you're wrong. And, Charlene, what about that man who cornered you at the party and what you told me he said? We need to find him, because it seems he's the culprit."

Charlene smiled. "Flo, I think you watch too many Lifetime movies. But you're right, so let's start with square one: this house. Then I'll go after him."

"Now, how're you going to do that?"

"He was invited to the party. I'll have to get Mona's guest list," Charlene said.

Flo scrambled to gather her purse and keys and headed to the front door at a fast clip that had Charlene running to catch up with her. "Look, don't push yourself, and don't you lift anything heavier than a pencil. I mean it." She sent her patient a stern look.

At the door, Flo turned back to Charlene. Her patient looked so very small and so very frightened. *My God, she's so terribly alone in this drama*, Flo thought. "I'll go get your sister. Charlene McDonald, art teacher…yes, I can see that now," Flo said, squeezing Charlene's cold hand before scooting down the driveway to her gas guzzling, eighteen-year-old car.

In the two hours that Flo was gone Charlene checked every nook and cranny of Corinne and Tyler's house. She found shipping invoices in Tyler's office for materials and other items, but with no way to make copies, she stuffed them into her bag. When her eyes lit upon a picture on Tyler's desk her hand froze.

All these years later, Tyler still kept his and Corinne's wedding picture on his desk. Charlene's eyes glanced about the desk and another picture stood out. Tyler and Corinne were standing in front of Mills Shipping. It was a modern four-story building with a large warehouse to the left, each boldly showing the company name. It struck Charlene then that she had no idea what Corinne did. Did she work there with Tyler, she wondered?

Her sister's smiling face in the picture told her to check there.

―⁂―

The small but heavy box Flo brought back to Charlene was handled with the utmost care. With Flo at her heels, Charlene carried the box up to Corinne's bedroom and lovingly placed it on the shelf in front of the awful red/orange wall. When Flo had called her an hour earlier telling her she'd gotten her sister's ashes, Charlene asked for one more favor. She asked

Flo to go to a mortuary and purchase an amber-colored urn. Only that color would do.

With Flo standing beside her, together they read aloud a Psalm from Corinne's Bible, which had been sitting on another shelf. "You're home, Corinne. Now, guide me to find who did this terrible thing to you. I love you, and I'll carry that love in my heart until I see you again," Charlene said quietly.

You get more flies with honey than with vinegar.

Charlene replayed the words Flo had said as they drove back to the Mills house. On Wednesday evening Trish, Terri, and Charlene decided to have a barbeque. Dinner was sure to be a relaxed event out on the patio. Since she'd taken her meals in her room since last Saturday morning after she and Tyler had that fight, Trish and Terri were delighted when her spirits seemed lifted and she joined in to help with the barbeque.

With burgers, hotdogs, and steaks slowly grilling, all three women were dressed for the warm summer evening in matching shorts and bright neon colored T-shirts, courtesy of Terri.

Expecting the rest of the family to come home any minute, Charlene decided to teach them and the twins, as well as Daisy and Flo, the latest steps in a popular line dance everybody loved doing back in Virginia. Being able to do the moves without the use of her crutch, Charlene danced her heart out. With the twins mimicking her steps, her laughter rang out with theirs.

With the aroma of food sizzling on the grill, loud club music, and tiki torches lighting up the backyard and patio, Mona, Melvin, Ryan, and Tyler joined them on the patio. Excitedly, Mona clapped her hands in time to the music and, soon, she too joined in the impromptu line dance, dragging her husband along with her. Ryan and Trish joined in also.

Tyler was left alone, watching the group. He couldn't take his eyes off his own wife as she happily danced. With the twins copying her moves, how could he not laugh? He was transfixed just watching her and was unable to move his feet to join them.

"Come dance with us, Daddy! The steps are easy and fun," Shelly called out to Tyler as he stood watching Corinne's body move.

Then she called out to him and his heart raced.

You get more flies with honey than with vinegar. Charlene smiled. Her eyes captured and held onto Tyler's from across the stone patio. "Yes, come dance with us, Daddy," she said, picking up the stereo remote and restarting the CD again.

How could he not? Her call was music to his ears. Crossing the patio, Tyler fell into step beside his wife. Laughing when the twins grabbed hold of his legs, encouraging him to move, Tyler was surprised when Corinne moved suggestively around him as she kept in step with the music. He'd gotten a good view of her shapely legs and backside.

Winded and laughing from dancing, Daisy and Flo retreated to the house. Then Mona and Mel dropped out, as did Trish and Ryan, and finally Terri propelled the twins to the table to eat.

Secretly, Tyler was glad to see Corinne out of her room because, according to Flo, her depression had returned. "Where'd you learn this dance?" he asked, keeping in step with her.

Charlene fumbled for an answer. "Oh, it's a new line dance I saw on television. But I do need to rest now." When they walked over to the patio, the only seats left were side-by-side. When he began filling her plate, Charlene frowned at the mound of potato salad along with a burger and hotdog. "Hey, that's way too much food," she said, accepting the heavy plate.

"You should eat it. You need more meat on your bones," Tyler said before biting into his hotdog, which he'd topped with every condiment sitting on the table.

"My bones are fine. You can ask Flo and Dr. Holland."

"I'm just used to seeing you a little thicker," Tyler mumbled around a bite of his hotdog.

Charlene didn't think Corinne looked thick at all when she'd seen her. "You like thick, Tyler?" Charlene asked, watching his eyes widen as he chewed his food.

With everyone looking on, probably with bated breath, he thought cynically, Tyler wiped his mouth before answering her. "Yes, I like thick, sometimes."

"Hum, sometimes," Charlene repeated around a mouthful of potato salad. "And so, other times what do you like?"

Tyler raised his eyebrows quizzically at her dancing eyes. "Don't you know?"

"Nope, I have a faulty memory from brain trauma, remember?" Charlene pointed to her head and winked at a smiling Mona across the table. "So tell me how else you like 'em, Tyler?"

He thought it odd that she was in a teasing mood. It had been a very long time since she'd teased him about anything, and he liked the banter with her. "I like 'em cute and attentive," he said, mocking her but also thinking she was certainly trying to be both tonight.

"Yeah, that's how I like 'em, too," Ryan said, kissing Trish's cheek as she ate hungrily.

Charlene nodded. "Okay, so thick, cute, and attentive. Not saucy, hot, and sexy, hum."

"And you…?" Turning, Tyler gave her his full attention.

Running her eyes up to the sky, thinking, Charlene sighed. "I like em' sweet and thoughtful." When Shelly scrunched up her face and asked what they were all talking about, Charlene answered, "Grown folks business, honey," without breaking eye contact with Tyler.

"Oh, is that what this is?" Tyler asked, watching her bite into her burger with catsup dripping down her chin. He watched her lapping unsuccessfully at it with her tongue. For reasons he didn't want to dwell on he wished to feel her lips on his again. Redirecting his thoughts, he picked up her napkin and wiped her chin.

"There you go again wiping my face." Charlene chuckled, and when he asked what she'd meant Charlene went on to explain that she'd remembered someone touching her face. Now, recognizing his cologne, she asked if it really was him.

"Yes, it was me."

So as not to be left out, Melvin ran the back of his hand down Mona's cheek. "Well, I happen to like 'em sweet, loving, and kind." Mona smiled in agreement.

"You all are so bor-ring in what you like if you ask me," Terri sang out, and then slurped her iced tea. "I happen to like 'em not too tall, hot, and with just a smidgen of chest hair."

While the adults gave Terri an indulgent look, Shelly bit into a hamburger and then spoke. "Are you guys talking about hamburgers or hotdogs?"

Terri couldn't hold back. "Yeah, Shelly, we're talking about meat!" Terri just barely escaped Ryan's hands and the playful thrashing that would have followed.

"Let's dance again, Mommy," Shane suggested.

Taking the napkin from Tyler's hand, Charlene wiped her fingers and helped Shane from his seat. Walking over to the stereo, she found several slow melodies to play, and, to Shane's delight, she helped him up on a small stone table so that they were eye-to-eye. She gallantly bowed to him. "It would be my pleasure to have this dance with you 'cause you're so darn cute." Charlene dropped her head to his small shoulder and was totally happy when he threw his little arms around her neck.

Unconsciously, Tyler let his eyes trail over Corinne's body. He thought she was downright sexy even if she thought she wasn't. He fought unsuccessfully to keep his eyes from the movements of her body. But several minutes later, Melvin suggested Tyler could perhaps fill in for Shane so he could finish his dinner. Tyler didn't miss his father's wink.

With all eyes on him, Tyler got up, walked over to Shane, and tapped him on his shoulder. "May I cut in," he said, then lifted a disappointed Shane down to the ground. "Go finish your dinner, Shane." Turning back, Tyler repeated her words. "It would be my pleasure to have this dance 'cause you're so darn cute." Then he added, "Unless you don't want to."

Charlene watched Shane poke out his bottom lip back at the table. "But Shane's upset."

"He's okay. He's a boy, and his heart will get broken from time to time," Tyler said, reaching out as she stepped into his arms. "It'll toughen him up."

Charlene stepped slowly into his embrace. "Did you toughen up?" She wondered if he'd toughened up and enacted a plan of revenge against Corinne for her adultery.

"Um-hmm," he murmured. "They're watching us back at the table, you know."

Charlene glanced over his shoulder. "Um-hmm," she murmured, moving closer as his arms tightened. She looked up at him. "Tyler, do you really want Shane to get hurt and toughen up?"

Tyler chuckled. "So you want him to grow up to be the sensitive punk we talked about?"

"No, but don't you want him to grow up happy and loving and to know it's okay to show his softer side?" Charlene asked. She was positive that's what Corinne would have wanted. "I wouldn't want him to be shunned or hurt." *Not like I was as a child.*

Tyler eased her body closer. "He'll be fine because he'll have a hovering mother and grandmother playing on his softer side. But he'll also have me to combat that," he said. Tyler inhaled her scent. "And I'm starting with football camp next week." He grinned; it was nice holding her in his arms. It had been so long.... "I'm picking up his football gear tomorrow."

"What? You can't be serious?" Charlene's eyes widened, surprised that their bodies were touching so intimately. Then realizing he was teasing her, she reached up and plucked his ear.

Enjoying the feel of her in his arms, Tyler fought to control the stirrings of his body when she rested her head against his chest. It struck him anew that they had rarely danced during their marriage. They rarely did anything except argue, and in most cases they didn't even do that. It had been a strained, silent indifference on both of their parts, but mostly on his.

Uh-oh, this isn't good. Charlene squirmed, having to rest her hands on him again. He must have sensed what she'd been thinking and created a little space between them, but not before she realized how good it felt to be held in a man's arms again. When the music ended, she quickly returned to her seat and to the curious pairs of eyes that had watched them dancing.

As the evening wound down Charlene asked Tyler about his day. She was probing his work ethic, but she picked up nothing more than his commitment to working harder to keep revenue steady and the staff employed. When Melvin said that Tyler was an excellent choice for CEO, Charlene noticed Ryan bristling. Tyler ignored it. She wondered what that was all about.

"Maybe I can come back to work." While searching Tyler's office back at the house, Charlene found a roster of Mills employees. Corinne's name was on it in the administration department. "I can start tomorrow, and maybe only work half a day. For pay, of course."

"You're salaried, of course you'll be paid," Ryan said tightly. As head of the human resources department at Mills Shipping, Ryan secretly thought that if Corinne returned to work, there was the possibility that she could push Tyler over the edge...not good for the CEO.

Charlene didn't get a chance to respond when Terri started another loud, heart thumping musical selection and pulled both her sisters-in-law onto the patio for another line dance.

Tyler fought hard not to gawk at his wife's sexy curves as she danced. He couldn't remember seeing her so funny and carefree before.

One other occupant at the table watched Tyler's reaction to his wife with great interest.

———

Later that evening, Charlene returned to her bedroom after helping the twins with their nightly baths and prayers. When she'd first arrived at the house she was profoundly happy to learn that it was Corinne who'd taught them the little prayer. It was the same prayer that she and Corinne had been taught to say as children.

Tonight Charlene asked Shane and Shelly to include a prayer for a special friend of hers who was in heaven. Although they were full of questions as to how her friend ended up in heaven, Charlene promised to tell them one day soon, but also reminded them of their promise not to tell anyone she wasn't their real mother.

In her bedroom, Charlene knelt to say her own prayers. Her heart was heavy as she asked for forgiveness and guidance.

Tyler appeared in the doorway and found her kneeling with her head bowed at the foot of the loveseat. He waited until she'd finished. "I haven't seen you do that in a long time, Corinne."

My name is Charlene. "I never stopped, ever," she said quietly, repeating Corinne's parting words to her that awful night.

"Can I talk to you for a few minutes?"

"Sure." Charlene got up and sat in the loveseat. She prepared herself for whatever he had to say. When he sat beside her in the narrow seat and reached for her hand, Charlene sensed bad news. "You've changed your mind about me returning to work, haven't you?"

"No. I just wanted to let you know that you don't have to worry about finances. After the divorce I'll take care of you financially, so don't concern yourself with that." Tyler halted, bracing himself to bring up their last argument. "I also wanted to tell you that I will not keep you from seeing the kids. You're good for them, and they love you." Tyler gave her hand a squeeze. "I should have said that before."

Charlene felt it best to say nothing, so she just nodded her head.

Sitting together and holding hands seemed surreal to Tyler. He couldn't remember the last time he'd just sat and talked with Corinne. In the growing silence he blurted out, "So you like 'em sweet, and what else was it?" Turning, his eyes dropped to hers and then lower to her lips.

Before he began speaking, Charlene was seconds away from getting up from the loveseat. She needed distance because the pull to him was so great that she'd wanted to rest her weary head on his shoulder, strong and solid as it was. "I said I liked sweet and thoughtful," she said.

"Right, well, I hope on some level during our marriage that I was at least both for you," Tyler said, meeting her eyes again.

Charlene remembered Corinne telling her that Tyler was indeed thoughtful and sweet. That is, in the beginning of their marriage. Then he became more focused on the business and the twins, but not on her. "Yes, you were." Charlene saw no reason to say otherwise.

Tyler brought the back of her hand up to his lips and kissed it. Turning even more, he cradled her cheek. "I also should have told you last Saturday that I still think you're beautiful and sexy. I don't want you to think negatively about yourself. You're here and you're alive...and we all thank God for that," he said quietly.

Charlene exhaled. "Amen to that," she said. "And...and I'm sorry you were hurt, but thank you for staying by my side in the hospital, talking and forcing me to open my eyes."

Pulling back, Tyler smiled. "Ah-ha! So you really did hear me talk about punishing Shane for throwing those carrots?" The light flashing in her eyes told him she did.

"And Mona chasing you with her shoe for breaking her gazing balls." Charlene grinned. "Yeah, I heard that and more."

"She threatened to break my balls, too. It's a terrible thing to say. Jeez, my own mother." He laughed shortly. "I'm worried about you, and I'll always be concerned about you."

"You know what, I was a sickly child. I was pitied by so many people and my friends. I'm not like that anymore. I'm stronger, and now more than ever I'm determined to live," Charlene assured him with a shrug of her shoulders. "Nothing can stop me, not now."

Tyler leaned forward, stunned by her admission. "You never talked about your childhood. Why were you sick?"

That was hard for Charlene to hear, but she already knew that Corinne hadn't talked about her past or told anyone that she had family, alive and living in Virginia. *Both desperately missin' her.* "My mother had a difficult labor birthing me. She died minutes after I was born."

More surprise registered on Tyler's face. He caressed her cheek. "Oh, I'm so sorry. Why didn't you ever tell me this? You only said that your parents died years before we met."

Catching herself, Charlene was unable to explain why she'd told him that. "It-it was too painful for me to know that I'm alive because she died. It's still really painful for me." Charlene tried to pull her hand from his, but he wouldn't let go. She wanted to get up and move away from the close confines that were becoming strained and contemplative.

"Oh, baby," Tyler said, wrapping his arms around her. He was sorry for a pain that she carried alone. "I wished you'd told me," he said as he dropped a kiss on her temple.

Charlene couldn't hear him. "You forgot I can't hear you in my left ear," she said. Pulling back, she reached up and touched his left ear. Her hand lingered for several seconds.

"I said I was sorry," Tyler said. The desire to kiss her was so overwhelming when her warm hand touched his ear in a tender, gentle way, Tyler did just that. He kissed her.

The sensuous swipes across her lips shocked Charlene motionless. Steeling herself, she simply let him kiss her. She knew it wasn't about her. It was for Corinne, and he was just sharing an empathetic moment for what she'd disclosed. But seconds into the kiss, she found herself kissing him back because he'd begun waking up desires she'd held in check for a very long time.

Their kiss swiftly progressed into a deeply passionate one with Tyler pulling her onto his lap. His hands tentatively molded to her curves.

Charlene struggled to hold her body rigid. *This is wrong on so many levels. Okay, it's just a simple, considerate kiss a husband would share with his wife, right?* With that thought in mind, she returned the kiss. It wasn't a mystery as to what he wanted. And then playing the role of his wife suddenly became all too real, too consuming. Although she fought against it,

Charlene was affected by his touch so much that when he lifted her T-shirt up and touched the swell her breasts, she could only think how wonderful it felt and not how wrong it actually was.

Breathing heavily, Tyler took in the sight of her. She wore a simple, thin, opaque bra, not the lacy, colorful ones he'd seen her wear before.

Charlene pushed away her feelings, pushed them to the farthest recesses of her mind, because he was her sister's husband. *He was.* With that thought, reality slapped her in the face, and that's when she opened her eyes, unsure when she'd closed them. She saw that his eyes were fixated on her breasts, which almost appeared bare in the flesh-tone hue of her bra. Glancing down at his hands lifting to caress them, Charlene was immediately repulsed. The scars and bruises covering her breasts and torso loomed and appeared ugly, disgusting her.

How could she have forgotten how she looked naked?

Mortified, Charlene lifted her wide eyes to his. She sensed what he had to be thinking...that she was horrible, repulsive. She didn't blame him. Who'd want to touch the bride of Frankenstein? But a bigger worry for her was that she shouldn't have allowed him to kiss her again. She knew it was wrong, and yet she'd allowed it and actually enjoyed it.

It was a stupid thing to do. A soft cry escaped Charlene as she pushed Tyler away. She began frantically tugging her shirt down, which suddenly didn't seem long enough. It ended up catching on the back clasp of her bra. She turned away from him, forgetting that scars marred most of her back, as well.

"Look at me, please," Tyler said.

"No, no, and please don't say anything. I already feel sick. Just leave!" Charlene was almost to the point of screeching. "Th-this shouldn't have happened!" *It shouldn't have.*

Tyler was positive her scars went beyond the physical. "Look at me," he demanded. He'd seen the healing gashes and the scars. He was prepared for what he saw, but only then did he realize her scarring was far more extensive than what he'd read in Flo's report. Her words from Saturday breakfast slammed into his head. *And Shane wants to compare scabs.* Now he fully understood the meaning behind her words. It caused a hurtful ache in his stomach. She'd told him…told everybody how messed up she felt. "You're alive and you're beautiful. Please look at me," he whispered to her back.

"No." She heard movement and hoped that he was leaving. She needed him to leave.

Tyler pulled her shirt down to cover her back. When she still refused to face him, he reached for the robe lying on the back of the loveseat and eased it around her. He smiled sadly when she quickly, but angrily, punched her arms through the sleeves. "Now will you turn and look at me?" And when she finally did Tyler's heart did another bizarre flip-flop to see the humiliation in her eyes.

"Are you happy now?" Charlene snapped, avoiding looking into his eyes. When he said he was and that he'd enjoyed the kiss, Charlene searched his face and fumbled to get herself out of the tight situation she'd put herself into. "Our situation remains unchanged," she said.

"Yes, I know." Tyler was stopped from saying anything more when he heard Shelly calling out for him.

"Tyler?"

Charlene snorted, hearing Shelly call her father by his given name. Smart-alicky. That's what her father used to call Corinne when she did something to tick somebody off. Charlene was positive that's what Shelly was doing again. She also thought her niece had perfect timing.

Dropping his head in exasperation, Tyler pinched the bridge of his nose. "Why does she keep calling me by my given name?"

"Tyler? Daddy?"

Cringing and not waiting for her to respond, Tyler gave his wife a quick kiss to her now-red lips. "I'm going to find one of Mona's shoes," he chuckled, finally coaxing a smile from her. "Just teasing," Tyler said as he left.

Charlene's immediate thought was that she'd just complicated an already complicated situation. But more importantly, she realized Flo's words had a drawback, a dangerous one.

"Damned stupid flies," she murmured. Flo had suggested she get closer to Tyler for two reasons. First, so she could find out if he'd had any involvement in Corinne's death and second, if he didn't then when the truth about her identity came out he'd find some room in his heart to allow her to have a relationship with her niece and nephew.

"Well, I certainly have his attention now, don't I?" Charlene huffed and flopped down. Dropping her head to the back of the loveseat, she raised her eyes to the ceiling. "Lord, if you got a minute, I need to bend your ear one more time tonight."

CHAPTER 14

The following morning, as Charlene rode to Mills Shipping with Tyler, she asked questions about the business and listened with rapt attention as he explained about several new contracts that had been secured since her accident. As he talked, Charlene admired the picturesque coastal highway and realized that she'd seen little of California since she'd arrived.

Forcing his mind off her choice of work clothes— a plaid button-down shirt, jeans, and flat summer sandals—Tyler was struck by the fact that she seemed relaxed. He'd even thought he liked not seeing her usual office attire of suits and dresses. "You look comfortable."

"Oh." Charlene knew Corinne dressed up for work. Her closet was full of business clothes, whereas her own closet back home in Virginia was full of jeans and pullover tops, appropriate for art classes and cleaning her classroom. Her fellow teachers often commented that she looked like a student herself. "Since I'm only working half a day I just threw this on. It's okay?"

"Yes." He thought it was perfect. She looked care-free and still sexy as hell.

"I had to make sure I wore something that covered everything, you know," she said, then wished she hadn't mentioned anything at all. Sliding her eyes across to his, she wondered if he'd thought about their encounter last night. She sure had, a lot.

Tyler thought the shorter hair style and the fact that she wore no make-up, only heightened her beauty. *When did I stop noticing that,* he wondered. "You look great, actually."

⁓

For Charlene, the morning was spent painfully smiling at all the strangers who came to greet her. To her shock, she'd found out that Corinne managed the computer department. She was responsible for preparing the shipping invoices and manifests. *Good Lord.* Charlene had hoped that Corinne just had a menial task as the boss's wife, not run an entire department of eight staff members whom she supervised.

When Tyler escorted her to Corinne's office, Charlene was struck by another wave of grief. It was so strong her feet halted in the doorway. But the feeling grew even stronger when Tyler pulled out the chair to the desk and waited for her to take her seat. Immediately, Charlene saw pictures of the twins with their mother on the desk. One picture was taken in their sunroom as lush green plants surrounded them.

Picking up another picture Charlene smiled sadly. Corinne was holding the twins. They were just tiny babies bundled in identical blue and pink outfits. For a split second, Charlene saw herself, because that's exactly how she'd looked eight years ago, with her hair pulled back and wide bangs hanging over her forehead. She also thought she looked rather geeky, too.

"You love that picture," Tyler said. He sensed she was feeling apprehensive. He knew he was. "Hey, listen, don't push yourself today, take it slow. I'll be in my office if you need me." Walking to the door, Tyler stopped when she whispered that she was scared.

Charlene really was scared that someone would catch on that she wasn't Corinne.

Tyler walked over and sat on the edge of her desk. It was the second or third time she'd said that, and it somehow unsettled him. "Don't be scared. You spent very little time here in the office because you preferred working from home on your laptop. No one is expecting you to jump right in and pick up where you left off."

He'd misunderstood. "What exactly was I working on, do you remember?"

Shrugging his shoulders, Tyler glanced at the desktop computer. "I don't know. But just turn your computer on and check your calendar before the accident." Avoiding her eyes, he reached across the desk and turned the computer on.

Charlene watched closely as he typed in Corinne's password. She'd recognized the name immediately. It was the name of their first and only dog, Hailey. "My memory lapses are so bad. Tell me, did I like it here?"

Rounding the desk and bringing her to her feet, Tyler gave her a chaste hug. "It's going to be okay." Releasing her, he gazed into her eyes. Oddly, he'd wanted to kiss away the worry lines from her forehead. He'd done that while she was in a coma. "Like other things, you didn't like being stuck in the office all day. You only worked two, maybe three days a week but you ran this department very efficiently. Without it Mills Shipping couldn't survive."

Charlene was surprised to hear that. "Really? So what other things didn't I like much?" *What else didn't Corinne like, besides intimacy?*

Inhaling deeply, Tyler hesitated several seconds before answering her. "Let's just say things that involved me. It was those very things that sent you searching elsewhere."

Charlene reflected on his words. "Then why am I still working here?"

Tyler decided to be honest with her. "At the time of your accident I hadn't fired you yet."

Shocked, Charlene recoiled, unable to hide her reaction. "Fired? Why?"

Weighing his words, Tyler eased back from her. "Because I no longer trust you, and, like I said, this department is vital to the operation of this business. You know my father is entrusting this place to me. Within a few months, when he officially retires, I'll be solely responsible for the family business. That ultimately makes me responsible for our wealth and the employment of a lot of people, and frankly I cannot trust you not to retaliate when I…" Tyler stopped, not wanting to rehash the issue of their divorce.

Charlene understood perfectly. Not only had he thrown her sister out of her home, but he was about to fire her from her job as well. And for what, she fumed inside…because Corinne had cheated on him. "When you file for divorce," she finished for him, defeated.

"Yes, that was the original plan."

"So why am I here, now?" Charlene asked with panic rising. *Bastard.* "If nothing has changed…or has it?" She didn't think for one second their recent friendliness or his lustful attraction to her had changed his mind, not one bit.

Running his hand down his face, Tyler stared at her. Something had changed, and it wasn't that she'd almost died. It was something else. It was him who seemed to be changing, and he didn't want to. He was going to remain firm in his decision to file for divorce. Unlike Corinne's other dalliances and affairs that he'd ignored and let slide, this time he'd seen pictures of her infidelity, and that cut him far more deeply than any of her scars. "No, nothing has changed. I'll be in my office if you need me," Tyler said as he walked to the door and closed it behind him.

Staring at the closed door, Charlene felt the unfamiliar urge to scream. She made a fist instead. "I *won't* need you, Tyler Mills, but Corinne sure did, right up until you crashed her world," she said with renewed resentment of him.

———∾———

On her third day at Mills Shipping, Charlene had done little more than read through a ton of emails, which presented another problem…she didn't have her reading glasses, so her task was hampered by squinting, thus giving her a headache. She'd made a mental note to ask Flo to pick her up a pair from the drug store.

When Melvin tapped on the door, Charlene was delighted to take a break. He carried a cupcake on a small plate. He waved it teasingly under her nose. "Wow, for me?" Taking the plate from his hand, Charlene licked at the frosting.

"Well, missy, if it wasn't before it sure is yours now," Melvin said and chuckled.

"Sorry, I guess I'm a bit of a pig, aren't I?"

"No, you're not. You're rebuilding your body, and since you know how he likes 'em, maybe you should take heed and thicken up some," Melvin said with a wink.

After pondering what Melvin had said, Charlene shook her head. "Tyler is proceeding as planned, and I'm A-okay with that, Melvin."

"I don't think you are. You're as miserable and, pardon the expression, as pent up as he is, and the both of you are driving the family nuts." Ignoring her wide eyes, Melvin sat in the chair across from her desk. "You're both stubborn and pigheaded. But I think both of you have realized just how fragile life can be." He studied her troubled face.

Taking a swipe of frosting and sticking her finger into her mouth, Charlene was saved from responding.

"Listen, I know I've been the reason Tyler's spent so many hours working here, but in the long run it's good for him. He's ready now to take the reins, but he doesn't want to yet. You want to know why?"

Charlene shrugged her shoulders.

"Because to some degree he doesn't trust his instincts, and he doesn't trust that he's ready to be at the helm. Tyler's cautious and he's good. That's why I chose him to take over. But sometimes, by being too cautious, one hesitates when the goods are staring him in the face." Melvin sat forward and arched an eyebrow at her.

"I'd swear I think you're not talking about the shipping business anymore."

"I'm not." He chuckled and met her eyes steadily. "Go ahead and play innocent, but I've already figured it out, missy," Melvin said, pursing his lips.

With her mouth suddenly dry, Charlene almost choked on the sweet frosting and cake now stuck in the back of her throat. *Oh, my God…he knows! What can I say? Absolutely nothing,' but confess and throw myself at his feet. Beg for forgiveness for deceivin' all of them.* Getting up and coming around the desk, Charlene wrung her damp hands and knelt before him. "Melvin, I-I didn't mean to hurt anyone. Please believe me, I didn't mean any harm by…"

"What's wrong?" Tyler asked, coming in and finding his wife in tears at his father's knee.

Clutching her trembling hands in his, Melvin stood her up and gently patted her back. "I didn't mean to get you all frazzled." Meeting Tyler's questioning gaze, Melvin lifted his shoulders in a shrug. "All I was saying is that sometimes we don't see a tragedy as a second chance. You two stubborn adults have little ones who need the both of you, the good and the bad. Both of you need to think about what you're doing and how your decision will affect your family and your little ones." Unfolding her from his arms, Melvin handed her over to Tyler and quietly left the office, closing the door behind him.

Charlene thought she'd throw up right there as she stared down at Tyler's Italian leather shoes. *Stupid me. I was about to tell Melvin everythin' and he wasn't even talkin' about me!*

"What happened?" Tyler asked, guiding her over and easing her down onto a sofa-style seating arrangement a few feet away from the window.

Charlene gulped in air and rubbed her aching eyes. "Nothin', I mean nothing, really."

Tyler got her a bottle of water from the mini refrigerator in the corner. Sitting beside her, he twisted off the cap before passing her the bottle. He knew exactly what his father was talking about. It had been the same speech his mother and Trish had been giving him. He waited for her to take a few sips of water, but was surprised when she gulped down almost the entire bottle and then burped afterward. Chuckling, Tyler patted her back. "You sound like the twins."

Charlene was hot, tired, and still sick, but it didn't stop her from asking him to bring her the unfinished cupcake sitting on the desk. She was so ready for the truth of her identity to come out. But it was still too soon because she hadn't gotten anywhere near finding out who killed her sister or why. Eating the cupcake, she cared little that he watched her. Then it did bother her and she told him so. "Stop eyeballin' my cupcake. I'm not givin' you any. Melvin brought it for me," she said around a mouthful of the delicious cake.

Tyler burst out laughing. "I like the Southern accent you added for effect. But for your information, there's a whole tray of them in the staff lounge."

Caught off guard, Charlene realized again the effort it took to hide her accent. "Oh, yeah," was all she could muster.

Reaching out and picking candy sprinkles that had fallen to her shirt, Tyler explained that the staff had planned an impromptu luncheon to celebrate her return.

"Oh, how nice, but why would they go to so much trouble?" she asked, forcing away his hand, which was caressing her shoulder. She guessed it was a normal thing for a husband to do with his wife. With his arm on the back of the sofa, Charlene listened as he reminded her how generous and kind the staff members were. He'd asked if she'd read her get well cards from them.

Charlene did read a few, but not many because they were all meant for Corinne. "I read some," she said.

"Well, since they couldn't send flowers, they sent in a donation to your favorite charity…the neo-natal unit at the hospital. The donation card is at home," Tyler said.

Charlene had been listening attentively. Hearing that, she guessed Corinne had involved herself in that charity because they'd had to spend the first few weeks of their lives in incubators, having been born three weeks early. Only Charlene had stayed longer, by another four weeks, until her lungs fully developed. "I'll read the card as soon as I get back to the house," she said quietly, lifting her eyes to his handsome face. "So what's on the lunch menu?"

"Pink frosting," Tyler mumbled as his gaze dropped to her mouth.

Charlene scrunched up her face. "Oh, do I have frosting on my nose or my chin?"

"Not your nose," Tyler said, watching her lick her bottom lip. Dropping his hand to her back he nudged her closer and leaned forward. "You missed. It's on your top lip and your chin."

"Oh." Charlene could say nothing when in that instant his tongue slowly, sensuously glided across her upper lip. He didn't stop there. Fighting back a giggle at the ticklish thing he was doing, she whispered, "Why waste a napkin, right…ah, did you get it all?"

"Uh-uh," Tyler murmured, capturing her lips just as her hands came up to stop him.

Lord, get me out of this. Charlene's mind tumbled over as fast as her stomach did cartwheels. When it was apparent that he was going to kiss her, she steeled herself, and when his arms tightened around her she turned her head away.

Oh! This idiot has a lot of nerve, and now he's thinkin' about his selfish needs again.

Charlene reeled when Corinne had told her that she and Tyler hadn't been intimate in a very long time and that she really didn't care if she never slept with a man again. She'd confided that she just didn't get into the whole sex thing, and that Tyler basically had left her alone.

Charlene had shared with her twin that that was where they were opposites, because she thoroughly enjoyed intimacy. That's why Charlene thought she could pretend to be Tyler's wife—she'd been assured there would be no intimate contact between them. But here she was again letting Tyler pull her onto his lap.

Tyler paid no attention to the buzzing of the inner-office telephone calling them to the staff luncheon. His hunger wasn't for food at that moment…it was coaxing another kiss from his reluctant wife.

Charlene struggled inwardly. Would Corinne have let this intimacy happen if she didn't want it? Charlene doubted it, but Tyler expected her to be receptive despite everything else. *Not!*

Tyler was beyond thinking it was a bad decision on his part to go down this path, but he'd wanted to kiss her again and couldn't explain it. *Yeah, I do…it's been months.* His hands roamed down her back to her hips…her body felt incredibly wonderful.

Fighting against the flames of desire, Tyler sank back against the sofa. He'd nuzzled her neck and finally captured her lips. On another level, he hated succumbing to whatever spell she'd cast over him. *What's going on*, he wondered. 'Head trauma…expect some behavior changes.' Dr. Holland's warnings rang loudly in his pounding head. *Yes, that's what this is*, he thought. But Tyler suspected her actions were more than just behavior changes. She acted as if she wanted him to kiss her, but he knew differently. Was she faking, as usual? That thought alone forced Tyler to sit up quickly, but he didn't release his hold on her.

Charlene met his assessing gaze. He seemed angry at something he'd started.

"Ah…sorry, you two," Melvin said, after knocking on the door and entering. Looking mischievously embarrassed for having caught them in an intimate moment, he smiled broadly. "Well, I'm in here now, so Tyler, you might as well let her up and you two come on into the lounge for lunch." Melvin chuckled. "And don't kill the messenger, we did call."

The instant Tyler's hands slackened on her hips, Charlene scrambled up from his lap and flew out the door in a flurry. All the while, Melvin's laughter was ringing behind her as she frantically searched the hallway, wondering in which direction the ladies' room was located.

She'd wanted to gulp more water and wash down the cupcake lodged in her throat. It had obviously shut off her airway, thus making her lightheaded to the point she'd lost control with Tyler. Yeah, that sounded plausible, she reasoned with herself.

~~~

Having acclimated herself to the layout of the office, Charlene worked until five o'clock each day. Since it had become apparent that Tyler wanted some level of intimacy with his wife, Charlene was more than primed to work around the clock.

She found Corinne's secretary, Anita, to be efficient but reserved and watchful. When Charlene requested a file containing recent manifests, she'd thought the young woman's hesitation was no cause for her to worry. But she did find it disconcerting, and planned to keep a low profile around Anita.

Attempting to understand the data in the thick ledgers, Charlene would have sworn it was written in Chinese with codes for everything.

Then…bingo!

She spotted the business name she'd previously gotten from Corinne's laptop, TM Hunt Enterprises. When her hand trembled, Charlene scrolled back to several emails in which Corinne had expressed concern about some shipments of containers and other property.

Shipments. Property. The words bounced around in Charlene's head. They mingled with the words the man at the party had whispered in her ear. *Mr. Hunt knows you have his property and he wants it back…or we're both dead.*

Frantically flipping through the ledger, Charlene found a tab for TM Hunt Enterprises. The next shipping date for the company was scheduled for June 26, and, as indicated by his bold, neat script, Tyler had approved the shipment.

Glancing at the calendar, Charlene realized it was already June 2. From previous emails she'd read, Corinne had been concerned about that date of June 26.

Thinking back, Charlene recalled that Corinne had said her lover had been an integral part of whatever was going on. She'd confessed that his business was used as a cover…for what? Charlene noticed the manifest file showed an order for twenty-five hundred containers. "Could this be connected to what you were killed for?" she said. She was so deep in thought she was unaware that Tyler had just walked into the office.

"What did you say you would kill for?" Tyler was sitting across from her desk.

Quickly closing the ledgers and stuffing her notebook in her bag, Charlene nervously said the first thing that came to mind. "A drink, yes, um, I would just kill for a cosmopolitan. Oh, hell. I'd even go for a shot of whiskey. It's been months, and so, yes, I'd kill for either right about now," she flubbed.

"Whiskey…cosmos? When did either of those become your choice of drink, Miss Mojito?" Watching her hands nervously patting her chest, Tyler pushed away the vision of the two of them on the sofa. He'd thought of little else since their noontime kiss a couple of days ago. He couldn't help recalling his father teasing about their 'frolicking' after she had run off, leaving him to face his father alone. So not cool, he thought.

"Oh, who cares? Cosmo, mojito, anything with spirits, um, liquor, I mean…" Charlene squirmed and quickly remembered Terri referred to alcohol as booze. "Booze, yes, booze."

"You're on anti-seizure and pain medications. Neither can be mixed with alcohol, so don't even think about drinking any booze, okay?"

"I guess I'm just getting a little frustrated, that's all." Truthfully, she was, and now her new worry was how Tyler was involved in any illegal activity.

Noticing a blush on her face, Tyler sat down on the edge of her desk. Cupping her cheek with his hand, she felt warm. "You've worked two full days. You're pushing yourself," he said.

Oh, no. Charlene fidgeted when his thumb traced her chin. Scooting the chair back, she quickly got up to put the ledger on a shelf behind Corinne's desk. "So, I-I guess it's quitting time, huh?" She was careful to keep her back to Tyler.

"Yes," Tyler said, coming up behind her and taking the heavy ledger from her hands and placing it on a shelf. Bringing his hands down he caressed her shoulders and dropped an arm around her waist. "Are you using a new perfume?" he murmured against her neck.

Trapped in his embrace, she cleared her throat and tried to side-step him. "No, no perfume. Just a body lotion, and why are you concerned about what I have on?" Charlene asked, dropping her eyes to her bag near to where they stood. *Oh, no.* Her papers were sticking out.

Switching sides, Tyler nuzzled her right ear. "Because whatever you've been using lately seems to be having an effect on me...or is that perhaps your plan?"

Wriggling out of his arms, Charlene stepped around the desk. "Now, why would I do somethin' like that? I-I don't remember, but have I done that before?" She stumbled.

"Not for me you haven't," Tyler quipped, following her. His playfulness disappeared. "I got your lack of interest. I can't say what the other guy got. Well, actually, yes, I can say."

Ignoring what he meant, Charlene snatched up her bag. "I'm ready."

Seeing her face crumble, Tyler bristled for bringing up something that was obviously a source of uneasiness for both of them. Following her into the hallway, he leaned forward. "Sorry," he whispered in her right ear.

"The shipment scheduled for June 26 will be the last shipment to Mexico. That's still the plan, isn't it?" James Smith said from the confines of his car. The sensitivity of his cell phone call was so important and illegal that he didn't dare take a chance of anyone walking by his office inside JS Computer Sales and overhearing him.

"Yes, that will be the last one," the person on the other end of the cell phone replied, noticing the nervousness of the other. "What's the problem now?"

"No-nothing. I'm just stressed with everything and people have died. Listen, I-I didn't sign on for this, and now I stand to lose everything. My business and my…" Blowing out a breath, James hit the steering wheel hard with the heel of his hand, and then rubbed his hand across it as if sorry he'd done such a thing to his beloved BMW.

"And your lover, right? James, you must realize she was never yours to have. Why can't understand that?

Corinne Mills is another man's wife. And, since we must talk about her again, what did you find out? I trust you approached her at the party as planned?"

"Yeah, um, yeah, I did...but only briefly." James closed his eyes, remembering their brief encounter and the feel of Corinne's body. "Yes, it's definitely her, and I gave her your message, that you knew she had your property and that you wanted it back," James said, beginning to feel sick in the stifling hot car.

"What did you say exactly?"

"I said exactly what you told me to say. That it was a matter of life or death if she doesn't give it back to you."

"I don't think those were my words; however, they'll do. I'm not concerned about you, James. You're done what I've asked, and in turn you've provided a means to get my merchandise to its destination without so much as a truck stop inquiry. And, I might add, you've been compensated handsomely."

"What about Corinne? I-I don't want anything to happen to her," James pleaded.

"I told you, nothing will happen to her. I just want my property back. I want what she stole from me. Have you checked for it?"

"Yes, and I didn't find anything. You know she's still recovering, right?" James paused nervously. "Listen, Mr. Hunt, she's suffered a lot of trauma, head trauma, too, and according to Tyler, some, um, memory lapses. Actually a lot of memory lapses, so maybe..."

"What are you saying…that Mrs. Mills now has a convenient case of amnesia?"

"Yeah, well, you might say it's something like that."

"Did she remember you when you approached her at the party?" Mr. Hunt was getting fed up with James and his whining. In the grand scheme of things he thought James Smith and Corinne Mills had become little nuisances that he planned to deal with, once and for all, after the last shipment was safely on its way.

"Yes, she remembered me," James said, unconvincingly even to himself.

"Good." Mr. Hunt was through talking. "I'll be in touch with you."

Hearing the disconnect signal on his phone, James started the car and turned the air conditioner on full blast. Resting his head on the backrest, he thought back to his encounter with Corinne at Ryan and Trish's anniversary party. Yes, he was sure that she remembered him. How could she not? They'd been hot and heavy for several months. He did wonder about that lookalike, but he was positive Corinne didn't have a twin. What he believed was that she'd had a girlfriend who'd bore a remarkable resemblance to her. So much so that the poor woman had been snuffed out by Hunt's henchman/associate/driver. He was only supposed to give Corinne a little scare, not run her off the road. James was on the verge of tears thinking about the dead woman, whose only mistake was being out with Corinne that night.

James thought back to when he'd gone to the hospital to check on Tyler shortly after Corinne's accident. He'd asked Tyler if he needed any help contacting Corinne's family. But Tyler, in his sorrow and shock, had reaffirmed that Corinne had no family at all.

James closed his eyes. He thought back to when he'd gone to Tyler and Corinne's house. It was the day after her accident. He'd gone there to console and commiserate with Tyler, his friend of ten years. James's wife, Mia, had sat with a distraught Tyler after hearing about the injuries Corinne had suffered in the tragic accident that occurred minutes after he'd left her. When Tyler told James that he and the twins were moving in with his parents temporarily, James had returned to the house and disarmed the alarm code. There, he'd spent time searching where he thought Corinne might have hidden Mr. Hunt's property—the original shipping invoices that showed what was really shipped via Mills Shipping. He knew she had them, but he'd found nothing.

Corinne didn't just have copies of the doctored invoices that were used in place of the originals…she'd had the shipping crates that contained Hunt's merchandise flagged for tracking. When the FBI originally contacted Mills Shipping, ordering them to cancel all business with TM Hunt Enterprises, Corinne hadn't, at James's encouragement.

Corinne had asked James to get her high-tech tracking devices that Mr. Hunt knew nothing about.

James wished she hadn't gone to Mr. Hunt demanding that he pull his containers back. Then she'd thrown in her ace. She'd told Hunt that she knew what he'd been transporting via Mills Shipping.

When Corinne had threatened to expose Mr. Hunt for his shady and highly illegal business, she had no idea what connections the man had. James was now positive Mr. Hunt had ordered Corinne to be *dealt* with. But then Corinne had told James that Mr. Hunt cornered her, threatening to go to Tyler and tell him of their affair, and all the while demanding his documents. But James knew Corinne had covered her tracks. She'd gotten the tracking devices to plant in the shipping containers that would transport Hunt's merchandise. The problem was, James didn't know if she'd actually installed them. If she had, there was no way for him to know which containers had them…Mills Shipping had thousands of containers, and only Corinne knew which companies used what containers and what was shipped in them.

Finally turning down the air conditioning in the car, James remembered the feel of Corinne's body. Yes, it was her, thinner, but definitely her. Still, he wondered about the other woman. He thought perhaps Corinne had family after all, maybe even a sister, and the Mills family didn't know.

Or she was simply a guest at the hotel who happened to be out at the same time Corinne was.

CHAPTER 15

By mid-week, Charlene was exhausted and thoroughly stressed.

She'd had back-to-back follow-up doctor's appointments that added to her stress. She'd failed the hearing test again, and Dr. Holland told her the damage to her inner ear was most likely permanent. Although the broken leg and arm had healed, the residual pain persisted, especially in her leg, resulting in her continued use of painkillers. Topping that off, she'd have to remain on anti-seizure medication despite the fact that the seizures had lessened.

But at the end of the week her spinning head kept her in bed most of the day. She was comforted by the twins. But one look at their faces and Charlene knew they thought their clone/alien 'mother' with the big head and funny eyes was coming apart. She assured both that she was fine despite their doubtful expressions and Shelly checking to see if green goo was leaking from a hole in her head.

She'd pushed herself going to the office, and decided to take a few days off. But she wasn't sorry for going because she'd discovered so much about her sister, including that she was a smart, savvy business-woman.

Corinne had been well liked and respected by her colleagues and staff. She'd made a lot of money for Mills Shipping. Reflecting back on their meeting, Charlene now guessed when she offered to pay Corinne back one thousand dollars as a partial payment of what she'd sent to cover their father's burial, it was probably just pocket change to her, whereas for Charlene it was the bulk of her meager savings. But she'd also found out that Corinne was a force to be reckoned with. Her excellently drafted, but scathing emails were proof of that.

Charlene could only smile when she'd read them. But her smiles faded when she came across shipping orders for TM Hunt Enterprises. The one thing that troubled Charlene was that Corinne's correspondence with the company became more insistent in the last six months leading up to the night she'd been killed.

In one such email, Corinne had virtually threat-ened the president, Mr. Hunt. She'd written, "If the order of June 26 is not cancelled, I'll be forced to inform the CEO, M. Mills and Interim CEO, T. Mills, of the continued partnership. This is my last and final warning…" That alone told Charlene that it was highly probable that Tyler had no idea what was going on with TM Hunt Enterprises.

But why wouldn't he know? He signed the invoices.

Upon further checking, she found out that Corinne had attempted to cancel several other orders for Hunt Enterprises. Comparing the invoices to the database on Corinne's computer showed nothing out of order. Everything matched up…or so Charlene thought.

When she compared the same invoices against what was on Corinne's laptop, they were completely different; nothing matched up. The merchandise, which should have been filing cabinets according to the invoices, were listed on the laptop in a series of codes: PA's, DA's and AAR's. The code sequences would change with the next shipment, and there were six in all.

After checking other invoices, Charlene realized that Tyler and Melvin signed off on every contract for shipping services. It was then a spark flared in her brain and wouldn't die out. It was an oddball thing, as her father would say, but for the life of her Charlene couldn't understand why Corinne would have two sets of invoices for supposedly the same orders that were buried in a file on her laptop computer. She also struggled to come up with a reason why Corinne would have threatened the president of T.M. Hunt Enterprises by exposing him to Tyler and Melvin if they had a business contract.

Sitting on the patio scrolling though Corinne's emails, Charlene glanced up to see the twins several feet away. She watched Shelly hovering over Shane's paint set as if she was interested in seeing what he'd been painting. But all the while, with her left hand Shelly was pouring out his little containers of paint down into the grass. Dropping her head back down and pretending she didn't see Shelly's dirty little deed, Charlene was surprised when Shelly turned her head in her direction to see if she'd been caught.

At first Charlene grinned at Shelly's antics, recalling how Corinne used to play those types of dirty little tricks on her when they were young…and just like that, the spark that had flared moments ago in Charlene's head now burst into a smoldering fire.

A disturbing picture surfaced in her brain about what Corinne *could* have done, whether intentionally or not. Charlene couldn't help but wonder if her sister had set up Tyler's family business to take the fall if the FBI found out that Mills Shipping was still dealing with T.M. Hunt Enterprises. A confidential partnership was how Corinne had referred to the business dealings in her emails. That's why Tyler and Melvin don't know anything about it, Charlene thought to herself, stupefied.

If it was true, it was an unimaginable act. No way would Corinne do such a thing. But then, how would she know? Her adult twin sister, for the most part, was a stranger to her. Flipping back to the copies of invoices she'd taken from Corinne's office and comparing them to what was on the laptop, Charlene became chilled.

The evidence didn't lie. "This has to be it," she mumbled. If what she was seeing was true, then Corinne had put a plan into action that was illegal and devious and likely was the reason she'd been killed;

Hunt stood to lose plenty and face criminal charges if caught.

"But why would she do such a thing? Mills Shipping is her children's future…" The minute those words spilled from her lips she recalled what Tyler had told her that first day she went to work in Corinne's office. "Until your accident, I hadn't fired you yet…I no longer trust you," he said. He'd also said that Corinne's department was vital to the operation of the business.

Yes, it was unimaginable that Corinne could do such a thing to sabotage the business. Charlene scrolled back to an email she'd read and disregarded. In that email Corinne hinted that she most likely would not remain at Mills Shipping. It was addressed to James Smith. *I anticipate termination before everything is over*, Corinne had written.

It was too much of a stretch of Charlene's imagination, but glancing up again and watching Shelly now happily dancing around a pouting, tearful Shane, Charlene realized that Shelly did that dirty little trick to get even with Shane for something he'd probably done to her…something that she'd probably brewed and stewed about and, just then, got back at her brother where it hurt him the most. Yes, Charlene felt that even more as she listened to Shelly protesting her innocence. "There's Corinne's favorite phrase again, 'never, ever,' " Charlene said. *Yes, Shelly has Corinne's streak of gettin' even with someone who'd done her wrong.*

Charlene wondered sadly what innocent thing Shane had done that would make Shelly pour out some of his water colors. What innocent things had she done herself that caused Corinne to act the same way when they were young girls?

With the twins now arguing, Charlene decided to intervene, thus giving her brain a rest. She went inside the kitchen and returned minutes later balancing three ice cream cones. Next, she turned the stereo on and soon began dancing barefoot in the cool lush grass with the twins giggling at her antics. Their squabble was over and done with.

A few minutes later, Charlene had another thing that caused her a great deal of stress.

Seeing Tyler suddenly step out onto the patio, she dropped her eyes to her ice cream cone. Since he'd last kissed her, she'd kept her distance whenever he came around. Her lies were weighing her down. Pretending and lying, she realized, was exhausting.

In the office she'd managed to stay clear of him and apparently he'd been doing the same because she'd seen very little of him this past week. As Tyler leaned over to sample Shelly's ice cream cone, Charlene turned her back but continued dancing. If what she believed was true, then it would appear Tyler wasn't involved in Corinne's death.

Tyler watched Corinne dancing barefoot to the old-school music. She immediately stirred something in him. In fact, he'd been conflicted about her since she'd come home from the hospital. He couldn't say what it was, but a feeling had begun escalating in him the second she'd awakened from the coma and he stared down into her frightened amber eyes. He'd never seen her frightened of anything. After kissing the twins, Tyler stood up and walked over to her. "Hi," he said.

Still dancing and enjoying her ice cream, Charlene greeted him, "Hi. How was work?"

"Good. Everybody asked when you're returning," Tyler said, watching her. "They miss you." He wouldn't confess to it, but he'd missed passing by her office to find her busily typing on the computer. He frowned when a vision of her flashed in his head…she'd been wearing eyeglasses as she peered into the computer monitor. Tyler shook the image away, recalling the doctor constantly checking her eyes and the injury to her forehead. Yes, it was possible that Corinne's vision had been affected, hence the eyeglasses.

"Hmm, really? I don't think Anita misses me all that much," Charlene said, realizing he didn't sound like he was in any hurry to fire Corinne. *Has he changed his mind?*

"Anita's okay. She has attitude issues at times, but she's good as your assistant."

Charlene's mind latched onto what he'd said. "Hey, um, has Anita kept the shipping invoices and every-thing on track…you know, since the accident?"

Seeing her ice cream dripping, Tyler leaned forward and lapped it from the cone and from her fingers.

"Um, good," he said. "Yes, she has. Just call and have her email you the report. They should be on your computer because she sends me a spreadsheet."

"Oh. So Anita has access to my computer and the email files, right?" Charlene thought about Anita's critical and often sly glances at her.

"Uh-huh. Are you going to finish that ice cream cone or do you plan to let it all run down your fingers like Shelly's just did?"

The sensation of Tyler licking her fingers shocked her system. It also pulled her thoughts from Anita and those invoices. "Well, you seem to be enjoying this more than me. Here, you take it." When she handed it up to him, Tyler closed the distance between them, easing one arm around her waist while his other hand lifted hers and held the cone up to his lips.

For Charlene it was a very sensual thing, and she found herself swaying to the music as she watched him lap up all the remaining ice cream. When his eyes slid to hers, Charlene quickly pulled her hand away and proceeded to take several bites of the waffle cone until it was all gone. "Sorry, but I like the cone best," she said when she'd finished it.

"You've developed a sweet tooth and…you've missed again," he said.

"Huh?" Charlene mumbled around a full mouth.

Dropping his head, Tyler whispered against her lips. "You've got ice cream here," he licked at her bottom lip. "And here," he did the same thing to her chin. "And some here," he murmured against her lips. "Sweet."

Uh-uh. Not again. Charlene's reserve was melting as fast as the ice cream had. When his hand eased around her waist, she found she couldn't escape from dancing with him. She decided to stay on task. "Hey, Tyler, will you let me know when you're going to fire me, you know, just so I can prepare and everything?" Charlene held her breath, waiting for his answer.

Firing her was the last thing on his mind in that instant. "Honey, you're excellent at what you do. Mills Shipping would be lost without you, and, so, no…I'm not going to fire you. Besides, Ryan would love running your department instead of HR. No, you're staying put."

Charlene gawked at him. "Bu-but wait, you said…"

"I know what I said, but Dad and I are not so blind that we can't do what's right for the business. Actually it's the right decision for all of us."

"But you said…" Charlene began, wearily.

Tyler pulled back and laughed at her pained expression. "Do you *want* me to fire you?"

Charlene could only shake her head no, because suddenly too many thoughts hit her all at once. If Corinne had known how he felt, would she have tried to sabotage his family business? Charlene thought she probably wouldn't have gone through with it.

For several minutes they continued dancing until they heard snickering coming from Mona, Terri, and the twins, who were all watching them from the patio. They quickly sprang apart.

"Aw, don't stop," Terri said, crossing the patio. "You guys look so good together, all relaxed and hot. I bet I know what's going to happen next." Playfully, Terri threw her arms around her brother. "Don't worry, Tyler, I'll yell out pointers through the door to the both of you since it's been a while," she teased.

Charlene whooped Terri on the backside for her comment, which she chose to ignore, then walked over to Mona, who was sitting with the twins. "Hi, Mona. How was your meeting?" she asked.

"Wonderful. This year's society gala will be a spectacular event. You will come, won't you, dear?" Mona smiled as she accepted the kiss her daughter-in-law gave her.

"I don't know. When is it?" Charlene watched Tyler remove his jacket and sit down beside her. He was too close, she thought.

"Mid-September. The weather will be perfect for dancing under the stars," Mona said, arching an elegant eyebrow at Tyler.

Mid-September seemed so far away. Time was slipping by all too quickly. Charlene realized she had little time now because the last shipment was scheduled in just over two weeks. Then what, she wondered. One thing for sure; she couldn't continue to deceive the people she'd come to love.

"Aaww, nooo," Shelly whined. "These are my favorite shorts, Mommy!"

Seeing that Shelly had ice cream on the front of her shorts, Charlene rushed over to her. "No problem. I'll put them in the wash tonight and they'll be all clean and you can wear them tomorrow. How's that?" Charlene asked a pouting Shelly. It was obvious that Shelly didn't like not having all of her clothes to pick from.

"You know, I probably need to go back to the house to get a few more changes of clothes for all of us, huh?" Tyler was looking at his wife as he spoke. "See, even Mommy's taken to wearing jeans and T-shirts all the time."

Shane and Shelly sent Charlene a knowing grin. They'd told Charlene previously that their "real mommy" didn't dress the way she did. "I'm comfortable," Charlene said, lifting Shelly in her arms. She hugged the little girl and moved away from everybody. Then she whispered in Shelly's ear, "You did a bad thing with Shane's paints. You have to apologize, and you're going to give me $5 of your allowance money so I can buy him some more, understand?" Charlene's heart tilted when Shelly nodded shamefully and laid her head on Charlene's shoulder briefly before she was handed off to Daisy to get washed up.

Terri, who'd been dancing on the patio, walked over to Tyler, laughing. "You're busted, brother, and your wife told you a thing or two, didn't she?" Terri snickered.

Tyler responded to Terri's teasing by pulling on her braids. "It's still early. I'll drive out to the house, grab some more clothes, and be back by dinner," Tyler said, hand dancing with Terri.

Having listened to their exchange, Mona suggested Tyler take his wife with him, adding she would know what clothes the children needed. Mona said she didn't mind it one bit if they brought all of their clothes, because she loved having her entire family under the same roof.

"What're you going to do when Ryan and Trish move out and get their own place?" Tyler quipped crossing the patio.

"Oh, that's not going to happen anytime soon," Trish said, stepping out onto the patio with Ryan following close behind.

Mona tossed her head at Tyler. "Ha, busted again! It's just not your day is it, Tyler," she said, sending him a wide grin.

"Well, we know at least for the next eight months or longer we're staying put, aren't we, *baby*," Ryan said. "Guys, we're having a baby," he said impishly.

For several seconds no one responded, but when it finally sank in, Tyler was the first to offer congratulations. He did so by lifting his brother off the ground in a bear hug, while the women surrounded Trish with hugs and squeals of joy.

Charlene wished them a beautiful, healthy baby. When Trish said she'd love to have a set of twins, Charlene couldn't muster up a response.

Thankfully, Tyler came to her rescue. "Ryan, all I can say is be prepared to keep the house stocked with

every kind of potato chip you can find. Make sure
Daisy keeps them in the pantry or you'll be driving to
the mini-market at two in the morning or face pure
hell. I suggest you map out all the nearby stores." Tyler
laughed and sent his wife a wink.

Charlene waved a dismissing hand at Tyler. She
would've loved to have been with her sister during her
pregnancy.

When Shane asked Trish just how the baby got
inside her belly and gawked at her stomach, the adults
were hard pressed to hold their chuckles in.

"Son, we'll talk real soon," Tyler said, holding out
Charlene's chair. "Let's get the heck out of here now
before Shane demands the details," he whispered to
her.

───◆◇◆───

When they arrived at the house, Tyler went into his
office while Charlene went upstairs to the twins'
bedrooms. Gathering armloads of clothes from each,
she deposited them on a large table in the second floor
hallway.

To her dismay Corinne's relaxed clothes were too
fancy for Charlene's taste, and most were too big.
Spotting the amber-colored urn on the shelf, Charlene
realized that although she was still grieving the loss of
her twin, she was oddly at peace now that she had
Corinne's ashes. She hoped one day, when everything
was out and in the open, maybe she'd get to take
Corinne back home to Virginia, where she belonged.

Hearing Tyler in his room, she got up and walked across the hall.

Standing in his doorway, she watched Tyler at his closet deciding which ties to take. "Take that blue and gold one. It looks nice," she said.

"Oh, yeah?" He watched her come further in his room. "How about this brown one with the gold strips?" he asked, lifting another tie from a long tie rack which held well over two hundred ties in a long, neat row.

Making a face, Charlene shook her head. "Looks like an old man's tie." Moving past him she glanced at the vast number of suits and shirts he'd collected and hung up on the door. It hadn't made a dent in what remained in his closet. Charlene proceeded to select various ties to coordinate with the suits and shirts. When finished, she stepped back. "What do you think?"

"I like them." Tyler watched her walk around his bedroom, touching various things.

"This room doesn't feel happy to me." Glancing across at him, she said, "I don't think you were happy in here," she said quietly.

Crossing his arms over his chest, Tyler couldn't hold back a smirk. "You think? Were you happy in your room across the hall?" He didn't think for one second that she was as miserable in her room as he was in his.

"The room, um, my room if you will, doesn't feel happy, and neither does it feel sad. It's just a room. But the twins' rooms feel happy to me. I can tell they were happy."

"Yes, they were."

"I'm sorry," Charlene said, picking up a picture of Mona, Melvin, and the twins.

"This is the first time you've been in here."

That wasn't news to her ears. Corinne had told her that they'd slept in separate bedrooms. "Oh, right. I, um…" All at once she was tired of saying that she didn't remember things. She remembered plenty. She remembered her childhood years with Corinne and her father. Despite having so little, those times were real and loving for her, and she missed both her father and sister terribly.

Watching her movements, Tyler noticed her limping slightly. "You okay?"

"My leg's just twingin' a bit, that's all. Too much dancing earlier, I guess."

Tyler shook his head, not understanding her. "Twingin'? What do you mean? A spasm?" he asked. At her nod, Tyler went into the bathroom, returning seconds later with two pain relievers and a glass of water. "This should help take the edge off until we get back to the house. Come sit down for a while," Tyler said, helping her down on the edge of the bed.

"Thanks," she said, taking the pills and sitting beside him. Charlene couldn't say why she felt so out of sorts, but suspected that it was realizing how far her sister had gone in her awful plan. Or perhaps it was the news that Trish and Ryan were expecting a baby, and wishing that Corinne had called her personally to share that wonderful news with her all those years ago. "Hey, its wonderful news about Trish and Ryan, isn't it?"

"You bet it is. Compared to our loud and wild kids, can't you see their baby? All quiet and shy like them?" Tyler chuckled. "It'll give Ryan plenty to focus on besides my business."

"And you know Shelly will probably try to push their kid around until he or she gets old enough to push back." Before long they were laughing together at that very picture. "I'll miss it," Charlene said quietly. And she knew she would because she'd either be alone back in Virginia, or she'd be sitting in jail for her deception.

Tyler liked hearing her laugh. "No, you won't. You'll be around to witness all the chaos."

Closing her eyes against the sting of unwanted tears, Charlene exhaled. "No, I won't."

Instead of answering, Tyler ran his hand down her back.

So there, in a room that Charlene discovered Tyler wasn't happy in, she felt his strength lifting her. She also felt an odd sense of comfort knowing Corinne was at peace. Yes, she wanted whoever was responsible for killing Corinne to pay with their lives, but gone was that initial blinding anger and rage, in part because she really didn't believe that Tyler was involved. Charlene's anger had been replaced with a need for justice. When Tyler leaned over and kissed her cheek, repeating that she would always be a part of his family, Charlene wanted to believe him, but she knew she wouldn't be.

"We're family, baby." Tyler couldn't help but kiss the lips that seemed to beckon him.

Charlene didn't stop him. She was glad to feel something besides pain and grief.

The kiss that followed was passionate for both Tyler and Charlene. Moments later, when they pulled apart, gasping, each sensed their actions this night would change their lives forever.

She knew she shouldn't let things get out of hand, but Lord help her, Charlene's resolve completely disappeared. Admitting that she wanted him would be foolish on her part. Making love to him would be a mistake of monumental proportions that could potentially hurt both of them. Still, it didn't lessen her desire for him. If anything, she wanted him more because she knew, ultimately, when he found out that she wasn't Corinne, he would hate her for playing such an underhanded and conniving trick on him, on all of them. Still, when she claimed his mouth and her hands circled his neck, for the first time in months Charlene's grief gave way to the comforting arms of a man...a solid, caring, and handsome man.

A man she knew she shouldn't be with. He was, after all, her sister's husband.

Making out with the woman whom he'd soon be divorced was something Tyler hadn't planned on doing. But he knew that's all this was, a make-out moment. He also knew the games Corinne played;

when she backed off and left him wanting and pleading for her, Tyler knew he'd feel ten times angrier. He would kick himself for being weak and for allowing himself to fall under her spell. Still, knowing all of that didn't stop him from lifting her up on the bed with him, all the while keeping his lips locked with hers in a kiss that was eager, frantic, and soulful. And yet, he was preparing himself for her to push him away and halt everything.

Corinne always did at this point.

Moving so that he was on top of her, Tyler dragged his lips up from hers. "You need to stop because this isn't happening," he said, gazing down into eyes that appeared honest and full of longing.

Running her hands up to his face, Charlene caressed his forehead as she remembered him caressing hers in the hospital. Her fingertips traced his thick, black eyebrows and his soft mustache. "Why are you always telling me what you think I know?"

"Because I know you," he said and attempted to push away from her, but she held firm onto him. "Let's go, and you *don't* want this." Her downcast look struck him as peculiar. "You don't, right?" he asked her again, almost afraid she would agree and knowing that she would.

"Why do you keep telling me what I want or don't want? I'm not made of stone, you know," Charlene said, meeting his eyes.

"Are you saying you're turned on, or are you faking again for my benefit?" Tyler couldn't hold back the harshness of his words. "Been there, done that. I don't want that," he said.

There were two things Charlene couldn't stand.

One was anybody telling her what she couldn't do, and the other was being called two-faced. That's exactly what Tyler had done. "First of all, I have no need to fake anything for a jackass such as yourself, and second, don't you know how to tell if a woman is faking? Most *real men* do. There's one sure-fire way to know, if only to quell your suspicions and doubts."

"First of all," Tyler said with laugher in his voice, "are you saying I'm not a *real man*, and second, just what exactly are you saying?"

"You know exactly what I'm saying." In that instant Charlene had done a dangerous thing and she couldn't take it back. She'd issued him a challenge. Now she had to stand up to his response to it.

Without taking his eyes off of hers, Tyler flipped her over so that she sat atop him and dragged his hands up to her breasts. They felt wonderful, heavy. Her nipples were distended. Then, drawing one hand downward, he unfastened her jeans and watched her inhale quickly, drawing her bottom lip between her teeth. "If you need to stop me, then now would probably be a good time," Tyler said as he gazed up into her beautiful face, a face he'd constantly seen in his dreams since she'd awakened from the coma.

Charlene poked a finger down onto his chest. "Why don't you just shut up and man up to the task?"

And so he did. He found her body hot and ready, and he couldn't pull his eyes away from her face as he swallowed the lump in his parched throat.

Stupid, stupid. Stop this now. It had been so long since she'd felt a man's touch. Her old boyfriend, Mark, had never ignited the consuming fire that Tyler had done with a few kisses and an intimate touch. Moving against him, Charlene issued another challenge. "So now what? I'm like this and you're like that…" She leaned forward, caressing his lips with her fingertip.

"My God, what're you doing to me?" Tyler prayed for control. He was also fighting the desire to rip her jeans off and take what she seemed to offer…what he most definitely wanted. *No, no, she doesn't want this. She doesn't want me! She never did…not like this.* In his haste to pull his hand from inside her jeans, Tyler scratched the back of his hand against her zipper. "Let's get back to the house and get some attention to your leg," he said through tight lips.

Leaning forward Charlene kissed his face, purposely avoiding his lips. Then she traced the contours of his full lips with her tongue. "My leg is okay now, but I'm out of sorts, Tyler."

Loving the feel of her hands touching his face and her lips moving teasingly against his, Tyler lost his ability to speak coherently. "What?" When her hand slipped between their bodies and caressed him, he knew he'd give her anything and everything she wanted. He was embarrassed for wanting her as much as he did.

Dropping her forehead to his, Charlene seemed to lose the strength that was holding her upright. "I'm so tired. I'm tired of struggling and searching…and everything, can't you tell?"

"Yes, and I'm tired of fighting, too. I'm a man, and I'm tired of wanting you and knowing I'm not the one you want. You only want me because I'm here and available." His anger resurfaced when he wondered if this was how she acted with her lover, the man she obviously did want. Tyler tried to untangle her limbs from his, but only ended up causing her to sit high atop his midsection.

Charlene grinned sheepishly. "Oh, I like this position."

"Since when?" His eyes narrowed when she leaned forward and loosened his tie.

"Since right now," she said, unbuttoning his dress shirt.

"Oh, you like this." Tyler sounded doubtful, making half-hearted attempts to still her hands.

"You tell me," Charlene said, pulling his shirt from his slacks and undoing his belt. When his hands captured hers, she moved her hips against him and watched him draw in a raspy breath. "I don't want to be in control. I want you to call it, play-by-play."

Tyler was totally under her spell. "You mean like basketball?" *What am I saying?*

Charlene leaned forward and kissed his chest, nipping at his flesh until his hands clutched at her, pulling her closer to his body. "I don't think this is anything like basketball, but you know I'm ready to play, don't you?"

He knew what she meant. Unfortunately, Tyler was beyond the ability of uttering a verbal response. He was fighting not to lose control under her assault. His mouth was drying out from having to gulp air into his lungs, and tasting her was a definite way to moisten his mouth. His hands came up under her shirt and in one move pulled it up and over her head.

His hands outlined the curves of her breasts. He watched her, still waiting for the moment when she would change her mind and turn her back to him. But when her hands covered his encouragingly, Tyler knew she wouldn't be running from him. Unhooking her bra seemed a clumsy task, as if he'd never done it before, and when her breasts lay bare for him, Tyler sensed her sudden hesitation.

He massaged and caressed her. He watched her eyelids grow heavy and finally close. He thought she was absolutely beautiful, scars and all, and he wanted to let her knew that. "Corinne…"

No, no, please don't say that. I'm not her. I'm Charlene. My name is Charlene McDonald. Corinne is…dear God…she's gone. Holding back a sob from the wrenching pain in her heart, Charlene covered his mouth with her hand to stop him from calling her by her sister's name again. There was no point in pretending where things were going, and at that point she didn't want to stop. Yes, it was selfish and wrong. She knew that, but she couldn't stop. "Will you forget about the hurt of the past and give me tonight? Right here, right now, let's make this a room you can have a good memory in. Can you do that for me, please, Tyler?"

When tears shimmered in her eyes, Tyler honestly knew he would give her whatever she wanted. When he nodded his heart lifted knowing that she did want him, only him…for tonight, that is. It was enough.

He took little time undressing her, and, when she attempted to pull the covers over her nude and scared flesh, Tyler stopped her. "You don't need to do that. You're beautiful, every inch of you. But I guess I'm going to have to show you," he said tossing his own clothes aside.

Charlene believed him.

She believed him because he did make her feel beautiful, inside and out. Having grown up with low self-esteem, Charlene expressed herself in her sexuality. She didn't shy away from what she wanted and what felt good to her, but she never saw herself as beautiful. So the scars on her body would have made her want to recoil from any man's touch. But they didn't. At least they didn't at that moment, when she watched Tyler's beautifully naked body move over hers and, ever so slowly, kiss every scar on her body.

Losing herself, Charlene wished for a life with the twins and Tyler and his family. His touch made her want forever with them. What else did she have? *Absolutely nothing*. When he reached the heart of her spirit, Charlene didn't hold back and she didn't try to cover the cry that rushed up from her lungs. It brought tears to her eyes and a smile to her lips when Tyler joined their bodies together in the most intimate dance she could ever imagine.

This wasn't just making love, Tyler thought. It was something else...something new and foreign. Something powerful...

His body went on a spiritual journey. He was connecting with her, this woman, his wife, on a totally different level, and it was unlike any other time they'd made love during their marriage. He'd never wanted her *this* much because she'd never really wanted him, not like she wanted him tonight.

Capturing her lips, her moans took on a new meaning to him. Her softly cooed words both stimulated and thrilled him. Her hands held onto him tightly and passionately, and the legs that circled his waist moved with him in a perfect symmetrical frenzy, pushing him beyond anything he could ever imagine. Tyler knew he would never forget what she'd asked of him...give her tonight. In fact, she'd pleaded for the night and he gladly gave of himself...and when he couldn't hold back any longer and his body strained and trembled for release, Tyler's hoarse cry came up from his gut, shocking even him. God help him, he wanted tomorrow night and the night after that, as well.

~~~

Later that evening, Charlene's eyes fluttered open.

Tyler's face came into view and her eyes went wide. Lying on his side, she was surprised to find him awake and caressing her fingers. Her eyes moved over his face. A handsome face, she thought. Mocha complexion, warm chestnut brown eyes, full lips, a neatly trimmed moustache framing them so perfectly, and a dimple in his left cheek. Any warm-blooded woman would find it difficult to turn away from him. He was tall, and his body was solidly built and muscular. No wonder she was all over him like nobody's business. Her body was still aflame from their second round of lovemaking. It was exhilarating, and her cheeks flamed when she thought of her brazenness.

"I can only imagine what you're thinking about with that look," Tyler said, teasing her.

"Okay, I'll bite, tell me."

"Yes, you did bite me," Tyler teased, grinning when her jaw dropped.

"I'm sure I didn't, but I must have been terrible."

"Baby, you were definitely not terrible. I don't think I can get up."

"You got up earlier." Charlene grinned, recalling when she'd told him she wasn't on any birth control. That sent him jumping up and rummaging in his closet for condoms. Forcing the sudden guilty thought of Corinne from her mind, Charlene did worry how to handle that situation. She didn't know what type of birth control Tyler and Corinne used when they were intimate. When Tyler joked that the condoms had been in his closet so long that he'd bet they had expired, Charlene took it from his fingers, squinted to check the expiration date, and then put it on him. Secretly, she was supremely satisfied by his reaction.

"We missed dinner and nobody's called us," Tyler said.

"Not even Shelly," Charlene said doubtfully. "They'll be scared."

Gathering her up against his body, Tyler kissed her forehead. "The kids are fine. You're the one who's scared. Tell me why?"

"What do you mean?" She was scared about what tonight really meant.

"Corinne, our kids are loved and cared for. They're protected, and, most likely, at this second talking Terri into sneaking sweet treats up from the kitchen," he said, chuckling softly as he intertwined his fingers with hers.

Raising her hand and covering his mouth with her fingers, Charlene felt another painful stab when he called her by her sister's name. *What have I done?* "Yes, and I should know about that, right?"

"You should since you were the one who snuck them those caramel popcorn balls last week, only to have Shelly fall asleep with hers and wake up with it stuck in her hair the next morning."

Laughing together, they recalled the incident and the following struggle as they washed Shelly's hair as she screeched and screamed. When Mona asked Shelly why she'd had sweets after she'd brushed her teeth, Shelly replied, "Mommy gave half of hers to me and I was saving it for breakfast."

Charlene became distracted by Tyler's touches and tender kisses. "You need to stop doing what you're doing." Of course she should stop him, but she didn't want to.

"Why should I? I'm hungry."

She didn't think he was hungry for food. Gathering the covers and clutching them to her chest, Charlene eased from his embrace and slid from the bed. "Let's go check out the cupboards. I'm sure we can find something to eat," she said, noticing his disappointment.

"Cupboards?" Tyler frowned at the word she'd used. "I cleaned out the refrigerator since we've been staying at my parents'." Tyler watched her awkwardly trying to put on her undergarments while holding the blanket around her body. Getting up, he tried to pry the blanket from her tight grip. "What'd I tell you earlier?"

It was different now. Everything was different now. She didn't want him to see her scars, not now when their passions had abated and they were no longer blinded by excitement and lust. It was a different story now. She couldn't explain it except to realize the colossal mistake she'd made by sleeping with him. "I-I can't remember."

"Uh-huh. I think that faulty memory is just a little too convenient for you right now." Easing his arms around her back, Tyler easily refastened her bra. "I meant what I said. You're beautiful, so please don't feel that you have to hide from me, okay?" Finally tugging the blanket from her tight fist until it dropped to the floor, Tyler kissed her, backing her toward the bed. "Let's stay here tonight," he murmured against the velvety skin of her neck. He wasn't ready to leave. He wanted to stay longer in the room where they'd just created a beautiful memory.

But Charlene stepped away from him. "You know, um, that's probably not a good idea," she said. Then, as quickly as she could, she gathered up her clothes and hurried into the hallway.

Don't push, Tyler thought. "Want to grab a burger before heading back to the house?"

"Okay," she called back from the bathroom. She knew staying the night meant sleeping together and making love again and again. Returning to the bedroom a few minutes later, Tyler told her he'd missed a call on his cell phone after all.

Forcing her attention from his beautiful naked body, Charlene heard him say it was James. Absently she repeated the name. "Oh, right your friend. He and his wife, Mia, sent that nice get-well basket, didn't they?"

"Right, and that's where those popcorn balls came from that ended up in Shelly's hair." Tyler laughed, watching her trying to suppress a giggle. He couldn't help but kiss her. "James and Mia have been anxious to see you, but I've been putting them off until you were ready. They're good friends and they've been really supportive after…" Tyler let his words drop off, not wanting to remember those horrific days when she lay in a coma and he was filled with remorse and guilt. He stepped into his slacks and put on a shirt.

Closing the buttons on his shirt, Charlene nodded. Inwardly she cringed, knowing she would have to smile through more visits from strangers and other opportunities to slip up.

CHAPTER 16

The following morning Tyler awakened to the twins jumping up and down on his bed.

"Wake up, Daddy! It's time to eat breakfast," they chanted loudly above him.

"All right, all right, just stop bouncing," Tyler said, watching them scamper down to the floor. "Go wake up Mommy, and don't do all that jumping on her bed, either." Tyler suspected Corinne would be suffering a love hangover, too. He certainly was, and he liked it.

Shane pulled Tyler's robe from the back of a chair and dragged it across the floor. "She's already up and making breakfast, Daddy."

"Waffles, Daddy! Waffles!" Shelly sang out as she pulled on his arm.

Corinne making waffles? That was as strange as…everything else, Tyler thought, dropping his feet to the floor. "Okay, you two, scoot and I'll go grab a shower." Seeing Shelly without shoes on, Tyler told her to go put her sneakers on before going downstairs.

"But I like not having shoes on, and my toes like it, too." Shelly danced around him, showing off her toes. "Look at my painted toenails. They look just like Mommy's."

"But, honey, shoes are good things so please put yours on," Tyler said, grinning down at her wiggling, coral-painted toes and waiting for the smart reply he knew was coming.

"Mommy painted my toenails the same color as hers, and you won't see them if I put sneakers on. Are you going to make her put sneakers on, too?" Shelly retorted, then whispered something into Shane's ear before both ran from the room giggling.

Closing his eyes, Tyler realized that Corinne did prefer to walk around barefoot lately. *Yeah, things were strange.* She was strange, he thought, and so was the children's habit of whispering to each other lately. Tyler made a mental note to speak to them about that later.

Thirty minutes later Tyler stood in the entryway to the kitchen as the rest of the family gathered in the dining room. He found his wife was indeed making waffles and was barefoot.

Coming up behind her, Tyler slid his arms around her waist and kissed her cheek. Memories of last night warmed him so much that he was moments away from whisking her upstairs.

Charlene had been so focused on working the large waffle iron that when Tyler came up behind her she just angled her cheek up to his lips. "Good morning," she said, then frowned at the wifely thing she'd just done. *I'm not his wife. I'm just the woman he slept with last night.*

"Good morning," he said, angling his head to kiss her lips, only to glance up to see an amused look on his father's face as he came into the kitchen.

As breakfast was being enjoyed, Terri commented on their absence at last night's dinner. "So, yeah, we had a mini celebration for Trish and Ryan's baby news. What happened to you guys?" By her suggestive tone, Terri had a pretty good idea what had happened. "Guess nobody needed any pointers or instructions from me, huh?" She directed her question to Tyler slyly.

Mona hadn't missed the tender looks that passed between the couple. "Yes, we missed you at dinner. Your father cooked a delicious steak," Mona said, sending a smile to her husband. "Did you two have dinner out, perhaps?" Her eyes danced.

"They had burgers and chili cheese fries at a diner," Shelly said, pulling her waffle apart with her fingers and stuffing it into her mouth.

Tyler grinned at his daughter. "And how do you know that, sweetheart?"

"She told us. She said you stopped and had burgers and fries and that's why you didn't get home in time for dinner or to put us to bed." Turning, Shelly said, "Isn't that right, Mommy?"

Charlene took that instant to put a forkful of scrambled eggs into her mouth. She simply mumbled, "Uh-huh." But inside, her body was humming. The look Tyler gave her over the children's heads was exactly the one etched on his face last night when he'd cradled her, just seconds before his body rippled. *Oh, my God.* So shocked at her train of thought, Charlene pulled her eyes away and, like Shelly, she stuffed a piece of syrupy waffle into her mouth.

Her actions, as well as Tyler's expression, made it obvious to everyone that the couple shared more than just burgers and chili cheese fries last night.

Choosing to ignore the looks, Tyler asked his father about his upcoming trip to Texas. He was going there to look over a small shipping company that was going out of business. He would offer a buyout, thus expanding Mills Shipping in that region.

Following breakfast, everyone headed into different areas of the house. Charlene decided to get back to Corinne's laptop.

Something Melvin had said during breakfast piqued her interest. He'd said he was going to inspect the containers to see if they could be fitted for devices. When she'd asked what he'd meant, Melvin explained that since they were so close to Mexico, they wanted to avoid illegal goods going across the border. Any business involved in smuggling would face prosecution and heavy fines, he said.

Charlene pulled up an email between Corinne and Hunt Enterprises. She'd attached a copy of a report from a mandatory truck stop just outside of Arizona. She'd demanded the president, Mr. Hunt, explain why the Mills truck was delayed for twenty-four hours.

Charlene scrolled back through several emails where Corinne specifically wanted to know what caused that truck to be held up for inspection at the truck stop. By the tone of Corinne's succeeding emails, she appeared apprehensive about their business arrangement.

As Charlene continued to check more documents and emails, she kept seeing references to computer equipment being shipped to Mexico…lots of computer equipment. "Okay, so where is this stuff coming from?" she wondered aloud. But it was right there, staring her in the face on the next few emails.

From Corinne's emails to a JS Computer Sales, Charlene surmised Corinne was acquainted with the owner. Well acquainted judging by her tone, which was friendly and often cryptically flirtatious. She'd often request the president of that company to call her on her cell phone to discuss what she'd called "matters of the utmost importance."

His response was found in Corinne's incoming emails; basically he'd told her she was overreacting and she had no cause for concern because he'd confirmed delivery. But Corinne's responses proved she was skeptical. In fact in one of her last emails before the accident, Corinne had written, "I no longer trust the association or shipments from Hunt Enterprises or Hunt."

His response to Corinne suggested that they meet for drinks. He'd written: "I have a little something for you." Charlene thought that sounded a bit personal;

it also had a familiar ring to it, but she didn't know why.

Deciding to take a break, she got up and went to her bedroom window, which overlooked the back of the house. Looking down into the garden, she wondered where Tyler was. She was actually glad he wasn't around. She needed time to process what had happened between them last night. Well, that is except for the obvious…they'd done what she shouldn't have allowed to happen, and she mentally reprimanded herself for letting things go so far, so fast. *Head trauma aside, I can be so dim-witted at times!* Spotting Terri and the twins down in the kiddy pool, she decided to join them. She left her bedroom but didn't make it that far.

Tyler was just about to knock on her bedroom door when she opened it to leave. "Hey, where're you off to in such a hurry?"

"Oh, I was just going to go hang out with Terri and the kids down at the pool," Charlene's breath halted when his hands ran up the sides of her ribcage.

"I have a better idea," Tyler said, picking her up and hiking her over his shoulder. He carried her to his room down the hall. There, he set her down on her feet and locked the door behind him. "Don't you want to hear my better idea?" he murmured, coming up behind her as she walked over to the window. His arms instantly wrapped around her waist.

Seeing the red scratch on the back of Tyler's hand and recalling how he'd gotten it sent heat rising up to her face and excitement tingling her chest. "Isn't this where we left off this morning down in the kitchen?" Charlene asked, dropping her head back to his chest and covering his hands with her own.

"Hmm, yes it is. I came to your room last night," he whispered against her neck.

After they'd returned to the house last night, Charlene showered and crept in to check on the twins. It was something she did every night. She loved watching them sleep. It was in those quiet moments that she felt Corinne was nearest. It was there in the quiet of night, while the children slumbered, that she talked to Corinne as if she was actually in the room with them. Last night she'd apologized for sleeping with Tyler. "Yes, I know, but I…" she stopped abruptly.

"You were checking on the kids. Aren't they precious when they're asleep?" he asked.

*My precious babies…*Corinne's voice echoed in Charlene's head.

"They're precious all the time. I've loved them from the moment I found out about them," she said. *When Dad shared Corinne's news…*Charlene turned in his arms. Standing up on her toes, she tilted her head up to accept the kiss he was primed to plant on her.

Their passions took over as soon as they kissed, and each wasted little time peeling the other's clothes off as they fell onto Tyler's bed. It was inevitable.

As Charlene watched him tenderly making love to her flesh, she died a little more inside because she knew it would all come to an end soon. It had to…it, too, was inevitable. What she was doing was ultimately wrong and Tyler would hate her, but no less than she would hate herself. Not only for deceiving the family, but because she'd committed the ultimate act of betrayal by sleeping with her brother-in-law.

When at last their passion was spent and Tyler dozed contently beside her, Charlene cried quietly. *I'm gonna pay for this as surely as I'm gonna pay for hurtin' you.* The words burned silently in her throat.

Drowsily, Tyler pondered his own conflicting emotions. Almost imperceptivity he felt her separating from him, physically and emotionally. Despite the magic that had happened between them last night and just moments ago, he knew without a doubt they were over.

Two days later Charlene was dressed in an outfit borrowed from Terri's closet. The yellow and blue sundress hugged her curves and was topped with a long-sleeved yellow cardigan that covered her scars. She and Tyler were meeting James and Mia for dinner.

Both couples arrived about the same time, but entered from opposite sides of the lobby. As James and Mia approached them, Charlene felt a sudden twinge of something resembling déjà vu tugging at the back of her brain. She shrugged it off, blaming it on her nerves and the fancy surroundings. Keeping up the "Corinne" charade was tiring and emotionally draining with the family. It was doubly hard with their friends.

As they met in the middle, Tyler nodded a greeting to James but took a step forward to give Mia a warm hug. Standing behind him, Charlene caught James's eyes and, just for an instant, she thought she saw *desire*! Before she could fully process those thoughts, Tyler had released Mia and pulled her forward to greet their friends.

Mia was a small woman with a short, fashionable haircut. Stylish, but understated, her designer outfit screamed money, but her voice was kind as she laid a perfectly manicured hand on Charlene's arm. "How are you doing, Corinne? It's good to see you out and about, isn't it, James?" she asked as she turned to look at her husband.

After a momentary uncomfortable silence, James recovered quickly. "She certainly does, and it looks like Tyler's been taking good care of her." His smile didn't quite reach his eyes. "So, what are we doing just standing here? Let's eat." He quickly steered a stunned Mia to the restaurant door.

Tyler frowned at James's odd behavior, but let it go with a shrug.

Charlene, on the other hand, had warning bells ringing in her head.

The foursome was escorted to a table by a large window overlooking the dark blue water. Over a beautifully prepared, outrageously expensive dinner, the conversation shifted to work between Tyler and

James. Charlene, still a little distracted by her nagging thoughts, was relieved Mia carried most of the conversation, keeping it light and friendly. She spoke about shopping trips that she and Corinne had taken together. Charlene feigned interest and smiled politely, hoping Mia wouldn't think her rude.

Later, when Mia stepped out to take a phone call, Charlene excused herself to go to the ladies' room. When she exited the stall and crossed to the sink to wash her hands she barely noticed the door quietly open behind her. But she was startled when she felt Tyler's hands sliding around her waist again and his lips nuzzling her neck.

Smiling, she closed her eyes, enjoying the feel of his hands slowly sliding up her stomach and cupping her breasts. Charlene dropped her head back and sighed. "You're insatiable." Then she turned her head and opened her eyes.

Charlene's smile immediately disappeared and was replaced by a look of horror and disgust when she realized that it wasn't Tyler caressing her body…it was James!

Furiously shoving him away from her, she swore at him. "What the hell do you think you are doing? Are you crazy? How dare you touch me like that?"

At first James thought Corinne was playing one of her hard-to-get games. Then he realized she was truly outraged. This was no game, and she wasn't pretending. Comprehension dawned. Could she be an imposter? No, it was her. He was positive. He knew her body.

At the same time Charlene was having her own epiphany, her own moment of clarity. This was the man Corinne was cheating with. This was "J." *Oh, my God, it's James. What am I gonna to do? How am I gonna to get out of this?*

James dropped his hand and stepped away from her, searching her face for signs of deception. "Wait a minute, what the hell did you just say?" James asked suspiciously.

Thinking fast, she had to convince him that she was Corinne. "I-I asked if you were crazy," she said, her voice shaking as her plan began to form in her mind.

"No, no, it was before that?"

Trying desperately to remember what she'd said and keeping the fear out of her eyes, Charlene's chest tightened painfully when James pushed her back against the long vanity table.

"You said 'you're insatiable.' What the hell does that mean, Corinne?" James spat through gritted teeth.

Slowing her fear, Charlene searched for something to say. "Look, James, this isn't the time or place. We need to get out of here and get back to the table before Tyler and Mia start to wonder where we are." Charlene tossed her head toward the door.

Ignoring her suggestion, James moved closer, pressing his face close to hers. "Answer me, Corinne!"

His eyes raked over her breasts. "You're sleeping with him, aren't you?"

The warning bells in Charlene's brain were now a loud, deafening symphony because she recognized his cologne. "He-he's my husband, isn't he?" There was no mistake, no lingering doubt that this was Corinne's lover...and Tyler's good friend. He was also the man who had accosted her at the party and whispered those threatening words to her.

"Don't feed me that bullshit, Corinne. Why are you sleeping with him? You said you didn't love him and that the two of you no longer had sex, so tell me why. Right now, damn it!"

Struggling to stay in the role, Charlene pushed herself off of the vanity and took a long, slow breath. "Listen, J...James, I'm...ah, living in the house with the family, so naturally..."

"That's a bunch of bull!" James angrily slammed his fist on the counter top. "I'm risking my life and my business so we can be together when this mess is done with and you're there sleeping with him," he sneered. "Why the hell would you do that?"

"I-I didn't." Charlene's hand flew to her chest. "I mean I didn't want to...James."

James' face shifted and his body relaxed as he pulled her into his arms again. "Oh, baby, he forced you, didn't he? That bastard forced himself on you, didn't he?"

"No, no, don't say that. Please, James, you're his fr-friend." Charlene struggled, cringing in revulsion at the wet kisses he pressed on her face, her neck, and her lips. "Tyler thinks you're his friend…honey," she said soothingly, knowing the only resemblance he had to honey was that he'd created one hell of a sticky mess.

"Don't say that. That son of a bitch is no longer my friend," James spat. "If he were my friend he wouldn't have tried to ruin me and my business. But we're going to be okay, baby. You and me, we're coming out on top," he said in a rush. "Fuck Tyler and his stuck-up clan."

While he was preoccupied with mauling her and cursing Tyler and the Mills family, Charlene was slowly easing closer to the door to escape this vile madman. "James, ah, we have to get out of here before someone comes in. We can't let that happen, you know."

"Okay, okay, but I need to see you. I've been calling the house hoping you'd pick up the phone, but you haven't. Try to call me on my cell phone later. We need to talk. You've got to give Mr. Hunt his property. All of it, Corinne," James said.

"His property…all of it?" Charlene hedged. She was almost at the door.

"He only thinks you have the original invoices. He doesn't know about the other thing."

"The other thing?" Charlene repeated, probing. "What do you think I should do?"

"Come on, Corinne. You have those devices. You should have given them to me before." James began to pace. "Just give them to me so I can erase the memory of you having used them." He glanced at the door when he heard a noise. "Call me," he said. With one last quick kiss, James released her. He cautiously opened the door, peeped out, then stepped out into the hallway.

Alone once again, Charlene crumbled against the vanity. She was nauseated, weak, and thoroughly disgusted. Remembering the conversation she'd had with Corinne about her lover, she'd said, "J was a sweet guy…he just got caught up with the wrong people, who began using his business as a cover…"

Charlene's mind raced as she desperately tried to digest and make sense out of what just happened. But the ugly picture came into focus. "James is a slimy snake," she hissed.

Back at the table, Tyler stood up as Mia returned and asked where everybody had gone. Tyler told her James had taken a call in the lobby and that Corinne was in the ladies' room.

"She's *still* in the ladies' room?" Mia asked, noticing his frown. "Tyler, what's wrong?"

Fearing that Corinne was ill, Tyler asked Mia to check on her while he waited outside the door. When Mia entered the ladies' room she found Corinne alone sitting in a chair at the vanity table. She was staring at her reflection in the mirror as if she was trying to figure something out. Barely responding or acknowledging her name, Mia hurried out to usher Tyler in, while she stood guard just inside the ladies' room door.

"Baby, what happened? Did you have a seizure?" Tyler asked, gently kneeling down by her chair and grasping her cold, trembling hands in his.

"No." Charlene was sick. Her breath came out in short bursts. She was having an honest-to-God panic attack…a first for her. She feared that her head was going to explode. *Okay, Charlene, get a grip. Now is not the time or place to fall apart. Pull yourself together. Get up so you can get out of here, then go home and figure out what the hell is going on.*

Looking into Tyler's face, Charlene realized sadly that Corinne hadn't acted alone. She'd been conspiring with James in a plot to destroy the family business. She looked over as Mia came back in and wondered if the woman knew about her husband's relationship with Corinne. Her instincts told her no. Another victim of her sister's deception, she thought. Taking a deep breath, she gripped Tyler's hand and stood up. "I'm so sorry…it's my leg. It's cramping badly." Charlene's leg really did hurt from James pressing her thighs against the vanity, but not as much as her head and her heart did.

When Mia suggested calling an ambulance, Tyler shook his head as he held onto his wife. "No, I think she'll be okay," he said. "But we should head home. It's been a long evening."

As the three of them walked back to the table to get Charlene's purse, James stood up, looking from one face to the other. "Hey, what happened? I came back to the table and everybody was gone. " His eyes settled on Corinne. "Is everything okay, or are you guys trying to leave me and Mia with this big check," he joked, tapping a finger on the slim vinyl sleeve containing the bill. "I only have fifty bucks on me," he said with a tight, teasing grin.

Mia rolled her eyes disapprovingly at his bad timing and insensitive joke.

Tyler reached into his wallet, peeled off some bills, and dropped them on the table. "This should cover it. Sorry to cut the evening short, but we're going to call it a night. Corinne's not feeling well," he said, looking at his wife to confirm that she was indeed ready to leave.

Honestly, Charlene couldn't wait to get out of there and away from James. "Yes, I need to take some medication." She took Mia's hand. "Thank you, Mia and I apologize for ruining the evening," Charlene said. Mia patted her hand compassionately, telling her not to worry about it and that the dinner was on them because it was a celebration for James anyway. She gathered up the bills and stuffed them into the breast pocket of Tyler's jacket.

"Celebration? What's up?" Tyler asked as he kissed Mia's cheek.

"We're celebrating a big order James just received. It's for two hundred computers, including software and everything," Mia said, proudly bragging at James's achievement. "Did I mention it's a major contract, cha-ching." She grinned boldly.

Tyler shook James's hand. "Congratulations. That's great. It probably doesn't make up for Mills cancelling that contract you had with Hunt, but I'm truly happy for you, James. I hope this venture is a profitable one."

As Tyler drove away from the seaside restaurant heading back home, Charlene not only had a much clearer picture in her mind about why her sister was killed, she knew by who…Mr. Hunt. Only Corinne, James, and this Mr. Hunt knew the shipping contract hadn't been cancelled with Mills Shipping.

And her instincts were right and were confirmed by Tyler's his parting comment to James. As far as Tyler knew, the contract with T.M. Hunt Enterprises was cancelled.

CHAPTER 17

Charlene was so close...

She was so close to exposing what had been going on at Mills Shipping. She'd even thought that maybe she could prevent the family business from facing criminal charges, as that would surely be the case if that last shipment crossed the border and made its way to Mexico.

With time of the essence, Charlene went into the office with Tyler on Monday. Recalling the drive back to the house following dinner on Saturday with James and Mia, Charlene asked Tyler to refresh her mind as to why the contract with James's company had been cancelled.

Tyler had reminded her that through another business partner, who'd been indicted for illegally shipping contraband into Mexico, they'd received information from the FBI when it was discovered that Mills had a newly signed contract with Hunt Enterprises. Tyler went on to explain that although Mills Shipping was set to make millions on the contract, it had been immediately cancelled when the FBI had informed them that Hunt Enterprises had switched the merchandise in the containers during transit.

A search by drug sniffing dogs at the mandatory truck stop only showed residue, but no drugs. The problem was, by the time the officials arrived, either the containers had been loaded onto another truck or they'd been washed and stripped. Tyler told her that other business was forced to close up following indictments and payout of large penalties. Sadly, he added, it also resulted in the loss of many employees as well as a sub-contract with James's computer company.

Charlene didn't think for one minute that the containers Hunt was sending to Mexico held legal goods.

After locking the door to Corinne's office, Charlene immediately went to work. First, she went through all of the invoices and manifests that Anita had sent to Corinne's computer. Sure enough, there was not even one order for TM Hunt Enterprises, unlike what was on Corinne's home laptop. But there were several standing orders for JS Computer Sales. From what she could tell it appeared that James's company was just shipping small units of computers to Arizona and New Mexico.

Charlene made copies of everything, even documents stored on Anita's desktop.

Getting to Anita's computer without arousing suspicion was a tricky task because she couldn't get Anita away from her desk. But since the young woman had been fighting a cold, Charlene finally convinced her to go home rather than risk spreading it to the rest of the staff.

When Tyler stopped by wanting to engage in a little private office hanky-panky, Charlene hustled him out of there so that she could get back to what she'd been doing…making copies.

By late afternoon Charlene had amassed a thick bundle of papers. Her plan was a simple one. First, she would tell Tyler what had been going on, and then…

Then what? Tell him his wife is dead and that I've been pretendin' to be her? No, that won't work. She'd considered contacting the FBI agent who'd handled the first investigation into Hunt Enterprises, but changed her mind when she realized she would be implicated with both Hunt and James. After all, Corinne Mills was an accomplice, and that's who she was supposed to be.

By Wednesday, Charlene was miserable. Her thoughts returned constantly to Corinne and Tyler. She wondered how Corinne could have fallen out of love with Tyler. He really was a good man, with a strong sense of family. He was a doting, loving father, and as a lover he was attentive, tender, and passionate.

To make matters worse, Charlene was just sickened that Tyler believed James was his friend. James was betraying Tyler and had been sleeping with his wife. Only then did Charlene wonder if it was James's anger about the canceled contract with Mills Shipping that caused him to put such a devious plan into motion. Could James have set out to destroy Tyler and his family's company over a cancelled contract? Or was he just a greedy, ambitious, traitorous snake who'd smiled in Tyler's face minutes after feeling up his wife in that ladies' room? Charlene believed James was all of that, and he'd pulled a willing, greedy, and vindictive Corinne along with him.

Since Charlene no longer needed the crutch to get around and the frequency of her seizures had subsided, Flo reduced her hours to only two days a week to monitor her vitals and keep up the physical therapy. On this day, Flo shared something she'd found out at the hospital the day before.

Flo told Charlene that she'd been called into a meeting with Dr. Holland. "Girl, Doc Holland said that Tyler had called him last week because he was concerned about some personality changes in his wife. Doc wanted to know if I'd detected any changes in your behavior other than what we'd expected to see in a patient who'd had a head trauma," Flo said.

Charlene knew it wasn't good if Tyler was suspicious. "What behavior changes was Tyler askin' about, Flo?" She feared the answer to her question.

"Well, Tyler told the doctor that you were almost like a different person. He'd said things were off, kind of weird and strange with you." Flo stared deep into Charlene's eyes until she dropped her head into her hands. Flo blew out a breath, having just figured out what strange things Tyler was talking about. Dropping down in a chair, Flo clapped her cheeks. "Oh no! The two of you did it, didn't you? Charlene, you were intimate with him?"

Charlene could only bob her head. The look on Flo's concerned face said plenty. By sleeping with Tyler she knew she'd jumped from the frying pan and into the fire. She'd used that "honey" Flo suggested, and it worked because Tyler certainly was attracted to her…too attracted, because they'd been intimate every day since the first night at his house. *Damned flies.*

As the week progressed, Charlene's deception hit a new low because she was positive everyone thought that "Corinne" and Tyler were headed for reconciliation.

On Saturday, Charlene prepared a picnic for the twins. She'd planned to take them to a nearby lake. They would talk there and she'd tell them the story she'd promised to tell them; the story about her friend who was in heaven. Seeing Mona coming into the kitchen just then, Charlene invited her along, too. "Please come with us, Mona, we'd love for you to join us."

"Okay, just let me change clothes and freshen up a bit. I'll even drive," Mona said.

The twins squealed joyfully as Charlene closed her eyes and let their laughter soothe her heart. This was it, and there was no turning back.

An hour later, as the foursome sat by the lake, Charlene took a deep breath and told them the story about identical twin sisters born just minutes apart. They were named Corinne and Charlene McDonald.

She told them how the sisters had grown up poor, how one sister moved far away to make a new life for

herself. How they'd lost touch over a silly misunder-
standing years earlier but later found each other again
and realized that they'd never stopped loving each
other. How their reconciliation was cut short by a
terrible, tragic accident. How a coma led to a case of
mistaken identity had prevented her from revealing
who she really was, forcing her to continue the
charade. But she didn't want to deceive them
anymore. She wanted them to know the truth. She
needed them to know the truth. Charlene wasn't sure
how much the twins were able to comprehend, but
seeing the compassion and forgiveness in Mona's eyes,
she knew she'd done the right thing and that Mona
understood her conflict and struggle. She also felt that
her confession had probably answered some question
in Mona's mind as well.

When she was finished speaking she waited for the
recriminations, the accusations. Instead, to her shock
and surprise, three pairs of arms embraced and held
her until finally she let go and released the tears of
grief she'd been forced to hold inside for three long
months.

When Mona finally wiped her tears away, she told
Charlene that she must tell Tyler who she really was.
The twins agreed. "Daddy won't be mad, Charlene."
Hearing the children address her by her given name
without anger or resentment, Charlene loved them
even more, if that was possible. She promised she
would tell him and the rest of the family soon, but

needed a few more days. They agreed to keep her secret for a little while longer.

On Monday, Charlene went back into the office. She took a huge risk making this phone call, but she had no choice. It was time. With her heart pounding in her chest and her foot tapping nervously under the desk, she waited for the call to be connected.

Mr. Hunt of T.M. Hunt Enterprises answered the phone immediately, having recognized the familiar number on his private line's caller ID. "It is so nice of you to call, Mrs. Mills. How are you feeling?"

At first all Charlene could do was clamp her lips together in an effort to force down the bile rising in her throat. His voice not only grated in her ear, but Charlene knew without a doubt this man had likely killed her sister. The telepathic thing she and Corinne had joked about that night was so strong now that she gripped the phone handset tighter. "I'm better now, thanks for asking," she managed to say stiffly.

"I assume you're calling me about my request. I trust you've read the email and we're in agreement to the terms."

Reading between the lines, Charlene assumed he was talking about the email he'd sent to Corinne the last time she was in the office. He was concerned about his next shipment. "Ah, yes, there's going to a scheduling problem that could delay, um, the pick-up…possibly by several days." Not sure he under-stood what she'd said because he remained silent,

Charlene waited tensely. The silence continued. "Did you understand what I just said?

Hunt was immediately on guard. What was she thinking having this conversation with him on the telephone? "That cannot happen, Mrs. Mills, and, furthermore, I'm still waiting for your reply to my request, my repeated request, about that other matter of great importance to me."

He wants his property back.

"Sorry, but it's not my decision about the schedule. You see, um, your order crosses into the upcoming holiday schedule," Charlene said, glad she glanced at the calendar and realized that the fourth of July was fast approaching. Hearing the man's sharp intake of breath, she hurried on. "So several of our drivers and warehouse workers will be on holiday the preceding week and several days after the fourth. Everything will be pushed back by several days."

"So I take it you'll be working with a skeleton crew then, correct?"

A what? "Yes, probably," she answered uncertainly.

"Then I suggest they handle my request. Let's meet to discuss this further."

Oh, no. "No, I-I can't do that." He asked if there was a problem, obviously not pleased. "You are aware that I'm still recovering, aren't you, Mr. Hunt?" Charlene asked, searching the desk drawer for something to settle her aching stomach. To her, even the man's voice was menacing. Meeting him could prove deadly. *For me!* "I'm unable to drive, so a meeting is out of the question."

"I trust you know you'll be satisfactorily compensated."

"Listen, I'm calling as a courtesy, and I have other calls to make regarding the change in the schedule…as I said, there will be a delay."

"How long, exactly?" Hunt asked tersely. Not liking what he was hearing, he was already checking his calendar and preparing to make several calls himself, starting with James Smith.

"Three days…maybe four."

"Um-hmm," he murmured. "What about the other matter?"

"What other matter?"

Hunt was cautious, paranoid, and suspicious. He had to be in the event the call was being recorded. He was thoroughly unglued that he'd even let the conversation proceed, but he needed answers. "You're usually so sharp and on point, Mrs. Mills." He paused for several seconds. "Ah, but then I've forgotten about that unfortunate accident. I do apologize, but I was referring to my property, Mrs. Mills."

"Oh, that," Charlene knew his next answer would prove to her that Corinne had been killed for those six original invoices on her laptop. "You'll get them, all six of them."

"Wonderful!" He breathed a sigh of relief. "When?" he asked sharply and expectantly.

"By the end of the week," she said slowly.

"I want everything, Mrs. Mills."

Charlene sensed he was threatening her and now wished she hadn't made the call. "Sure thang." She cringed when her accent slipped out. She prayed he hadn't noticed.

"Pardon?" Hunt snapped, but he had to remember she had suffered head trauma in that terrible fall. *Horrible mistake that was, she was supposed to die in that fall.* Unfortunately his trusted associate/partner had called him that night to inform him of a second woman, but he'd guaranteed him that it was Mrs. Mills who'd ran towards the cliff. Hunt's order was followed exactly. He'd ordered his associate to eliminate the friend and dispose of the body quickly. If Mrs. Mills survived the fall, she'd be putty in his hands because she'd know he wasn't playing games with her anymore. If she didn't survive, then James would have another source.

"Good day, Mr. Hunt." Charlene hung up the telephone. Her mind was firing like a firecracker as fragments of the plot struggled to come together in her head. The problem was she just couldn't seem to grasp them in a way that made any sense.

Over the next few days Charlene worked steadily, reviewing her notes, meticulously studying Corinne's emails, and examining every piece of evidence that she had collected. Something still seemed to be missing…something that would tie everything together.

Two nights ago, Charlene found herself too restless to sleep. She had so much on her mind…her confession to Mona and the kids, Corinne's affair with the loathsome James Smith, and her own affair with Tyler. She scolded herself for continuing to sleep with him. She'd opened Pandora's box and released all those conflicting emotions that they'd both been holding in. And she'd been praying that she would be able to find the proof that Mr. Hunt either killed Corinne himself or had ordered it done, and she wanted to save the Mills family business.

Finally getting up and looking out the window at the dark sky, a chill swiftly ran through Charlene. It was the sky she blamed. It looked much like it did the night she fell over the cliff. That night, as pain engulfed her body, she'd stared up at the glistening stars until they faded out.

Pangs of regret tightened her stomach. She'd come to California to reunite with her sister and to meet her niece and nephew, but Charlene blamed herself for letting so much time slip by. "Why didn't I call Corinne sooner? Why did I wait so long?" Even as she quietly said the words, Charlene knew it was because she just didn't want Corinne to reject her again. But more than that, Charlene had struggled to put Corinne's venomous attacks behind her, and it wasn't just that one day at her sister's wedding, either. It was all of Corinne's malicious remarks and hurtful put-downs she'd had to endure most of their lives together. Corinne's hatred and constant sarcasm had ultimately torn away Charlene's self-esteem and sense of self. But on the night they met, Charlene had put it all out of her mind and washed away the years of rejection from her own twin…or had she, she wondered.

"What're you doing up?" Tyler asked, coming by her room and finding her standing at the window. He crossed over to her and wrapped his arms around her shoulders.

Startled, Charlene just shook her head. "Can't sleep," she said, turning to him. Her first instinct was to move away, but she dropped her weary, aching head onto his chest instead.

Tyler didn't believe her. "Come on, it's well past your bedtime," he teased and walked her over to the bed. His intent was to leave her alone, but when she held onto his arm and gazed sadly up into his eyes, leaving her alone was the last thing on his mind. So he stayed, her head on his chest until she finally fell into a troubled sleep.

CHAPTER 18

On Monday evening with everyone relaxing in the living-room following dinner, Tyler and his father were discussing the purchase of the company in Texas. Tyler was half listening as his father expounded on the benefit. Melvin didn't seem to notice that he was carrying on a one-sided conversation.

Tyler's focus was on Corinne and whatever magical spell she'd cast over him. He simply couldn't get enough of her. At that moment, he was anxiously waiting for her to come in from her physical therapy session with Flo out on the patio.

Was he falling in love with her again? He didn't know. She confused him. He wanted to hate her for cheating on him, but he sensed that she was different somehow. He was seriously attracted to the "new Corinne," scars and all. He thought back to a couple of night ago when she couldn't sleep. He'd held her while she slept. Did he want to make love? Absolutely, but what she'd needed from him wasn't intimacy. She needed comfort, and he gave her that.

When he'd finally slipped from her room, sure that Corinne was sleeping soundly, Tyler walked smack dab into Terri tiptoeing up the stairs, shoes in hand, after being out at a club most of the night. He also didn't miss the odor of cigarettes and alcohol, either. "Busted," he whispered as she crept by him in the dimly lit hallway.

Mortified at being caught red-handed, Terri didn't have time to register her surprise at seeing Tyler emerge from Corinne's room because he chased her down the hallway to her room, threatening to spill the beans about her being out all night.

Since then, Terri had dropped innuendos about them "hooking up again." Was she right?

Forcing his mind back to the present, Tyler listened to Shane and Shelly, as they leaned over the coffee table making cards and affixing bright stickers to them. Although they'd been whispering back and forth again, he'd picked up on their conversation about two sisters who were twins like they were. "Charlene will like my cards best," Shane whispered.

"Charlene doesn't care what our cards look like. She just wants them for her scrap book," Shelly had responded.

Smiling as the children talked matter-of-factly about the person they were making cards for, Tyler joined in on their hushed conversation. "Who is Charlene? Is she a new friend at camp?" Tyler looked questioningly at the adults in the room.

His mother, he noticed, looked noticeably uncomfortable. Then, shaking his head, Shane answered. "No, Daddy, Charlene was sent to take care of us and she loves us…"

At that moment, Charlene and Flo walked into the dining room, having finished the therapy session. Each stopped in their tracks as they heard the conversation that was unfolding in the living room. Charlene stood completely still as she listened to Tyler questioning the twins, but her eyes probed Flo's with a silent plea.

Tyler decided he'd had enough of the children talking as if there was some type of ghost living with them. "Listen, you two stop fibbing right now. I also want you to stop the constant whispering you've been doing lately. It's not nice, so it stops today, all right?"

"But, Daddy, it's not a fib about Charlene. We're telling the truth. That's what we've been whispering about because it's a secret…a good secret," Shelly whispered. "But Charlene *is* living with us and she's my new BFF, and Mommy sent her here to take care of us, and you, too," Shelly said as if her explanation should have made sense to her father.

"Charlene said you would be upset, but don't be, Daddy," Shane said, coming over to his father. "She's going to take care of us because that's what Mommy wanted her to do."

"And Charlene has to keep her promise to Mommy. She just has to," Shelly added.

Apprehension, fear, and uneasiness hit Tyler with an energy that radiated heat up into his chest. He stood up quickly. "I said stop this…right now, both of you. I'm not going to tolerate you two telling lies, you understand me?" He looked from one set of amber-brown eyes to the other. "Answer me. Do you under-stand what I'm saying?" Tyler's voice had risen, angry that his children were outright lying. Then Shelly began to cry.

Leaning against the dining room wall, Charlene's heart twisted painfully to hear that. She was alarmed by Shelly crying and the panic in Tyler's voice. She gripped Flo's arm for support.

Back in the living room, Tyler's patience was stretched. "Shelly, stop crying and look at me," Tyler said. When his daughter raised a red, wet face to his, he refused to succumb to her beautiful but sad little face. He was standing firm this time. "Where is this Charlene person who, by the way, doesn't live here with us? And I don't want to hear any more foolish-ness about Mommy sending her here or anything about a promise." His heart twisted to see Shelly's bottom lip trembling, and he longed to pick her up in his arms and hold her.

Then Tyler watched Shelly point to his left. He turned to see that Corinne had come into the living room and was now standing beside him. "You heard? Our precious little children have taken to fibbing and telling tall tales."

Shane defended Shelly. "Tell him! Tell Daddy we're not fibbing, are we Charlene?"

Without taking her eyes off Tyler, Charlene answered in a quiet, but drained voice, "No, honey, you're not fibbing."

Tyler looked from Corinne to the twins and to the family who sat mesmerized in silence. What was wrong with everybody, he wondered.

Terri, who'd been chatting on her cell phone, snapped it shut to listen, all eyes and ears.

Still angry and crying, Shelly pleaded. "Tell him the story, Charlene! Tell him so he'll stop saying we're fibbing and telling tall tales because we're not, are we?"

Charlene looked at Shelly, then up at Tyler. Her time had just run out.

"Tyler, my name isn't Corinne." Charlene swallowed hard. "My name is Charlene McDonald. Corinne was my identical twin sister." Keeping her emotions in check, Charlene placed a hand on Tyler's chest and applied just enough pressure until he sat back down in the side chair he'd gotten up from.

Bemused, Ryan couldn't hold back a chuckle. "Corinne, this is absurd. You're obviously suffering an identity problem. That's all this is." He noticed his brother's shocked expression.

"No, Ryan, it's not an identity issue," Charlene said, gazing into Tyler's confused eyes.

"I'd never met you before, but I knew you'd married my sister. You see, years ago, Corinne hated how we'd lived and she wanted more for herself. She wanted a different life and she wanted money and all that it could bring her." Charlene glanced around at the rest of the family. "I didn't mean to hurt anyone, but when I was in the hospital I couldn't talk. All I could do was feel horrible pain. I'd begun to hear voices that comforted me and bathed my face, and still I couldn't wake up. I heard everyone so concerned about me, well…about Corinne, and I wanted to come out of that darkness. I struggled to come out, but I didn't know how. And when I finally did, all of you called me Corinne. I couldn't understand why you'd call me by my sister's name, but I knew that I was Charlene McDonald and not Corinne Mills, my twin sister."

"What the hell…" Tyler said, but was pulled up short when his father held up a hand to let her finish talking. It seemed everyone was spellbound listening to her.

"I hadn't seen Corinne in almost nine years. The last time I saw her she was standin' in the back of the chapel about to marry you, Tyler. She hadn't invited me or our father."

"What are you talking about? Corinne, you don't have any family," Tyler said with a sinking feeling in his chest. He listened as her voice changed ever so slightly and became stronger, more Southern, and his eyes flitted across to his family before coming to rest on her again.

Continuing past her pain, and tuning out Terri and Trish's whispered comments, Charlene told them about the first time she'd come to California…to confront Corinne on her wedding day. "I came to persuade her not to marry you if she didn't love you, but she had me arrested."

"It all started on our thirty-fifth birthday, on March 25th and I missed her so much and I knew she'd had a set of twins. A few times during those nine years she'd call and speak briefly to our father, but never to me. When he died eighteen months ago she'd sent me some money to pay for his funeral, but she didn't come home. But the night before we turned thirty-five, somethin' weird and wonderful happened for me. I picked up the telephone, called the airport, and scheduled a flight out here, to California. I didn't care if Corinne still hated me or not. All I cared about was seein' her and meetin' the babies I so desperately wanted to get to know." She glanced at the twins hovering by their father's knees. "They're not babies any more, are they?"

Shelly interrupted excitedly, her tears all but gone. "Tell him the weird part, Charlene!"

Charlene nodded at the little girl. "No sooner had I hung up the telephone, it rang again, right in my hand. It was Corinne. She was callin' *me*. I told her about the flight I'd just arranged and it would have put me here in two days, but she told me to stay put and that she'd call me right back. When she did, she told me to go to the airport at six-thirty the followin' mornin' because that's when my flight was leavin' Norfolk. She'd moved my flight up to get me here sooner. I-I can't tell you how wonderful it felt to see her. She was still so beautiful, even more than she was on her weddin' day…on your weddin' day." Charlene's voice wavered.

"Are you listening, Daddy?" Shane asked, grinning. "Listen to her funny voice, too."

Yeah, he was listening, Tyler thought. Initially, he thought Corinne's brain trauma had forced her to reveal another personality. But as he listened to the Southern drawl coming and going from her voice he couldn't stop from listening to her…and yeah, it was weird and strange.

Charlene continued. "I'd showed her the picture she'd sent to our father years ago when Shane and Shelly were only two." Charlene pulled the picture from a thin wallet in her pocket and passed it Tyler. On the back was written, "To Daddy, with all my love, Corinne."

Recognizing the picture, as well as the handwriting, Tyler lifted unbelieving eyes to hers.

"When we met in the lobby of that hotel, we were both stunned that we still look so much alike. We were even dressed alike, in white blouses and black slacks, and our hair was styled alike. Then we went up to her room 'cause she said she needed to talk to me. She asked if she could trust me. I said, of course, Corinne, you can trust me with anythin'. So she said, 'can I trust you to take care of my precious babies, and Tyler, if somethin' should happen to me.' "

Moving the children aside, Tyler stood up. "I've had enough of this shit, and I'm calling that quack doctor of yours, Corinne!" When he attempted to sidestep her, Charlene grabbed his arm and stopped him, knowing that she had to continue, she had to get it all out, once and for all.

"Yeah, Tyler, please call that cute Doc Holland, like right now, and tell him Corinne thinks she's somebody else," Terri said, snatching up the house phone and holding it out for Tyler.

"That's not necessary, Terri," Charlene said, but her eyes never left Tyler's face. "Corinne and I sat in her room and there she told me about your birthday present and why she was stayin' in that hotel. She'd said she'd always dreaded our birthday because it was a reminder of what she'd done to me, of how she'd pushed me out of her life. She deeply regretted everythin' and wished she could go back and change things. She also told me that she was in trouble. Tyler, I pleaded with her to tell you, and that's when she told me about the man who, um, she'd been involved with. But on her birthday night, she came home to tell you about him and to tell you why she was in trouble. She never got the chance because you gave her your birthday present." Her lips tightened, because try as she might, Charlene couldn't keep the rising rage at his cruelty out of her voice.

Tyler yanked his arm from her hand. "You're fucking nuts, you hear me!" he shouted.

Terri and Trish gasped as they held onto the twins in absolute shock, their thoughts reeling as the story unfolded and each realized on some level that it was true. They drew the children closer and propelled them up the stairs to their rooms. This was adult talk, and they were confused enough. Both hurried back to hear the rest of this fascinating story.

Ryan sat enthralled, exchanging disbelieving glances with his parents. He felt guilty seeing the frightened expression on Tyler's face. Yes, because on a personal level he was still miffed that his parents' had chosen Tyler over him to run Mills Shipping.

"No, Tyler, I'm not nuts. But I have to tell you everythin', though it hurts to repeat it all. Up in her room we talked for hours, all through the night, until Corinne's cell phone rang. It was him, her lover. He'd asked her to meet him down in the parkin' lot. I pleaded with her not to go. I told her that I would go to the police with her in the mornin' and report everythin'. I even suggested she come to you and beg for your forgiveness, but she said no. She said…" Again, Charlene's anger washed over her and she had to bite her bottom lip to keep from screaming at him. "She said you had pictures of them together. She said that you were divorcin' her and were gonna use the pictures to get full custody of the children."

Tyler could only stare back at her, unblinking, as a seething fury built up inside him. When he glanced around again it seemed that his family were still held captive as well.

Swiping at hot tears, Charlene saw everything replaying before her. "Just before she left the room, she said she'd never forgotten about me and that she'd always loved me. It was somethin' in how she'd said it that made me follow her. I went down to the parkin' lot, and, from where I was hidin', I saw Corinne sittin' in the car with a man, a tall black man." Charlene told about hiding in the truck and watching the black car slowly creeping around the parking lot.

"When Corinne got out of the car and looked directly at me, I sensed somethin' was terribly wrong. She used to say I was the one with that telepathy thing."

Feeling her leg cramping, Charlene ignored the pain but did sit down on the couch facing Tyler. Pain, anger, and grief pushed her to finish. "When Corinne stepped from the car, the man pulled off immediately and because I kept lookin' back at that car without the headlights on, I felt a sense of dread like somethin' bad was about to happen. It was so strong. I knew the man that got out of the back seat meant to do harm, and he did. I yelled for Corinne to run. I grabbed hold of her hand and we took off runnin' down the road. As we ran, Corinne glanced back at the car. It was aimin' for us and the man had a gun in his hand."

Tyler felt his breath catch. He was becoming light-headed listening to her because suddenly all of the things that he thought strange and weird about Corinne now struck him all at once as she…Corinne or Charlene…told her bizarre and absurd story. As a painful stab sliced through him, Tyler wondered how long it would take until he was able to breathe again, because surely he had stopped breathing and was hallucinating. This couldn't be real.

Charlene told of the black car slamming into her and sending her over the cliff, but that she hadn't fallen because she'd grabbed onto a thick tree branch sticking out from the side of the cliff. "I could hear Corinne's voice above me. She was mouthin' off at the man. She told him he wouldn't get away with what he'd done. Just before the branch I was holdin' onto broke, I saw an object come flyin' over the cliff. I recognized it immediately. It was Corinne's locket. She'd told me that she changed the picture every year. I remember reachin' for it because I knew it was important to Corinne. That's the last memory I have until I woke up in the hospital."

"This is such bullshit!" Tyler snapped incredulously, his hands balled into two tight fists.

Ignoring him, she said, "I didn't tell anyone at first, but then, I had to."

"And just who the hell did you tell this crap to?" Tyler sneered sarcastically, still not believing Corinne or the tall tale she was telling.

"I told Flo, because I needed her to do me a huge favor. You see, Tyler, that man killed my sister and put her body in a car and set it afire. I found that out by readin' the police blotters looking for a Jane Doe. When I read a particular one, I-I just knew it was her. I sent Flo to claim Corinne's ashes and bring her home," Charlene sobbed. "I told Flo to have the police match the remains with my blood samples from the hospital."

Quietly stepping into the living room, Flo cleared her throat and patted Charlene reassuringly on the shoulder. "Tyler, when I first heard this story I had a hard time believing it, too." Flo spread her hands. "I thought maybe it was a scheme to keep her children in a big divorce settlement; this is California, after all. I honestly didn't know at first. But I'm sorry, Tyler. That report checked out because I *did* have DNA testing run at the hospital. I had a friend in the lab rush a report for me, and the genetic markers of Charlene's blood samples taken *while* she was in the hospital are almost a match to the DNA obtained from the Jane Doe. I just now had that lab tech fax the report over to me when I heard what was going down in here." Flo passed the single sheet of paper to Tyler and retreated from the room.

Tyler stared down at words that made no sense to him whatsoever. He raised blank, unreadable eyes to Corinne or Charlene; hell, he didn't even know at that point. "And who else did you tell this story to?" he asked in a deceptively calm voice.

"She told me," Mona spoke up, "and then I told Melvin, but we'd suspected something long before Charlene told me." Mona stood and came to sit in a wingback chair facing Charlene. Ignoring the many pairs of eyes that followed her, Mona reached for Charlene's hand. "Do you remember me sitting by your hospital bed, or any of my chats?" Mona asked her.

Tyler gawked at his mother. This had to be a nightmare.

Now the one shocked was Charlene. She nodded slowly. "I remember you talked about your friend Helen and the twins."

"Yes, but sometimes I also listened to you talking, mostly incoherently. I called for the doctor a few times and he'd come in and say 'she's still in a coma, but her mind is struggling to come back.' " Mona rubbed Charlene's hands in her own. "You talked about Corinne as if you weren't her, honey. You often said, 'Corinne run,' and 'I missed you, Corinne,' and that's when I started to pick up that Southern accent. But I had to ask myself, why would this woman, who was in a coma and under sedation, call out for someone whom she's supposed to be. One day, I even told you that I thought you held many secrets."

Charlene was shocked. "Wait a minute, so this whole time…you're sayin' you knew I-I wasn't Corinne, even before the picnic at the lake? You knew I was livin' here lying to y'all?"

"That's right." Mona lowered her head to hide her tear-rimmed eyes. "But there was something else I noticed, dear. You see, in the hospital I spent days talking to the woman who I thought was my daughter-in-law. I'd begged for another chance…a chance to be her friend." Mona's face contorted briefly.

"Charlene, everything in life comes full circle…even *my* own deceit. You see, Corinne only tolerated me and that's because I saw right through her from the very beginning." Mona lifted her face to Tyler. "I knew she wanted to marry Tyler for her own selfish reasons. Mainly, she wanted his money and status befitting the wife of Tyler Mills. He was so enamored with her, nothing would sway him to change his mind. He was determined to marry her. So I made a deal with Corinne. I told her to make him happy and give him the children he wanted…and she did that. But I had to make sure that she had access to all the money she wanted. But a few years ago when I noticed that Tyler wasn't happy, I talked to him about it. He'd told me Corinne had stopped…" Mona glanced around the room and then chose her words carefully. "He told me she'd stopped being intimate with him. When I confronted her and threatened to cut off the money, Corinne reminded me of our deal. She said she'd given him babies and that had made him happy. She said it was the only thing that made him happy. Then she threatened that if I stopped paying her, she would tell Tyler everything and he'd end up hating me and she'd see to it I didn't see my grandchildren." Mona dabbed at her eyes. "Corinne constantly reminded me of that, my dear. She said she could destroy him, destroy us, take the kids and disappear forever. I couldn't take that chance…but you, Charlene, never brought it up, not even once."

A jumble of emotions permeated his brain. Tyler didn't know how to feel. He was shocked how his mother and wife had manipulated his life. When had he lost control? Right then and there, his entire world shifted on its axis. He could deny all he wanted, but it was true the woman sitting on the arm of the couch wasn't the woman he'd married. She was not his wife. "Enough of this," he said, lashing out in anger. He grasped the imposter by the arm. "Where's my wife? Where is she?" His mind was refusing to accept the truth. But his heart did.

Recoiling as he loomed over her, Charlene stood up. How dare he be angry at her? He had no right to be angry as far as she was concerned. "She died, Tyler. Don't you get it? Corinne's gone! She died right after her thirty-fifth birthday…" And finally Charlene's shoulders collapsed under the weight of it all. Suddenly, completely exhausted, her voice was devoid of feeling. "She died right after you threw her out of her own home, you bastard!"

This was insane. It was inconceivable that something like this could happen. He was living a nightmare. Tyler stared into her face, into her eyes, and he knew. He really knew. Somehow he had always known, but accepting was another story. She was telling the truth.

As if a veil had been lifted, he realized this was not Corinne Mills standing before him. Corinne would have never sat down in the driveway drawing flowers, and neither would she eat a burger and let the catsup run down her chin. Corinne would never roll around out in the wet grass with the twins…and Corinne had never given him such pleasure with a kiss or a shy glance. She'd never cried with such pleasure when he was buried within her.

In his head, Tyler heard his responses to the questions she'd asked him since he'd brought her home from the hospital, about work, about their friends…and the argument that Saturday morning. He and Corinne had never argued like that. Then there was that conversation in her room, when they sat on the loveseat and she'd told him about being a sickly child and how her mother had died…and Corinne didn't need eyeglasses when working on her computer. "Oh, my God." No, this was definitely not Corinne. "Where the hell is Corinne?" Tyler bellowed.

With matching anger, Charlene pushed him away. "Her urn is back at your house! It's in an amber box that matches her eyes, my eyes, and our mother's eyes. It's on the shelf in front of that atrocious wall, you idiot!"

Trish and Terri began sobbing. They were ignored by Charlene and Tyler.

"You get out of here and you stay the hell away from my children!" Tyler exploded.

Charlene laughed suddenly. "You know what, Tyler? You're really the predictable jerk I called you before, and you sound like a broken record!"

"Get the hell out of here!" He repeated, ignoring the shocking, disbelieving gasps, sobs, and comments of his family. His stomach was twisted in painful knots and his head pounded.

Charlene threw up her hands. "Oh, okay, I get it. I get where you're going with this again. It wasn't enough for you to banish one McDonald twin out of the house, so you're going for two. You make me sick!" Charlene hissed in his face. "If it wasn't for you, my sister, the only other relative I had besides those twins upstairs, would be here right now and she wouldn't have had to die at the hands of some clowns you were dumb enough to do business with. You thoughtless, heartless pig! How could you do that to her? She was your wife and mother of your children. How could you throw her out of her own home?" Charlene shrugged her shoulders carelessly, "And for what, because she sought comfort in the arms of another man? Trust me, Tyler, Corinne got more pleasure from her new wardrobe than she got from him or any other man!"

Charlene waved her hand to block out the intrusive image of the intimacy she'd shared with Tyler. "It didn't matter to her, Tyler. Don't you understand that? Corinne wasn't happy with herself, but she'd vowed never to go back to livin' without money again. And she did that because she didn't want you and your family to think less of her because she really *wasn't* like y'all…like you, the wealthy, smart businessman who was born in the lap of luxury with money to burn and with a silver spoon in your big mouth!"

Charlene snatched the wrinkled DNA report from his slackened hand. "This only proves that we were sisters and our DNA will match the twins, but don't you think for one second that I'm gonna turn and go away because of your meaningless threats? I won't. But you hear this, I'm keepin' that promise I made to Corinne, and I plan on seein' my niece and nephew and being in their lives!"

"The hell you will! I suggest you rethink any promises you may have made to Corinne, and if you go near my children, trust me, you'll suffer the consequences!" Tyler's wrath was so intense his breath came out in hot bursts. Surely, fire spewed from his mouth.

"There you go again with your pointless threats!" Charlene stepped dangerously closer to him, cocked her head to the side and chuckled. "Here's a news flash for you, Tyler Mills, I'm nothin' like Corinne was! I don't sit idly by and let crap happen to me and then brood and stew about it for months on end. You'd best believe that I do somethin' about it, and what I'm gonna do is make the bastard who killed Corinne pay. And when I'm done, and if I have to, I'll fight you in court because I want to be allowed contact with my niece and nephew. So trust me, buster, you'll be the one dealin' with the consequences of my actions, you got that? Otherwise, I don't give a damn about what you suggest or think!"

Everyone was on their feet, but Terri moved toward Charlene, her chest still heaving from emotion and exhaustion. Closing her eyes briefly, Charlene tried to calm herself. Tyler was standing absolutely still, watching her.

Charlene turned her back on him to address the rest of the family, who were still frozen in various stages of shock, disbelief and fascination. Only Mona seemed relatively calm in the face of the tornado that just devastated the people she'd come to love. Reaching for Terri's hand, Charlene addressed the family. "I owe y'all my sincere apologies for deceivin' y'all like I did. I honestly didn't mean to hurt anybody. I've grown to love y'all."

"I should have guessed you weren't Corinne in the hospital," Terri said, intrigued by the turn of events. She moved to study Charlene more closely. "You said my braids were pretty, and Corinne hated my braids. Is-is Corinne really dead?"

"Yes, I'm afraid she is."

"And you pretended to be her to catch the people who killed her," Ryan said.

Charlene nodded. "Yes, but to do that I needed to recover first and so..."

"You had to let everyone think you were her." Trish watched Charlene nod. "You do know that's criminal, don't you?" Trish watched the imposter bob her head again. "On the other hand, I'm shocked and saddened about Corinne." Trish turned into Ryan's waiting arms, sobbing.

"Where are you from, Charlene, and how do we know you're telling the truth? I mean, you look exactly like Corinne, and she never mentioned anything about having family," Ryan asked, unsure of everything he'd heard.

"I'm from Chesapeake, Virginia. Corinne and I were born identical twins. Corinne left Virginia a couple years after we got out of high school and came out here to California."

"What do you do, Charlene?" Trish asked quietly.

"I'm an art teacher, and I work part time for a wedding boutique." Charlene could feel Tyler's eyes burning into her. She felt his seething rage. She ignored both so that she could answer the family's questions. They deserved at least that, she thought.

"And you have no other family, none at all?" Melvin asked, sliding his eyes to Tyler's. He knew his son was in shock.

"No. Our father died almost two years ago. I spent the precedin' two years takin' care of him when he became ill. Our mother died after givin' birth to me," she said.

Tyler threw his hands up. "I've heard enough of this homespun bullshit. What exactly happened to Corinne?" Tyler asked her tightly.

"Corinne was murdered by a man she had a business arrangement with. She was trying to get out of it. She'd even threatened him and he came after her," Charlene said sadly. "He shot her on that road as I tumbled down that cliff." Charlene reached out to touch Tyler's arm. She knew the grief he was feeling.

Tyler moved aside. "Don't touch me," he said. His mind was reeling over what he'd just heard. Looking at the imposter only added to his anguish. He wanted her gone. "Mom, Dad, either she leaves this house tonight or I will, with my children. It's your choice."

Mona stood up. "Tyler, don't you dare threaten me, I won't stand for it! Now we have a situation that needs to be dealt with as a family. First and foremost, you all need to come to terms with the fact that Corinne is dead. She's no longer with us, and that hurts."

"Mom, this woman is an imposter." Tyler raked a gaze down the woman who'd duped him. "She didn't start this tale of a story until…" Tyler stopped and shifted his weight as he processed a thought swiftly running through his head. A sardonic grin replaced his scowl as he walked back over to the woman who'd passed herself off as his wife for almost three months. "Uh-huh. I get it now. You didn't start this tale until I took you to bed," he sneered.

Seeing that he was trying to shift the blame back to her, Charlene raised an eyebrow and snorted. "Oh, please! Get over yourself. Did you think I was so gullible that I'd risk everythin' to come here for the sole purpose of sleepin' with you? Well, dream on, you idiot! But since you want this aired right here and now, let me just say this, the woman you took to your bed was me." She thumped her chest. "That was me, Charlene, and I shouldn't have done that. I was wrong for allowin' it to happen." Seeing regret on his face, Charlene changed tactics. "Didn't you guess even then? Tyler, I hadn't seen or talked to Corinne in years, how would I know what she was like in bed? We couldn't have been that similar…or were we?"

Yes, in his heart and his gut, Tyler knew this Corinne was different in bed. She acted as if she wanted it. She acted as if she *wanted* him. She gave as much as she took, and she made him see better days ahead. "Yes. I knew something was different…it was off from her norm," he admitted slowly, yet sardonically.

Charlene felt he was mocking her. "Well, what the heck was it, because I know for a fact that I didn't swoon and sway when you touched me. Come on, tell…thanks to you, I have no more secrets from your family." She poked her finger into his chest, just as she'd done the first night they slept together. She was about to issue him another challenge.

"So come on, Tyler, don't be the sensitive punk you don't want Shane to grow up to be. Man up and tell me why you didn't even question the difference in your wife's behavior…the wife who'd previously shut you out?" she asked mockingly, knowing that she'd hit home.

In that instant, Tyler wanted to throttle her. How dare she throw his stupidity back into his face? "She wasn't usually as involved," he said tightly, his lips barely moving.

Charlene thrusts her hands on her hips. "Now, what's that supposed to mean, huh?"

Tyler threw up his hands in exasperation. "I don't want to talk about this shit anymore. Not to you, and certainly not in front of my entire family. I'm taking my children and getting the hell out of this house. You're more than welcome to stay here, but I'm done listening!" Tyler turned and stormed toward the door.

Both Mona and Melvin shouted for Tyler to come back. He ignored both.

Charlene wanted to punch his lights out. Instead she yelled at his back. "That's right, do what you do best! Walk away. You couldn't man up and face your wife, so you put her out. You're such a coward, Tyler!"

Hearing that, Tyler stopped in his tracks. He'd heard those same words from Corinne when he'd told her to get out of the house that terrible night a few months ago. Yes, she'd called him a coward, too.

Turning back, his swift strides forced her to back away from him as he rushed out the words he didn't want to say. "As far as sex went, she wasn't as involved in the act as you were!" Tyler enunciated. "Her attitude was take it or leave it, and in most cases that's exactly what I did. I left it and her because I was through asking her! Yes, she shut me out, so without drawing you a picture, lady, you were into it…or at least you pretended to be," Tyler said.

Recoiling with understanding, Charlene backed down. "I-I didn't pretend, Tyler. I never even referred to myself as Corinne. You all called me Corinne. But more and more I saw myself, my personality, the person who I am, dyin' inside and strugglin' to come out. It was becomin' an effort to speak slowly and deliberately so that I didn't have a Southern accent.

But you caught me a few times when I slipped. But you know what? That's exactly what Corinne did, too. It was still wrong of me to do what I did."

Irritated at his single-mindedness and knowing he would leave, Charlene relented. "Please don't leave. This is your home, your family, and I don't want the twins to be upset any more than they probably are right now." Reaching into her pocket, Charlene pulled out the two little ceramic kittens that had been on the windowsill in Shane's room. She'd meant to take them upstairs after explaining their meaning to the twins earlier. "Do you remember these?"

Tyler took one quick glance at the figurines. "They're yours…Corinne's." But he did recognize them. To Corinne, they were like gold and she allowed no one to touch them, ever.

"Did you ever look at the bottom of them?"

"Why would I?"

Turning them over in her hand, Charlene said, "Corinne's name on the bottom of one and mine is on the other. I made them in art class for our twelfth birthday. It's marked right on the bottom 'cause I did it. I was so shocked when I saw them back at your house, but I'm so happy Corinne kept them." Sitting them on the coffee table, she watched as Melvin leaned forward and carefully picked them up. Charlene couldn't imagine the truth would be so painful.

I've hurt these people somethin' awful.

"Tyler, we grew up with very little. Corinne and I were raised by our father, and he didn't have much. One day, she and I sneaked into this house at the end of our block that was being renovated. We walked around the large sunny rooms. It was going to be a real showplace when it was finished. We danced in the kitchen, our sneakers got all dirty from the sawdust, and then we ran out on the back porch. Out there, we found several cans of paint. Most of them were dried up, but we took the three cans back to our house and mixed all three cans together. We had orange, yellow, and some other reddish color. Anyway, we had enough paint to cover just one wall of the bedroom we shared. To us it was beautiful. It was fresh and new. Tyler, it's the same atrocious color that Corinne has painted on her bedroom wall."

Charlene looked back at the many sets of eyes staring at her. "It really was an ugly color, but when you don't have much, even an atrocious colored wall can bring you some happiness. For a little while, at least."

Letting out a harsh laugh at the absurdity of it all, Tyler again lashed out. "This is bull!"

Forcing herself not to cry, Charlene shook her head at his lack of compassion and understanding, but she also saw Tyler in a whole different light. She saw raw hurt. *Of course he's hurt.* "You know, I-I have to thank Terri for two things," Charlene said.

"Me!" Terri exclaimed defensively. "What'd I do now?"

"You were the only one who let me see just how extensive my injuries were. But you also told me somethin' that happened a while back that I think inadvertently put Tyler's relationship with Corinne on a more downward path."

"Oh, my God! What the heck did I say?"

"You said Tyler was going to move out of the house, but he didn't because she got sick."

"Right. I remember saying that," Terri answered.

"You said that you'd told Tyler about overhearing Corinne on her cell phone at midnight. She was speaking low and quiet and then she started crying saying how she 'couldn't believe she wouldn't see him again', and implied that she was talking to another man." Charlene reached for Terri's hand. "Corinne was talking to me. I called her at three in the morning when our father died. The three-hour difference would've made it midnight here when I called her. When I arrived here, Corinne told me she'd taken sick to her bed with grief over Daddy's death, but she said she couldn't come back to Virginia without Tyler finding out about us," Charlene said.

"Oh, no," Terri said, flopping down on the couch, realizing the mistake she'd made.

Charlene turned to Tyler. "Listen, I don't want anythin' from you other than to be allowed to see my niece and nephew. They're my only blood relatives. But I do want somethin' else from you, Tyler, some-thin' I've never asked you for." Charlene choked.

Tyler suddenly clapped his hands. The sound was loud and ominous as he crossed back to Charlene. "Okay, brace yourselves folks. Here it comes. I'll bet the imposter wants money. So how much money do you want to keep this fucking story out of the tabloids?"

That did it.

Eyes narrowed dangerously, Charlene slapped his face so hard the sound echoed around the room. "When I went over that cliff, I had on my best silk blouse and black slacks. When I'd offered to repay Corinne some of the money she'd sent for our father's funeral, she pushed it back in my hand and I put it back into my pocket, but before I left Corinne's room I put it in her small bag of toiletries. It was a thousand dollars in an envelope wrapped with a wide rubber band. It was all the money I had, and that's all I want from you!"

"I-I have Charlene's money, Daddy," Shelly called out hesitantly from the doorway, shocking everyone because no one knew she'd been standing there, or how much she'd heard.

"Oh, my God!" Tyler said, his face red and stinging from the slap, went to his daughter. He stooped down and gave her a reassuring hug before sending her upstairs to retrieve it. When she came back a few minutes later, he saw that she carried the box of items he'd collected from the hotel. "Honey, where did you get this?" he asked gently, taking the box from her. Until that moment, he'd forgotten all about it.

"It was in the back of your car when you picked me and Shane up from school one day. I didn't think Mommy would mind if I kept her things safe. But they're not all Mommy's things; some are Charlene's so I kept them safe for her," Shelly said.

Forgetting about the throbbing pain in her leg, Charlene leaned down so she was eye level with the little girl and hugged her tightly. "Thank you for keepin' my things safe. That was a wonderful thing for you to do, Shelly. Everythin' is okay, so you go on up to bed and say your prayers." Her little shoulders relaxed once she was assured that she hadn't done anything wrong.

"I won't forget. I'll say the prayer for your friend, but it's really for Mommy, right?" Shelly watched Charlene nod yes. "Tyler's mad, isn't he?" Shelly looked warily at her father.

"Yes, sweetheart, your daddy's upset, but he'll be okay because you love him, right?"

"Uh-huh." Shelly turned and hugged her father's legs. "It's okay, Daddy. We're not sad because Mommy's in a nice place," she said and left the room.

Tyler handed over a small folded envelope containing the bills. It was exactly as she'd described…tightly bounded in a crumbling enveloped with a wide rubber band around it.

Taking the envelope and clutching it to her chest, Charlene walked toward the great foyer leading to the front door. "I see Flo is ready to leave. I'll have her drive me into town. I'm so sorry about Corinne, and honestly, I didn't mean to hurt y'all. You have been gracious, supportive, and kind to me. Despite how y'all felt about Corinne and everythin' she'd done to hurt you, y'all forgave her. How sad that Corinne didn't realize how blessed and rich she truly was," Charlene said.

Mona reached out for Charlene, but she pulled away. "Please, please don't leave," Mona said.

The second he heard the front door close, Tyler sank to the couch. For a long time, no one spoke. Even Terri, who always had a snappy comeback, was oddly quiet.

Finally Melvin, who had silently listened to the entire exchange, addressed his family. "It's obvious to me that we, as a family, have a lot to think about and talk about. Many things were said here tonight that need to be dealt with. We are a family who gets through situations together, and that will never change."

Tyler now knew that it wasn't Corrine who had made him happy again. She was dead, and that knowledge caused him to break down and cry bitterly.

His family gathered close to embrace and comfort him.

CHAPTER 19

That night Charlene checked into a motel off the interstate.

Although her heart was heavy, Charlene was also glad everything was out. She could now breathe without grief, guilt, or rage. She missed the twins and the family and…she missed Tyler also, she admitted to herself. Despite the tragic circumstances she'd inadvertently developed feelings for him, even though he'd said some cruel and hurtful things when he'd lashed out at her two nights ago. To be honest, she'd said some pretty hurtful things, too.

Sitting in her room, Charlene didn't know what to do. She felt more alone now than ever.

Yes, the truth was out, but it didn't bring her any closer to avenging her sister's death, and she wouldn't stop until she did. Problem was, she needed her bundle of papers. She also had to come up with something to tell Mr. Hunt because the man had left several messages on Corinne's office voice mail. Charlene had been able to retrieve the messages because she was able to dial and retrieve them from Corinne's voice mail.

She had to return to the Mills house one last time.

~~~

The same night of the big blowout, Tyler had gone to his house. There on the shelf was the urn. On the lid was inscribed CORINNE MCDONALD MILLS, LOVING WIFE OF TYLER, LOVING MOTHER OF SHELLY AND SHANE AND LOVING SISTER TO CHARLENE. Something fell from underneath it and floated to the floor, a card maybe.

Bending to retrieve it Tyler saw that it was a picture. Identical twin girls were holding hands and standing in front of a tree. It was Corinne and yes, it was Charlene...twins about twelve years old. Returning the urn to the shelf, Tyler dropped down to a chair and let his eyes travel up the hideous orange wall. He didn't blink away the tears that blurred his vision.

"Well, now I know the story behind this awful color, Corinne," he'd said. "Why didn't you tell me? No wonder you weren't happy. How could you keep such secret? It shouldn't have even *been* a secret. Damn it. I can't understand why you would deny your only sister and father the beauty of knowing your children, or from sharing your life. We could have helped them." Tyler shook his head. "Oh, and now I know how you came up with Daniel for Shane's middle name. You said you'd just liked it. Now I know it was your father's name. Good Lord."

His heart twisted. "I'm so very sorry that you couldn't come to me, but how could I have been so blind? How could I ignore the aura of sadness that always surrounded you or your evasive answers about

your childhood? Why didn't I press you harder?"
Getting up, Tyler walked around the bedroom, as if
seeing familiar things for the first time.

Turning to leave, he glanced at the bed and
remembered the day he and Charlene fell asleep there
after her seizure. Somewhere in the back of his mind
echoed the whispered words 'I love you, Corinne.' He
realized that he hadn't said them. Charlene had
spoken those words.

Returning to the house, the family held a private
memorial for Corinne. They were not releasing
anything to the media since her killer was still out
there. Although the twins asked for Charlene
constantly, Tyler had no answers for them. He, on the
other hand, was surprised at how they were handling
their grief. They'd told him that their mother was in
heaven with the kitten and that she had sent her twin
sister, Charlene, to take care of them. In their eight-
year-old minds, that was sufficient.

Tyler and Melvin pondered what Charlene had
told them of why Corinne was killed, but trying to get
to the bottom of it was impossible. They didn't even
know where to start until Tyler contacted the police
and requested an investigation into the death of his
wife. He made it clear that he suspected foul play and
that it must be kept quiet for the time being.

With an immediate homicide investigation open,
Melvin and Mona demanded a speedy resolution.
Being one of the most respected, influential, and

wealthy families living in Baldwin Hills, California, they received prompt attention from the detectives.

First, Tyler was able to confirm and verify everything Charlene had told him. He'd been surprised when he'd called the hall of records in the small town of Chesapeake. The friendly clerk who answered the telephone delighted in telling him she knew of the family. And yes, the twin girls' daddy had passed on almost two years ago.

The police investigation had also provided Tyler with reports showing that Charlene was more than just the art teacher she'd claimed. She'd been barely out of high school when, at the recommendation of her teachers she'd received a full college scholarship. She went to college in Virginia. She was, in fact, an art authority of sorts, specializing in Native American culture and artifacts. Her expertise was often called upon at the discovery of tribal sites in and around the state.

"Not just an art teacher, are you, Charlene McDonald?" Tyler murmured and remembered how much Corinne liked Native American art. When he'd tried to engage her in a conversation about it, she'd clammed up. But she adored dream catchers and insisted on hanging them in the bedrooms in their home, much to the displeasure of the interior decorator she'd hired.

The homicide investigator, Detective Vernon, proved to be professional and extremely good at his job. He scheduled a meeting with the family to update them on the investigation.

———∽∽∽———

That same afternoon Charlene borrowed Flo's car to go back to the estate. She had no idea what she was walking into.

After ringing the doorbell, Charlene forced her tight stomach to settle down. Then Daisy appeared at the door. Unsure of her reaction, Charlene smiled hesitantly. "Hi, Daisy," she said.

"Hi Charlene, it's nice to meet you," Daisy said, stepping back so she could enter.

The grandeur of the foyer never failed to take her breath away. Charlene let out a nervous sigh. "Is Mona home? I kinda wanted to…"

"Oh, my dear." A relieved Mona rushed to the foyer and embraced the young woman. She seemed genuinely glad to see her. "Thank God, Charlene! We've been so worried about you. Why didn't you call and let me know that you were okay?"

"I'm sorry, Mona. I just didn't think I should," Charlene said, looking beyond Mona's shoulder to see that they weren't alone. "Maybe I shouldn't have come." She thought she'd pick a time to visit when everyone would be at work and the kids at camp, but then she realized there was a death in the family. But she was heartsick to see Tyler's grief-stricken face. He stood at the living room doorway with Ryan and two men in suits. One stopped talking when he saw her standing there.

In spite of everything that had happened between them, Tyler's heart beat faster at the sight of her. He'd expected their first meeting to be awkward and uncomfortable. He still felt a lot of resentment toward her, but he couldn't deny that he was glad to see her.

The two detectives followed his gaze to the young woman who had just entered the room. They shared a look, each knowing without a doubt that this was the twin sister of Corinne Mills.

Melvin reached for Charlene, drawing her into the living room. "Missy, it's good that you're here." He introduced her to the detectives and encouraged her to take a seat. She nodded her consent to answering some questions for them.

Each appraised her with guarded, watchful eyes. Detective Vernon spoke first. "You're Corinne's twin sister…identical twin, it appears," he said, glancing at the photos in his hand.

"Yes," Charlene said, feeling nervous and small.

"We know that you met with your sister on the twenty-sixth of March," the detective said.

Glancing from one to the other Charlene nodded. "I didn't lie about anythin'." When she heard the children playing upstairs Charlene stood up quickly. "Can I go see the children?"

"No," Tyler said quickly, but then caught the look his mother gave him. "Not yet," he amended.

Easing back down to the couch, Charlene listened as Melvin explained to her they'd contacted the police to investigate Corinne's death.

Detective Vernon continued. "We went to the hotel and obtained the surveillance tape of the parking lot and surrounding property the night Corinne Mills was killed. We also have on tape when you arrived and when your sister arrived, Ms. McDonald."

Detective Vernon placed the security DVD into the player. He'd already seen the footage and knew the family was going to be disturbed to see what they were about to see. He had already warned them that it was graphic, and he was glad the DVD had no audio.

Charlene didn't want to look. She'd relived the dreadful nightmare in her head repeatedly since coming out of the coma, and didn't think she could actually watch it. But once it started playing she couldn't help herself. Her emotions echoed the family's as they gasped in horror at the drama unfolding on the television screen.

Finally, Charlene thought, *I can grieve. I can cry openly and not hide my pain.*

Moments later, Detective Vernon clicked the remote off. "This clearly is not just the homicide of Corinne Mills that we've witnessed, but it's an attempted homicide of Charlene McDonald, as well." He turned to Charlene. "Ms. McDonald, do you know why your sister was killed?" He watched her nod slowly. "I need you to tell me everything your sister told you that night."

"I can't do that. Not yet," Charlene answered in all honesty.

Surprised by her response, Detective Vernon said, "If you're knowingly withholding pertinent information that can aid in a homicide investigation, I can arrest you until you cooperate."

Melvin spoke up. "Nobody is being arrested in this house is that clear, detective?"

"Mr. Mills, I'm conducting an investigation and Ms. McDonald here has pretended to be your daughter-in-law. Now she's withholding vital information. But I'm concerned for *her* safety, too. That DVD shows she was meant to die as well," Detective Vernon stressed.

"But that's not why you want to question me." Charlene met the detective's eyes directly.

"Smart of you, and very correct," he said.

Tyler listened to the exchange, now feeling worse for sending Corinne from the house after watching the tapes. He heard Charlene agreeing to meet the detective at the police station, but she said she wanted to talk to the family first.

Although the detectives were eager to take her statement, they deferred to her request on the condition that she come in for questioning. After accepting the detective's card and watching as they were escorted to the door, Charlene turned to the family. Seeing the renewed sorrow on their faces broke her heart. She

loved these people, and, on some level, she knew her
sister did as well. It was important that they knew it,
too. "Please believe me when I say that Corinne loved
this family, 'cause despite everythin', she spoke highly
about each of you," she said quietly.

Mona insisted everyone head to the dining room
for the luncheon Daisy had set out.

At the table, Terri broke the strained silence. "So,
um, Charlene, Tyler did some checking into your
background and stuff. Seems you're well known in
your hometown."

She wasn't surprised that they had investigated her.
"It's a small town," Charlene said, noticing Terri
seemed pensive and not her usual self. But then again
nobody was acting normally after what they had just
seen. How could they?

"Where're you staying?" Terri asked.

"At a motel off the interstate," she said nervously.

"We called Flo, but she wouldn't tell us where you
were so Tyler fired her," Trish said.

"Yes, she told me. I wish you hadn't done that,
Tyler, 'cause nothin' I did was Flo's fault," Charlene
said, refusing to meet his gaze.

Tyler didn't respond. He couldn't. The imposter's
voice was affecting him someplace strangely. He hated
the feeling...whatever it was.

"Which motel, Charlene?" Trish asked.

"I don't know exactly. Flo programmed her GPS
for me to find your house. I just know I'm twelve
point eight miles from here and then I turn left...no,

right." A nervous sound escaped her. "Well, if I turn too far right, I'll be in the Pacific Ocean and we know how that'll turn out."

"So you don't know how to swim," Ryan said, recalling the night she fell into the pool.

Charlene murmured 'no' and then rested her hands in her lap. She was nervous, and Tyler's silence was making her already frayed nerves worse. She knew he had to be wondering how she could have played such a cruel joke on him, on all of them.

Mona patted her trembling hand. "You have nothing to be afraid of. We're all family."

"But I'm not your family. I may look like Corinne, but I sure don't talk or act the way she did."

"Well, you did a hell of a convincing job pretending to be her, didn't you," Tyler said.

Charlene didn't respond, but noticed Mona's hand tightened around hers.

Mona chose to downplay her son's outburst. "Grief is a process that we get through in our own way. Some people lash out like Tyler just did, others may curl up into a ball and cry their hearts out, and that's okay, too. But I'm telling you all, my family, it will pass and we will have each other for support as we grieve for Corinne." Mona's eyes circled the table. "Charlene here has had to grieve the loss of her twin sister all alone and, I might add, silently for three months. So let's remember that, too."

Charlene realized it was time she began speaking. "I told that detective that I wanted to talk to y'all, but mainly I kinda wanted to talk to Tyler."

Tyler had been listening to the imposter's voice. He kept seeing her in his arms and dancing out on the patio. He had to swallow hard before responding to what she'd just said. "Unless it's about the investigation into my wife's death, I don't want to hear anything you have to say," Tyler said quietly as he focused on mixing his salad greens.

Fingering the pattern on the rim of her coffee cup, Charlene said, "I understand." After staring into the cup for a few seconds, Charlene struggled to pull her words forth, regardless if he wanted to hear them or not. She didn't have a choice. It was a matter of the life and death of two innocent people. To prevent that, she was willing to endure Tyler's outbursts.

"The night of Trish and Ryan's anniversary party, I went to the ladies' room. When I came out I walked over to admire the garden through the side window. There were these huge plants, beautiful things I'd never seen before and…" Charlene hesitated, and started again. "Out of the blue a man grabbed me from behind. Obviously, he thought he knew me." Charlene pressed on. "He pushed me against the wall and felt me up somethin' awful." Wiping at her eyes remembering the incident, Charlene shuddered in disgust. She told them everything the man had said, and did. "I-I couldn't move. I begged him to get off me, and when he finally did, he asked if I was Corinne or her look-a-like who'd burned up in that car." Glancing up, she found she'd had everyone's attention and quickly dropped her eyes.

Clutching her chest, Mona's mouth hung open in stunned disbelief. "Oh, my! I remember finding you shaking life a leaf. Why didn't you tell me what'd happened?"

"Because what he'd said told me that he knew what happened to Corinne. But, I wondered, how could that be if Corinne hadn't told anyone about me? From his words and his actions, well, it also told me he was Corinne's lover…and he'd been invited to the party."

With his attention now fixed on her, Tyler said nothing.

Charlene edged on. "It-it happened again when Tyler and I went to that restaurant a couple weeks ago. This man…he followed me into the ladies' room. After my initial shock of findin' a man in the ladies' room, particularly this man, I-I couldn't believe it. He still believed I was Corinne. So, to find out what he knew, I decided to play along, even though I was sick and scared and I couldn't breathe with his hands all over me, touchin' me like that. Then he got angry and lashed out at me…at-at her, Corinne, I mean."

Tyler's attention was on her. He was thinking he'd been there each time she'd been accosted.

"He was her lover, and I *knew* for sure that he was one of the last people to see her the night she died. He said he missed her and he would've gotten suspicious if I didn't, you know, accept or return his affections. So as Corinne, I pretended to, um, enjoy his advances." Charlene held her anger in check at the memory of James's hands on her body, but her tears fell.

Tyler's fist hit the table. "So all of this was going on and you said nothing? I came into that ladies' room to find you in a state of shock. Why the hell didn't you say something? Why didn't you tell me?" Tyler bellowed.

"Because…" Charlene swallowed, searching to find words to say what she needed to say.

"Because she knows who he is, don't you, Charlene?" Ryan interrupted and they all watched her bob her head quickly. "You must tell us, Charlene, so we can find this man."

Tyler lost it when she closed her eyes and shook her head. "Who the hell is it?"

Charlene hesitated before finally turning to face him. She knew it was going to hurt him, but she also knew she had to tell him. "Tyler, this man and Corinne, they have devised a plan to destroy you and Mills Shipping. The contract that you think is canceled with Hunt Enterprises…well, it's not canceled. It never was. There have been six shipments, and there's another shipment comin' up…" She reached across the two empty seats for him, but Tyler snatched his arm back. "I've checked Corinne's emails and a ton of invoices and I know she was tryin' to get out of it, because she either didn't trust this Mr. Hunt person or…"

"Who is it?" Tyler repeated in a tone that was now quiet and ominous.

Just tell him.

"Okay-okay, listen…James Smith isn't your friend. He wants to destroy you and the family business. He-he was Corinne's lover," she said quickly and watched Tyler sink back against the chair. "She didn't love him, Tyler. He was just somebody who…who…"

"Fucked my wife!" Tyler cut her off mid-sentence, not in the least sorry for his language when the picture of Corinne and her lover—his so called friend, James Smith—flashed in his head. *Son of a bitch!*

"Well, that, yes, but I think he used her to get back at you for canceling the contract with Hunt, which meant terminating business with him."

Melvin asked Charlene to tell them everything she knew. "Oh, good Lord," Melvin said when she'd finished. "Nobody is to take any action, is that understood?" He looked directly at Tyler. "Son, I mean it, don't do anything. Hunt is connected to some criminals, big time."

"And, that's exactly what Corinne told me that night, Melvin. She said that they were using JS Computer Sales as somethin'," Charlene said.

"So this is why Detective Vernon wanted to question you. Charlene, he was correct in saying that you're in danger. They don't know it was Corinne who died. So, yes, now your life is in danger," Ryan said.

Yes, on some level Ryan wanted to see Tyler fail as interim CEO, but all of that went out the window in the face of the tragedy that had happened. And now, he was fully aware of the ramifications of all that Charlene had just told them.

"That detective knows I'll avenge Corinne's death, and I will. But I'm not stupid, either. Those cops have no interest in me. If I go there and tell what I know, you're right, I won't be safe. I'll be dead." Charlene leaned forward and finally took a gulp of her now lukewarm coffee.

"We'll protect you here, Charlene," Trish said, her voice strong with conviction.

"Of course we will. You'll stay here," Mona announced, echoed by everyone but Tyler.

Charlene stood up. "No. I've upset your household enough," she said in a firm voice. Then she turned to Tyler. "Can I go see the children? Just five minutes, 'cause I've got to get Flo's car back to her." When he finally nodded, Charlene rushed from the dining room.

Seeing his brother reach for his glass of iced tea, intent on finishing his lunch, usually quiet and reserved Ryan chose that moment to have his say. "Tyler, how could you sit there and not comfort her just now? Didn't you hear her pain, didn't you feel it? You're the cause of it, and yet you sit there unaffected. I just don't believe you, Tyler. You've slept with that woman!"

"Well, sure, but then I thought she was my wife…my cheating wife!" Tyler had had enough of Ryan, too, and told him so. "And, Ryan, here's something for you…you stay the hell out of my business, both personal and work-wise." He watched Ryan push his chair back and drop his napkin to the table. "Yeah, I get that you're pissed off about me being picked for CEO, but that's Mom and Dad's decision. What's happened with Corinne or Charlene or whoever won't change that fact, so as of today your bullshit comments and innuendos cease, you got that, baby brother?"

"Yeah, big brother, I got that. But do me a favor and spare me your crap because what has gone down over the past two days is much bigger than you! Corinne was a member of this family, and she's dead. I grieve for her children and you. I hurt for all of us because this is heartbreaking, damn it! But do you want to see Charlene dead, too?"

"Of course not, and stop making me out to be an unfeeling monster. She deceived me, duped all of us. But yes, I recognize her pain as I put mine aside for my deceased wife!"

"Well, you could've fooled me," Terri accused, on the verge of tears. "Tyler, she sat here and bared her soul to tell us about some sicko assaulting her and you don't feel horrible for her or for what she had to deal with?" Pushing her chair back Terri got up, clearly distressed. "Do you have any idea how horrible I feel for telling you about overhearing her on the telephone? I insinuated she was talking to a man and crying, but she was crying over her father's death. I feel so responsible. But Corinne, I-I mean Charlene, was right. You're a jerk. No wonder Corinne hooked up with another man and it killed her!" Sobbing loudly, Terri ran from the dining room, her sandals slapping against the kitchen floor until she went out onto the patio.

Seeing his mother's tight lips, Tyler turned his fury on her. "Please, Mom, don't bother telling me that once again I've upset the family mealtime. I get it. But I don't care anymore!"

Mona and Melvin had let the siblings air what was troubling them. It was necessary. Mona nodded sadly. "Tyler, I can only imagine what you must be thinking, but you have to set things right, dear. First, you need to go out to the patio and tell your baby sister that she's not responsible for what happened, or rather what didn't happen in your marriage."

Mona was barely holding on as she spoke softly and reasonably, all the while struggling to control her frustration and annoyance with her eldest son.

"Then you march yourself upstairs and you tell Charlene that you're sorry for not stepping up to the plate and protecting her when she was assaulted, not once but twice, while you sat idly by with your indifference…that same indifference that sent Corinne running to another man."

Rising from the table, Mona walked over to where Tyler sat with his forehead dropped to the heel of his hand. "Then you do whatever you have to do to get Charlene to stay here. Because we all know her measly thousand dollars won't last long in this city, and it truly is a matter of life and death." Lifting his chin, Mona searched Tyler's sad and weary eyes compassionately. "We love you, and, just as we'll protect her, we'll also protect you, because *I know* what's really in your heart even if you won't admit it."

Melvin came up and rested comforting hands on Mona's quaking shoulders. "Come, Mona, we've got some calls to make, and I, for one, could use a stiff drink."

And then Trish left. Ryan trailed behind her, but not before laying a comforting hand on Tyler's shoulder. Tyler reached up and covered Ryan's hand with his own.

Feeling emotionally empty, Tyler glanced out the dining room window and spotted Terri pacing on the patio. She was angrily slapping at Mona's prize-winning pink rose bushes and sending the full blooms flying out over the lawn. "Shit."

He left the dining room to go talk to her first.

—∾∾—

Before she went to visit with the twins, Charlene slipped into what had been her bedroom for almost three months. There, she retrieved the manila envelope of documents she'd previously printed in Corinne's office. Next she logged onto Corinne's laptop and, with the portable data drive she'd gotten from an office supply store, copied Corinne's files..

Now sitting on the floor visiting with the twins, she was delighted to find them happily talking as they ate lunch and watched a DVD. Much to her relief, they didn't ask any questions or seem traumatized by the events that occurred several nights ago.

That was where Tyler found her thirty minutes later. "I need to talk to you in your room...um, the room down the hall," he said from the doorway.

"Sure. I'll be right there," she said pleasantly, not wanting to alert the twins to friction.

A few minutes later Charlene joined him in the bedroom. Not knowing what was coming she stepped inside and closed the door behind her. He had his back to her, and, after several long seconds waiting for him to speak, she rushed ahead defensively. "So, go on and get it off your chest. Tell me what a terrible person you think I am because, to some extent, what I did was unforgivable. But Tyler, as I explained before..."

Turning, Tyler cut her off. "I wasn't thinking that."

Hope filled her instantly. Maybe he'd forgiven the awful deception she'd played on him. "Oh, then what are you thinkin'?" She inched closer to him.

"I was thinking how much I dislike you," he said.

Hope was snuffed out in a flash. Poised to touch his arm, she let her hand drop to her side. "Oh."

"That's all you can say after what you've done?" Yes, he thought, she'd deceived him the most. *Stupid fool.*

"Well, I've just never had another person say that they didn't like me before, so I'm not sure what to say or what you want me to say."

"I want you to explain again how you could so easily pretend to be my wife. Your deception was deep and personal. And it didn't stop you from sleeping with your sister's husband, did it?"

Indignant, Charlene blasted back. "What about you, Tyler? You only took me to your bed because you felt guilty for throwin' Corinne out of the house! What about your deception and your birthday present? Don't you think that was deep and personal, too, for Corinne? You slept with *her* all the while knowin' you were still gonna divorce her, file for custody of the twins and then fire her from her job when she recovered, so don't you even talk to me about deception. Not to mention that I didn't have to twist your arm to hop into bed with me every chance you got!"

"Well, I wasn't acting a part when I…" Tyler didn't want to say when he'd made passionate love to her. "I didn't want to sleep with you, I mean her. I found it strange that I…" Tyler stopped short, knowing that he was about to admit he had developed feelings for her.

"That you wanted her? I understand that. I know it wasn't about me when we slept together. All that

passion and tenderness, I knew it wasn't for me."
Charlene hated herself for voicing what was deep in
her heart. In spite of how wrong her deception was,
she'd secretly wanted all that passion and tenderness
for herself.

"But I did sense that something was different. I
just didn't know what, and I certainly would've never
suspected that it wasn't my wife I was..." Tyler felt like
he was in a battle with himself. "That I slept with." In
fact he was still in a battle because, until a few nights
ago, he simply couldn't understand why he was so
happy with his wife or why he couldn't get enough of
her or why he was beginning to feel whole again. Even
now, as he stood talking to his wife's twin sister, gazing
into her bottomless, deceitful, amber-colored eyes,
Tyler's gut tightened remembering her laugher ringing
in his ears when they'd relaxed contently together,
caressing the other long after their passions subsided.
He'd never gotten a chance to do that with Corinne
because after she'd done her 'wifely duty' she'd made a
beeline to the bathroom, leaving him alone and filled
with regret for having had to ask her in the first place.

"Well, you said Corinne wasn't the involved type,
unlike me, right? That's kinda explainable. You see it'd
been such a long time since I'd been with a man...So
yeah, I'm the involved type, and I'm not apologizin'
for being me," Charlene said plainly. "I'm not sorry
that we shared that closeness, Tyler. It was wonderful,
even if it was wrong." Charlene's voice faltered. "I
missed being close to someone like that and just being

held. I was lonely, Tyler, even before I came here to California. I was just so lonely, can you understand that?"

Tyler would not say that it was wonderful for him as well, and neither would he say he understood the feelings of loneliness. He wouldn't tell her, but he definitely understood.

When he didn't comment and his gaze rested somewhere above her head, Charlene went on. "I hope your dislike of me doesn't prevent you from at least lettin' me see the children from time to time. Please don't do that, Tyler."

"I don't want to talk about that right now. I let you see my children because they've been asking for you. I came up to tell you that my family wants you to stay here."

Charlene searched his weary eyes. "That's not what you want, is it?"

Tyler wasn't going to lie. "No, it's not, but you need security and I need distance from you. I can move back to our…back into my house," he said, although the home he shared with Corinne was the last place he wanted to be.

Charlene thought if she did stay he could have all the distance he wanted. His parents' house was a freaking mansion with room to spare. "Then no, I won't stay. I've done enough damage," Charlene said and turned to leave.

"Charlene."

At last he'd said her name. Charlene thought him saying her name softly like that could erase everything wrong at that very second.

Turning to face him, she saw his conflicting emotions, but mostly she saw his regret and his grief. It was still too painful to see on his handsome face. "Thanks for lettin' me see the twins. And I'm real sorry you fired Flo, but please give her a good recommendation."

With that, Charlene turned quickly and left the bedroom.

CHAPTER 20

Two nights later, Charlene was sitting on the stone back step outside her motel room. She'd watched the sun set several hours ago and still she sat there wondering what to do. Clearly, she couldn't stay there much longer. She'd refused Flo's offer to stay at her apartment because the woman had her son and his family already living there with her. The motel would suffice for now. It was just a cheap motel on the beach with clean bedding, but no air-conditioning, which was why she'd been sitting on the step. At ten o'clock at night it was still hot out. She didn't think she'd ever get used to the heat here.

The motel was just a stop until she left California. She was going to leave before the end of the week. She was tired. She'd called Detective Vernon asking for him to give her one more day and then she'd come to talk to him. She was surprised when he'd readily agreed to her request.

Leaning against the doorframe, she watched the foamy caps riding against the black water off in the distance. She reflected how much her life had changed in three months. But it was time to leave.

"Flo's GPS needs recalculating or a better satellite service. This place is much further than twelve point eight miles from my parents' house," Tyler said from behind her. He'd been standing there watching her unnoticed for several minutes.

Looking up quickly, Charlene was surprised to see him there. "You know, I probably misunderstood that voice on the GPS thing talkin' the whole drive out there. It's the voice of a cartoon character," she said and smiled. When he said nothing more, she scooted over and patted the step and was relieved when he sat down beside her. Charlene glanced up at the dark sky waiting for another tongue-lashing from him. As tired as she was, she didn't think she had the energy to give it back to him.

Tyler watched various people stroll along the beach. Most were vagrants. "Have you had dinner?" He heard her soft yes, all the while downplaying his relief at having found her. It wasn't easy. After searching several motels and coming up empty, he'd finally given up and called Flo. Then he'd had to do more than give her a good recommendation. He had to pay her five thousand dollars. Money well spent, but he would've paid ten times that to find Charlene.

"I had chicken and rice soup. Why?"

"I was just curious." But he was concerned and frightened for her. Reaching into his pocket, Tyler pulled out her pain and anti-seizure medications. "I thought you might need these."

Charlene snatched the bottles and clutched them tightly. "Oh, I so needed this pain medication last night. I couldn't sleep at all. It was so bad I came out here at four in the mornin'."

"That's not safe," Tyler mumbled, focusing on her bare feet buried in the sand.

"I was okay. Nobody bothered me. So, ah, what brings you 'round these here parts, mister?" Charlene joked, adding to her most exaggerated Southern accent in an attempt to gauge his mood. It was pretty bad, she guessed, because he wouldn't even look at her.

"Not funny. Everybody's concerned about you." As was he, he thought silently.

"Tell them I'm okay. I'm a tough girl."

Turning and scrutinizing her small frame, his expression was doubtful. "Right," he said.

"What's happening down at Mills Shipping?" Charlene asked.

"Everything's under control." She asked about Hunt's June twenty-sixth shipment.

"The delay you gave him will stand, but there'll be another hiccup in the schedule." He didn't want to alert her to what the FBI and the police were doing quietly behind the scenes down at the office. "You feel like taking a ride with me?"

Guarded at the change in topic, Charlene stared at him. "A ride? It's ten o'clock at night."

"It'll be okay. I'll have you back in an hour or so." Checking his watch, Tyler stood up.

"Well, okay. Let me go inside and wash this sand off my feet first," Charlene said, taking the hand he offered to help her up. She felt she had no reason not to trust him.

Minutes later, standing in the stifling hot motel room, Tyler saw it was just that…a rent-by-the-hour hot box. There was a bed with no headboard, a dresser, a lamp, and a table with a hotplate and microwave. Each had to be fifteen years old, and the television set was just as old. In the trash he spotted an empty soup container and lots of tissues. He surmised she'd been crying. Turning when she exited the tiny bathroom, Tyler glanced at her T-shirt and blue jeans. "Do you have anything black, like jeans and a shirt?"

"No, sorry." They left the motel and walked to Tyler's car, which was parked up on the road. "Would you believe my suitcase has up and gone from that fancy hotel," Charlene said, talking because it took her mind off how good he looked. Dressed in black jeans, black boots, and fitted black polo, she had to force down the heat rising to her face.

"What do you mean?" Tyler asked, opening his car door to blasting music from inside.

Charlene gaped at Terri as she watched the girl climb from the driver's seat and into the back seat. "Terri, girl, what're you doin' here?" Actually, Charlene was glad to see the young woman who'd become her friend over the past three months.

"We gonna have some fun, so get in, Charlene," Terri said, grinning.

Tyler asked again about her missing luggage. "Oh, when I arrived at the hotel Corinne had arranged for me, I knew I wasn't gonna be stayin' there. It probably cost three hundred dollars a night. So I asked the desk clerk if he could hold my bag until I met my sister. He said okay, but I never went back down for it. I called a couple weeks ago and it isn't there. I think it's been stolen or thrown in the trash 'cause it was old."

Tyler knew the nightly rate for the five-star hotel started at six hundred dollars a night for a single. "I'll go by tomorrow and check. You need clothes?" He knew that she did because he'd seen her wear the jeans and pink T-shirt she had on several times before.

"I brought her a few things," Terri said, repeating what Charlene had told her previously, that she just couldn't bring herself to wear any of her sister's clothes.

A short while later, Tyler pulled up to the back of a garage and flicked his car lights. The large bay doors opened silently and light spilled out onto the road. Tyler got out of the car.

Charlene squinted at the building through the windshield. "What's goin' on?"

"It's okay. Come on." He held his hand out for hers.

"Yeah, Charlene, let's go inside. We have a surprise for you. It's going to make you feel all warm and fuzzy." Terri chuckled and all but pushed Charlene out the car.

Inside the garage Charlene spotted several men working on cars, mostly painting them, but as they walked deeper into the garage one car stood out. She knew that car! She recognized it as the vehicle Corinne had stepped out of that night in the parking lot. It was James Smith's car, jazzy and sleek. Tyler gave her a pair of goggles and gloves, telling her to put them on. When he held out a baseball bat, Charlene's jaw dropped. "What's that for?"

"Okay, it's like this." Tyler nodded toward the car. "That's James's BMW. That car is his pride and joy. It gets detailed every week, and it cost him over one hundred grand. It's customized to his specifications, right down to the heated seats for his flat ass. Now, for every single time that son of a bitch groped you and felt you up, take a swing at it."

"What?" Charlene laughed at such an absurd thing. "Are you crazy? I-I can't do that."

"And why the hell can't you, Charlene? Girl, that man is a dog. What he did to you was wrong and he's gotta pay." Terri snatched the baseball bat from Tyler and thrust it into Charlene's hand. "Now, batter up."

"But that car is so beautiful and expensive and…" Charlene said lamely, looking from the bat to the both of them.

"He grabbed your breasts!" Tyler had come up behind her and whispered hotly in her right ear. He jumped out of the way when she gave the hood a tentative whack. "Okay, so that's how we roll. Got it, Charlene? Now, he put his nasty, wet lips on your face and neck." He applauded when she hit the hood of the car harder this time; he could tell she was beginning to enjoy this.

It was then that it all became more real for Charlene. She watched them clapping and cheering her on, and had to angle her head because she could only hear it in her right ear. *Corinne's dead.* "Yeah," she yelled. Enraged, she whacked the car again.

Terri cheered. "Now that's what I'm talking about! Act like it's his head and hit it again!"

Charlene dug the ball of her foot onto the dusty cement floor as she poised to take another swing. Now that she knew what the objective was she was ready. It wasn't a home run she was going for; rather it was to demolish James's beloved car. Oh, yeah, she needed this.

After five minutes, Charlene was thoroughly exhausted but had exorcised James from her mind. She gladly accepted the bottle of orange soda pop Tyler passed her. "This is hard work."

Tyler blotted her sweat-drenched forehead with the sleeve of his shirt. "Yeah, but you missed some parts," he said, handing over a handful of bills to the two shop guys who'd cheered her on. After moving behind a protective area as instructed by the guys, the trio watched the two men rip the interior of the car to shreds with the blades of sharp utility knives.

When they were finished, Terri opened a small can of paint she'd retrieved from the trunk of Tyler's car. She happily painted out the words BITCH BOY on both of the crumbled side panels of the car. She posed beside the car when Tyler pulled out his cell phone and snapped a picture. The color was an atrocious mix of orange, yellow, and red.

"Ready for the second part?" Tyler asked Charlene.

"I'm almost afraid to ask," Charlene said, giving Terri a high five for the paint job.

"Then don't. Just watch." All three watched as the now unrecognizable car was loaded onto a flatbed tow truck, covered completely with a black tarp, and driven away.

A few minutes later, after following behind the tow truck, the trio watched as the chop shop employees silently unloaded James's wrecked car and placed it back where Tyler had had them pick it up an hour earlier...in front of James and Mia's front door. "Just so you know, I didn't do this for Corinne. She obviously wanted James by choice. I did this because you didn't make that choice, and James put his hands on you inappropriately," he said. "So how did it make you feel to trash his car, honestly?"

She longed to touch his hand resting on the gear shaft. "I feel relieved."

"I feel great," Terri called out from the back seat, passing Charlene a candy bar.

"Now for the finale," Tyler said, getting out of his car. Using a remote, he set off the rewired alarm in James's battered car and waited.

Within seconds, James came running from the house wearing only boxer briefs, black slippers, and white crew socks. He stared, unable to believe that the wrecked and ruined vehicle sitting in front of his home was his beloved beemer. He searched the street to see who was responsible for the senseless destruction of his beautiful car. Suddenly he spied Tyler leaning nonchalantly against his own car across the road.

At first, James couldn't comprehend why Tyler was there. Then fear, understanding, and, finally, rage penetrated his brain. Suddenly and without warning he bellowed and charged like a bull in heat.

Tyler stood his ground, shifting his body slightly to a more defensive posture as an enraged and out-of-control James advanced on him.

Out of sight in the back seat of the car, Charlene and Terri gripped each other's hands, watching wide-eyed and astonished as the drama unfolded in front of them. Charlene was alarmed at the fury and pure hatred on James's face as he loomed ever closer to where Tyler was waiting. *I'll bet Corinne never saw this side of lover boy*, she thought to herself. Just for a moment she worried about what would happen to Tyler. She needn't have.

Tyler watched and waited until he could practically see the whites of James's hate-filled eyes. Just before James reached him, Tyler drew his arm back and swung his fist, releasing all of the anger, hurt, pain, and frustration he had been holding inside. His fist struck James squarely in the nose, instantly breaking it and dislocating his jaw. The impact was so hard that it lifted James completely off his feet and he landed on his back, legs sprawled, out cold in the middle of the road.

Tyler stood over the unconscious man, holding his throbbing and rapidly swelling hand. He knew that by tomorrow he was going to be in a hell of a lot of pain, but damn it, it was worth it. He smiled through the pain, quite pleased with himself. His smile faltered when he realized that he would have to explain to Mia what he had just done. Another innocent person victimized by greed and selfishness. He was tempted to throttle James. But seeing that the man hadn't moved, Tyler felt a twinge of disappointment. He guessed he would have to be satisfied with James's jaw wired shut and the pretty boy's face disfigured. He could live with that.

During the drive back to Charlene's motel, Tyler told her how devastated Mia had been when he informed her about James and Corinne. Naturally, she was upset. He tried to be as brief and as gentle as he could; he owed her that much. They had been friends for many years. She certainly deserved better than James, Tyler thought.

Later, Tyler also told Charlene that the F.B.I was actively investigating James's company and Hunt Enterprises again. He added that Detective Vernon was assisting in the investigation.

Charlene now knew why Detective Vernon didn't seem so eager to question her again.

———

The following afternoon Charlene borrowed Flo's car again. This time she drove out to Tyler and Corinne's house. On the solitary, scenic drive she reflected on what'd happened the previous evening. They'd stopped for ice for Tyler's bruised hand. With Terri driving, Charlene gently held the ice cubes to his swollen knuckles. Feeling the warmth of desire stirring inside of her, she didn't dare meet Tyler's eyes. She had always abhorred fighting and violence, but seeing Tyler making a stand, knocking James out with a single punch, had given her a charge. He'd been defending her honor. He'd done it for Corinne, too, but mainly he'd done it for her. No one had ever done that for her before and she found his chivalry sexy as hell. She just hoped he couldn't read all that in her eyes.

He'd told her to go in and pack up her few things. Although Charlene tried to argue, she relented when both he and Terri insisted she stay at a decent hotel or they were taking her back to their parents' home, by force if necessary. Charlene discovered that resisting the Mills siblings was futile. So they agreed on a respectable hotel that offered some security.

Arriving at Tyler and Corinne's house, Charlene let herself in with the extra key that'd been in Tyler's room at his parents' home. She'd taken it when she went to retrieve the papers.

It was that afternoon that Charlene discovered something extremely useful.

She'd gone into Corinne's bedroom. "Okay, sis, I've come here because I have this peculiar feelin' that you left somethin' here for me to find. Now, I'm kinda thinkin' it's a clue to what you'd told that man you had that night up on the road," she said out loud as she stood in the middle of the room. Closing her eyes, Charlene recalled that Corinne had told the man that she'd seen to it that he got caught. "Okay, that musta meant you'd set a trap, so what was it?"

Moving around the bedroom, Charlene fought to recall another memory of that night. When it hit, her eyes widened and she stopped in her tracks. "Wait…it was in the hotel room…what was it that Corinne had said?" Having stopped in front of the vanity dresser, Charlene eased down on the stool and glanced up at her reflection in the mirror. Absently, she wondered if Corinne had ever envisioned her face. It was something Charlene had done herself many times over the years. Waving off another pang of grief, Charlene casually opened Corinne's jewelry box and spotted her sister's collection of lockets. There were seven in all.

Smiling sadly at another distant memory, she recalled what Corinne had said. "Every year I get a new locket and put a new set of pictures in it."

Charlene's smile suddenly disappeared. She picked up the lockets one by one and opened each locket. "Seven lockets," she whispered. "The twins turned eight years old in January, so where's the eighth locket?" She searched the jewelry box. "Where's the one that Terri showed me in the hospital…"

More of Corinne's words from that awful night came back just then and replayed themselves in Charlene's head. *I have a micro-memory card with tons of data and documents. I've saved it all.* But Charlene remembered being so excited staring at the tiny pictures of the twins that she'd tuned out some of what Corinne had said. Only now, she heard it.

A chill snaked down her spine, causing her skin to prickle as she held onto another memory. It was the second she'd fallen over the cliff. "I fell when I reached for…that locket!

"Oh, my God. That's it. That has to be it," Charlene said in a rush and looked up at the mirror again. For a split second, it seemed her reflection smiled and nodded. Goosebumps covered her forearms. Charlene jumped up and rubbed at her eyes, not believing what she thought she saw. She was too frightened to look into the mirror again so she glanced wide-eyed around the room instead…checking to make sure no one was in the room with her.

She thought she had to be hallucinating. Yes, that was it! But still, her smiling face had stared back at her when she knew she wasn't smiling or nodding. Perhaps, she wondered if her strange vision was because she was close to getting the information that her sister died for…because Corinne had thrown it over the cliff in the hope that Charlene would catch it.

Maybe she wasn't hallucinating after all.

━━∾∾━━

Furious that his shipment had been delayed, Mr. Hunt was at a point where he didn't know who he could trust. He knew it certainly wasn't the man on the other end of his cell phone. Impatiently, he tried to focus on what James was saying. "What…car accident?"

As painful as it was for James to talk past his wired jaw, broken nose, and missing teeth, he hated having to repeat the lie he'd just told Mr. Hunt. "I-I said I had a car accident. My-my car is…it's to-totaled."

"James, I don't care about your problems, least of all your automobile issues. I'm scrounging around to find other means of getting my shipments out. Now unless you can tell me that you can persuade your girl-friend to do something about that on her end, then you're wasting my time," Hunt said, his patience long gone for the man who'd become a whining pest.

James balled his hand into a tight fist. He'd been trying to contact Corinne all day and still she hadn't called him. She had to know what Tyler did, he thought. "Mr. Hunt, ah, I'll get your shipments to go through Mills Shipping as planned. Just give me a couple of days. I-I have another contact and I'll arrange a pickup of the co-containers as we planned."

"And what about her? Has she turned on you, James?" Hunt listened closely, noticing hesitation in James's voice.

"No, no, absolutely not! She's still, um, she's still re-reliable." James winced painfully. In his mind, he was no longer one hundred percent sure about Corinne's loyalty.

"All right, I want confirmation of the containers no later than tomorrow."

"Sure, um…" James hedged, grimacing as pain shot from his jaw to his bandaged nose.

"What now?" Mr. Hunt didn't hide his irritation or annoyance with James when he mentioned money. "Are you crazy, trying to have this conversation on the phone?"

"I need to know that, well, that everything is still, you know, okay." James relaxed when Hunt said everything was okay and disconnected the call.

———

After leaving Corinne and Tyler's house, Charlene stayed busy. First, she went to the office supply store and made an extra copy of the invoices and emails. But before she returned Flo's car, Charlene had one more stop to make. She had to go back to the Mills house to get Corinne's locket…the eighth locket.

Charlene had a pretty good idea where the locket was. It had to be somewhere among the box of things that Shelly had so carefully looked after. Arriving at the house at the exact time she'd planned, Charlene was sure no one would be home except for Daisy. Sure enough that was the case. "Hi, Daisy."

"Hi, Charlene, come on in." Daisy hugged the young woman. "I sure miss you around here. It's just not the same, you know."

"Yes, I-I know. Um, Daisy, I came by to bring Shane a new paint set and I got Shelly some of that silly putty stuff she likes. Would you mind if I just took it up to their rooms so they'll be surprised when they get home from camp today?" As she spoke, Charlene had been inching toward the staircase.

"Oh, sure, go on up," Daisy said before hurrying back to the kitchen where her afternoon soap opera was playing on television.

——~~~——

Two hours later, sitting on her bed in the Holiday Inn, Charlene sat surrounded by well over one hundred pieces of paper. With everything laid out according to dates, she'd bundled up one set and packed it into her bag, while the other set she would prepare to be mailed to an FBI agent whose business card she'd found in Corinne's office.

Wishing she had more time, Charlene put on her reading glasses and finally pried open the eighth locket. Pushing away a pang of heartache, it was soon replaced with the knowledge that Corinne had seen her children's beautiful faces moments before she died. She'd opened the locket and kissed the tiny pictures before she'd gone down to the parking lot to meet James.

"Could it really be this easy? Lord, I sure hope so," she mumbled. Then, using the end of a safety pin, Charlene pricked around the picture several times to lift the insert holding Shelly's picture. A very small, flat object fell into her hand. Picking it up she realized it was a microchip of some kind, and it was in the tiniest Ziploc bag she'd ever seen. Next, she went to work on the other frame holding Shane's picture. Sure enough, there was another tiny Ziploc bag with another microchip. "Now what in the world are these things?" Holding the plastic bags up to the light, Charlene couldn't make heads or tails of them but she knew where to start checking: the public library just two blocks up the street from her hotel.

Thirty minutes later, sitting at a computer terminal in the library, Charlene searched the internet for microchips. She had a slight headache and prayed it wasn't a precursor to a seizure. She quickly scanned more sites until she found what she'd been looking for, or so she thought. From what she could tell, the microchip could be accessed by simply putting it into a slot on a computer. Charlene couldn't imagine such a tiny thing could fit into any computer, but read on.

When a young boy about sixteen years old sat down to use the computer terminal beside her, she decided to elicit his help. "Excuse me, but do you know if a computer can really have a space to hold a tiny microchip thing like this," she asked, pointing to the one on the monitor.

The student took one look at her monitor. "Yeah, sure, but that's not a microchip, miss. It's actually a micro-mini scan disk and it can hold gigabytes of data." Seeing that the pretty woman probably didn't understand a word he was saying, the student smiled politely. "Okay, a disk like that can hold a bunch of information, you know, like documents and pictures, but that one there is primo. They're just coming out on the market. You don't need a computer if you've got a reader or digital camera."

"Huh?" Charlene still didn't quite understand him.

"Okay, um, first, do you have a micro scan disk like that one?" When the woman nodded the student was excited. "Jeez, you do? Then I've got my camera." He then explained so that she could understand. "The pictures will be super sharp. Do you know what hi-def is?" He doubted she did. Too bad, he thought, because she sure was pretty. Not smart technically, but pretty.

"Yes, hi-def is a really clear picture, right?" Every television in the Mills' house was hi-def.

Scrunching up his face, the boy laughed. "Well, okay, yeah," he said.

"Yes, so you have a camera that maybe I can see what's on my micro thingy?"

Laughing again the student said, "I sure do. Say, where're you from anyway?" he asked reaching into his weighted down backpack and pulling out a small camera.

"Virginia," Charlene said, handing him one of the tiny Ziploc bags.

"Oh, you've from the country, huh? I could tell by the way you talk," he mumbled as he pulled out a pair of plastic, cotton-tipped tweezers and carefully removed the disk. He then inserted the disk into his camera. "My parent's went to Virginia once. The brought back a lot of ham." The boy laughed suddenly. "Oh, I get it now, Virginia Baked Ham!"

"Um-hmm. What's your name?" Charlene watched him press several buttons on his camera, which was only slightly bigger and thicker than a credit card.

"Everybody calls me Web Man because they think I'm a computer geek because I can do a lot on the internet. The name sucks, right?" She said no and asked for his given name. "Oh, my name is Tyrone," he said.

"Okay, Tyrone, I'll give you one hundred dollars if you can print out for me what's on that disk, and I'll give you another hundred if you do this one, too,"

Charlene said and pulled out the other plastic bag from her pocket.

"You got a deal. So what's your name, miss?" She told him. "Well, Miss Charlene, let's start printing," Tyrone said, reaching back into his backpack again.

Charlene grinned when he pulled out a full pack of copy paper and a large plastic bag containing an assortment of wires and adapters from his backpack.

———⁓———

On the pretense that Corinne was still alive but was extending her recovery at home, Tyler had issued a memo to the staff advising them that two temporary assistants had been hired to pick up where Corinne left off. Truth was, they were FBI agents named Mallory and Ron. They'd come to the Mills offices to search for evidence indicating Hunt was still using their shipping services. Problem was, so far they found nothing.

Reporting their findings to Tyler and Melvin in a meeting, Tyler grew uneasy hearing that Corinne's office computer had been stripped clean. In fact, she'd never logged onto it.

Hearing that, Tyler gave them Corinne's laptop. There they found only traces of document names. The actual files and documents had been deleted. For the sake of time, the agents suggested Corinne's laptop be taken to their headquarters for further search and analysis.

But Tyler already had an idea what'd happened to Corinne's documents.

———

At seven o'clock that evening Tyler knocked on Charlene's hotel room door. When she opened the door, he backed her into the room. "Where is it?"

Charlene was thankful that she'd had the fore-thought to hide all the documents she got off the chips, which included manifests and pictures. She'd put them into the half-sized refrigerator in her room for safekeeping. "What you talkin' about?" She was surprised to see him. "Did James buy himself another car that we can demolish?" she asked inno-cently.

Instinctively he knew she was hiding something. "I know you deleted those documents from Corinne's computer, but you're smart, Charlene. You wouldn't have just deleted them if you thought you'd need them in your own little investigation. Sound familiar to you?" Tyler asked, not letting her sidestep him. He stepped closer, forcing her to back up.

Uncomfortable with his nearness, Charlene ducked beneath his arm. "Stop cornerin' me." She decided she wasn't going to pretend that she hadn't deleted the documents from Corinne's computer when she'd gone to the house to get the papers. "Tyler, if somethin' happens to me, I'll make sure those who I believe are responsible for killin'

Corinne will be held accountable and brought to justice."

Tyler stared down at her beautiful face. "Don't give me that. Isn't that the same thing you said that Corinne tried to do? And look what happened to her. Don't be stupid. Just give me whatever is was that you got off both of her computers, and I want all of it."

"Whoa. Wait a minute. What you mean both of them? What're you talkin' about?"

"Her office computer was replaced. The one you used isn't hers. Neither she, nor you, have ever logged onto it. So you tell me what's going on?"

"I don't know." Charlene's mind spun. "I only deleted a file of invoices and emails from Corinne's laptop, that's all, honest." He didn't believe her and proceeded to search her room.

Charlene followed him around the room as a more troubling thought surfaced. "Tyler, you know the last time I used Corinne's office computer. I couldn't have switched it."

Abruptly ending his search, Tyler thought. A twisted picture of sabotage had already formulated in his mind based on the information the FBI agents had already given him. He'd even wondered how far back Corinne and James's plans went.

Charlene guessed what he'd been thinking and held back the instinct to reach out and touch his arm compassionately. She knew he'd flinch away from her again.

Without another word, Tyler turned and walked out of the room.

━━∿∿∿━━

From the time Tyler left, Charlene had pulled out her notepad and had been writing out and studying the sequence of codes she'd found on Corinne's computer. They just had to mean something, she thought.

It was three o'clock in the morning before she finished scribbling down the codes. Finally something stood out that caused her brow to furrow. Mills Shipping containers all began with the letter P or D preceding a number.

Retrieving her chilled packet of papers from the refrigerator, she dumped them onto the bed. Sorting through the pile for the invoices, she noticed they all were for office furniture.

At first Charlene didn't know why the pictures had been taken. They only showed large boxes labeled office desks, chairs, and filing cabinets, but on a closer look, that stuff was being picked up from the back of James's company. The time stamped in the bottom corner of the pictures showed it was two forty-five in the morning. "Who picks up stupid office furniture at that hour of the mornin'?" she mumbled aloud. But Charlene's mind was running double-time to keep up with all of the fragmented pieces of information. It was there in front of her…she needed to concentrate harder to see it.

Straightening up quickly, she pushed all of the papers further back on the bed. Next, as if playing a game of solitaire, Charlene began to pluck individual items from the scattered pile.

In the first row she laid out pictures of the Mills Shipping containers. There were six in all. Next, copies of the original invoices were placed on the second row. There were six invoices. This was followed by several emails dated just before and immediately after the shipments were picked up. Lastly, the final row was made up of the pictures of the furniture boxes being picked up from JS Computer Sales.

Shrugging her shoulders, she said, "Okay, so what's the big to-do? I don't get it. What am I missing that Corinne had gone to such lengths to hide? There has to be more to this…wait a minute." Suddenly, Tyler's false accusation filled her head. It had to be sabotage of some sort, calculated and well planned out. Something more was going to happen.

"Okay, so Corinne was havin' an affair with James and…" Charlene remembered Tyler and Mia escorting her from the ladies' room to the table and Mia saying they were celebrating a big contract James's company had received for several computers.

"So why the pictures of the shipping containers? What's the significance of them," she mumbled. Charlene thumbed through the remaining pile of papers until she came up with an email Corinne had sent to James. Struggling through the cryptic wording, Charlene understood that Corinne wanted James to get her tracking devices, six in all, that she would personally pick up and activate.

"Now how would she do something like that?" But thinking like Corinne probably had, Charlene grabbed up her notepad and tore off six blank pages. Then she placed them, one by one, on another row of her solitaire layout. With her heart racing, she proceeded to write one code on each of the solitaire stacks. "Oh, my God!" The picture suddenly fell into place.

All six codes tied back to the Mills Shipping containers. James's company was the pick-up point for dummy boxes marked 'office furniture' that were transported to the Mills warehouse and loaded for transport…all legal, with doctored invoices and manifests that would show office furniture.

The picture that had formed in Charlene's head turned ugly, and she had an idea what was really in those boxes. She'd figured out what Corinne's sequence of letters meant. D-Drugs, M-Money and AAR- Automatic Assault Rifles. Charlene couldn't figure out what PS stood for.

Turning and flopping down onto her solitaire layout, shocked, Charlene grimaced. "And that's why they killed you, Corinne. This information could bury Hunt and James."

Making a tight fist, her face soured. "So now I have it. But there's one more thing that I need to do." According to one of Corinne's last emails to James,

she'd indicated she would activate the tracking devices
while the shipments were en route. "So wait, that
means she would have activated them by
computer...but she hadn't, and now those containers
are delayed."

With a sinking feeling in the pit of her stomach,
Charlene didn't believe that Corinne would go to such
lengths and not walk away without something. "No,
she wouldn't. But she did want two things: her children, and, knowing she would soon be fired, she
wanted money...PS stands for payments," she said,
her heart plummeting.

Charlene pulled a small piece of paper from her
purse. It had been tucked in Corinne's Bible. At first
she thought the information unimportant, but now
she unfolded the piece of paper and studied Corinne's
writing. Charlene realized what it was. It was a bank
account number. It was an account in the name of
McDonaldson. The PIN was their father's birth date.

It all seemed to fit. Charlene shook her head in
disgust. "This is ridiculous. Damn it, Corinne, how
greedy were you?" Sensing she had no time to waste,
Charlene gnawed on the inside of her lip, deep in
thought. "I need to find out, but who can I call now
to help me?"

Digging into her purse again, she pulled out
another piece of scrap paper. Ignoring the fact that it
was four in the morning, she dialed the phone
number on the paper.

CHAPTER 21

At eight-thirty the following evening, Tyler was still in his office working. He'd often worked late when large shipments of merchandise were prepped and loaded onto the Mills trucks. It was generally a noisy process since so many workers had to be on hand, and tonight was no exception. With the warehouse managers, Donte, Darrell, and Maceo, following a tight schedule, the process was timed and well planned, and the forklift operators were quick to fill the containers. Mills had thirty forklifts, and twenty-seven of them were on the move tonight.

From his office, Tyler could hear the clamor and ruckus going on down on the docks, four floors below his office. It didn't bother him at all.

Whenever they were down a man or two, he'd go down and help out. As part of his training to one day be CEO, his father had made sure Tyler learned every aspect of the business from the ground up. Closing his eyes, he recalled how he'd met Corinne. She'd been hired to work in the offices as an administrative assistant.

Tyler realized he'd missed a lot of things lately. With an unsettling thought, he realized he missed his wife…only it wasn't Corinne he missed. He was saddened deeply that the mother of his children was dead. It didn't even seem real that they wouldn't see her again. He didn't miss her as his wife because she'd stopped being that many years ago. They just existed in a large fancy house and shared nothing except the children.

But he did mourn her. And yet, Tyler couldn't explain what had happened since he'd brought Charlene home to his parents' house to recover.

His world had suddenly opened up again and he'd become excited to rush home…not that he hadn't done that before, eager to see his children. In fact, he'd spend hours down on the floor playing with them. But he'd also missed the simple act of sharing his life with his wife.

He was secretly jealous of Ryan and Trish, the closeness they shared, the obvious love.

He'd even thought he was falling in love all over again with the woman he'd married years earlier, only it wasn't his wife. It was Charlene he'd unknowingly fallen in love with, and he wasn't alone, it seemed. The rest of his family had grown to love Charlene, too.

"How could I not know? Yes, Charlene was right. I'm such a stupid idiot," Tyler said to himself. With renewed frustration, he got up from his desk and strode over to the window. He thought about going home, but since Shane and Shelly were at a sleepover, he didn't feel much like going home and being smothered by his mother, Trish, and Terri. Although loving and supportive, they were driving him crazy with their barrage of questions about Charlene.

He'd really had some explaining to do the night he almost broke his hand on James's face. His mother and sister-in-law had fussed over him while Terri regaled them with an exaggerated version of his exploit. His mother clucked disappointedly at her son resorting to 'street fighting like a thug.'

Absently looking down at the activity going on below him in the warehouse, Tyler flexed his still-sore hand. A movement caught his eye. He wondered if the same warehouse worker he'd reprimanded last month for drinking a beer while working was at it again.

He watched the man drop low and come up along the side of one of the containers set to be filled with crates. Next, he watched the worker climb inside the container. "Damn it."

Thinking of all the possibilities, all of them dangerous, Tyler snatched his suit jacket from the coat hook and hurried from his office. His intention was to fire the idiot on the spot. Tyler didn't care if they played loud music or basketball in their down time. On many occasions he joined them, but he had zero tolerance for drinking. It was a safety hazard for every person on the docks and the worker, Jimmy, knew better.

Once on the ground floor and out on the container holding area, Tyler was careful of his footing as he steered around hundreds of pallets and ropes scattered about. He went to the empty container he'd seen the worker climb up into and called out to him. He shined the wide angled flashlight he'd brought with him into the container. "Jimmy…" Tyler's breath left him in a rush. His mouth dropped open when he saw Charlene crouched down at the back end of the container with her arm reaching into the area above the wheel well. "What the hell…?"

Busted. That's what Charlene thought as she came to her feet and slowly walked toward the open door. When Tyler held his hand up to help her down, Charlene struggled to come up with an explanation.

Tyler could only gape at her contrite and red face for several seconds. Then he let loose. "You start talking right now, because I'm getting a very disturbing picture in my head!"

You should've seen the picture that was in my head, Charlene thought. Wiping perspiration from her forehead, unknowingly leaving dirt smudges on her face, she went into an explanation. "Okay, but you really have to listen to me. That shipment, you know the one you said had a hiccup, well, it's still being shipped…tonight. The truck is gonna be switched in Arizona, and, Tyler, your two truck drivers who run that route, well, they're gonna be killed in that switch and their poor bodies dumped." That was another tidbit Tyrone had found on the disk, a link to a phone call Corinne had somehow recorded where Hunt made the order to his henchman.

Tyler gaped at her, unconvinced, trying to absorb all that she'd said. He realized he had no reason not to believe her. Still…"But that cannot be, unless…"

"Unless somebody workin' at Mills is on Hunt's payroll," Charlene said breathlessly.

Just then both of them turned quickly, hearing footsteps running in their direction.

Recognizing who it was, Tyler threw his hands up in exasperation. "Shit! What are *you* doing here?" He grabbed a heavily panting Terri by the arm.

Pursing her lips, Terri sent a guilty-as-ever look up to her brother. Wheezing and trying to catch her breath, she bent over, her braids swaying as she dropped her elbows to her thighs. "Sorry, Charlene, but I had to hustle it back over here from where that other container was because I saw something. I'm not saying they're big rats, but trust me, they're big four-legged, furry things that scared the you-know-what out of me." Finally standing upright, Terri frowned impishly up at Tyler and shrugged her shoulders. "How ya doing, Tyler?"

Tyler gasped. "What? How am I doing? Are you out of your mind traipsing around down here?" Pulling Terri over to stand beside Charlene, Tyler could only mutter incoherently for several seconds. "It's dangerous, damn it!"

Terri waved a hand. "Please! Who you telling? I almost got ate up by giant rodents, and you know they would have chewed off my toes first." She began stamping her feet to ward off anything that may have been crawling nearby. "You need some serious pest control down here."

"Then you should have worn proper shoes if you were going to be involved in some type of covert ops on a dock!" With his patience past the boiling point, Tyler stepped back, looking up at the container. He knew this particular one was going to Arizona, but didn't know it was for Hunt. He wondered how Charlene knew that. Just then he noticed that her right hand was balled up. "What's in your hand, and what exactly were you doing up in that container?" He'd already figured whatever she'd been doing was part of her own investigation…and she'd involved his feeble-minded, thug-wannabe younger sister.

Charlene hesitated. "Tyler, didn't you hear me? You've got people, who knows how many, on your payroll who're probably workin' for…"

"Oh, right, and did she tell you what's going to happen?" Terri asked, still stamping her feet.

"She told me," Tyler answered Terri, but kept his eyes on Charlene. "What's in your hand, Charlene?" When she made no move to show him, he took her hand and gently pried her fingers open. He immediately recognized the single tracking device. "Shit," he swore, but had no time to question her further when he heard a group of warehouse workers coming up behind him. From their conversation, he knew they were ready to load that container.

Putting a finger up to his lips, he eased them quietly back into a dark niche between the containers.

Combined with what Charlene told him and what the F.B.I was doing, then yes, he would agree he had employees on the take. Turning, he spotted one of the managers, Maceo, going over the manifests with the loaders. When the man looked up and saw Tyler, he immediately stopped in his tracks. The man's shock registered on his face.

"Hiya, boss. What ya' doing there?" Maceo asked, surprised to see Tyler.

"Hey, man, I just needed to make sure this container was labeled correctly. We don't want any delays at the truck stops." Tyler felt Charlene shift behind him. He winced. Feigning interest, he listened as Maceo agreed, but assured him that he would recheck the paperwork. All the while, Tyler was concentrating on keeping his body rigid. He simply couldn't understand what Charlene and Terri were doing behind him. *Probably looking for somewhere to run off to...so now they're scared?*

It started with a fluttering of her right eyelid and then a twitching in her shoulders. *Oh, please no...not now...*

In the dark alcove, Charlene could do nothing but stare at the back of Tyler's jacket as she felt a seizure grip her. Praying that she didn't alert the men talking to Tyler, she was struggling hard to control the shivering and twitching of her body. Several times she'd attempted to reach out, trying to grasp the back of his jacket that was dancing before her eyes, fearing she would fall to the ground. She couldn't even wipe the blood running from her nose. She couldn't alert Terri because the girl was probably busy scanning the ground for rodents. *Please, please stop…*

Tyler suggested Maceo get him a copy of the shipping invoice and begin loading up the next container to avoid any delays. When the three men were far out of hearing distance, only then did Tyler turn around, ready to throttle both Charlene and Terri.

One quick look at Terri's terrified face made him change his mind.

As best as she could, Terri had grasped Charlene's arms and had a hand clamped over her mouth in an attempt to keep her still and quiet. That is, after Terri looked up from the ground several seconds before and realized that Charlene was having a seizure.

"Aw, Charlene," Tyler said. When Terri dropped her hand away, he saw Charlene holding her lips in tightly and knew she'd been doing that to keep quiet as he'd told her to. Instinctively, he pulled her into his arms and whispered that she was going to be okay and that he was getting them out of there.

Charlene couldn't respond because she'd just passed out in Tyler's arms.

—∾—

Charlene's eyes fluttered open. Glancing around slowly, she realized she was in her hotel room. Trying to remember what could have happened, she looked up to see Tyler coming out of the bathroom carrying a wet face cloth and glass of water. "Tyler..." She saw the front of his shirt, smeared with blood. "What..."

"It's okay. You had a seizure down at the dock." Tyler noticed her struggling to remember, then sat on the edge of the bed and wiped her face. "Here, drink some water," he said.

Speaking was difficult and her muscles ached. But Charlene had another worry with Tyler in her room. "Can I have some ice, please?"

Tyler frowned. "Ice?"

"Yes, please, it really helps. Um, there's a machine right down the hall."

"Okay." Tyler picked up the ice bucket from the dresser and hurried from the room.

The second he left, Charlene got up on shaky legs and pulled her two packets of documents from the refrigerator and dropped them behind the nightstand. When she heard him returning, she quickly got back on the bed just as he came through the door.

Dropping several ice cubes into her glass, Tyler lifted her to a sitting position again and passed the glass to her. After draining her glass she handed it back to him. "It's good for you to drink a lot of water," he said and went to refill her glass with more water.

When he returned he sat on the bed facing her again. Charlene's eyes focused on his watch. "Is that right? It's one-thirty in the mornin'?" When Tyler confirmed the time was right, Charlene looked puzzled. "That can't be right. I went down to the dock at seven with…"

Tyler tilted his head to the side. "Um-hmm, with Terri, yeah, I know. I sent her butt home, but not before she told me the two of you had installed those tracking devices in the shipping containers. You had six of them, didn't you?"

"Yes, Terri and I split them and I had one left. It was in my hand when…"

Tyler raised his hand. "And you were going to put it in that last container bound for Arizona, right?"

"Yes, but…Oh, my God, Tyler, did I tell you what's gonna happen to those two truckers who make that delivery?"

"Yes, you did. How did you know about that?"

"I told you I'd been doin' my own investigation, but, Tyler, that last trackin' device…" Her memory was jumbled and couldn't remember if she'd put it in the container or not.

"I took care of it," Tyler said.

Sitting up, she gawked at him with unbelieving eyes. "You did it?"

"Yes, I did it," he repeated. "Where did you get them?"

"They were in a little jewelry bag of Corinne's you'd picked up at the hotel," Charlene said, glad that she'd had the forethought to open the bag when she'd gone to the Mills home to drop off the play items for the children. She'd spotted the box on Shelly's dresser. When she opened the jewelry bag she found the eighth locket, as well as six little electronic things. Sensing they may have been important, Charlene took them. She didn't know what they were or their importance until she met with Tyrone at the library.

"Well, while you've been out, the FBI and the authorities here in California and in Arizona have been hard at work. They've made several arrests already."

"Really? Who did they arrest?" Charlene took the wet wash cloth from his hand and wiped absently at the bloodstain on the front of his dress shirt.

"The dock manager, Maceo, was arrested at the warehouse. His girlfriend is Anita, and she was arrested at her apartment." Tyler was saddened that Corinne's assistant could be connected with her homicide. "She was all packed up, preparing to leave town in a couple of days."

Charlene couldn't help but feel his anguish. "I'm sorry, Tyler," she said.

"It's not your fault. Both James and Mr. Hunt were also arrested, but neither are talking. The FBI was waiting for them to meet tonight. They'd been monitoring their calls and knew about a money exchange tonight. Lots of money, but both have told the FBI the money that was to be exchanged was payment for new computers for Hunt Enterprises." As hard as it was for him to say, Tyler had to tell her the rest. "Anita has talked to the FBI agents, and, according to her, it was a preset meeting the night James and Corinne met down in that parking lot. He was supposed to get some invoices from her. When she said no he called Hunt, who'd had his henchman waiting nearby in that black Lincoln you spotted. Hunt gave his point man the go ahead to…to hurt Corinne if she balked, and she did."

Charlene had already suspected that. "They'll go to jail for a long time, right?"

"I don't know. Hunt is a smart man, and not much was on Corinne's office computer. Anita had been instructed to replace the hard drive and then shred the ledgers, but the FBI was able to open a link on Corinne's laptop and switch on the tracking devices that you'd installed."

"Okay, but that doesn't tie James and Mr. Hunt to the other stuff, does it?"

"What other stuff are you talking about?"

He doesn't know exactly what the shipments were. Hesitating momentarily, Charlene then leaned over, reached behind the nightstand and passed Tyler one of the packs of documents. "I believe this is all the evidence the FBI will need to keep them in prison for a long time." Explaining the documents as Tyler pulled them from the envelope Charlene saw that he, too, was astounded to see the proof of Corinne's level of deceit, all to destroy him. But to be on the safe side, Charlene was keeping that extra set.

Tyler glanced up after scanning the papers. Noticing they were cold, his eyes slid to the mini refrigerator before coming back to her. "I guess she didn't trust her lover, did she?"

"No, she didn't. I think she knew he would sell her out for the money and so she set out to gather all of that evidence that showed Mr. Hunt and James were using Mills Shipping trucks to safely transport drugs, money, and weapons out of the country." Charlene had to tell him the rest. "Tyler, she did it because she knew you were going to fire her. She also knew if you filed for divorce you would demand custody of the twins. Even if nothing was ever proven, Mills Shipping would be irreparably damaged. It would be ruined by the scandal and you still might have even faced charges. The media would've had a field day. She was banking on the fact that no judge would grant custody to a father facin' possible jail time. But really, Tyler, Corinne and James, they did it for the money. *She* did it for the money," Charlene said.

Tyler angrily shoved the papers back into the large envelope. "What money?" he asked. "I have her bank accounts under mine. Corinne made a decent salary, she had a savings account, and, according to my mother, she paid Corinne, too. So, what money are you referring to that she'd go to these lengths for?" He shook the large envelope.

Charlene told him about the information she'd had Tyrone find for her.

After pulling the scrap piece of paper Tyrone had jotted his number on before she'd left the library a couple days ago, Charlene had called his house. The next day they met back at the library and Tyrone had let out a whistle as he gawked at the monitor.

"Jeez, Miss Charlene," he'd said. "This is a bank account in the islands. Do you know how much money you have sitting in there?" he'd asked in amazement.

"No, it's not my account. It's my sister's, and she died tryin' to protect it," she'd said.

"Well, I'm sorry about your sister, but her account has a cool five and a half million dollars sitting there. Oh, man!" Tyrone whistled, puffing out his pimpled, cocoa-brown cheeks.

Even as she told Tyler, Charlene just couldn't fathom that kind of money. As tainted as it was, her twin had died for it. The thought of it only sickened her more.

Seeing that Tyler was becoming more despondent, Charlene reached for his hand. He didn't pull it away this time. "Tyler, as much as she could, Corinne loved you and the twins. The problem I believe, is that she just didn't love herself. I picked up on that the night we met. Initially all she could talk about was the fancy California parties she went to and her fabulous house, her designer clothes and luxury cars...all superficial trappings. I tell you, I couldn't relate to any of that stuff. I thought she was speakin' a foreign language and I had to keep bringin' her back to talk about the twins, and about you and your family."

Tyler was still reeling from the documents. "What are you saying, Charlene?"

"I'm sayin' that, as much as she was capable of, Corinne loved you. She did all of that," Charlene said, pointing to the papers in his hand, "because she was angry and hurt. That's a bad combination for someone who'd grown up havin' to fight for everythin' and struggled for years to keep that information from comin' out."

Tyler silently agreed with Charlene's assessment of her sister. Standing, he pulled out his cell phone and called the senior FBI agent, Ron. He'd instructed him to come to the hotel and gave Charlene's room number. He added he was holding all of the evidence they would need to "bury those bastards for two lifetimes."

CHAPTER 22

The following morning was a beautiful sunny Saturday...perfect flying weather.

Charlene sat in the small area designated as the breakfast nook at the hotel. She sipped her coffee and munched on a blueberry muffin.

In a matter of hours she'd be leaving California. Her heart was heavy as she reflected on how much her life had changed in the few short months since she'd arrived that fateful day back in March. She was going back home still alone and with scars, both inside and out.

Charlene reflected on how excited and nervous she'd been to see Corinne again, and, much as she'd hoped, they did let all the stuff in the past go. In actuality, she was the one to let it go. She mourned Corinne deeply, but she no longer felt that Corinne had the better life. Having to walk in her sister's shoes for the past few months, Charlene realized that her twin sister had been a lonely, deceitful, and manipulative woman who didn't have the capacity to love anything besides her children and material things. To her previous way of thinking, Corinne had it made...only she didn't. She didn't possess the capacity to love the man she'd set out to get, and, when she realized her affairs didn't hurt or torment him because he'd become indifferent, she set out to destroy him. Charlene was no longer angry at Corinne as she'd been in the past. It no longer mattered to her.

But Charlene also felt blessed because she'd met and fallen in love with her niece and nephew…and, she silently admitted to herself again, she'd fallen for their father as well. Sighing, she knew she would miss the comfort of his arms, the swelling of her heart, and the tightening in her stomach whenever he walked into a room.

But she no longer felt so terribly alone. She had 'kinfolk,' as people said back home. She knew her two little kinfolk loved their Auntie Charlene. She hoped they wouldn't forget her.

Recalling the brief conversation she and Tyler had after the two FBI agents left her room, Charlene was uncertain if he would let her visit the children from time to time, or let them come to visit her. All she asked for was to be a part of their lives, in any capacity. He'd said they were all grieving and he didn't want the children confused.

"I understand, but would you at least think about it?" She'd watched him shrug his jacket on and gave a slight nod. It gave her a little bit of hope. It was almost three in the morning before the FBI agents left. About to leave himself, Tyler had asked if she was going to be okay.

"Um-hmm," she'd mumbled and got up from the chair to walk him to the door. When he'd stood directly behind her, Charlene turned. She'd wanted to tell him that, somehow, she'd developed feelings for him. Charlene never really had the time to fall in love with any man, but what she felt for Tyler was intense. It made her sad and happy and torn.

She realized she was wrong. He was her brother-in-law and he was grieving. He needed time, and so did she. *How insensitive can I be?* But watching conflicting expressions cross his face, Charlene could only wonder what he was thinking about as they stood at her hotel room door. Whispering his name, her hand had come up to cover his.

Charlene hadn't expected Tyler to kiss her, but when he did she was relieved that for the moment he didn't hate her. With his hands tenderly caressing her face, she felt no desire to stop what felt wonderful and, at that moment, so right. His sorrowful moan tore away at her.

Charlene wasn't going to be ashamed for wanting him. But when the kiss ended, she saw the turmoil on his face and knew it was obviously a mistake. "Tyler, you know we're both under a lot of stress and we're both grievin' a terrible loss…"

He couldn't meet her eyes, but he'd said in a quiet, raspy voice that he didn't want what was happening. Charlene knew what he'd meant. He didn't want her. She placed a finger over his lips. "You're absolutely right. We shouldn't even be going down this road again. I never should have," she said.

But now, several hours later in the light of day, as Charlene pinched off another piece of blueberry muffin, she knew she wouldn't forget the brief moments they'd shared before he'd turned and walked out of her room.

Following breakfast Sunday morning, Tyler sat with the family in the living room. He listened as Shelly and Shane talk endlessly about their sleep-over, but his attention drifted back to the early morning hours when he'd kissed Charlene's pliable and willing lips. He'd wanted her so much. *So why the hell didn't I say that,* he chided himself, forcing away the image of her the last time they'd made love.

What Tyler had really thought about as he gazed down into her face was that her eyes always appeared different to him, smiling, inquisitive, and hopeful. Even as he'd made love to her or sat and had a quiet conversation, her eyes reflected what she'd been feeling. He'd trusted her and she'd given him hope; for what, he didn't know.

When he'd lifted his hand and caressed her cheek, he knew he'd never seen Corinne like that, and he hated the direction of his thoughts. He'd compared the sisters when there was no comparison. Corinne never made him feel hopeful or even wanted, but Charlene did.

Whatever fervor that had claimed Tyler, he wasn't prepared for it. He'd pulled her into his arms and his lips claimed hers the second she touched him. He had been wrong to kiss her and he knew it. But she felt so good, and he'd missed her since she left his parents' home. Tyler recalled dragging his lips from hers and kissing her cheek, an apology on his lips. Stopping was the last thing he'd wanted to do, but he'd pushed himself away from her, trying desperately to quell the fire his body was straining to ignite. The only solution he saw was by leaving. So he left.

Forcing his eyes open as the twins' chatter surrounded him, Tyler glanced up to find Terri staring at him over her cell phone. She'd been giving him sly grins all morning long. When his cell phone vibrated in his pocket, he pulled his attention away from her. Tyler checked the message. Terri had just texted him again. "So did the two of you do it after you sent me home?"

She'd started at breakfast with her little comments and texting. Tyler waited for Mona to become distracted and then plucked several grapes and lobbed them across the table at Terri, smacking her soundly in the head, thus effectively silencing her.

"So, Tyler, dear what are you doing today?" Mona had been watching his sadness, which was evident on his face even though he tried to hide it. After having heard the details of Terri and Charlene's escapade last night, Mona gave Terri an annoyed glance. But she too was eager to know what had transpired between Charlene and Tyler.

"I'm taking Shane and Shelly to the amusement park. You want to come with us and maybe ride in a tea cup?" Tyler said and forced a smile, teasing his mother. He knew she was deeply concerned about him and tried to lighten the moment.

"Thanks, but I'll pass. I'm actually having lunch with an old friend today." Mona smiled. "She called me out of the blue. Nice, wasn't it?"

Getting up, Tyler hugged his mother. "Yes, it's very nice."

"Tyler, honey, what about…" The door chimes forced back words Mona guessed he didn't want to hear. She would have asked him about Charlene again.

"Auntie Charlene!" The twins' squeals of joy drew everyone's attention to the doorway.

The moment she stepped into the room Charlene was wrestled to the floor by Shane and Shelly. Had it not been for Tyler's quick response, she would have dropped the large box she carried with both hands. "Hi, um, thanks," she mumbled up at Tyler from the floor.

"Would you like to get up?" he asked, grinning at the children's excitement.

"No, I'm fine." Turning her attention to the kids, Charlene listened with rapt attention as they told her about going to the amusement park with Tyler and Terri and invited her to come along. "Actually, I can't go. I have to leave today." Blowing out a breath, she pulled them close. "I love you two so much, and you know that I love you as your Auntie Charlene, right?"

When each nodded, Charlene realized they were a-okay. "And you know I was never a clone or an alien mother, right?"

"What?" Both Ryan and Trish looked flabber-gasted.

"Long story, I'll tell you later," Tyler said as her words echoed in his head. *I have to leave today.* He was disheartened that she was actually leaving.

"Don't forget about the wires." Charlene caught Tyler's eye and both grinned awkwardly.

Returning her attention to the giggling twins, she said, "I wanted to tell you that I've carried you in my heart since the day I found out that your mother was havin' y'all. I'll always carry you there, but..." She paused dramatically. "I'm also carryin' you on my person." At their frowning faces, Charlene straight-ened out her leg and pulled up the bottom of her jeans to reveal a tattoo of a rose on her inner ankle. She'd gotten it several days ago. "Isn't it cool? I have both your names on it." Charlene watched their little fingers tentatively touching her leg, fascinated, but careful not to touch the tattoo or the antibacterial cream covering it. Pressing her lips together tightly, Charlene lifted watery eyes to the family looking on.

"Did it bleed and hurt, Auntie Charlene?" Shane asked excitedly. "Can we get one, too?"

"Yes, it did hurt, but it was a nice hurt, and no, you can't have one, but I got you some fake ones." Charlene pulled out two butterfly tattoos from her pocket and gave one to each. "And in that box your Daddy is holdin' are the baby flowers I promised y'all. They're ready to be planted in the ground, and they'll grow back every year if you take care of them."

"And here I thought it was just a box of dirt and weeds," Tyler said, finally helping her up from the floor and passing the twins the box. "Now be careful and take it out on the patio."

"We will." Gingerly holding the box between them, the twins were about to run off.

Charlene was heartbroken. "Hey, come back here and give me a goodbye hug." When they did, she struggled to keep her tears in check. She watched them carefully carry the box to the patio before turning to face the rest of the family. *This is so hard.*

"My heart is so heavy and I feel so sad today, but I'm so happy I got to know y'all. Maybe one day, um, I can come back and see y'all and the twins. They really are the only family I have left." Watching their faces fall, Charlene edged on. "I, um, wanted to say I'm sorry again for deceivin' everybody with my lies. It wasn't intentional, but lovin' y'all is intentional, and maybe one day I hope you might want to see me again, too," she said quietly.

Mona embraced Charlene tightly. "You little minx. You think you know everything, but we already

love you and you're more than welcome to stay here,
now. Please, Charlene, stay."

Charlene eased out of Mona's arms. "I can't,
Mona. I have a home to get back to and my job. My
life, as lonely as it is, is back there, but a huge part of
my heart I'm leavin' here, but thank you, Mona. I-I
wanted to tell you that in all my thirty-five years, I've
had several women that I've called mama from time to
time, but really, I've had no mama," she said and
kissed Mona's cheek. "But now I'm happy to add you
to the top of my list of mamas. Now, I believe you
have a lunch date you need to be gettin' ready for,
don't you?" Swiping at her eyes, Charlene grinned
impishly.

Mona squeezed Charlene's hand, not wanting to
let go. "You called Helen, didn't you?"

"Yes, indeed. I surely did that. See, I remembered
hearin' the regret in your voice and how you'd been
missin' your friend. She misses you, too. I think she's
as nervous as you are, but, Mona, you've told me
many times over the past three months that life is
precious. So don't you waste it on stuff that don't
matter no more." Charlene brightened suddenly.
"Helen said she'll order cosmopolitans in my honor.
Yum." Grinning boldly, she kissed Mona's cheek
again.

Terri had been holding back her own tears. "Oh,
man, I'm going to miss you so much, Charlene. If I
come to Virginia Beach on holiday break can I look
you up?"

"You better," Charlene said and smiled. She hugged her then whispered thanks to Terri for helping her last night.

Trish, Ryan, and Melvin all took turns hugging Charlene and speaking so encouragingly that Charlene truly felt they would miss her. Tyler had yet to say anything.

"I kinda owe the biggest thanks to Tyler," she said.

"I somehow doubt that," he said, suddenly uncomfortable and on the spot.

"Well, I do. Did I ever mention that I thought you were a movie star who'd come in my hospital room by mistake?" Charlene couldn't hold back the giggle that bubbled in her throat, made worse by Terri's sudden laugh. "But then I realized you weren't and that you belonged there. It was your voice and your face that I remember most. It was your words that pulled me from that dark place and forced me to open my eyes, so I do owe you a thank you," she said.

Tyler wanted to touch her face and erase the sadness in her eyes. He wanted to tell her to stay. He wanted to apologize for all the awful things he'd said to her. But he didn't do or say any of that. With his throat constricting, he simply leaned forward and kissed her cheek. "You're welcome."

What had she expected, she wondered? That he would pick her up in his arms and beg her not to go and then whisper his undying love for her into her good ear? Stretching up and accepting his chaste kiss, Charlene was unexpectedly shy with everyone watching them. Why, she couldn't say; after all, the family *had* been privy to all of the intimate details of what had transpired between them.

The waiting taxi driver, idling in the circular driveway, blew the car horn, startling everyone.

· Stepping back, Charlene walked to the door and opened it. She turned to blow them a kiss before walking through and closing it quietly behind her.

· Tyler closed his eyes briefly to suppress the instinct to go after her. When he opened them, the sympathetic eyes of his family were watching him. "I'll go change for the park…"

Charlene stood on the other side of the door for several seconds, forcing her wildly beating heart to slow down.

Just leave…walk down the steps to the taxi and just go.

But she couldn't go, not just yet.

Charlene turned the door knob and rushed back into the house just as Tyler turned and walked up the first step. Running past the surprised family and up two steps, she stopped and faced Tyler.

"What the…" Tyler managed to say when she'd suddenly appeared before him.

Not giving him a chance to push her away, Charlene threw her arms around Tyler's neck. She kissed him soundly on the mouth, and when she felt his arms ease around her waist, tightening as he returned the kiss, only then did she let go of the breath she'd been holding since she stood on the other side of the front door, staring out at her taxi cab.

Neither Tyler or Charlene seemed to notice the hoots and whistling behind them.

Finally, Charlene eased from his embrace, walked back down the stairs and retraced her steps to the front door. There, she turned and adjusted her T-shirt in a most dramatic fashion. "So…that's how we thank a gentleman properly in the South," she drawled.

Then she was gone.

For several long seconds no one dared to move as they stood watching the door expectantly. Each wondering, hoping, Charlene would come back.

She didn't.

CHAPTER 23

The week before the end of August in Chesapeake, Virginia, was steamy, almost as steamy as the sultry jazz music coming loudly through the speakers of Charlene's old stereo.

Sitting in her dining room working on wedding invitations for a fellow teacher, her mind once again drifted to another reference to California. There was no humidity, she reflected, and forced herself from dwelling on what could never be.

In the seven weeks since she'd returned back home, Charlene had immersed herself in what was familiar. Although lonely, she was somewhat content. She'd called and talked to the twins only five times, each time calling when they would have just come in from day camp. She listened intently as they talked about camp and the friends they'd made. When she asked them how their father was, each said the same thing. "Daddy's okay."

She knew in time they would forget about her as they grew up. There was nothing she could do except take Tyler to court and fight for visitation, but she didn't want to do that. To her way of thinking, she'd caused him and his family enough grief. She didn't want to add to it. For the time being, she was content to have brief phone conversations, which she figured would eventually stop altogether when the twins got too busy to talk to her.

The gold tassels she carefully tied to the one-hundred-and-eighty-seven wedding invitations were a necessary task. Aside from the fact that she was getting paid to do it, Charlene needed the chore to keep her mind occupied. With school reopening in two weeks, she'd been milling about, looking for things to keep her busy since she'd returned to Virginia.

One thing she did was repaint almost every room in her house. With the help of two friends, Liz and Wesley, who'd been her constant companions, the old house seemed brighter.

Whereas Tyler and his family had to keep the news of Corinne's death quiet until the FBI captured all parties involved with her homicide, Charlene, on the other hand, returned to town and told everyone, starting with her church family. With the town being the size it was, very little was kept secret for very long. The memorial service she'd had was beautiful and brief, but the repast held in Corinne's honor lasted for hours.

As she worked on the invitations, Charlene felt oddly anxious and hoped she wasn't about to have a seizure. She hadn't had one since the second night after returning home. It was brought on by the stress of her ever growing mountain of bills...all had come past due while she was in California. She'd had no other choice but to deplete her meager emergency savings to pay them.

After returning home armed with a copy of her medical records that Flo had obtained for her, Charlene had gone to see her own doctor. After reading the thick file, he'd sat back and stared at her. He knew she'd suffered a great deal and told her she'd recovered so well because she'd had such excellent medical care. Recalling Melvin's words, Charlene quipped, "It was the best money could buy."

With possible permanent hearing loss in her left ear and a tendency to seizure, Charlene was forced to wear a medical alert bracelet, but that was okay with her. She was alive. She was lessening her dependency on the pain medication and had sought more cost-effective approaches to controlling her pain, which included acupuncture and yoga. She believed both were working. Her body was still scarred, but it didn't bother Charlene one bit. She was alive.

She was nervous about an upcoming medical appointment. Charlene's doctor had referred her to a hearing specialist for evaluation of a cochlear implant, an electronic device that might restore hearing in her left ear. He'd also told her that she'd been added to Tyler Mills's health insurance and that would cover all of her future medical care.

Taking a break from the wedding invitations, Charlene got up and walked into the kitchen. Although slight, a breeze circled above her from the ceiling fan, causing her hair to flutter around her head. That's when another feeling of apprehension swept over her. "Just nerves with school starting soon, that's all this is," she mumbled.

———

The plane ride from California to Virginia was uneventful, but Tyler was nervous. He'd come to Virginia on a mission...

Tyler's plane had landed two hours ago in Norfolk and he'd rented a car for the twenty-minute drive to Chesapeake. "So what am I doing," he said inside the interior of the rented Lexus. But he knew exactly what he was doing. It was something he'd dreamed about doing for the past seven weeks.

He'd come to see Charlene.

Pulling the car to a curb at a small park just outside of town, Tyler was surprised to see it full of people. What had he expected to see on a steamy Saturday afternoon? His eyes scanned the crowd of people hanging out and enjoying the beautiful, but hot, day. From what he'd seen so far, he liked the friendly town. He could see Corinne growing up there.

Tyler hadn't thought too much of Corinne other than the fact that she'd been terribly unhappy and that he would not see her again. Shane and Shelly seemed to accept that she was somewhere watching over them, making sure they behaved themselves.

Reflecting back, Tyler had such high hopes for him and Corinne and for their marriage. Even though they had married within months after meeting, he believed he'd loved her. It was only after they'd returned from their honeymoon that Corinne had confessed that sex just wasn't something she could get that all that hyped up about. She apologized for not being up front with him. It had been a crushing blow to Tyler's ego. That's why he'd been so hurt to find out about her affairs. Only now could Tyler agree that Charlene had been correct. Corinne wasn't happy with herself and she looked to find comfort, not sex, elsewhere.

But Tyler believed Corinne's unhappiness stemmed from her harboring a past that should never have been a secret. He simply didn't understand why she'd felt the need to hide the fact that she'd grown up under circumstances that were not her fault. Poverty hadn't been her choice. In retrospect Tyler realized that Corinne's quest for money and what she perceived as something better was what left her, for the most part, miserable. She connected to no one emotionally except for the twins, and he resented her for depriving them of their grandfather and aunt for eight long years.

Over the years, he'd been miserable himself because he'd come to love Corinne, despite the fact that she wanted nothing from him. Occasionally, he'd discreetly sought the arms of women for companionship and intimacy, but those relationships had been unsatisfying.

All Tyler ever wanted was to come home, play with his children, tuck them into bed, and make love to his wife. Only it wasn't like that. It had never been like that.

Watching children playing in the park a few feet from the rental car, Tyler could remember when he'd thought there might be a second chance for his marriage. He'd thought to put everything aside and been willing to make another go at it. It was the day he'd come home to find his wife sitting on the concrete driveway drawing flowers with Shane and Shelly.

Only it wasn't her.

He clearly remembered his heart soaring as he stared into her upturned face. He'd sat down and attempted to draw what he thought was a family tree with the four of them standing under it, shielded and protected from the harshness of life.

But it wasn't Corinne who'd made his heart soar or who'd thoroughly chewed him out at breakfast when he'd stayed out most of the night, or the one who'd given him the greatest pleasure he'd ever experienced in her tender arms.

It was Charlene that he'd fallen in love with.

It was Charlene who'd been the reason that he'd adjusted everybody's schedule back at Mills Shipping so that he could leave and travel to Virginia. So now, almost three hours later, he still hadn't gone to her house. He was delaying going to see her because he was nervous. He couldn't put it off any longer. "Okay, I'm here, I'm ready. I've waited long enough..." he said, pulling the Lexus away from the curb. "I've negotiated million-dollar deals, so I can do this."

Fifteen minutes later, Tyler walked up to Charlene's front porch.

Jazz music greeted him through the open screen door. The front of the house reminded him of her. It was colorful with potted plants on both sides of the porch. Glancing to his right, he spotted a large tree and clearly remembered the picture he'd seen of Charlene and Corinne as young girls standing under the then-sapling, holding hands. The picture now sat in a frame in Shelly's bedroom and a copy was in Shane's.

Looking for a doorbell and not finding one, Tyler knocked. When he didn't get a response, he stepped into the cool foyer. Because of his height, he could see over a railing that separated the hallway and the dining room. He spotted Charlene's bowed head. She was working on some cards while loud music filled the house. Tyler's heart lurched, knowing she'd lost the hearing in her left ear.

Curiously, Tyler's attention was drawn to the living room to his right, specifically to the mantle above the fireplace. He was lured to a lovely picture of Charlene, Corinne, and a man he assumed was their father. The man was handsome and he guessed the girls to be about sixteen. They were indeed beautiful girls with identical eyes, hairstyles, and smiles.

Another picture, set slightly apart, held him spellbound for several seconds. Without a doubt, Tyler knew the attractive woman in the picture to be Charlene and Corinne's mother. She was lovely and the spitting image of both of them…and of Shane and Shelly. Her familiar amber eyes held a mysterious, almost mischievous glint.

Pulling his eyes away from the picture Tyler circled the homey living room. Although there were few furnishings, what Charlene had appeared traditional and well tended-to. The paintings hanging on the walls drew his eyes. Most were colorful landscapes. The faint smell of paint suggested she'd recently painted the room.

Turning to a far corner, he spotted two pictures of Shane and Shelly sitting on a table, proudly displayed, he thought. Tyler hadn't seen the pictures before and picked them up for a closer look. He noticed Charlene had captured them just as he saw them. Shelly's mischievous grin lit up her face. He looked back at the picture of their grandmother. She too, had that grin. Tyler smiled.

The picture of Shane showed him thoughtfully studying something in the grass. *Probably a bug he planned on catching.* It was uncanny, but Tyler realized that his children's expressions matched both of their grandparents and he felt wonderfully connected to the couple he hadn't had the fortune to meet.

Hearing the phone ring, he glanced up just as Charlene rushed into the kitchen to answer it. Not wanting to frighten her, Tyler stepped back into the entry foyer. There, he stood watching her shadow move about in the kitchen, which was straight ahead toward the back of the house. He listened as she talked about baking cookies for some upcoming event. The thought of anybody baking anything in all of Chesapeake in that humidity made Tyler shake his head.

When she left the kitchen and lifted her eyes, his world suddenly shifted back on its axis. For the first time in seven long weeks, his heart thudded loudly in his chest with excitement.

Charlene stopped dead in her tracks when she saw Tyler standing in her entryway holding a bag in his hand. She quickly closed the distance from the kitchen doorway to the front hall. It was no further than thirty feet, but Charlene didn't remember closing the distance. She didn't think he was real, so she reached out her hand and touched his chest. "Tyler…?"

"Hi."

"Hi." *He's really here.*

The sound of her voice made him smile. "You look great, Charlene. How are you?"

"Well, right now I'm shocked to see you." She was immediately alarmed that something might have happened back in California. "Is everybody all right back home?"

"Yes, and we all miss you." Tyler realized this was harder then he thought it would be.

"Oh. Well, I certainly miss everybody, too. How're the kids?"

"Wonderful. I brought pictures with me," he said over the music.

"Great." Trying to control her nervousness, Charlene gave up. "Okay, Tyler, I'm really freaked out to see you. I mean I'm glad," she said, realizing that he'd spoken loud because the stereo was so loud. She rushed into the living room and turned it off, then returned to the foyer.

His eyes took in every detail of her. "Did I ever tell you that I liked the sound of your voice, Charlene?"

"Huh?"

"It's just one of the things I like about you," Tyler said, his eyes never leaving her face.

"But you also said you disliked me and...well, you had good reason," she said.

"Charlene, do you remember Mona saying that grief was an individual thing?" When she nodded, he continued. "For me, I initially directed my grief at you, just as you'd blamed me for taking Corinne away. We were both wrong, and I hate myself for letting you walk out of my parents' house twice. I, um..."

Stepping closer, Charlene rested a hand on his arm. "What're you sayin'?"

"I'm trying to say that I'm sorry, and I bought you something I think you should have. Something I feel belongs here." As difficult as it was for him, Tyler just didn't think it was appropriate to tell her how he felt...at least not yet. He reached into the bag in his hand.

"Oh, what is…?" Charlene legs almost gave way when he pulled the small amber-brown urn containing Corinne's ashes. "Oh, my…Tyler, are you sure?" She lifted the box from his outstretched hand with both of hers.

"Yes, I'm positive. Where will you put it?" He looked into the living room at an empty space on the mantle.

Charlene followed his eyes and smiled. "Perfect," she said, carrying the urn and placing it on the mantle between the two photos. "Welcome home, Corinne," she said. Turning, she threw herself into his arms and hugged him tightly. "Oh, thank you, Tyler. Thank you so much." His cologne filled her with longing, but she also noticed how warm he was when his arms circled around her. Stepping back, she frowned at his suit. "Are you warm?"

"Oh, God, I am," he said shrugging out of his jacket. "You don't look hot at all." Actually, he thought she looked better that hot. She looked great.

Chuckling, Charlene took his jacket. "I'm used to this humidity. Come on back into the kitchen and I'll get you a glass of lemonade. Sorry, I don't have air-conditionin'."

"Do you want it?" Tyler followed her, admiring the first-floor rooms that opened into a large kitchen. All white appliances greeted him, and, like the living room, nothing was new.

"Why? You want to buy me air-conditionin' units or somethin' like that?" She passed him a tall glass of lemonade and then opened a bag of cookies.

"Yes, something like that," Tyler said, reaching in the bag and taking several cookies. He turned to admire one wall of her kitchen. Behind the stove a five-foot-high sunflower had been painted on the wall. He turned back to her. "It's a daffodil, isn't it?"

Charlene laughed, knowing he'd been teasing her and remembering the day she sat in the driveway drawing chalk flowers with the twins. "So tell me about Shane and Shelly."

"They're fine," he said, pulling a slim box from the bag. "A gift for you." Tyler slid the box across the table to her. "And I have pictures of everybody on a CD," he said.

Lifting the lid off the gift box, Charlene stared at the material for several seconds before lifting the item from the box. It was an elegant, white silk blouse, almost a duplicate of the one she'd worn to California. "It's beautiful, much finer than my other one. Why'd you do this?"

Gazing into her eyes, Tyler leaned in closer. "Is that a Southern thing to ask when a gentleman comes bearing a gift for the lady of the house...a very beautiful lady of the house?"

Charlene felt her kitchen shrinking around her until all that existed was the two of them. "Thank you. It's lovely," she said quickly. "Come into the dining room. I-I was working."

Watching her nervously, yet carefully, place the blouse back into the box and exit the kitchen, Tyler smiled and followed her. He was remembering the words of the females back home, including Shelly. Everyone told him go get Charlene because he loved her.

Stepping into the traditional dining room, Tyler realized what she'd been doing when he'd spied on her from the foyer and living room. Picking up one of the wedding invitations he smiled. "I know this flower is a rose," he said. "Are there purple roses?"

Taking the delicate invitation from his hand and sitting down, Charlene grinned. "It's not purple, it's lavender. I have to finish this by tomorrow, and I have twenty more to do."

Sitting across from her, Tyler absently picked up a tassel and saw that she'd been tying the delicate ribbons together and attaching them onto the invitations. "Is this a hobby?"

Okay, so now he's completely fillin' up my dinin' room. "Hardly, I get paid for doin' this. When I'm not teachin' during the summer, I help out my friend. She owns a bridal shop."

He'd remembered hearing that before. *When?* It was the night she'd confessed who she really was. Tyler glanced around. "Just so you know, the FBI confiscated that money that was in Corinne's island account. It was the payoffs she'd received from Hunt. Oh, and I also got in touch with Tyrone the Web Man."

"You did? Why?"

"I had a gift for him also."

"You're kiddin'. What'd you get him?" Charlene was surprised that he'd remembered her telling him about the teenager who'd helped her at the library. She picked up on the quirky look he presented her. "What?"

"A fully loaded laptop computer from a company that's going out of business," he said. "While James is sitting in a jail cell awaiting trial, Mia filed for divorce and has been liquidating JS Computer Sales. Everything's going dirt cheap. Need anything?"

Charlene gave him a doubtful look and turned up her nose. "How's Mia doin'?"

"She's fine. She told me that she'd suspected something was going on between James and Corinne. But the night the four of us went out for dinner, she said she didn't feel it and guessed that she'd been wrong all along. After you left town, the story of the events surrounding Corinne's death was released to the media."

"Were you guys okay?"

"Yes, and we got a lot of support. Since we'd already had a private memorial for Corinne, we asked in lieu of flowers and cards that donations be made in the name of Corinne and Daniel McDonald to the Cedars Sinai Hospital's Neo-Natal Unit." Tyler passed her an acknowledgement card for donations totaling several hundred thousand dollars.

Charlene clutched her throat. "Daniel? My father?"

"Uh-huh." Tyler squeezed her hand compassionately. "Oh, I also have a photo from Terri, but I have to destroy it after you see it." He knew he was throwing a lot at her all at once.

"Why?" Charlene mumbled absently, in shock at the number of zeroes on the donation card. The fact that his family had included her father had blown her away. It took her a few seconds to follow what he'd said next. "Picture from Terri...what is it?"

"It's incriminating," Tyler said, pulling the photo from his pocket and showing it to her.

Suddenly, both laughed to see Terri's saucy pose as she stood beside James's demolished and once-beloved car.

"So where's your computer? I'll show you the pictures." Tyler laughed suddenly. "Even camera shy Trish, proudly showing her little belly, posed for pictures for you."

Swallowing the lump in her throat, Charlene smiled. "Ah, sorry, I don't have one. But if I can keep the CD, I'll take it to the library and look at it. I can print them, too."

"Hmm, no doorbell, no air-conditioning, no computer, and still no shoes. Charlene, you're not a very modern girl, are you?" He watched her glue a tassel to another invitation.

"No, I'm not, but I can play a mean harmonica," she said and grinned at his lifted brow.

"Really?"

"Really. My dad taught both Corinne and me how to play." She plucked the tassel from his hand. "And stop messin' with these."

Tyler captured her hand and rubbed his thumb across her fingers. "I miss you, Charlene."

"Huh?" Her eyes flew to his smiling ones and Charlene was once again mesmerized by the look in his dancing eyes.

"I said I missed you," he repeated. Leaning forward, Tyler moved the little glue thing to the side, yelping when a drop of glue landed on the back of his hand. "Ouch! What is that?"

Charlene didn't pretend it wasn't funny. It was. "That's hot glue," she said, lifting his glass of lemonade and pressing it to the back of his hand. Longing hit her with unexpected force when she recalled rubbing the ice cubes on his bruised knuckles after he'd knocked James out cold.

"Jeez. I hope that stuff comes with a warning label," he said, taking the glass and rubbing it across the back of his hand.

"It does. So about what you were sayin' before…"

Recovering, Tyler sipped from his glass before responding. "I said I missed you a lot and I've been worried about you. Why haven't you called?" When she explained about talking to the twins, Tyler shook his head slowly. "You didn't talk to me. Did you want to?" He watched her nod slightly. Just as he leaned close, intent on kissing her lips, a man's voice called out a greeting from the front of the house.

"Hey, Charlene, you back in the kitc—" The uniformed officer stopped mid-stride when he spotted her sitting in the dining room with a man. He immediately offered an apology. "Oh, sorry." He was caught off guard by the appearance of her male guest, who'd just stood up.

"Hiya, Wes, how's it going today?"

"Good," he said, his eyes never leaving the man now standing on the other side of the table.

"Wesley, this here is Mr. Tyler Mills. He's…he was Corinne's husband. Tyler, Wesley Jackson here is one of our town's finest deputies," Charlene said. She watched the two tall and handsome men shake hands. She felt dwarfed sitting there.

Wesley's demeanor immediately shifted to friend mode and he offered a sympathetic handshake. "Mr. Mills, you have my deepest condolences. Corinne was a lovely person."

"Thank you, Deputy Jackson," Tyler said, still uncomfortable receiving condolences.

"Call me Wesley, everybody else does."

Charlene snickered. "No, we don't. We all call you Barney behind your back, Wes," Charlene said, gluing on another tassel before looking up at an embarrassed Wesley. "Go grab yourself a glass of lemonade and some cookies and come join us."

Tyler sat back down. The deputy and Charlene seemed close. He'd watched the man watching her and wondered just how friendly they were. When Wesley returned from the kitchen and peeped over her shoulder at the invitations, Tyler's heart sank when the deputy kissed the cheek she'd offered up to him…like they were used to doing it. He remembered the first time he'd kissed her cheek like that. It was the morning she'd made waffles. It was after their first night together. *Damn.* He heard the deputy admiring the invitations.

"So what brings you by this early, Wes? You don't generally make it up at this side of town until your shift's about to end." Charlene gave Wesley a wink.

Tyler didn't miss it, and neither did he miss their obvious rapport.

"Well, Miss Mary across the road called down to the station and reported that a fancy car had been parked outside for quite a while. She reported that something peculiar was most likely going on." Wesley popped a cookie into his mouth and tilted his chin across the dining room table to Tyler. "I take it that's your vehicle, Tyler?"

"If you mean the Lexus, then yes. It's a rental." Tyler was crushed. He was too late. He wasn't so blind that he couldn't see that Charlene had already moved on. His instinct was to go get in that rental, drive back to Norfolk, and take the next plane back to California.

"Well, it sure is a nice one." Wes watched Tyler closely.

Charlene picked up on the tension in Tyler and was quick to dispel it. She also knew how protective Wesley was of her. She thought to quash what was some kind of territorial turf between them. "You know, Tyler, years ago Wesley fancied himself in love with Corinne."

"Really?" Tyler murmured quietly, noticing the man's embarrassed grin. He wanted to hit him. Hard. His knuckles started to itch.

"Now, Charlene, we were just classmates, that's all we ever were." Wesley bristled.

Ignoring him, Charlene continued. "Tyler, my father beat Wesley with the end of our yard broom all the way up the road when he caught them up on the hill after their prom. They were in the back of Wesley's mama's new Chevrolet. He tried to break it in." Charlene lapsed into a fit of giggles.

"Charlene!" Wesley was beyond embarrassed in front of this stranger.

"Oh, come on, Wes, everybody knew what y'all had planned on doin' after the prom 'cause you'd gone up to the Quik-Mart and brought condoms!" Charlene's laughter came out in ripples, forcing her to cover her mouth several times. "I heard Daddy tellin' Miss Ann, who was his lady friend at the time, that it was a whole box of rubbers!" Charlene laughed harder.

"You know, I'd wish you'd stop telling that tale, Charlene," Wesley huffed, unable to meet Tyler's serious eyes or Charlene's merrily dancing ones.

"I'm sorry, Wes, but it's just so funny, and it's true 'cause I'm the one who told Daddy what Corinne was plannin' on doin'." Charlene turned to Tyler, feigning a whisper. "You see, Corinne thought it was time to lose her you-know-what."

Tyler wasn't fazed. He was still reeling from their obvious relationship. And he still wanted to punch Wesley in the nose.

Wesley struck back at Charlene. "Well, she didn't lose it to me, Chatty Cathy, but I did hear a rumor that she liked another guy at school. Anyway, I mean no disrespect Mr. Mills. Corinne was a nice girl and she'll be missed greatly. Corinne's twin here was just jealous because she didn't have a date for her prom."

Tyler watched a shadow flit over Charlene's face before it disappeared.

"It wasn't that I didn't have a date, Deputy Barney," she stressed. "It was that we could only afford the one dress, and, of course, Corinne insisted on wearin' it first. Now how would I look showing up at my prom a week later with the same dress on? I'm glad I didn't go," she huffed.

Tyler decided to intervene in what he suspected was an ongoing and somewhat comical feud between them. It also saddened him that Charlene hadn't gone to her prom. He could imagine an eighteen-year-old Corinne insisting on wearing the dress first and showing it off, probably spitefully. "So who has pictures of the prom? I'd like to see them."

"I do." Having finished the invitations, Charlene got up and moved the box of invitations over to a built-in wall cabinet. As she passed behind Wesley's chair, she paused when he lifted his glass of lemonade to his lips.

Tyler knew what she was about to do before she did it. He'd been in that position himself. He bit back a laugh seconds later when Wesley glared up from the wet stain spreading across his uniform shirt to her retreating back.

"Aaww, Charlene, you did that on purpose," Wesley whined as he wiped at his shirt.

Following an hour of looking at photos and reminiscing with Charlene and Tyler, a hesitant Wesley prepared to leave. He offered to guide Tyler out from Charlene's street to the main road. "So, um, if you're staying in town a while, I can recommend several nice hotels or a bed and breakfast spot for you, Mr. Mills," he'd said.

"Oh, I never asked, are you stayin' for a visit, Tyler?" Charlene asked hopefully.

"I thought I'd stay a couple of days. Check out the town where my children's relative lives." He'd wanted to say, check out where she lived and yes, where Corinne had grown up as well. It would be closure for him.

"Great, you can stay here. It definitely won't compare to your house or your parents' estate, but I have empty rooms and food in the fridge."

"Charlene, um, what about your peeping neighbors?" Wesley's face was full of meaning.

"When have I cared what my neighbors thought of me? A few of them are still put off 'cause I painted the window shutters red." She waved her hand in the direction of the front door.

Tyler liked the red shutters. It was one of the first things he'd noticed about her house. "Thank you, Charlene. I'd love to stay."

—∿∿—

Following a light supper of pasta salad, Charlene decided to take Tyler out to see the town at night. They stopped at a local nightclub at the encouragement of one of her girlfriends she'd spotted at the internet café where she and Tyler had gone to look at the pictures on the CD.

"I'd swear those kids have grown several inches since I last saw them," she said, sitting across from him in the small nightclub. But no sooner had they arrived than many of the locals turned their focus on the two of them.

"You haven't been out much since you've returned home, have you, Charlene?" Tyler asked, recalling the number of people who'd come up to her and given her sympathetic hugs. Even in the small club many watched them, and he watched her fight back tears. He understood.

"No, not really. Just to the market, the doctor, and church, that's about it. It feels weird because the same people we ran into earlier, and even the ones here now, they all knew Corinne. Most of them knew that I'd gone out to California to see her. I know they're all wonderin' how I'm doin', but it's still weird, this grief thing. For you, I know it's more recent and fresh."

"Yes, but honestly, Charlene, I'd grieved for the Corinne I met nine years ago. I can't forget the beautiful woman who became despondent, sad, and deceitful, but as the mother of my children, I grieve for them and the senseless loss of her life."

"Have you forgiven her, Tyler, for what she did to you and tried to do to the business?"

"Yes." And he had. "I had to forgive her if I wanted to get on with my life. I realized what you told me that last night in your hotel room was true, no doubt about it. Corinne was miserable, and she didn't like herself. But I have to tell you that my being here for only a day and looking at the photos in your family albums and hearing all those people speak so kindly about her…I know on some level that she was happy here. I don't think her heart ever left this town or you or your father." He reached for her hand when she twitched her lips and sniffed.

"Thank you. I think I needed to hear that. I feel so alone without her presence, and, of course, my dad's." Charlene pulled her hand back from his. "It's tough."

"Yes, I know."

"Would you still have divorced her? You know, after she'd recovered?" Charlene asked.

"Yes, but I wouldn't have taken full custody of Shane and Shelly because she *was* a good mother and she loved them," Tyler said.

Just then the club owner came over, a fellow Charlene introduced as Ricky. After giving Charlene a crushing hug, he turned to Tyler. "Mr. Mills, it's a pleasure to meet you." Ricky hurried off and up to the small stage. Seconds later, Ricky announced that the evening would be dedicated in memory of their friend and his first girlfriend from high school, Corinne McDonald Mills.

Hearing that, Charlene's mouth dropped open and she sent Tyler an amusing lopsided grin. "I'll bet it was him who Corinne lost her 'you-know-what' to and he used to be really, really fat…and he had a jheri-curl in high school." Charlene dissolved into a giggling fit.

Tyler's laugh was mingled with hers, just as old-school tunes filled the club.

~~~

Arriving back at her house, Charlene showed Tyler the second floor, which consisted of a large bathroom and three bedrooms, one with a small bathroom attached.

"This was my father's bedroom. I've made it into my art room, of sorts." Walking into the second bedroom, she said, "This used to be Corinne's room. It's just a guest room now, and, don't worry, there are no ghosts livin' up in here," she said.

"And where's your room?" Tyler asked, running a finger along her jaw line.

"Well, you'll only see it briefly 'cause you'll be sleepin' in *this* guest room." Charlene angled her head back, stepped into the hall and walked to her bedroom.

Stepping inside, she waited for Tyler to enter. "This was the room that Corinne and I shared growing up...it's just my bedroom now."

Tyler's chest sunk in. The atrocious orange wall remained. Since that exact color also remained on the wall back at his still-closed-up house, it confirmed to him that Corinne's heart never left Virginia or her father and twin sister. It wasn't just talk. "She never really left, Charlene, and you've kept that color," he said.

"Yes, I've always been happy with it," Charlene said.

"Yeah, me too, now," Tyler said, noticing a large flower had been painted in the corner of the wall. He smiled, recognizing that it was a daisy.

Each said goodnight and walked to their bedrooms.

CHAPTER 24

At seven o'clock the following morning, Tyler awakened with a jolt. He'd actually thought perhaps Charlene had come into the bedroom and lightly touched his arm, but looking around he saw that he was alone.

Getting up from bed, he went into the small bathroom connected to the bedroom. Glancing around, Tyler was again surprised to see a blue bathtub, blue toilet, and blue sink. When he'd first seen them yesterday, he realized he'd never seen a blue toilet before. After brushing his teeth and washing his face, he was surprised how rested he was despite the three-hour time difference. It would be four o'clock in the morning in California.

Through the open bathroom window screen he heard a variety of sounds…bugs and birds and the intermittent swishing of a sprinkler somewhere nearby. He could tell it was going to be another beautiful, but hot, day. It already was. Opening the curtains over the blue sink, Tyler inhaled the morning air and immediately spotted a little white bird of some kind. It captured his attention as it stood out on a dark green leaf of a large tree in the backyard.

He whistled at it, and, oddly the bird returned a soft chirp. It made him smile.

After donning a pair of jean shorts and a T-shirt, he went down to the kitchen. The house was quiet and bright. He guessed Charlene was still asleep since they didn't get back to her house until after midnight.

After filling the coffee maker, Tyler stepped out onto the back porch. There, Charlene sat with her feet up on a railing. "Charlene?"

Pulling her attention from the little white bird nestled up in the tree, Charlene was surprised to see him up so early. "Good mornin'. You're up awfully early."

Crossing over the porch, Tyler sat down at the small bistro table across from her. He couldn't help but notice her tanned legs or the tattoo on her ankle with the twins' names. "Despite the time difference, I feel rested. What are you doing up so early?" He gazed out over the neatly cut grass and the colorful shrubs lining the walkway.

"It's not early to me. I've been up for a couple of hours and I put the laundry out to catch the mornin' sun." Actually, she'd been unable to sleep with him so close by. Memories of the two of them making love were still so vivid in her mind that Charlene was forced to get up and keep herself busy, lest she go pounce on him.

He watched her point to the side of the house where a clothesline was strung up. Fragrant sheets and towels swayed with the light morning breeze. Tyler inhaled the pleasant scent of clean linens. "Nice, but do you have a clothes dryer?"

"Yes, and although that makes me a modern girl, I happen to like nature's way better." *Lord, he is handsome.* "Did you have a nice time down at the club last night?"

"Yes, I did. So many hands shook mine, but everybody was really nice. So how come you wouldn't dance with me last night when I asked you? You know I knew the steps," he teased, recalling her swiftly shaking her head when everyone began a line dance. It was the same line dance she'd showed him on the patio at his parents' home.

"Like Wesley said yesterday, Tyler, folks do talk."

"Yeah, um, about him, I, um…well, I think he likes you. He's sweet on you." Tyler knew he was searching, but her answer mattered greatly as to how their conversation this morning would play out. "I do believe that's a Southern saying, right?"

"Give me a break!" Charlene huffed with a wave of her hand. "Wesley is like my cousin, and I don't mean kissin' cousins, either. What that nutcase is sweet on is the girl that lives about five houses up the block. She lives in the house where Corinne and I stole those cans of paint from." She snickered. "But that's why he comes by so often. He's hopin' to catch a glimpse of her, and, for real, he's gettin' on my nerves with that mess. I told him if he doesn't just ask her out on a date or somethin' then somebody else is gonna beat him to the punch and he'll be kickin' his own butt for waitin' so long, you know what I mean?"

Oh, yeah, I know. Tyler smiled broadly, revealing even white teeth. "Hey, your house feels happy to me…all of the rooms," he said out of the blue.

Charlene perked up and dropped her feet from the railing. "That's a nice thing to say." She watched him grin before rushing back inside to fix them cups of coffee.

Tyler returned a few minutes later, slightly out of breath from having run back up to the guest bedroom for another gift he'd brought for Charlene. On the porch, he passed her a cup of coffee and kissed her cheek. "Just like you like it, looking like a cup of steamed milk," he teased and resumed his seat at the small table. "Can I ask you a question?"

Charlene nodded, but could see he was hesitant. "You can ask me anythin'."

"Okay, that night back in California, when you told us who you were…you said that you blamed me for Corinne leaving you. What did you really mean by that?"

Setting her coffee cup down, Charlene met his intense eyes as she geared herself up to admit an awful truth, a truth she would only admit to him.

"For all those years since Corinne left, I needed somebody to blame. So I blamed you for showin' her what it was like to have such a privileged life. You showed her what it was like to have money and the finer things that kept her away and from comin' back here. Each time I missed her, like at holidays and birthdays, I had to come up with excuses to say why she hadn't come home, even when our father died. She didn't come back because she didn't want to.

"Tyler, everybody comes back home. Some just for a quick getaway, others move back here when life in the big cities prove too much…but people always come back home. Corinne never did 'cause she selfishly just didn't want to. I was more embarrassed than anythin' else, especially at our father's funeral."

Try as she might, Charlene couldn't hold back the hard edge that laced her words. "How dare she not come back for even that? She didn't need to send me money to help me bury him. She needed to be here. *I needed her here*…with me. On some small scale I kinda wanted to show folks around here that Corinne did care and that she did still love us." Refusing to give in to an emotional outburst, Charlene sipped her coffee and then sat her cup down.

"Oh, Charlene, I can understand why it was easy to blame me for keeping her away."

"Yes. But I also knew I was wrong. I couldn't be angry at her for wantin' a better life. I understand that, but what I couldn't understand was how she could forget about us…forget about me. We surely didn't forget her. My father always talked about his daughter livin' a grand life out there in California, and the sicker he became the more he talked about her. But when I came to your house, I realized I'd been blamin' the wrong person. I shouldn't have blamed you. It was her choice to act as if we didn't exist. But that night we talked, Corinne apologized and cried a river of tears because she felt enormous guilt for doin' that. It was then that I realized how miserable and how unhappy she was. She said she hated growin' up poor and that she would never, ever go without again. She said that I couldn't understand that. I guess she was right, because I was okay growin' up without because I never wanted riches and fancy things. She also told me that you could never understand that, Tyler."

Tyler had listened to her without interrupting. "I would have never judged her or looked at her differently for how she'd grown up. If I had known about you, I would have helped you and your father." Tyler sipped his coffee and then moved the cup aside. His eyes searched her for understanding. He got it and caressed her cheek.

"Actually, I think I knew you weren't Corinne from the beginning. I thought it was odd that I'd been having these strong feelings for my wife. It started the moment I went to the hospital and saw her lying in a coma. I felt intense guilt for what I'd done that sent her from the house that awful night. But day after day, I sat by that hospital bed and prayed for her eyes to open. I prayed to be given a chance to right the terrible thing I'd done. So when your eyes opened and silently spoke to me, I knew I could never walk away from you, not ever."

"But you didn't know it was me. You thought I was Corinne."

"But I knew *something* was different. In the limousine ride from the hospital to my parents' house you told me that you were scared, remember? In fact, more than once you said that to me. Corinne was never scared about anything." Tyler blew out a steady breath. "Listen, I'm not making a comparison, Charlene, because there is none. To me you look different than she did. You felt different and wonderful to me and I felt different and wonderful being with you, kissing you, sharing with you, and being inside you. I've ached for you…and the day you left after planting that kiss on me, I've longed for you like no other."

With her heart thumping faster, Charlene could only mutter one weak word. "Oh."

Tyler turned to look out over the lawn again. He inhaled the freshness of a new day and he hoped for a new life with this woman that he loved and adored. He felt like laughing. Yes, he felt that hope and promise of a future. It was right there in her eyes.

And he was about to grab hold of that lifeline. He felt giddy just thinking about it.

"It feels peaceful here, kinda like…oh, I don't know, like I want the twins to come here and run out there in the yard and to fall asleep in the rooms upstairs. Take their baths in the blue tub." Tyler chuckled. "But more than that, I want us to always want to come back here, you know, for a quick getaway or a vacation or a second home. Can they do that, Charlene? Can we all do that?" Tyler turned back to her.

She misunderstood what he'd said. "Do you mean it? Y'all can come here, really?" Then replaying his words in her head something snapped. "Wait a minute! What do you mean?"

Getting up and gathering her up in his arms, Tyler laughed. "I have a condition."

"Condition to y'all comin' for a visit? Okay, you name it." With her heart doing a double-dutch stomp in her chest and her knees knocking as his words sank in, Charlene was holding back what she'd wanted to do since spotting him in her foyer yesterday. She'd wanted to throw her arms around him, kiss him senseless, and tell him how much she loved him. How much she loved the twins, and his whole family.

"I have two conditions, actually," Tyler said.

"Okay, I can do two."

"Okay, the first one is really a declaration. It's from my heart and soul."

Oh my God. "Tell me."

"I love you, Charlene. I wanted to tell you that the second I saw you yesterday. I'd rehearsed it and…well, pretty much what you want to tell Wesley to do about the girl up the street, it's exactly what everybody, including Shane and Shelly, have all been telling me. But I was giving you time to, ah…"

"To what?" Charlene whispered, her eyes dancing across his face.

"I was giving you time to miss me and hoping you'd think I was how you liked em'. You know, a sweet and thoughtful kind of guy." Tyler lifted his thick eyebrows, recalling the cookout on the patio when she'd talked about the kind of guy she liked.

A burst of happiness fluttered in her chest. "Oh, Tyler, I've missed you. I began missin' you the night I left your parents' house. Then you showed up and sat down on that motel step beside me. And you're every bit as sweet and thoughtful as ever. I've thought about you every day, but I felt so guilty for wanting you and for loving you. I thought it was wrong…until I saw you yesterday and knew it just couldn't be wrong because I feel so wonderfully happy."

Tyler hugged her tightly. "And I knew it wasn't wrong to have fallen in love with you the second you rushed back in the door and planted that Southern thank-you kiss on me. I've lived it over many times the last seven few weeks. So okay, we love each other and I'm happy. Are you happy?" Tyler's heart raced with her pronouncement.

"How 'bout this cute and attentive woman, who is not so thick, show you just how happy she is," Charlene said and threw her arms around his neck and kissed him soundly.

Finally easing her back and giving her two more quick kisses, Tyler laughed. "I have one more condition," he said.

"Oh, that's right, you said you had conditions. Tell me." Charlene was beside herself. She couldn't keep still, and her knees were still knocking together.

"I need a date for Mona's society gala thing in a few weeks." Tyler couldn't stop grinning at her. His heart was overflowing.

"Oh, a date, huh?"

"Yes, but I was thinking you'd go more than as my date. I was thinking you'd go as my fiancée." When he felt her trembling, Tyler eased Charlene back to her chair and glided his hand down her arm again, this time stopping at her hand and slipping an engagement ring on her ring finger.

"When I told my mother that I was coming to propose to you, she sent me to the jewelry store. I took Shane and Shelley with me. I told the jeweler I wanted a stone that perfectly matched their eyes." Tyler chuckled. "You should have seen them, Charlene, they were holding their eyes wide open with their fingers." He mimicked how they'd done it. "So do you want to marry me, a man with children and a ready-made, crazy, quirky, in-your-face, but loving family?"

When her tears finally fell, only then did Charlene realize the engagement ring was a perfect amber stone. It was the exact color of her eyes as well, and she knew that Tyler indeed loved her and he was offering her a family. His family.

"If you'll take me, scars and all, then yes, I'd love to marry y'all," Charlene said, accepting Tyler's passionate kiss.

...and when a light breeze swirled above them, each gazed up at the perfect blue sky.

The little white bird each had spotted earlier took off from its perch on the leaf and soared high in the sky into a puffy white cloud.

Then it disappeared.

ABOUT THE AUTHOR

Born and raised in Baltimore, Maryland, Bernice Layton works full-time and is an avid reader of novels, mostly romantic suspense. She is a member of Romance Writers of America and happily resides with her husband. She is the mother of one daughter, NaTiki, who inspires her to keep writing with this phrase in mind, "All things are possible with love and friendship, and the endless possibilities of past, future, and present encounters.

This is Bernice's third published novel for Genesis Press, Inc. Her debut novel, *Promises Made,* was released on 11/04/2008, and her second novel, *Crossing the Line* was released on 4/6/2010. Bernice plans to write several more books. You can visit her at **www.bernicelaytonauthor.com**, **www.myspace.com/booksbyb**, or email her at **booksbyb@yahoo.com**.

2011 Mass Market Titles

January

From This Moment
Sean Young
ISBN-13: 978-1-58571-383-7
ISBN-10: 1-58571-383-X
$6.99

Nihon Nights
Trisha/Monica Haddad
ISBN-13: 978-1-58571-382-0
ISBN-10: 1-58571-382-1
$6.99

February

The Davis Years
Nicole Green
ISBN-13: 978-1-58571-390-5
ISBN-10: 1-58571-390-2
$6.99

Allegro
Adora Bennett
ISBN-13: 978-158571-391-2
ISBN-10: 1-58571-391-0
$6.99

March

Lies in Disguise
Bernice Layton
ISBN-13: 978-1-58571-392-9
ISBN-10: 1-58571-392-9
$6.99

Steady
Ruthie Robinson
ISBN-13: 978-1-58571-393-6
ISBN-10: 1-58571-393-7
$6.99

April

The Right Maneuver
LaShell Stratton-Childers
ISBN-13: 978-1-58571-394-3
ISBN-10: 1-58571-394-5
$6.99

Riding the Corporate Ladder
Keith Walker
ISBN-13: 978-1-58571-395-0
ISBN-10: 1-58571-395-3
$6.99

May

Separate Dreams
Joan Early
ISBN-13: 978-1-58571-434-6
ISBN-10: 1-58571-434-8
$6.99

I Take This Woman
Chamein Canton
ISBN-13: 978-1-58571-435-3
ISBN-10: 1-58571-435-6
$6.99

June

Inside Out
Grayson Cole
ISBN-13: 978-1-58571-437-7
ISBN-10: 1-58571-437-2
$6.99

2011 Mass Market Titles (continued)

July

The Other Side of the
   Mountain
Janice Angelique
ISBN-13: 978-1-58571-442-1
ISBN-10: 1-58571-442-9
$6.99

Holding Her Breath
Nicole Green
ISBN-13: 978-1-58571-439-1
ISBN-10: 1-58571-439-9
$6.99

August

The Sea of Aaron
Kymberly Hunt
ISBN-13: 978-1-58571-440-7
ISBN-10: 1-58571-440-2
$6.99

The Finley Sisters' Oath of
   Romance
Keith Thomas Walker
ISBN-13: 978-1-58571-441-4
ISBN-10: 1-58571-441-0
$6.99

September

Except on Sunday
Regena Bryant
ISBN-13: 978-1-58571-443-8
ISBN-10: 1-58571-443-7
$6.99

Light's Out
Ruthie Robinson
ISBN-13: 978-1-58571-445-2
ISBN-10: 1-58571-445-3
$6.99

October

The Heart Knows
Renee Wynn
ISBN-13: 978-1-58571-444-5
ISBN-10: 1-58571-444-5
$6.99

Best Friends; Better Lovers
Ceyla Bowers
ISBN-13: 978-1-58571-455-1
ISBN-10: 1-58571-455-0
$6.99

November

Caress
Grayson Cole
ISBN-13: 978-1-58571-454-4
ISBN-10: 1-58571-454-2
$6.99

A Love Built to Last
L. S. Childers
ISBN-13: 978-1-58571-448-3
ISBN-10: 1-58571-448-8
$6.99

December

Fractured
Wendy Byrne
ISBN-13: 978-1-58571-449-0
ISBN-10: 1-58571-449-6
$6.99

Everything in Between
Crystal Hubbard
ISBN-13: 978-1-58571-396-7
ISBN-10: 1-58571-396-1
$6.99

Other Genesis Press, Inc. Titles

2 Good	Celya Bowers	$6.99
A Dangerous Deception	J.M. Jeffries	$8.95
A Dangerous Love	J.M. Jeffries	$8.95
A Dangerous Obsession	J.M. Jeffries	$8.95
A Drummer's Beat to Mend	Kei Swanson	$9.95
A Good Dude	Keith Walker	$6.99
A Happy Life	Charlotte Harris	$9.95
A Heart's Awakening	Veronica Parker	$9.95
A Lark on the Wing	Phyliss Hamilton	$9.95
A Love of Her Own	Cheris F. Hodges	$9.95
A Love to Cherish	Beverly Clark	$8.95
A Place Like Home	Alicia Wiggins	$6.99
A Risk of Rain	Dar Tomlinson	$8.95
A Taste of Temptation	Reneé Alexis	$9.95
A Twist of Fate	Beverly Clark	$8.95
A Voice Behind Thunder	Carrie Elizabeth Greene	$6.99
A Will to Love	Angie Daniels	$9.95
Acquisitions	Kimberley White	$8.95
Across	Carol Payne	$12.95
After the Vows	Leslie Esdaile	$10.95
(Summer Anthology)	T.T. Henderson	
	Jacqueline Thomas	
Again, My Love	Kayla Perrin	$10.95
Against the Wind	Gwynne Forster	$8.95
All I Ask	Barbara Keaton	$8.95
All I'll Ever Need	Mildred Riley	$6.99
Always You	Crystal Hubbard	$6.99
Ambrosia	T.T. Henderson	$8.95
An Unfinished Love Affair	Barbara Keaton	$8.95
And Then Came You	Dorothy Elizabeth Love	$8.95
Angel's Paradise	Janice Angelique	$9.95
Another Memory	Pamela Ridley	$6.99
Anything But Love	Celya Bowers	$6.99
At Last	Lisa G. Riley	$8.95
Best Foot Forward	Michele Sudler	$6.99
Best of Friends	Natalie Dunbar	$8.95
Best of Luck Elsewhere	Trisha Haddad	$6.99
Beyond the Rapture	Beverly Clark	$9.95
Blame It on Paradise	Crystal Hubbard	$6.99
Blaze	Barbara Keaton	$9.95

Other Genesis Press, Inc. Titles (continued)

Other Genesis Press, Inc. Titles (continued)

Other Genesis Press, Inc. Titles (continued)

Other Genesis Press, Inc. Titles (continued)

Other Genesis Press, Inc. Titles (continued)

Path of Thorns	Annetta P. Lee	$9.95
Peace Be Still	Colette Haywood	$12.95
Picture Perfect	Reon Carter	$8.95
Playing for Keeps	Stephanie Salinas	$8.95
Pride & Joi	Gay G. Gunn	$8.95
Promises Made	Bernice Layton	$6.99
Promises of Forever	Celya Bowers	$6.99
Promises to Keep	Alicia Wiggins	$8.95
Quiet Storm	Donna Hill	$10.95
Reckless Surrender	Rochelle Alers	$6.95
Red Polka Dot in a World Full of Plaid	Varian Johnson	$12.95
Red Sky	Renee Alexis	$6.99
Reluctant Captive	Joyce Jackson	$8.95
Rendezvous With Fate	Jeanne Sumerix	$8.95
Revelations	Cheris F. Hodges	$8.95
Reye's Gold	Ruthie Robinson	$6.99
Rivers of the Soul	Leslie Esdaile	$8.95
Rocky Mountain Romance	Kathleen Suzanne	$8.95
Rooms of the Heart	Donna Hill	$8.95
Rough on Rats and Tough on Cats	Chris Parker	$12.95
Save Me	Africa Fine	$6.99
Secret Library Vol. 1	Nina Sheridan	$18.95
Secret Library Vol. 2	Cassandra Colt	$8.95
Secret Thunder	Annetta P. Lee	$9.95
Shades of Brown	Denise Becker	$8.95
Shades of Desire	Monica White	$8.95
Shadows in the Moonlight	Jeanne Sumerix	$8.95
Show Me the Sun	Miriam Shumba	$6.99
Sin	Crystal Rhodes	$8.95
Singing a Song...	Crystal Rhodes	$6.99
Six O'Clock	Katrina Spencer	$6.99
Small Sensations	Crystal V. Rhodes	$6.99
Small Whispers	Annetta P. Lee	$6.99
So Amazing	Sinclair LeBeau	$8.95
Somebody's Someone	Sinclair LeBeau	$8.95
Someone to Love	Alicia Wiggins	$8.95
Song in the Park	Martin Brant	$15.95
Soul Eyes	Wayne L. Wilson	$12.95

Other Genesis Press, Inc. Titles (continued)

Soul to Soul	Donna Hill	$8.95
Southern Comfort	J.M. Jeffries	$8.95
Southern Fried Standards	S.R. Maddox	$6.99
Still the Storm	Sharon Robinson	$8.95
Still Waters Run Deep	Leslie Esdaile	$8.95
Still Waters…	Crystal V. Rhodes	$6.99
Stolen Jewels	Michele Sudler	$6.99
Stolen Memories	Michele Sudler	$6.99
Stories to Excite You	Anna Forrest/Divine	$14.95
Storm	Pamela Leigh Starr	$6.99
Subtle Secrets	Wanda Y. Thomas	$8.95
Suddenly You	Crystal Hubbard	$9.95
Swan	Africa Fine	$6.99
Sweet Repercussions	Kimberley White	$9.95
Sweet Sensations	Gwyneth Bolton	$9.95
Sweet Tomorrows	Kimberly White	$8.95
Taken by You	Dorothy Elizabeth Love	$9.95
Tattooed Tears	T. T. Henderson	$8.95
Tempting Faith	Crystal Hubbard	$6.99
That Which Has Horns	Miriam Shumba	$6.99
The Business of Love	Cheris F. Hodges	$6.99
The Color Line	Lizzette Grayson Carter	$9.95
The Color of Trouble	Dyanne Davis	$8.95
The Disappearance of Allison Jones	Kayla Perrin	$5.95
The Doctor's Wife	Mildred Riley	$6.99
The Fires Within	Beverly Clark	$9.95
The Foursome	Celya Bowers	$6.99
The Honey Dipper's Legacy	Myra Pannell-Allen	$14.95
The Joker's Love Tune	Sidney Rickman	$15.95
The Little Pretender	Barbara Cartland	$10.95
The Love We Had	Natalie Dunbar	$8.95
The Man Who Could Fly	Bob & Milana Beamon	$18.95
The Missing Link	Charlyne Dickerson	$8.95
The Mission	Pamela Leigh Starr	$6.99
The More Things Change	Chamein Canton	$6.99
The Perfect Frame	Beverly Clark	$9.95
The Price of Love	Sinclair LeBeau	$8.95
The Smoking Life	Ilene Barth	$29.95
The Words of the Pitcher	Kei Swanson	$8.95

Other Genesis Press, Inc. Titles (continued)